THAT NIGHT HARRY STYLES REGAINED
CONSCIOUSNESS.

His eyes opened—confused, unfocused, frightened.
He saw lights, colors, shapes, but everything was distorted, the surreal images of a nightmare.

He felt the water that enveloped him, the weight and
resistance of it ... *its suffocation.* Instinctively he
groped for the surface to breathe. But no breath came.

He screamed, as if the alarm of his voice would wake
him from this nightmare. But no sound came.

And then he felt something, someone, forcing him
back underwater, into its warm suffocating envelopment, and his nightmare was totally realized ...

TALES OF TERROR AND POSSESSION
from Zebra Books

HALLOWEEN II (1080, $2.95)
by Jack Martin
The terror begins again when it is Halloween night in Haddonfield, Illinois. Six shots pierce the quiet of the normally peaceful town—and before night is over, Haddonfield will be the scene of yet another gruesome massacre!

MAMA (1247, $3.50)
by Ruby Jean Jensen
Once upon a time there lived a sweet little dolly, but her one beaded glass eye gleamed with mischief and evil. If Dorrie could have read her doll's thoughts, she would have run for her life—for her dear little dolly only had killing on her mind.

ROCKINGHORSE (1743, $3.95)
by William W. Johnstone
It was the most beautiful rockinghorse Jackie and Johnny had ever seen. But as they took turns riding it they didn't see its lips curve into a terrifying smile. They couldn't know that their own innocent eyes had taken on a strange new gleam.

JACK-IN-THE-BOX (1892, $3.95)
by William W. Johnstone
Any other little girl would have cringed in horror at the sight of the clown with the insane eyes. But as Nora's wide eyes mirrored the grotesque wooden face her pink lips were curving into the same malicious smile.

Available wherever paperbacks are sold, or order direct from the Publisher. Send cover price plus 50¢ per copy for mailing and handling to Zebra Books, Dept. 1885, 475 Park Avenue South, New York, N.Y. 10016. Residents of New York, New Jersey and Pennsylvania must include sales tax. DO NOT SEND CASH.

EXPERIMENT
THE

RICHARD SETLOWE

ZEBRA BOOKS
KENSINGTON PUBLISHING CORP.

*In memory of my father
Ernest Setlowe*

Every great advance in science has issued from a new audacity of imagination.

—JOHN DEWEY
The Quest for Certainty

Acknowledgments

There are several medical experts who generously educated and advised the author during the researching and writing of this book. I am deeply grateful to them—

Virginia Armon, Ph.D.; Bruce R. Bodell, M.D.; Gerald W. Gardner, Ph.D.; Howard M. Grindlinger, M.D.; Murray Grossan, M.D.; Charles M. Grossman, M.D.; Jay D. Hyman, D.V.M.; LCDR D. A. Ingrum, MC, USN; Thomas Muziani, C.C.P.; Martin J. Nathan, M.D.; William R. Sweetman, M.D.

PRELUDE

Epic events in man's evolution are, more often than not, heralded by very ordinary circumstances.

"Ninety-three KHJ with all the good sounds this beautiful Sunday afternoon here in Southern California. Fair September skies, eighty-four degrees downtown, in the nineties in the valleys. Lotsa smog, but what the hay, we're from Los Angeles and we're tough. We won't breathe air we can't see. Right? Right on."

The radio report was followed by a "golden oldie" titled, "Feelings." The throbbing ballad hung in the hot arid air, as if it were a physical element like the automobile exhausts from the Ventura Freeway, the .36 parts per million ozone count, the sweet resinous pollen of the lemon trees or the oily smoke from the backyard barbecue.

Ruth Styles had, in this her thirty-fifth year of life, developed an acute sensitivity to all the different air particles about her home in the San Fernando Valley suburb of Encino. The sight of her husband Harry, hovering over the smoking barbecue, was reminder enough that there was something malignant in those particles.

Harry stood an inch, maybe two, under six feet, and he had not long ago been a husky man. But now his blue shirt hung loosely on a frame recently wasted by cancer. The aftermath of the disease was evident in the gaunt hollows of his face and in his pale skin. Yet his movements reflected none of the painful, resigned caution of a sick man. He skewered the plump franks, flipped the thick hamburgers with quick decisive movements of his right hand while balancing a half-quart can of beer with his left. Harry Styles gave every impression of a man who still believed in his own immortality.

"Daddy, Daddy, that one." Four-year-old Christopher, as blond as a sunbeam, bobbed eagerly at his father's side and pointed out a hamburger beginning to singe around the edges.

"Aha!" Harry flipped the hamburger with a theatrical flourish. It was a game that father and son played at the barbecue.

Ruth watched them a moment, then continued to set a redwood picnic table. The table was heaped with baskets of stone-ground whole-wheat hamburger and hot dog rolls, bags of natural-style potato chips prominently labeled "No Preservatives Used," overflowing bowls of homemade coleslaw and carrot and raisin salad, pitchers of homemade lemonade sweetened with unrefined sugar, and baskets of fresh fruit. Ruth's preoccupation with natural and organic foods had developed simultaneously with Harry's illness and accelerated with the prognosis of the disease.

She studied the abundant table, spread before her like the overflow of a cornucopia, as if drawing some healing magic from the array. Then she turned back toward her family.

Alongside the pool, thirteen-year-old Brenda Styles, in a polka-dot bikini, lay stretched out on an air mattress sunning herself and reading. Or rather she was cramming *Silas Marner* for the next day's quiz in freshman English, all the while her tapping toes kept the beat to the music blaring from the transistor radio propped next to her.

Brenda had inherited her mother's black satin hair and alabaster skin, a lustrous milky flesh whose lack of pigment resisted the baths of sunshine and Swedish Tanning Secret to darken it.

Christopher, on the other hand, had Harry's genes, an inheritance of fair hair that bleached to a pale lemon silk and skin that darkened as if doused with a walnut stain after a summer in the sun.

The third child, David, aged eleven, suddenly surfaced from the depths of the pool, thrashing the water, sputtering and choking.

"For Chrissakes, Davey, you're splashing me," his sister complained loudly.

The boy wore a diver's face mask, at the moment flooded with water, and he ripped it off in a panic for air.

"Hey, Dad, the mask is too big," David yelled. "It keeps flooding."

"The mask is the right size. You're not clearing it right."

A dog, a shaggy black mutt that had been slumbering in the shade of the picnic table, lunged to the pool's edge, barking excitedly at David. The dog danced about the edge, as if threatening to plunge in, but each time he approached the lip, he dropped down on his forepaws, then back-stepped away from the water.

"I'm trying to clear it, but it doesn't work," David complained. "Will you show me again? Please."

"Okay."

Ruth anxiously looked at her husband.

"Honey," Harry called out to her, "will you watch the hamburgers while I give Junior Jacques Cousteau there a snorkle lesson?"

"Harry, I don't think you should."

Harry smiled at his wife and dismissed her alarm with a wave of his hand. "It's all right. I'm not going to swim forty laps. I'm just dipping into the water. It's warm enough and I won't get a chill. Hell, all the time I was in the hospital, all I thought about was lying in that pool with a cold beer and the hot sun on my skin."

"Is that *all* you thought about?"

Harry laughed. "Well, maybe it was the second thing on my list."

Ruth indeed looked lovely. She wore a long white cotton piqué dress. The gingham ties that nipped the waist emphasized the weight she had lost in the last few months. That loss was due to the strain she'd been under, and the tension showed in the lines now etched in her face.

Ruth had bought the sun dress at Joseph Magnin for Harry's homecoming from the hospital. At the same time she had gotten the sports outfit Harry now wore, a chambray shirt-jacket with a drawstring hood and matching swim trunks. It evoked images of a man who

14

surfed and jogged along the beach. Ruth had bought it for Harry to convalesce in.

He unzipped the jacket and removed it, stripping to his bathing trunks. A livid red scar ran all the way from his back across his side to the center of his chest, as if he had been all but literally cut in two.

The sight of the scar brought tears to Ruth's eyes. The hooded surfer's jacket was false hospital room cheer, like a Hallmark get-well card that cajoled: "You'll be up and running around in no time." But the scar stated incalculable pain, irreparable damage. Beneath the blue chambray optimism, it was the reality of how deeply Harry had been mutilated.

Harry reached down and took his son's small hand. "Okay, Chris, let's get wet and show your big brother which end is up."

"Yay!" The kid bounced and skipped at Harry's side. Christopher was a stocky child, with stout arms and legs, but at four he still had his baby potbelly. His suit invariably slipped below this little pot, precariously hanging on to the chubby cantilever of his behind.

Harry gingerly eased himself into the pool, testing the water temperature with his foot, then slowly stepped in and lowered himself all the way down to his neck, although the water at that end was only three feet deep.

Christopher belly-flopped into the pool with a great splash, dog-paddled over to Harry, and hung around his neck, kicking vigorously.

The shaggy black dog began barking excitedly. He dipped a paw tentatively into the water, then sprang back yelping with renewed frustration.

"Come on, Groucho. Come here," Christopher coaxed the dog. "It won't hurt you. Come here."

The pool was fifteen yards long—"A thousand dollars a yard," as Harry frequently commented—and the ground for it had been broken fourteen months before, right after Harry's last salary raise. It had been filled just a month before the first devastating medical report.

"Why is Groucho scared of the water?" Christopher asked. The thought of being frightened by the pool, especially when his father was there with them, was something totally alien to the boy's understanding.

"Because your brother, the great animal trainer, tried to teach Groucho how to swim by just throwing him into the pool when we first got him. It terrified the poor puppy."

"But we won't let him drown. I'll teach him how to swim."

"He doesn't know that. In the back of his mind, all he remembers is being suddenly dropped into this cold wet mysterious stuff and not being able to breathe and choking and not knowing what was happening."

Harry treaded his way along the edge of the pool to where Brenda lay. Her round behind in its polka-dot bikini loomed up like a beach ball. Harry reached up out of the water and gave the beach ball a playful swat with his palm.

"You've got your mother's behind, Bren, honey. You're going to be a heartbreaker."

Daddy! Brenda sat up, shocked, at once embarrassed and flattered and confused. She glanced at her mother, who laughed.

Brenda settled back down. "Meet my father, the dirty old man," she said to no one in particular.

Harry treaded water into the deep section of the pool, where David was hanging on the side. He eased Christopher's grip off from his neck and placed the child's hands on the lip of the pool. "Hang on here and practice your kick," he told the four-year-old, then took the face mask David held out to him.

"The trick is to press at the top like this." Harry demonstrated, putting on the mask. His voice, with his nose sealed off, had a thick congested sound. "Then blow the air out through your nose. The air pressure forces the water out through the bottom."

David nodded.

"I'll go underwater and fill the mask up and you watch me clear it."

"Okay."

Harry submerged and sat on the bottom of the pool. In a moment David joined him, his face a few inches from his father's, peering at him intently through the blurring green water. The boy's long black hair swirled and drifted about his head in the eddies generated by his sculling hands and feet.

Harry pulled the mask away from his face, allowing the water to fill the mask. Then he pressed it against his forehead with the tips of his fingers and exhaled through his nose. The water in the mask began to recede.

On the surface, Christopher hung on the edge of the pool trying to peer into the mysterious depths to see what his father and brother were doing. Brenda sighed and struggled to refocus her drifting attention on *Silas*

17

Marner. Ruth sipped a tall glass of lemonade and critically surveyed the flower garden she had landscaped about the pool. She had, at first, assiduously cultivated it. Now the neglected rosebushes were badly in need of pruning, the camellias were wilted for lack of deep watering and feeding.

The surface of the pool suddenly exploded as Harry broke water choking and coughing. He yanked off the mask trying to get at the air, but was unable to catch his breath. His body was convulsed by spasms as he gasped hoarsely for air.

"Daddy!" Christopher, delighted at his father's emergence, let go of the side of the pool and dog-paddled over to Harry, clutching at him for support.

David surfaced by his dad and looked at him a moment in confusion. "Hey, Dad! What's the matter?" Then the boy wailed in alarm. *"Ma!"*

Ruth dropped the glass she was holding and sprang to the pool side. One look at Harry choking and fighting to breathe and stay afloat while a terrified Christopher clung to his neck and she leaped into the pool, her long white sun dress billowing about her like a parachute.

She struggled to hold Harry afloat, swallowing water herself, gasping out, "David . . . grab Christopher . . . *Brenda!"*

Brenda stretched out as far as she could reach and caught her mother's grasping hand. Then the girl got a grip on Christopher's chubby arm and hauled the terrified child over the edge, while Ruth and David supported Harry. He was making terrible retching sounds, the sound charged with the deep pain convulsing his body.

"Oh, my God, Harry!" The anguish and helplessness in Ruth's face reflected a pain as great as that racking her husband. Blood now appeared at Harry's mouth. It bubbled at his lips and splattered Ruth, the bloody froth violently spitting, foaming, and ebbing with each agonized gasp for air.

1

Fifty yards from shore, a half-dozen surfers sat astride their boards, bobbing listlessly in the swells, their eyes squinting seaward, searching for a gathering comb of water.

The sky was overcast, bleeding all color from the landscape. The sky, sea, and sand seemed made of the same muted gray element. A veil of mist hung on the surface of the water, and the surfers rising up into it on glassy swells looked as if they were levitating into thin air.

Karl Steinhardt watched them a while, then kicked at the thick wet sand and trudged on through it. A towering, gaunt figure, white-haired, with a deeply lined face. Head bent, he stalked the beach, searching the shoreline like a shell collector. At one point he stopped and stooped to examine the olive-green shell of a kelp crab, then again kicked at the sand and continued his stalking.

Kicking sand. That is what his late wife Johanna had

always called his long ruminative treks along the beach. When his brain had become numb with study, analysis, classification, research, experiments, and dissections, he had always fled to the beach. Beaches on the Skagerrak outside Oslo and on the Baltic Sea south of Stockholm, the dunes of Massachusetts, the tidal flats of Chesapeake Bay, and now the gleaming white Pacific sands of Southern California. The wandering pocks in the sand that were obliterated at high tide were the footsteps of his career.

Steinhardt searched the landscape about him. To the south the foothills swelled up out of the water, rolling to the distant peaks. The town of Marejada spilled out of a sun-baked valley of the California coastal range right to the edge of the sea. The red tile roofs of the Spanish-style homes that predominated in the town looked like a cluster of russet stones that had been washed down the arroyo in the past winter's rain.

But to the north, toward Los Angeles, the land's advance from the sea was gentler, creating a broad, gleaming beach that stretched for miles to a distant fog-shrouded point of sea cliff. Steinhardt trudged on in that direction.

A massive wood and steel pier loomed over him. It thrust like a pointing finger from the beach into the sea for a quarter of a mile. It was the landmark of the Institute of Oceanography. Alongside its barrel-thick pilings, four scuba divers waded ponderously into the water, laboring with iron tanks, lead weights, nylon-mesh specimen bags, and plastic slates. Except for the surfers and divers, dressed in thick black neoprene wet suits against the chill, the beach was deserted.

The divers submerged in a brief eruption of bubbles and Steinhardt was totally alone. He walked on, head bent to the ground, shoulders hunched, hands clasped behind his back. Here at the water's edge Steinhardt was not searching for the carapace of kelp crabs but for the answers to fundamental questions of life. At the interface of land, sea, and air he sought the primal rhythms of creation, the rhythms to which all life played harmony and counterpoint.

In the past, after kicking at the sand and slugging through the soft oblivious dunes, the answers had always spontaneously come to him. It was as if the synapses in some as yet uncharted folds in his brain had attuned themselves to those primal rhythms and decoded the messages they carried, as a radio receiver tunes in and decodes the information in radio waves.

But today no answer came from the sands he kicked or the echo of the surf in his ears. Nor would it come. For the question he asked was not one of biology or medicine but of destiny. Should he go on with his research? Had he already gone too far?

Steinhardt turned and slogged through the sand back toward the campus. At the edge of the beach and up the slopes of the hill beyond it were the Insitute of Oceanography's sprawl of disparate buildings—monolithic concrete block offices and classrooms, Victorian wood-frame houses, Quonset huts, red-tiled haciendas. The size and architectural style of each building gave a historical balance sheet of the institute, its ebb and flow of endowments, state appropriations, private gifts, and military research grants. The largest and most impressive building was the most recent, a three-story, surreally modern structure. Its steeply slanted, raw concrete walls looked as if they had been carved out of the bedrock of the hill from which the building jutted out and from which it traced its extreme bevels and contours.

On the seaward side, the offices facing the ocean opened onto balconies that ran the width of the building. Above Steinhardt, a white gull sailed over the beach. It glided without beating its wings and settled gracefully on the topmost balcony just opposite Steinhardt's office.

He looked up at the white gull curiously. Perhaps its choice of his office balcony was an omen.

Aaach! He kicked at the sand in disgust. *An omen.* How easily the confused mind slips into mysticism. On the brink of a major breakthrough in his work, he was hesitant, uncertain, assailed by grave misgivings. They bogged him down like the soft sand through which he now labored, sinking ankle-deep, the sand spilling into his shoes and making every step an effort. Steinhardt headed back to his laboratory, back to his unfinished work, that work which he had begun to distrust.

The front door of the research building burst open and Mark Matsuda, Steinhardt's assistant, ran out. He vaulted down the three steps leading to the beach walk in one stride, ran a few steps, then, spotting Steinhardt, slowed his pace, as if such a raucous approach was an outrage.

"Dr. Steinhardt!" Matsuda was out of breath and excited. He had apparently run down the entire four flights of stairs from their office.

"Dr. Steinhardt, the University Medical Center

23

called. Dr. Bernstein said for you to call him as soon as possible."

"Jaaa." The word came out as a long breath. The fate of his life's work was going to be resolved after all. His question was to be answered not by mystic seaside revelations but by the personal tragedy of another man, a total stranger.

2

How many times had Dr. Morris Bernstein made this same decision—ten times? A hundred? Each time he had blocked it from his memory, so that now the agony was as acute as it had been the first time.

Bernstein studied the patient lying on the bed of the intensive care unit of the University Medical Center. He checked the oscilloscopes and digital read-outs again, desperately searching for a deviant flicker. There was none.

"Nothing's functioning on it now," Bernstein said finally. "It's over."

A second doctor standing beside Bernstein nodded gravely in agreement, as if grateful the decision wasn't his to make.

It was just such decisions, such pronouncements, that had prematurely aged Bernstein. He wearily rubbed his furrowed forehead and tight, freckled scalp. Now in his mid-fifties, he looked over sixty years old. At sixty, should he live so long, he would look like the emaciated, wasted eighty-two-year-old corpse that lay on the bed before him, making its mechanical parodies of life.

"The family won't give permission to pull the plug," the other doctor said. "They say it isn't the will of God."

Bernstein shook his head as if acknowledging some grotesque joke. He looked about him at the machinery that imitated life. A mechanical respirator, the heavy piston in the transparent plastic cylinder pumping air in and out of a tube inserted directly into the old man's throat, did the work of lungs and a diaphragm that no longer functioned. An electronic pacemaker galvanized the heart that no longer had the ability to maintain its own beat. The dialyzer sucked the blood from the man's wrist into a stainless steel cabinet where cellulose membranes substituted for the failed kidneys. And hanging bottles dripped glucose, electrolytes, vitamins, proteins, fats, and water into translucent tubes that shunted into translucent veins the nutrients that the disease-ravaged stomach could no longer absorb.

"Will of God, huh?" Bernstein said. He smiled, but it was irony, not humor, that twisted his lips. He turned and hurried from the intensive care unit, fleeing through the swinging doors.

In the anteroom Steinhardt paced impatiently. He whirled at the sound of the door opening. Bernstein, preoccupied, was startled to find Steinhardt waiting for him.

The gaunt, towering figure of the Scandinavian moved forward and seized the doctor's hand, his right hand squeezing Bernstein's palm, his left gripping the smaller man's forearm. The blue eyes eagerly searched the other man's.

Bernstein nodded. "Yes, Karl," he said softly, acknowledging the other man's unspoken question. "Yes."

Harry Styles sucked greedily at the oxygen, his pained gasps making a harsh rasping sound. Gradually his panic quieted, the vertigo subsided, and he relaxed and sank back into his pillow, waving the oxygen mask away.

"That better?" Ruth asked.

"Yes. Thank you." Harry's voice was a labored whisper.

Ruth replaced the oxygen mask in its holder by the head of the hospital bed. There were bubbles of perspiration on Harry's brow. She gently wiped them with a tissue and then kissed Harry lightly on the temple, as if testing the degree of his fever.

There was an intimacy in the gesture that made Bernstein, standing in the doorway, feel as if he were intruding. He said nothing but stood politely waiting for them to be aware of his presence.

Harry Styles had weakened so quickly in the last few weeks that the sudden momentum of his illness seemed to have also physically drained his wife. Ruth Styles had visibly aged, as if her vitality and health were inseparably linked with her husband's. Now they sat silently holding hands, their fingers entwined, the wasting hulk of a once handsome blond man and a beautiful woman whose milky skin and black silky hair now were both dry and lusterless, man and wife fading together like cut flowers.

"Can I bring you anything from home?" Ruth asked.

"A carton of cigarettes."

Her laugh was meant to be polite, but even that

effort failed and tears coursed freely down her cheeks. She buried her face in her husband's shoulder.

"Oh, Jesus, Harry, what the hell am I going to do without you?"

He lightly stroked her hair.

"I'm not going to die," he said in a hoarse whisper that gathered strength and conviction from his mounting anger. "I refuse to die."

Bernstein knocked on the open door. Ruth sat up and dabbed at her tears as he entered. The physician nodded and smiled—that smile heralding sympathy, condolences, tragedy—first at Ruth and then at Harry.

"How are you feeling today, Mr. Styles?"

"Weaker than I felt yesterday. Stronger than I'm going to feel tomorrow."

Steinhardt stood behind Bernstein, the shaggy white head looming above the other's bald pate, the blue eyes riveted on Harry.

"Are you in any pain?" Bernstein asked.

"Only when I breathe."

"A great kidder," Bernstein said to Ruth. Noticing the direction of her gaze, he then waved his hand. "This is Dr. Steinhardt, an old colleague and friend. The ivory tower of medical research. He is going around with me to observe medicine in its mundane practice." He picked up the chart hanging from the foot of Harry's bed and studied it, sharing it with Steinhardt.

"Tried to give my body to medical science," Harry whispered. "They rejected me."

"What sort of research?" Ruth asked Steinhardt.

With great reluctance Steinhardt looked up from the chart and summoned a shy smile. "Very basic work in respiration and oxygen assimilation," he said. The voice was deep and resonant, the diction precise, and the speaker's native Norwegian was a nuance rather than an accent. "I'm working at the Institute of Oceanography."

"Mr. Styles here is involved in aerospace research," Bernstein interjected quickly.

"Ah, yes." Steinhardt nodded.

"Just nuts-and-bolts electronics." Harry made a weak, deprecating wave. "Avionics."

"But you have been much more successful in your field than we have in mine," Steinhardt said expansively. "You have men cavorting on the moon. We can't get them more than a couple of hundred feet down into the ocean without putting them into armored pressure cookers."

Harry gestured weakly, pointing to something behind Steinhardt. In a frame on a nightstand was a Kodacolor print of Ruth Styles and three children posed beside a tent on a Sierra lake. Next to it was a detailed model of the Apollo spacecraft, the replica looking more like a child's top than the command module that had carried men to the moon and back. That and the photograph were the only personal effects evident in the hospital room. Steinhardt studied both as if they were important, even critical, to his mission, before turning back to the ashen, wasted man in the bed.

"You worked on the moon landings?"

Harry nodded, a bob of the head and a small weak smile.

"Harry was also the head of the team that developed the guidance and navigational system for the space shuttle." Ruth Styles volunteered the information in a

29

soft, low voice that was vibrant with pride.

"Ah!" Steinhardt's appreciation was emphatic, as if it had some great significance for him.

"Just a subsystem within a system within a system," Harry whispered. "But my claim to immortality." Harry turned to look at his wife with great affection and lifted her hand to his mouth to kiss it lightly. "That," he whispered, "and our children."

For the first time since entering the room, Bernstein turned his full attention to Ruth Styles. Despite the sleepless grief that had etched the skin about her eyes with spiderwebs of lines and drained the flush from her face, she was a beautiful woman.

Bernstein was disturbed. It was not Ruth's beauty that suddenly made him anxious, but the way she totally possessed her husband. He and Steinhardt would have to confront that, and the expectation of that emotional tug-of-war depressed him, draining the excitement Bernstein had experienced just a few moments before.

"He's relatively young."

Bernstein nodded. "He started smoking two packs a day in college, and he told me that the pressure and deadlines of his work had him up to three and sometimes four packs. That, and living in the Los Angeles basin all his life. He's probably accumulated as much lung pollution and stress as a man of eighty."

Steinhardt and Bernstein hurried down the corridor of the hospital. The polelike figure and the short, pudgy surgeon made a Mutt-and-Jeff-ish procession, Bernstein taking two jogging steps to each one of

Steinhardt's strides, amid a flux of doctors, nurses, orderlies, and visitors.

"But his heart is still strong," the scientist commented.

"There's very little oxygen in his blood for it to circulate," Bernstein said. "We took out the right lung three months ago. Apparently there'd been a simultaneous involvement of both lungs, but on the left lung it must have been microscopic and we missed it on the biopsy. In any case, it was centrally located so we couldn't have done a lobectomy." He and Steinhardt had previously discussed the case in detail, but Bernstein once again went over all he had done as if seeking absolution for his failure to save his patient.

"He's still alert. How much more time does he have?"

Bernstein shrugged. "A month at the most. If you're going to get his permission you haven't any time to waste."

They entered the hospital lobby, packed with forlorn visitors carrying flowers and books, dismissed patients waiting impatiently in wheelchairs for cars to arrive at the entrance to pick them up.

"I anticipate Mrs. Styles will be my major obstacle," Steinhardt said.

Bernstein nodded. "Karl," he said softly, "even if Styles and his family consent, I doubt very much if the committee will ever agree to the procedure." He was referring to the committee on research involving human beings. "It's too experimental. Too far out."

Steinhardt looked down at his colleague. "In that event perhaps we can have him transferred to a naval hospital."

Bernstein was surprised. "Will *they* let you do it?"

Steinhardt shrugged. "Most of my funding comes from the Office of Naval Research. The rest from the National Science Foundation. Neither, I'm quite sure, has the vaguest idea what exactly it is that I'm doing. My last two papers have yet to be published. They are, no doubt, somewhere at the bottom of a huge stack of other research papers awaiting publication on the desk of the editor of the *Journal of the American Society for Experimental Biology*. How many people really are interested in 'Oxygen-Carbon Dioxide Diffusion Across Transplanted Silastic Membranes'?"

Steinhardt smiled, and like Bernstein's own smile, the scientist's was an expression of irony rather than cheer.

He seized his friend by the shoulder in a warm grip, shook his hand, and then was across the lobby and through the main door in three great strides.

3

When Ruth Styles returned home that afternoon she drifted vaguely from room to room not really looking for anything in particular.

Ruth was alone, and the silence in the normally noisy house was strange and disorienting, distorting her sense of place as if her meanderings were in a dream from which she would wake; this anesthetized world suddenly would shatter with the explosion of the alarm clock summoning Harry to work and thrusting her back again into the noisy, tactile reality of her life.

Christopher was being looked after by a neighbor; David and Brenda were at school. The children were the perimeters of Ruth's life now. She went to the hospital in the morning and came home in time for the children's return from school. After dinner with the children, she returned to the hospital to resume her deathwatch.

Ruth harbored no shred of hope, clung to no straw of faith in the spontaneous remission of the tumor. Twice before in her life she had passionately believed in such things, and twice her faith had been devastated.

The first time had been when her father was stricken with cancer. With each operation, each course of chemotherapy, each radiation treatment, each vague statement that her father felt a little better today, she had had hope. But inexorably, relentlessly, he had weakened, his flesh shrinking on his bones as it was consumed from within. In five months he was dead.

When Ruth was told that Harry had lung cancer, she had reacted to the diagnosis as though she had been told her husband was dead. She refused to be comforted by the doctor's optimistic plans for surgery. Although Ruth encouraged Harry's desperate hopes, she herself remained numb with dread.

When Harry returned from the hospital with his lung removed and then slowly gained strength, she had had a giddy surge of hope. Perhaps they had gotten it all. She and Brenda had gone out and bought a huge poster photo of John Wayne. "Real men only need one lung," she had inscribed on the poster. Harry had hung it over his desk in his study. Then it had all started again, the dry hacking, the constant clearing of the throat, the occasional vomiting, and the cough day and night.

Ruth wandered into the bedroom. Groucho was sleeping on the bed. The dog stirred, looked up guiltily, then jumped off the bed and slunk forward, his tail downcast but wagging supplicantly, expecting a scolding.

Ruth did not have the will to rebuke the dog. She knelt down and hugged him, drawing comfort from his warmth and fur, even from his musty doggy smell. Groucho snorted happily and licked Ruth's face. She stood up and then wearily sunk down on the bed. She longed to sleep.

Ruth had shared this bed with Harry until the day he was finally taken to the hospital. She had shared the sleeplessness, the incessant cough and shifting for a comfortable position, the vaporizer to ease the breathlessness that only got worse. She had administered the cough medicines, the lozenges to soothe his raw throat and the countless glasses of water and cups of hot rosehip tea in the middle of the night. She had adjusted the pillows to try to help his chest pains and rubbed his back to ease the ache there. And when Harry finally fainted into an uneasy sleep, she lay next to him listening to the dry, grating snore with its echoes of a death rattle.

There had been no rest for her. Even when, totally exhausted, she managed to fall asleep for a few hours, she always awoke with a stabbing sense of guilt for having somehow abandoned Harry.

Harry, seeing her exhaustion, tried to get her to sleep in one of the other rooms, but Ruth refused to take even that small step toward abandoning him. All too soon he would be utterly alone, when she would be helpless to either share or ease his sleepless nights, the pain, the insatiable struggle for breath.

Harry's rapidly decreasing lung capacity first affected his walking, and then he was restricted to bed. He increasingly needed oxygen to breathe. He could not drink enough to keep hydrated and needed intravenous fluids. Ruth wanted to nurse him at home rather than abandon him to the impersonal care of a hospital. It was Harry who insisted on going. It was because of the boys.

Brenda fussed about her father, coming in unbidden

to read to him or just to wipe his hot, moist forehead. But David and Christopher watched from a distance, increasingly remote.

"I'm becoming their aged invalid grandfather," Harry said the night before he was taken to the hospital, and he cried. He and Ruth huddled close together, silent. Brenda had come and looked into the dark room and then left without saying a word.

It was almost time to pick Christopher up from Mrs. Levine. Ruth got up from the bed and listlessly wandered into the study, a fourth bedroom in the rear of the house that Harry had converted for his work. The nearest telephone was there.

Behind the desk was the John Wayne poster. "Real men only need one lung." It now represented all their betrayed hopes, all Ruth's anguish. At the sight of it, she felt a rush of fury. She sank down at Harry's desk and cried, her deep sobs causing the dog at her feet to whine and bark.

4

Steinhardt was at the hospital early the next morning. Bernstein escorted him to see Harry, then left the two of them alone.

Harry, at first, had difficulty following what Steinhardt was trying to explain to him. He'd had a bad night, one of his worst to date, and the pain and coughing had kept him from sleeping. He kept the oxygen mask on most of the time Steinhardt was talking to him, and the doctor's references to his research on oxygen-carbon dioxide diffusion got confused in Harry's mind with the oxygen he was breathing.

Then Steinhardt produced the schematics, and Harry's technically trained mind immediately focused on them. He was fascinated. The schematics were like the cutaway diagrams of a human head and torso used in TV commercials to demonstrate the efficacy of aspirin or nasal sprays. However, the anatomical detail was considerably greater, especially the cross-section detail of the manufactured implants.

"That's ingenious," Harry said in a labored whisper

that still conveyed his admiration.

"It's hardly an original invention. The basic design is approximately four hundred million years old," Steinhardt noted, then added, "except for the elaborate arrangement of the blood vessels *here* in the anterior comb to form a countercurrent heat exchanger." He pointed to that section of the drawing.

"Ingenious," Harry repeated. "An artificial gill." He stared at the drawings in his lap.

"It would allow a man to literally breathe oxygen directly from the water as fish and other aquatic animals do." Steinhardt's voice was muted, but his eyes betrayed an intense excitement that made Harry hesitate to ask the question that came to his mind.

"But why is it necessary? What's wrong with the scuba lung?"

"Any apparatus that uses compressed air or gases is too limited in depth and range. Below two hundred feet pressurized nitrogen, which constitutes eighty percent of air, becomes a drug causing nitrogen narcosis. Pure oxygen under pressure is toxic, so mixtures of oxygen and inert gases like helium must be used for deep dives. However, when the diver ascends to the surface too quickly, the pressurized gases in the blood are released in bubbles. It's the same effect as when you open a bottle of beer or soda pop. But bubbles in the blood can be fatal. They create the bends and embolisms. In order to get a man down to four hundred feet for only fifteen minutes of work we must encase him in a suit of armor and afterward take two and a half hours to gradually decompress him."

Steinhardt shrugged. "Obviously, this isn't very practical, if you want men to explore greater depths or work on oil drilling or mining operations."

Harry sat propped up on three pillows, a position that somewhat eased the pressure on his chest and allowed him to breathe with slightly less difficulty. Over the plastic proboscis of the oxygen mask, he stared at the tall, gaunt Scandinavian, who was patiently explaining the basics of diving physiology to him as a teacher might instruct a not particularly quick student. Harry was as fascinated by this intense, brooding man as he was by the lesson.

But why was Steinhardt explaining all this to him? At the edge of his consciousness, Harry already knew the answer. It both horrified and enthralled him.

Steinhardt was still talking. "Yet there would be no limits to our ability to explore and work underwater, either in time or depth, if we could absorb oxygen from the water directly into our bloodstream as the most primitive fish does." He paused and studied Harry, examining the masked face to determine whether or not the other man was following him.

Harry said nothing. He felt a little light-headed. Perhaps in his excitement he'd taken in too much oxygen too quickly. He slipped off the mask and consciously tried to calm his breathing. In a few moments he relaxed, as the oxygen-carbon dioxide level in his blood reached a more normal ratio.

Harry put his hand on the drawings of the artificial gill. "How long has this work been going on?"

Steinhardt shrugged. "General Electric developed the thin silicone membrane in the early sixties. Bodell, a researcher in thoracic and cardiovascular surgery in Chicago, described what he called an artificial gill in 1965 using Silastic capillary tubing developed by Dow

Corning. It was a device to oxygenate the habitats of rats underwater." The scientist gave a small smile, one that briefly illuminated his face with a humor and warmth Harry hadn't seen before.

"From such modest origins, worlds are conquered," Steinhardt said.

"In 1966, just a year after Bodell published, Ayes was awarded a patent on a gill-type underwater breathing device. However, the major medical breakthroughs have come about in just the past decade. In open-heart surgery both the heart and lungs are bypassed. The blood is totally oxygenated outside the body. Efficient artificial gill-like devices about a liter in size are now standard in heart-lung machines. My research has been directed at getting back to biological basics. Using the same silicone materials and surgical techniques, I've developed an artificial gill that can be implanted in mammals. It will sustain them underwater for prolonged periods."

Steinhardt had been talking with great assurance and authority, but now he suddenly fell silent. He gave Harry a shy, hesitant smile and sat there staring at him as if he were embarrassed to say anything further. He glanced down at his shoes and then looked back at Harry with the same awkward smile.

Harry returned a grim smile. "You're looking for a volunteer," he whispered.

Steinhardt nodded. "It's never been implanted in a human yet," he said reluctantly. "It is at best a very dangerous operation. One in which there are countless more unknown factors than known." He shifted his glance away from Harry, avoiding the sick man's eyes.

Harry trembled. He sucked deeply at the oxygen

again to relax, but the hollow ache of fear in his gut remained.

He slowly lay back against the pillows, his heart pounding, and watched Steinhardt. The research scientist obviously didn't have Bernstein's bedside manner. He didn't have his colleague's experience of hour-by-hour confrontations with cancer, strokes, bedsores, chronic pain, death, suicidal patients, grief-stricken families, the constant bleeding, howling maelstrom of the dying and dead. How was it that Bernstein had first introduced Steinhardt? "The ivory tower of medical research."

Harry was painfully aware that his fear and Steinhardt's embarrassment had the same source. "You need an already condemned man to volunteer," he said finally.

Steinhardt nodded, and his acknowledgment was in itself an anguished apology. "I'm sorry," he said softly. "But the most we could hope for the first time is to get preliminary data on the amount of carbon dioxide and oxygen diffusion taking place across the silicone membranes of the gill. We would not even begin the operation until the patient had slipped into a final coma."

For a long time the two men were silent, and neither looked at the other. Then Harry pulled aside his oxygen mask and spoke. "What you're saying is that I'll never regain consciousness," he whispered. "Never know whether or not the operation, the experiment, was a success."

Steinhardt nodded. "As a research scientist yourself you know that no experiment is a failure," he said. "We often learn more from those that don't succeed than from those that do."

After Steinhardt left, Harry lay still, his hands nervously playing with the drawings. The scientific authority had confirmed his death sentence. Harry's fear of death suddenly bordered on panic, and only his physical weakness kept him from screaming.

He had not given Steinhardt an answer. To do so would have meant accepting his own death. Harry might academically acknowledge the fact that he was going to die, eventually, and he had dutifully made all the necessary arrangements to provide for Ruth and the children. But those preparations had no more emotionally accepted his immediate death than had the insurance policies he had taken out when he was healthy.

As a drowning man, Harry still clung to whatever straws he could grasp. And in medical fact, Harry was drowning. Periodically fluid had to be withdrawn from his chest cavity, his lung tapped, to ease his breathing. It is said that drowning men see their entire lives flash before their eyes, and as Harry's consciousness cycled from periods of pain to periods of quiet and back to pain, Harry did in fact review his life.

He did not think about his wife or the children. They were sources of contentment, and there was nothing there in his life he would change if he could. It was in his career, in the sum total of his professional life, that he had been frustrated. Now he mentally worried that unfulfilled void in his life as if it were an unfilled tooth.

Before he had become ill, Harry at thirty-five had been middle-aged, not physically but psychologically.

He was at a point of perspective in his life where the past assumed meaningful patterns and the future fortuned its logical limits. He would have had a solid, financially comfortable career in engineering management in the aerospace industry. But he had come to accept that without a Ph.D. he would never realize his original ambitions of exploring and expanding the frontier of science. His job was to engineer other men's explorations. For Harry, work had become an increasing drudgery.

On weekend afternoons he and David often plunked down in front of the TV set to watch reruns of "Star Trek." It was their favorite program, often nonsense of course, but Harry was always strangely moved when the announcer intoned: "Its five-year-mission: to explore strange new worlds; to seek out new life and new civilizations. To boldly go where no man has gone before."

Harry had frequently considered going back to Cal Tech for his doctorate. But when, in the privacy of his study, he had drawn up a realistic budget to support Ruth and the three kids and his studies, he had despaired.

A month before the cancer was diagnosed he had again gone to his study. It had been a particularly frustrating day at work. This time he had drawn up a second budget—one based on mortgaging the house, Ruth's working, canceling his life insurance, and using the money they'd saved for the children's college. He'd do his graduate work at UCLA, the state university, rather than the more prestigious but expensive Cal Tech, a private school. This budget had worked, but he had never discussed it with Ruth. It sat in his desk drawer, the blueprint for a dream irrevocably deferred.

Now, in death, he was being offered the participation that had eluded him in life. The macabre irony of this didn't escape Harry, and with the little breath he had left, he summoned up a joyless laugh. But the laugh emerged as a hoarse bark that broke down into a pain-racked cough.

5

That afternoon Ruth got a call from Dr. Bernstein. Would it be convenient for her, he wondered, to stop by his office before her visit to her husband? Dr. Steinhardt wanted to discuss something with her.

"A new course of treatment for Harry?" Ruth asked wearily.

"No. I'm afraid the prognosis remains pretty much what I described to you before."

"Then what's it about?"

"I'd rather Dr. Steinhardt explained it to you. It's complicated."

Ruth agreed, and an appointment was made for ten the next morning. Though exhausted and numb, she was still curious. She remembered vaguely that Steinhardt was involved in some sort of research but couldn't recall anything else about his work. Yet her mental image of the doctor was quite vivid. She remembered the towering frame, and above all, his face and eyes. To Ruth, Steinhardt's penetrating eyes seemed neither kind nor cruel; they simply absorbed and totally accepted everything, like those of a young child before learning to be critical, when the world is only a source of constant wonder.

But there was no sense of wonder in Steinhardt's eyes the next morning when he met Ruth in Bernstein's office. The scientist in fact seemed very ill at ease. After greeting her, he blurted out, "Mrs. Styles, please know you have my sincerest sympathy. My own dear wife Johanna died just a few years ago of cancer. I know the anguish, the feeling of helplessness you're experiencing."

Ruth was surprised. The sudden grief and pain in Steinhardt's face was so poignant that she couldn't look at him; she felt as though she'd dissolve into tears. She looked down and said, "Thank you." And after a moment, she asked, "What was it you wanted to discuss with me?"

Steinhardt briefly outlined the research and experiments he had been conducting with silicone membranes to reproduce the oxygen-carbon dioxide diffusion that takes place across the gills of aquatic animals. His voice was low and vibrant, as if what he was explaining was of life and death importance. And the slight Norwegian accent seemed to heavily underline the grave scientific import of the procedures he was detailing. Ruth was confused, having lost the thread of what Steinhardt was explaining almost at the beginning. She was mesmerized by his eyes.

Steinhardt suddenly paused, as if he had reached a significant point in his exposition. He studied Ruth in silence a moment, then reached down and opened a frayed black leather portfolio at the desk. From it he withdrew the medical illustrations of the man with the gill implant.

Ruth had only a glimpse of them as they traveled from the portfolio to Steinhardt's lap. But a glimpse was all Ruth required, one vivid horrifying picture that jelled those thousand confusing words. She was three steps ahead of any further explanation before Steinhardt said another word.

"No! Never!" Ruth shouted.

Steinhardt looked up in astonishment. He glanced at Bernstein to see if the doctor had said or done something to trigger Ruth's outburst, but Bernstein only returned his look of bewilderment.

Ruth pointed an accusing finger at the medical drawings in Steinhardt's hand. "I will not allow Harry to be a guinea pig in some grotesque medical experiment."

Steinhardt perceptively stiffened, as if Ruth had delivered a personal offense, but his voice remained patient. "Medically, there is nothing particularly grotesque about this procedure, Mrs. Styles. Today we routinely replace arteries with Dacron tubes and rebuild shoulder joints, hips, and leg bones with Vitallium metal. We totally reconstruct jawbones and hip joints with Cerosium ceramics. The implanting of atomic-powered heart pacemakers, electronic bladder stimulators, and plastic eyeballs is commonplace."

Ruth shook her head, an abrupt, angry shake. "No!"

Bernstein looked from Ruth to Steinhardt and back to Ruth, his troubled eyes reflecting both her grief and the scientist's disappointment. "But, Mrs. Styles, your husband has indicated he wants his body donated to medical science."

"He thought he might donate his kidneys or his eyes to someone who needed them," she said in a whisper, almost at the point of tears. "Please, let's just let nature take its course."

Steinhardt was not going to relinquish that easily. "You did not let nature take its course when Mr. Styles's right lung was surgically removed. Nor when he underwent a painful series of radioactive cobalt treatments and chemotherapy."

Ruth looked up and met Steinhardt's eyes and, for that moment, there were neither tears nor compromise in her eyes and voice. "He's suffered enough. We've all suffered enough. Now I want him to die in peace."

After leaving Bernstein's office, Ruth immediately found a ladies room. She shut the door to a stall, sat down, and put her face in her hands and wept, her tears triggered as much by a sense of shame as of grief.

In her encounter with Steinhardt, she'd felt she couldn't continue to look him in the eye. She could no longer look anyone in the eye, for at any moment she felt she was going to break down into tears. But it was not just her vulnerability to tears, as acute as an exposed nerve, that made Ruth self-conscious. It was the knowledge, finally admitted to herself, that she wanted Harry to hurry and die.

His death had been what she had once most feared, but now that it was inevitable she wanted it to come swiftly and pass on. Death was no longer terrifying. It had become a nagging presence that tormented, humiliated, and exhausted her and Harry in a thousand obscene ways each day. It stank, the sweet, noisome smell of catheters, bedpans, and bedsores that no amount of caustic disinfectants and pine sprays would dispel.

Twice a day Ruth dragged herself to the hospital to watch the once beautiful blond man she had loved, the robust father of her three children, agonizingly being consumed and transformed into the same skeletal specter that her father had become. To keep from going mad, she had had to anesthetize every joy, every hope and dream for which she had once lived.

Were Ruth alone she might willingly have died with Harry, like some faithful Hindu widow throwing herself on her husband's funeral pyre. But there were three children who were growing, each as inexorably storming the future as Harry, in his fate, relentlessly sank into death.

Whether the future beyond Harry's death would be barren and lonely for her or would hold new opportunities, a new life, Ruth did not as yet even allow herself to speculate. But the future was there, and if nothing else it promised release from the present. Ruth wanted Harry to die as swiftly and easily as possible, and she would battle anything that delayed his death.

6

Harry had lost a great deal of weight and had weakened considerably since he'd gone to the hospital. In his struggle for breath he had been barely aware of the harrowing change in his appearance. Ruth had shaved and groomed him daily on her visits so he had no practical reason to look into a mirror. He was not by nature a vain man, but now he registered his decline in the shocked silent faces of his three children as they lined up alongside the bed. Their reaction caused him deeper pain than the cancer in his lung.

Harry had asked Ruth to bring all the children. He wanted to tell them formally that he was very ill and he was probably going to die. He felt that if *he* told them, it would somehow be easier for them to accept. But when they were standing beside the bed, he found he couldn't speak. David and Brenda, his two dark-haired beautiful oldest children, were rapidly maturing into reflections of their mother. Blond and cherubic Christopher was the image of himself as a boy. Harry looked at them and his throat caught. Emotionally he simply didn't believe he was going to die. He couldn't tell his children that. Instead he looked at the three grave, silent frightened faces of his children and whispered, "I want you each to know I love you very much. You know that, don't you?"

He looked at Brenda. The girl nodded and then began to weep.

Harry looked at David, and the eleven-year-old whispered back, "Yes, sir, I love you too."

Christopher stared back at his father, the child's eyes wide and awestruck.

Harry motioned to his daughter. "I'm not contagious." Brenda leaned forward and kissed her father on the cheek, a timid but affectionate kiss. Then she buried her face in Harry's neck, her tears splashing his face.

Harry sat up and took her face in both hands, staring at her with bright fevered eyes before kissing her on the forehead.

David solemnly took his sister's place at the head of the bed. He hesitated a moment, then dutifully leaned over and kissed his father on the cheek. With as much strength as he could muster, Harry squeezed his son's shoulders with pale gaunt hands.

Christopher now moved beside Harry's pillow, the child's tangle of blond curls and his enormous wondering eyes barely peeking above the white-sheeted hummock of the high hospital bed. Ruth, watching in the background, moved forward and lifted Christopher so that the four-year-old could reach his father. "Daddy!" Christopher cried out. He clutched at Harry, throwing both his stout little arms about his father's head, choking off his air.

Alarmed, Ruth yanked the child away. "Daddy can't breathe." Her momentary panic infected the child, who looked from her to Harry with now confused and frightened eyes.

With great pain, Harry forced himself to sit up and reach out toward the boy. He kissed the blond head and worried little face, comforting the child. "If he smothers me," Harry gasped in a choked whisper, "that's the way I want to go."

Ruth ushered the three children from the hospital room. Harry, his face contorted with anguish, watched them leave, then grasped for the oxygen mask. The effort and emotional excitement of the brief meeting with his children had exceeded the capacity of his strength. He was near collapse.

He literally gulped oxygen, his breaths panicked and pain-racked. His head cleared, but the oxygen did not relieve his distress. Instead it seemed to dissolve the last restraining thread of Harry's self-control, triggering sobs deeper and more agonized than his desperate gasps for oxygen. The hoarse sobs and crying were muffled by the plastic oxygen mask, and the tears flowed abundantly down his wasted face, collecting in the oxygen intake of the mask, making a muted blubbering sound like that of a heartbroken child.

That afternoon Harry was placed in an oxygen tent, a plastic canopied affair that fitted over the bed and enveloped him in a cool, moisturized atmosphere that was 50 percent oxygen. They also gave him Dilaudid, a narcotic, for the increasing pain.

The drug made Harry more than comfortable; he felt

as if he were floating, suspended weightless. With curious detachment Harry became conscious of his breathing, the desperate in and out pulse of it, the flare and ebb of energy his breath ignited as if each inhalation were the puff of a bellows on a dying ember. The insistent, automatic rhythm of it, in and out, up and down, seemed to be reverberating to all the other rhythms that surrounded him, heartbeats and respirators, all harmonics of the rising and setting of the sun, the ebb and flow of the tide.

The afternoon sunlight streamed through the window and the plastic sheeting of the oxygen tent, the light fracturing and the motes swirling like bubbles, coalescing into a shining fluid stream. Harry's body, with its weight and pain, dissolved away and he drifted up into that stream as if he were some elemental aquatic creature. Ahead was a shining luminous sea. He swam eagerly toward it, propelling himself with an instinctive whipping motion. All about him he sensed countless other flagellating creatures all frantically racing toward the same goal. Faster, faster, faster. He had to stay ahead of the others. To be first was everything. To be less than first was oblivion. Suddenly he was at the shining sea; he plunged into the blinding light and was consumed in ecstasy. His identity dissolved, all knowledge of being a separate distinct being instantly melted from him. He became the light, an element of the shining sea.

Harry lay still on his hospital bed. It was a long time before he came back to himself. He was still trapped in the enfeebled body of Harry Styles.

When Dr. Bernstein looked in on him later that evening, Harry tried to describe the experience.

Bernstein at first listened with great interest, then dismissed it. "The drug Dilaudid sometimes produces hallucinations. So does anoxia."

Harry shook his head. "No. It wasn't a hallucination. Or a dream. I really relived it. They're all there somewhere, aren't they? All the memories of the womb and birth?"

Bernstein nodded. "Yes, but that would have been before your brain or memory had developed."

"But my brain, my whole body, they all developed from the nucleus of that very first cell, didn't they? It just divided up and redivided."

"Well, yes."

"That very first cell is *me*. I know what it knows. The memory is still there. It was buried or suppressed. Maybe the drugs, or my condition, released it. But it was no hallucination. I really experienced it."

Harry sank back against the pillows. In the shadow of death he was convinced he had relived his own conception, the primal moments of his life. He lay on his bed, his mind beyond pain or discomfort, filled with wonder.

"I don't want the children here again."

Ruth had to press her face against the thin plastic sheeting of the oxygen tent in order to hear Harry. Despite the oxygen tent his voice had become weaker, his breath more labored than even the previous day.

"I don't want them to remember me this weak and sick," Harry continued with great difficulty. "It's only going to get worse."

Ruth said nothing but sat perfectly still, her chair

drawn up against the bed. Only a barely perceptible nod indicated that she had heard her husband.

Through the plastic Harry could see Ruth clearly, but the waves and bows of the transparent material created strange distortions in her face, as if Harry were underwater. The cooled, humidified, oxygen-charged atmosphere that enveloped him and the hum of the electric motor that circulated and cooled the air in the tent isolated him from Ruth and the rest of the hospital room. His illness and medical technology had already removed him, by degrees, beyond the pale of normal life, as if gradually conditioning him to the final isolation of death.

Harry restlessly shifted his body in a futile effort to breathe more easily, but even that slight movement brought a great shock of pain. Despite the constant pain, he had deliberately cut the drugs he'd been taking in order to clear his mind. He did not want to be drugged and befuddled. He had a decision to reach, and now he had reached it.

With a feeble gesture of his hand, he motioned Ruth to lean closer. "I want Steinhardt to do the experiment," he whispered.

"Oh, my God, Harry." Even through the distorting plastic sheet Harry could plainly see the shock registered in her face. "Why? Why? It won't change anything."

Harry was silent. Ruth strained forward against the plastic partition, her eyes intent on Harry's face, waiting for an answer.

"I want to be the first," he said.

7

The cypress logs in the fireplace crackled and exploded. They shot up geysers of steam and sparks, protesting that they hadn't had enough time to dry before being burned.

The view of the ocean that Steinhardt had so painstakingly framed by cutting down the cypress was now shrouded in darkness and night fog. The picture window only reflected back the flames and the gaunt figure of Steinhardt hunched over an old book.

Steinhardt removed his glasses, wearily rubbed his eyes, and let his glance drift about the dark paneled study. The walnut-stained bookcases and the tiers of leather- and cloth-bound books walled the room from floor to ceiling.

It was the eclectic collection of a lifetime—his ancient university and medical school texts in Swedish and Norwegian, the standard medical references in English, and shelves of scientific tomes in German, French, and English that had been published in very limited editions. There was, in addition, a concentration of philosophic works from Aristotle to Teilhard de Chardin, including the complete published works of Emanuel Swedenborg, the eighteenth-century scientist, philosopher, and mystic. Steinhardt's Swedenborg collection, including volumes *Oeconomia Regni Animalis* and *Regnum Animale* in the original Latin text, was one of the most comprehensive outside the Royal Academy of Science in Stockholm.

The heavy leather-bound volumes were the cache of a secret alchemist still hunting for the philosophers' stone that transmuted base metals to gold and indefinitely prolonged life. After a lifetime of medical and biological research Steinhardt had realized that each discovery ultimately turns out to be merely the opening of a Chinese box revealing another box within, another mystery.

Like Swedenborg, Steinhardt had come to the belief that the basic principles of nature correspond to larger, ultimately divine patterns. Each transaction of the lungs and heart, each whip of the bronchial cilia was, when understood, the key to cosmic secrets.

At the age of fifty-seven, Swedenborg had had a profound spiritual revelation, thereafter abandoning science to devote his life to writing Biblical prophecy. Steinhardt, in his sixties, had yet to experience a divine revelation. This evening he felt only a bone-deep weariness. He once again rubbed his eyes, replaced his old-fashioned half-lenses for reading, and concentrated on the page before him from Swedenborg's "Clavis Hiero-glyphica."

There is no motion without *conatus,* but there is *conatus* without motion. For if all *conatus* were to break out into open motion the world would perish, since there would be no equilibrium.

Conatus. For Swedenborg, it meant the motive force in nature that corresponds to the will in human minds. It transcended both man and nature, originating in the Infinite.

The sharp ring of the telephone jarred Steinhardt from his meditation. He stared at the phone in confusion. He was a reclusive man who seldom received calls at night.

The phone rang a second time, and he reluctantly pushed himself up from the chair.

It was Ruth Styles. "My husband will let you perform the gill experiment on him." Her voice on the phone was tense, angry, frightened. "He'll be your guinea pig." Her voice broke and there was an audible sob on the line. "My God, I don't know why. He's suffered so much already. Why does he insist on doing this?"

"Mrs. Styles, I don't entirely understand why he wants to myself. I've spent my entire life in research in comparative physiology. In a rather narrow specialty. And yet I've seen time and time again men suffer any pain, often risk their lives for . . ."

"I don't want Harry to suffer anymore," Ruth Styles interrupted him. "He's in great pain now. I can see it in his face even when he's asleep. I don't want him made into one of those vegetables that you keep alive with machines."

"Mrs. Styles, you have my solemn word we won't prolong his life artificially a moment longer than we have to to collect our data. I totally sympathize with your feelings. I lost my own wife less than three years ago. I believe I mentioned that to you."

There was silence on the other end of the line. Steinhardt wanted to say a great deal more, but it was not the time. He had known with certainty that Styles would agree to the operation. But he couldn't explain why to Ruth Styles in her present state of pain and confusion. Perhaps he might never be able to explain it to her.

"I greatly appreciate your calling, Mrs. Styles. I know how difficult it is for you. I'll stop by and see you and Mr. Styles tomorrow. Dr. Bernstein and I will make all the necessary arrangements."

Steinhardt said good night, hung up, and stood, with his hands leaning on the oak desk, staring at the shadows in his study.

For a quiet man Steinhardt knew too many men who had died violently, and at this moment he felt their ghosts surrounding him in the writhing shadows cast by the fire. There were the B-29 bomber crews, faint with high-altitude anoxia, who had crashed and burned. Nordstrom, who had frozen to death in Spitsbergen studying lichens, and Ramenofsky, who had fallen from a cliff of ice in Antarctica while searching for Ordovician fossils. The divers who had died in agony of the bends, and the old veteran diver Matsui, who—knowing what tortures awaited him on the surface if he made a rapid emergency ascent—had chosen to drown silently in the depths.

"Yes, Mrs. Styles, I've seen time and time again men suffer any pain, often risk their lives for . . ."

It is the special power of lonely old widowed men to conjure up the ghosts of events past, and in the solitude of his study Steinhardt called them forth. He desperately needed the momentum of their lives flowing into his, the reassurance that the next experiment was the logical progression.

This time he was not just opening another Chinese box. He was entering the sanctum sanctorum. He was violating the primordial nature of man cast in God's image. And Steinhardt was terrified of the consequences.

8

Bernstein studied the photographs, then reluctantly passed the pictures down the conference table to the doctor on his right.

Bernstein had seen the photographs innumerable times before. They were standard in texts on embryology. The first was a grainy head and shoulder side view of a three-year-old girl with small, irregular, ulcerlike openings in the side of her neck. The second displayed a boy, five years old and very pale, with similar branchial clefts.

The pictures were passed from hand to hand, studied, and passed on. The thoracic surgeons, anesthesiologists, heart-lung machine operators, and scrub nurses now gathered around the conference table had, like Bernstein, seen them before, but now they viewed them with a sense of revelation. Before the photos had been studies of birth defects, biological calamities to be bemoaned and, if possible, surgically corrected. Today they were heralds of a new world.

"The development of all embryos reenacts the basic

stages of evolution." Steinhardt sat at the center of the table. Even seated, the scientist towered above the others in the group. "At five weeks old the human embryo has four distinct gill clefts at each side of the neck. A tail, curving upward toward the head, heightens the external resemblance to a fish, but the similarity is even more pronounced in the internal organs—the heart, blood vessels, kidneys, and brain."

Ontogeny recapitulates phylogeny. It was a natural law everyone in the conference room had recited in high school biology class. The development of an embryo repeats the stages of the evolution of its species. Thus a fertilized human ovum is at first a unicellular organism like an amoeba and then, in progressive stages, the embryo resembles a sponge, a worm, a primitive fish, and in many characteristics, a reptile, before it becomes a distinct mammalian embryo and finally a human fetus.

"After a short existence of two weeks, the gill arches disappear and the embryo advances from a stage potentially adapted to aquatic respiration to one that anticipates the breathing of air," Steinhardt continued.

"Early in the second month the arms and legs appear as buds, as the future human retraces the evolution from fish to amphibian. And by the end of the eighth week the tail has usually been incorporated into the spinal column. The primordial gills and gill pouches evolve into the pharynx, larynx, tonsils, middle ear, and other related structures."

Steinhardt paused while a second set of schematics of embryos at five and eight weeks was passed about the room.

"Oxygen is, of course, supplied by blood from the

mother's circulation. But the fetus's existence is totally aquatic. It is immersed in amniotic fluid, which is strikingly similar in composition to seawater. The fetus breathes the fluid in and out of its lungs, and studies suggest some oxygen is absorbed this way. At birth, air is substituted for the fluid, and respiration becomes deeper and more sensitive.

"However, on occasion normal development goes awry. There are numerous reported cases of infants being born with their embryonic tails. In a parallel birth defect, children are occasionally born with vestiges of their embryonic gill clefts still evident. Their lungs are fully developed, and the gill openings are usually corrected by a simple surgical procedure and skin graft."

Steinhardt searched in the recesses of his frayed leather portfolio and withdrew still another set of photographs and drawings. He studied them silently, frowning, then as if having reassured himself he looked up. "The embryonic studies and the birth defects are invaluable to us in this procedure, because they indicate exactly where the artificial gills should be implanted. Where they are biologically most likely to be accepted by the body."

Steinhardt passed the final set of schematics around the table, stirring a renewed shuffle of diagrams, photographs, coffee cups, and cigarette packs. The majority of the medical personnel in the room were on duty, and the briefing was squeezed in between rounds of the surgical ward. About half the people were smoking, most notably Bernstein. The thoracic surgeon smoked almost incessantly. He smoked with the same confidence with which he moved about the wards and hospital beds infected with galloping diseases, as if he believed that along with the antibodies he had built up to contagious bacilli and viruses, he had also developed an immunity to the carcinogens of tobacco smoke. The ashtray on the table in front of him was already choked with butts and ashes, and despite the air conditioning a stale, pale-blue aureole appeared to encircle his head. The scrub nurse who sat on his left, a nonsmoker, constantly fanned the air in front of her face.

About the table there was a great deal of comment and moving of chairs as the doctors and technicians left their seats and clustered around the new schematics. Their interest was more than academic. They were the operating room team that had been selected for the actual implant.

"The gills themselves are composed of what?" Ben Harrison asked. Harrison was the chief surgical resident. He was a thin, tense man, always overworked and harassed by the responsibilities of his job, but there was no one Bernstein would rather have on the other side of the operating table.

"The main structural elements are composed of the same silicone rubber now routinely used to replace leg tendons and ear and nose cartilage. The capillaries are Silastic, a liquid-impervious, oxygen-permeable silicone membrane with which researchers have been working some years now to construct artificial hearts and lungs." Steinhardt gave a small bemused smile. "There are no secret ingredients. I have made no new discoveries. A tuna fish created the basic design."

"Why a tuna fish?"

"It is one of the few warm-blooded fish. That is, its body temperature is higher than that of the surrounding water. As much as twenty degrees higher. And its banks of muscles develop forty times the power of more typical fish the same size. Its gills are therefore designed to take in oxygen much more effectively to meet those greater metabolic demands."

"Dr. Steinhardt, what do you think the chances of success will be for this operation?"

"Success?" Steinhardt was puzzled by the word. "Our purpose in this first experiment is only to get data on the amount and efficiency of the oxygenation that takes place using this design and these materials. Does the device damage flowing blood, breaking up cells, leading to damage to other organs, the kidneys, the brain, the bone marrow? We must find this out. It's not a question of success or failure. In all experiments we learn something. Perhaps that we're totally on the wrong track." He smiled faintly.

"What about the patient?"

"I think my colleague Dr. Bernstein can best answer that."

Bernstein rose from his chair, feeling compelled by being addressed by the title "colleague" to attain a somewhat greater stature. "Well, in the present prognosis of the disease the patient would probably not live out the week. He's presently lapsing in and out of coma. This procedure won't alter his eventual death forty-eight hours one way or another. Both he and his family are aware of this, but they have agreed to the experiment in the interest of medical science. The patient is a research engineer and, in fact, is highly motivated to make what he feels is a final contribution."

Behind his glasses, Bernstein's eyes, habitually moist

by nature, glistened with tears, a reaction to his fatigue and the irritating cigarette smoke as much as any sentiment, but it transformed Bernstein's brief comment into a eulogy. He bent his head and sat down.

"Actually you're all involved in much more complicated procedures as a matter of daily routine in your heart and lung operations," Steinhardt continued. "You totally bypass both vital organs and completely oxygenate the blood in what is in essence an artificial gill within the heart-lung machine. The blood cells are considerably damaged in their transportation through the tubing and pumping machinery, as you're aware. I'm simplifying this surgical procedure and oxygenating the blood in the manner nature first did. If you'll look at the operation in this way, it won't seem quite as exotic or alien to you."

After the briefing Bernstein and Harrison accompanied Steinhardt to Harry's room to check on their subject's progress toward death. Harry's skin had taken on a pronounced bluish tinge that no amount of oxygen cleared up.

Outside the hospital room Steinhardt pronounced, "If the experiment is to produce any results at all, the operation must be performed within the next forty-eight hours."

The two surgeons both nodded in agreement. "I'll schedule it for the day after tomorrow," Harrison said, scowling. Harrison's habitual expression was, in fact, a dark scowl, no matter how agreeable his actual reply was. Like the deep, harassed lines in his brow, the scowl seemed to have been permanently etched into the flesh of his face.

After the two men had seen Steinhardt into the elevator, Harrison turned to Bernstein. "He makes it sound like the most natural and inevitable procedure in the world. Infinitely more natural than, say, implanting an atomic pacemaker in some guy's chest. Then I think, 'Holy shit, we're going to try and implant *gills* in some guy.'"

Bernstein nodded and smiled. "The committee on human research had the same reaction."

"How the hell did you get it past them?"

"We almost didn't. I had to really stick my neck out and put it on the block to get them to approve. Christ, but he's a total innocent when it comes to hospital politics. In that respect he hasn't learned a thing in thirty years."

"You've known him *that long?*"

Bernstein nodded. "Since my residency at Massachusetts General."

Harrison checked his watch. "You through cutting for today?" he asked.

Bernstein nodded.

"Let me check by my office for messages. Then let's get the hell out of here and have a drink. I want to hear about this."

Harrison and Bernstein went to Walsh's, a quiet neighborhood bar near the hospital, an old hangout where the stained wooden floors were still swept with sawdust.

They ordered drinks and Bernstein recounted his relationship with Steinhardt. But what could he tell Harrison really? The merest outline. He'd known Steinhardt for thirty years but he knew the man hardly at all. They had met, as Bernstein had said, when they were both surgical residents in Boston. But Steinhardt was several years older, already an experienced surgeon who had taken his training in London during World War II and was working as a senior resident in an American hospital to acquire a license to practice here. He had, while in England, already done significant research in high-altitude anoxia in bomber crews.

"Ben, you ever wanted to be anything but a surgeon?" Bernstein suddenly asked Harrison.

"No."

"Not a football player, a novelist, a movie star?"

"No."

"A psychiatrist?"

"God forbid."

"Me neither. Nothing but a surgeon." Bernstein held up his two hands, examining them, turning them first palm up and then studying the backs. "With these we're artists in flesh. We're healers. We're God. Right?"

"Right!" Harrison agreed emphatically.

"Maybe, if we have a flash of brilliance. Or if we're lucky. We come up with a new technique, a new procedure that goes into the books. It all adds up to a career. But for Steinhardt, it was never enough."

The waitress brought them another round of drinks. Bernstein lit another link in his chain of cigarettes and for a moment watched the plume of smoke. The practice of surgery had never been enough for Steinhardt. Bernstein, in those days, couldn't see beyond his next bowel resection, but Steinhardt's mind was already somewhere else. Bernstein's wife Selma used to call him the Viking. Steinhardt always had an air about him that any moment he was going to plunge into an open longboat and sail due north, defy the Norse gods and giants, and go explore Niflheim, the mythical frozen land of the dead. What Steinhardt did, in fact, was get a research grant to trek into the Arctic to study the physiological adaptation of the Eskimos to below-freezing climates.

Bernstein took a good healthy slug of his drink and ordered another round. What did he know? He was just a workaday chest cutter. But Steinhardt was doing fundamental studies of respiration, circulation, and metabolism.

"When did you run into him again?" Harrison asked.

Bernstein shrugged. "You know how it is with old friends. A letter here and there. A Christmas card. We've never really been out of touch." Every few years, if they were in the same place or passing through for a conference, they might get together for dinner. They'd talk about work. Steinhardt would recount whatever exotic research he was doing at the time. Bernstein remembered his excitement while describing how he'd dissected over a hundred sea snakes to find out how they absorbed oxygen from seawater without gills. Sea snakes in the South Seas and Eskimos in the North Pole. There was a part of Bernstein's soul that ached to traipse off on adventures with his towering Nordic friend.

But now that Bernstein thought about it, he recalled that they talked mostly about his own work. Steinhardt had kept up with the literature. He was particularly interested in the then new heart and lung bypass procedures. After Steinhardt joined the Institute of Oceanography he would on occasion look over Bernstein's shoulder during operations. But the surgeon didn't know what he was working on until after Steinhardt's wife died. Then he plunged completely into his research. Perhaps it was a way of assuaging his loneliness or grief. Or maybe Steinhardt suddenly felt he didn't have many years left himself. Bernstein knew that feeling. In the pit of his guts he knew that feeling. He peered intently through the thick lenses of his glasses at Harrison across the table. What the hell, Harrison was practically a kid. There was no way Bernstein could describe the desperation of that feeling to Harrison. But it drove Steinhardt.

Then one day Bernstein received a call from Steinhardt asking if he could drive down to the institute and have dinner with him. He laid out all his cockamamy gill research. Steinhardt had already designed and made up the prototype. He had gone to the plastic fabrication shop that made the oxygenators for the heart-lung machine. He and the biomed engineer first did a mathematical model based on Steinhardt's studies. How much surface area of blood did they need to expose? Then a computer had designed the gill. Steinhardt stood over the plastics technician personally supervising her applying the Dacron velour on the tubing. And then he set up a complete surgical lab at the institute. But he needed Bernstein's help. He needed his finely honed surgical skills.

Bernstein had been both frightened and enraptured. The idea of a man breathing water like a fish appalled him. But Steinhardt's work was undeniably a fundamental breakthrough. Aside from underwater diving—in which Bernstein had little interest—the artificial gill was a key step in the development of a functional prosthetic lung. Bernstein had had heady visions of scientific immortality. He cut down on his surgical practice and spent afternoons, evenings, and week-

70

ends working with Steinhardt. "We did a lot of dogs and monkeys," he told Harrison.

"Dogs and monkeys with gills," the resident said with wonder in his voice. "Son of a bitch! That's when he began looking over your shoulder on every pneumonectomy, laryngectomy, coarctation, and transplant. You said it had to do with his research on embolism."

"It did," Bernstein insisted. "Embolisms, bends, narcosis. The whole spectrum of diving diseases. You eliminate them all by bypassing the lungs and oxygenating the blood directly in a gill."

Harrison shook his head and stared down at the table. "His whole life," Harrison said. "It's as if Steinhardt has been preparing for this one procedure his whole life."

"In a sense that's true of all of us, isn't it?" Bernstein said. "Even that poor son of a bitch guinea pig Styles. If we ever do anything that's significant, that lives after us, everything is preparation for it. Even our blind alleys, gropings, and failures."

"You've had too much to drink." Harrison laughed.

"Shit, I haven't had enough to drink," Bernstein said. "Two more and I'll have a goddamn cosmic vision."

"Two more, Morris, and you'll pass out."

"That's when I'll have the goddamn cosmic vision. On my way head first into the spittoon." He looked around the bar. "There aren't any more spittoons. When I was a student in Boston, all the bars had spittoons. Big brass spittoons. Goddamn works of art. I miss the spittoons in bars. That's why I don't drink much anymore, Ben."

71

"Also, you have a low tolerance for alcohol, Doctor."

Bernstein turned back to Harrison, and the brown, tear-bright eyes behind the glasses were sober and unglazed. "I'm scared, Ben."

"Scared? Scared of what?"

"I don't know. This whole *mishegaas.*"

"Something wrong about it?"

"No, nothing's wrong. What could possibly go wrong? I just have this premonition."

"A premonition of what, goddammit?"

"I don't know. It's just a premonition. Look, I've been into people's hearts, lungs, larynx, and bowels, what, three thousand times. I'm entitled to a premonition."

"You're entitled," Harrison agreed. "You're one of the great chest cutters. No doubt about it."

Bernstein held up his hands, examining them as he had earlier, first holding the palms up to the light and then the backs.

"Then why, this once, after three thousand times into the goddamn chest, am I suddenly afraid to use these hands?" he asked.

9

At six-thirty on the morning of the operation, Harry Styles suffered a pulmonary hemorrhage. He was rushed to the operating room, sweating, breathing frantically, and coughing up blood, the blood bubbling at his mouth in a red froth. Emergency calls were made to Steinhardt and Bernstein.

When they arrived at the hospital, Styles was already stretched out on the operating table, his chest and abdomen bared, shaven, and painted mustard yellow with antiseptic. Harrison and the nurses were bending over him.

"What the hell are you doing, starting without me?" Bernstein asked, bursting into the operating room.

"I was afraid he was going to expire in the hall," Harrison said. "He was choking on his own blood and turning a terrific blue. We rushed him in here to get him on oxygen. We're cutting this a little close. You'd better get on with this operation as expeditiously as possible, or your patient may not last long enough to get him on the machine."

Bernstein carefully probed Styles's abdomen with his fingers, feeling for muscle tension.

A soft asthmatic wheeze punctuated each stroke of the respirator, as a rubber bellows forced a mixture of oxygen, nitrous oxide, and ethane through a tube down the patient's throat and into his one remaining lung. The anesthesiologist stationed at the head of the table studied a stainless steel console of gauges measuring the patient's tidal volume and respiratory rate and then looked up at Bernstein.

"He's paralyzed," the anesthesiologist said. "I've given him four milligrams of Pavulon."

"That should do it." Bernstein nodded. "But we've got to be extra careful with Clancy around. She damned near killed a patient of mine the other day. A coronary bypass. We were already into the chest and she rubbed against him on the pretext of handing me a hemostat and he got a giant erection. The blood drained out of his heart into his groin just like that, and he went into shock. It took eight units of blood to reprime his heart."

The scrub nurse, Agnes Clancy, the object of the eight-unit erection, was a plain woman in her early forties with the figure of a pine board. Her sensuality was part of the elaborate and obscene mythology that Bernstein had fabricated about members of the operating room team. The longer they worked with him, the more elaborate and obscene was the myth, embroidered over the years amid heart valve replacements, pulmonary embolectomies, and pneumonectomies. The stories were needed to break the tension of exhausting twelve- and sixteen-hour stretches of surgery. They were never mentioned outside the sterile walls of the operating room. Outside they would be misunderstood.

The fantastic stories were the libretto to the music that issued from a cassette player on the table next to the heart-lung machine. Bernstein's preference was saccharine old show tunes, lush Mantovani strings, schmaltzy movie scores.

Bernstein nodded to Harrison, who stood across the table from him. "Go ahead and open him up. Give us lots of room to work in."

Harrison started the incision at the base of the throat, slicing in a line down the middle of the chest to just above the navel. He did not have to cut through much fatty tissue to expose the breastbone, as the patient had become emaciated by his illness.

"Bovie."

The severed blood vessels were sealed by the spark from an electric cauterizing needle.

"The Black and Decker."

The scrub nurse handed Harrison the sternal saw, a stainless steel instrument similar to a workshop electric hand saw. The cassette was playing an instrumental version of "If I Loved You," but the throbbing strings were drowned out by the grating whine of the blade as it sawed through the breastplate, tearing the bone into two halves. Bernstein reached over and gripped each side of the sternum, forcing the two halves apart.

Without a word Clancy dressed the exposed bleeding cross sections of bone with a wax and then draped a sponge cloth over each of the cut edges.

"A little wider, please," Harrison instructed Bernstein. He slipped the stainless steel blades of a retractor into the gap between the two halves of the breastplate presented by Bernstein, then turned a screw knob that forced the blades apart until there was a nine-inch-wide hole in the patient's chest, exposing his pulsing heart.

"Enough already," Bernstein said.

"You wanted lots of room to work in."

"Any more and you'll shatter his ribs." He peered into the chest. "Shit, what a mess. Let's get him tied off before he bleeds out."

"It's lousy exposure to work on the lung."

"Yeah, but going through the chest gives us our best shot to hook up the pulmonary vessels on both sides."

"If you say so," Harrison muttered. "It's my first gill implant."

Bernstein grunted. Above the green surgical mask, his eyes shone with the intensity of his concentration, part of the astounding transformation that occurred whenever he began to operate. At bedside, his sympathy and concern for his patients was deep and sincere. His melancholy brown eyes seemed always on the verge of tears. But when he donned his surgical mask, his basic personality seemed to change. He became a cool, facile technician. The patient, dressed and draped in sterile sheets that revealed isolated organs, was no longer a human being in pain. Bernstein was confronted only by the imperfect machinery of the flesh that had to be corrected with speed and exacting skill.

He rapidly isolated the hemorrhaging vessel, tied it off, and drained the chest cavity. Then he reached in and grasped the throbbing heart muscles in his hand. He looked up to study a television monitor on the wall. The picture showed electrocardiogram and pulse readings as horizontal waves.

76

"This guy is still strong," Bernstein said over his shoulder. Behind him Steinhardt loomed, his white head just brushing one of the disks of the lights that canopied the operating table. "I did a dissecting aortic aneurysm last Tuesday on a seventy-five-year-old who was so weak we would have killed him if we cut his hair."

"What happened?"

"The operation was a success, but we couldn't get him off the machine. He went into fibrillation every time we tried to get him restarted on his own again, and he just never came out."

Bernstein pushed the heart to one side to expose the left lung. "Take a look," he invited Steinhardt. "It's a wonder he's breathing at all."

Steinhardt examined the lung, noting the extent to which the tumor had destroyed it.

"If we touch it, it'll fall apart," Bernstein said. "It won't hold a stitch. We might as well take the lung out. He's dead if we do and dead if we don't. He'll be on the heart-lung machine from here on out; so he won't be using it. Removing it will make the hook-up cleaner. What do you think?"

Steinhardt studied the devastated lung, then nodded reluctantly.

Bernstein turned to Harrison. "We won't bypass the heart. Let him pump naturally as long as he's able. It'll prevent problems, and we'll be able to keep him on the machine that much longer. We'll tap into the outflow tract here and the left atrium here. Can you hear me, Tom?"

The medical technician seated behind the desk-sized stainless steel console of the heart-lung machine stirred. "I hear you, doctor: We're not bypassing the heart. Just the lungs."

"So bring him on the machine very gently. Just enough pressure to get the blood to and from your machine. I want his heart to work as normally as possible."

"Gently. I got you."

Harrison made an incision into the base of the artery that conducted the blood directly from the heart to the lungs, and the plastic cannula to the heart-lung machine was inserted. A surgical hook-up was made with a second tube from the machine and the left atrium of the heart, the chamber into which the freshly oxygenated blood from the lungs normally flowed.

"Okay, let's go on the machine very gently."

"Very gently," repeated the heart-lung machine operator. The machine had already been primed with a chemical "cocktail" compatible with blood. It contained, among other things, an anticoagulant to prevent blood clotting, a diuretic, an electrolyte, albumen, anesthesia, and muscle paralyzers. Now a throttle was opened and the patient's blood flowed through a long transparent tube into the machine and through a web of polymer membranes, where it mixed with oxygen and carbon dioxide gases. The oxygenator, about the size of a quart bottle, was the "lung" of the heart-lung machine. The blood then circulated through a rotary pump, the "heart," which forced the blood through another plastic tube back into the body.

"We're on bypass," the machine operator called out.

Bernstein nodded and turned to Harrison. "I'll take it from here, Ben."

Up to that point, Bernstein had delegated the routine

of the operation to the resident surgeon. Now he appeared to hesitate. He looked first at Steinhardt and then at Harrison. His eyes, framed by the surgical cap and mask, were the only clues to his expression. They were distant and somber.

"The hook-up is complete," he said to the anesthesiologist. "You can turn off the respirator."

The anesthesiologist clicked a switch. The heavy rubber bellows sighed and sank toward the bottom of its transparent plastic cylinder like an exhausted piston. The pressure gauge peaked at 500 milliliters and then slowly bled down to zero.

Bernstein reached into the chest cavity with his hand and at his touch the lung collapsed. Harry Styles had taken his last breath.

10

The pink stone castle of the mermaid's kingdom, its towered walls wavering in the invisible currents in the water, loomed in the gloomy distance. Before it, half buried in the sand on the bottom of the sea, lay the shattered wreck of an eighteenth-century brig. Above its splintered foremast hovered a beautiful fantailed Japanese goldfish, its popeyes staring unblinkingly back at Ruth Styles.

Harry had bought the goldfish and created the fairy-tale seascape for Brenda's fifth birthday. The delight and care with which he had arranged the sand, the ship, and the castle made Ruth wonder whether he was giving his daughter a birthday present or passing on his own childhood fantasies to her.

On Brenda's sixth birthday, Ruth had bought her a ceramic mermaid, a brightly painted figurine with blond hair. The little girl had ignored it. She had never placed it in the bowl and eventually the figurine had disappeared.

One afternoon Ruth had heard Brenda in the living

room talking to the goldfish, scolding it for some imagined misbehavior. Ruth then realized, as Harry had known all along, that Brenda was the mermaid princess. Not only was the painted ceramic figure a usurper to her throne but its concrete artificiality was also a threat to the existence of the kingdom itself and the powers of enchantment that had created it.

The original goldfish had died years ago, and Harry had immediately replaced it. The goldfish bowl sat on an end table in the living room, and the sovereignty of its kingdom had passed, in succession, from Brenda to David to Christopher. Ruth had never entered its realm.

The night of the operation Ruth sat staring at the goldfish, expecting at any minute to receive a call from the hospital telling her that her husband was dead. There were no hopes to be nurtured, no plans to be made. All she could do was wait.

Ruth had prepared the children for the news. The afternoon after they had all last seen their father at the hospital, she had gathered them around her in the living room. The doctors had done all that they could to cure him, Ruth had told them, but there was a very good chance that their father would die. The children had wept; Christopher clung to her as if she too might leave them.

This evening, Ruth had once again told them. But this time the children were all silent. She tried to encourage them to talk, to ask questions, but there were no questions. There was only the silence of her children, as each retreated into himself.

Ruth looked up. Brenda was standing in the door-way watching her.

"Ma, do you have a picture of Daddy I can have?" The girl walked slowly into the living room. "You know, one before he got sick."

"Yes, I'm sure I do. There's a box of them in the study."

She and Brenda went into the study and searched through the cache of loose photographs. There were bunches of pictures that Ruth had never gotten around to pasting in albums. Pictures of each of the children at every age. All the children together. The dog. Her and the children. But there were only three or four photos of Harry.

Brenda carefully studied them. Was the image of her father already dimming so that she needed a photograph to keep it alive in her memory? Or did the child need to replace the too cruelly vivid picture of her father in the hospital that she could not forget? Brenda finally selected a snapshot of Harry, the incompleat angler, awkwardly trying to fish. Ruth had taken it during a family camping trip to Yosemite. Brenda took the picture to her room, leaving Ruth alone in the study.

On the desk was the framed Kodacolor print of Ruth and the children that Harry had taken on the same camping trip. It was the picture Harry had kept in his office and the one he'd taken to the hospital with him. Ruth had removed it from the hospital room that morning.

It had always seemed to Ruth a happy picture, she and the children beside a tent pitched on a Sierra lake. But now it seemed ominous, foreboding. Harry was not in the picture. She and the children were alone in a wilderness.

Ruth picked it up and took it to the living room mantel, and then went to check on her other two children. Both boys had gone to bed that evening without their usual protest. When she entered their room, Groucho, a black shadow at the foot of the bed, jumped up and gave a low rumbling growl before he recognized her and came to the door.

Christopher was a tangle of bedclothes and limbs as if he'd been sleeping very restlessly. Ruth rearranged the sheet and cover and tucked him in. He muttered groggily and then fell immediately asleep. Even asleep, the sun-bleached flaxen head buried in the pillow, the boy was the carbon copy of photographs of Harry at that age. As she stared down at the boy, Ruth experienced a surge of joy, poignant and bittersweet, at the recognition that even as Harry died he remained so visibly alive in this child.

She felt David watching her. The older boy was not asleep but lay in the next bed perfectly still, his eyes wide open.

"You all right?" Ruth asked.

"Yeah." Then the boy asked, "Are *you* all right?"

"As well as can be expected." Ruth bent over and gently brushed the long black hair from her son's forehead and kissed him. "Get some sleep," she said softly. "School tomorrow."

She left the room, and the dog, who had trailed at her feet from bed to bed, again settled down with a grumbling sigh at his post at the foot of David's bed.

There was still school tomorrow. Ruth didn't know whether Harry would die that night, or the next day, or the day after that. So there was still school tomorrow. The children were so quiet and frightened. They had been that way since the last visit with their father at the hospital. As much for their sake as her own, Ruth wanted it over and done with. She had already done her mourning and grieving. Cancer does that to you, she thought. You mourn and grieve and agonize with each day's dying so that when death finally comes it's a relief for the survivors. Harry's illness had at first terrorized her, but it had eventually become her oppressor. She had become its slave, obediently performing all the odious tasks it demanded, silently suffering its torments.

Ruth reentered the study and went to the liquor cabinet. The bottle she took out was almost empty. She poured what remained into a glass and sank into a chair at Harry's desk. It was late, and the hospital had not called yet. They would probably not call until the next day. She had to get through the night.

11

Bernstein swiftly excised the lung. He pulled the bloody organ from Styles's chest and dropped it into a stainless steel basin that Clancy held out. "There goes his jogging," Bernstein said.

Harrison routinely examined the chest cavity, probing about the heart and blood vessels, searching the pleural walls. "That's it. I don't see any other signs of cancer. Apparently it was still localized in the lung. Not that it makes much difference at this point."

Bernstein nodded. Then slowly, as if the movement itself were a weighty decision, he raised his head to stare at Steinhardt, who stood hovering behind Harrison. "So much for phase one," Bernstein said.

Steinhardt now moved into position over the cavity in Styles's chest. Harrison, his part of the operation over, stood off to one side to observe.

Operating very slowly and meticulously, Steinhardt and Bernstein cut out the windpipe and bronchi that had once brought air into Styles's lungs and sewed closed the trachea. Then they cut new channels from the chest cavity into the neck, paralleling the path of the carotid arteries, the critical blood vessels through the neck to the brain. The pulmonary arteries and veins that had once serviced the lungs were sewn into place at the base of the channels. Bernstein nodded to Steinhardt. "And that's phase two."

Bernstein checked the patient's vital signs, all of which remained strong. Then he and Steinhardt began the third and critical stage of the procedure, the one for which there was no medical precedent. On each side of the patient's neck four distinct lines had been drawn in blue dye, marking the position of the gill clefts in the birth defects and embryonic studies.

Steinhardt's scalpel now traced one line, cleaving the flesh and transforming the line from blue dye to blood. The sternocleidomastoid muscle of the neck was then retraced, and a broad passage cut through the neck directly into the windpipe.

The artificial gill Steinhardt sutured into the trachea resembled a Chinese fan. The rigid ribbing was spanned by laminations of wispy translucent membranes, each a web of exceedingly delicate capillaries.

The surgeon made an incision down the length of the neck, behind the collarbone and into the chest. Then artificial blood vessels made of Dacron were planted into these channels and drawn through into the chest cavity, where they were sutured to the pulmonary arteries and veins that had formerly gone to the lungs.

Working together, Steinhardt and Bernstein cut and sewed the artificial blood vessels to valves on the artificial gill, then cut the ties. The transparent membranes of the gill filled with blood, transforming it into a delicate red fan, pulsing with a vivid, primal beauty.

86

For a moment Steinhardt and Bernstein stared at each other.

Then they set to work transplanting the second gill, then the third, and fourth, each operation proceeding without difficulties, and each procedure swifter and less hesitant than the one before it.

Bernstein sewed the last incisions still open in the neck, then turned to Harrison. The operation at that point had been going on for fourteen hours, but there was a strain and exhaustion in Bernstein's eyes that Harrison had not seen in the man after twice that long in the operating room.

"Ben, would you please close up," Bernstein asked.

"Of course." There was little left to do except the routine of joining the split sternum with stainless steel sutures, sewing the chest, and preparing the chest drains.

Since the beginning of the operation, a green sterile sheet had been hung and pinned tight just below the patient's jaw line. It formally separated the surgeons from the anesthesiologist or, more to the point, separated the sterile working area of the surgeons and nurses who had scrubbed for the operation from the unsterile place of those who had not scrubbed.

Bernstein now ripped off his surgical mask and walked around to the anesthesiologist's station and stared down at Styles, seeing the face of the man for the first time since the operation had begun. The patient was no longer dressed and draped into an isolated impersonal organ but was a mutilated and mortally wounded human being. Bernstein, his face unmasked, was not the supremely efficient and detached technician whose every movement Harrison had been carefully studying. The exhausted surgeon now somehow seemed as naked and vulnerable as the patient before him. His face reflected back the dying man's pain and mute anguish.

For the tenth time that evening, Harrison checked the patient's electrocardiogram, arterial pressure, and urine output. Just then Bernstein walked into the room. "The lab finished the analysis of the blood sample," he said, handing Harrison the report.

Harrison looked it over. The patient's oxygen, carbon dioxide, and electrolyte levels were all within safe limits.

"How's he doing?" Bernstein asked.

"Stabilizing."

"Stabilizing," Bernstein repeated and shook his head. "After having his chest sawed open and his lung cut out. After having been inflicted with a half-dozen other equally mortal wounds and been injected with five or six different deadly poisons to paralyze his mind and body, the patient is stabilizing."

Harrison nodded. "The medical miracle isn't modern surgery but the human body's ability to recover from its outrages." The operation had, to his surprise, gone almost routinely. There had been no dramatic, heart-stopping ventricular fibrillations. Many open-heart operations he and Bernstein had performed had been trickier.

Harrison relaxed into a chair and studied the patient stretched out on the bed. The only visible movement was the rotating head of the heart-lung machine pumping the blood from its silicone rubber oxygenator back through the tubes in the patient's abdomen. They had decided to allow Styles's condition to stabilize for a period rather than proceed with the next phase of the experiment immediately after the trauma of surgery. Now they were taking turns keeping a medical watch.

"You know, Morris, all this arcane crap about tuna fish and four-hundred-million-year-old Devonian period designs, it's all just a lot of academic masturbation on Steinhardt's part. His artificial gill is just another development of the medical technology that's become commonplace in the last ten years." He pointed to the heart-lung machine. "Christ, the invention of new blood oxygenators has accelerated so fast that the Patent Office's classifications are obsolete as soon as they are published."

"What did you do, run a patent search?" Bernstein asked.

Harrison shrugged. "I had an idea I wanted to check out."

"What happened?"

"Somebody else had the idea first."

Bernstein grunted an acknowledgment.

Harrison looked over at him and scowled. "For Chrissakes, Morris, go to bed. You're about to collapse. I'm watching him."

It was a moment before Bernstein moved. "Yeah, you're right. Tomorrow's the big day," he said in a voice that croaked with exhaustion. He patted Harrison's shoulder, muttered "Good night," and shuffled out.

The room was now eerily silent. There was not even the asthmatic bellows sound of the mechanical respirators or the labored gasps of the patients that resounded from one bed after another in the intensive care unit outside. Here there was only the soft whirling sound of the heart-lung machine forcing the oxygenated blood back into the patient's arteries and veins.

Jesus Christ. Harrison suddenly understood what had so frightened Bernstein the night they'd been drinking. Harrison stared at the patient on the bed, the same fear now gripping him.

12

The night of the operation Steinhardt couldn't sleep. He sat up reading *Oeconomia Regni Animalis,* Emanuel Swedenborg's treatise on the human body as the kingdom of the soul, in the hope that the eighteenth-century text would drug his brain into sleep. But something in Swedenborg's writings kept haunting him, flitting into consciousness like a gadfly buzzing in and out of his field of vision. To designate the human soul, Swedenborg had used the term *anima,* which in Old Latin had originally meant "breath." Jung also had used the same term *anima* to denote the inner personality attuned to the unconsciousness. Were they, and the ancient mystics, declaring that there was an inseparable union between the human soul and breath? Steinhardt read until dawn before he finally dozed off, only to sleep fitfully, plagued by nightmares.

When he got to the hospital the next morning he quickly examined Styles, who was still in a coma, and immediately began setting up the experiment. Steinhardt felt enormously energetic, despite his lack of sleep. Before this day ended, the years of work would come to a culmination. The doubts and corrosive fears that assailed him would be resolved.

He breathed deeply in a deliberate effort to dissolve the knot of fear and anxiety in his stomach. He had to retain a detached scientific objectivity, but his surging blood conspired against him.

His assistant Mark Matsuda arrived, and together they installed a large Plexiglas tank alongside the bed. The tank was seven and a half feet long and deep and wide enough to easily accommodate a man. It had a heater and bubble oxygenator similar to those in large tropical fish aquariums. Steinhardt and Matsuda had filled the tank with a sterile saline solution and were adjusting the temperature when Bernstein and Harrison returned.

"Why ninety-three degrees?" Harrison asked.

"That's the water temperature experiments indicate will cause the least shock to the system," Matsuda said.

Matsuda was a man in his mid-twenties, unusually tall and brawny for a Nisei. He had been a competitive swimmer as an undergraduate at the University of California. He had begun working with Steinhardt as a research assistant during his Ph.D. candidacy in marine biology. When Steinhardt asked Matsuda to continue to work with him after he had been awarded his doctorate, Matsuda had considered it a greater honor than his advanced degree.

He now bent over Styles's comatose body, affixing postage-stamp-sized medical sensors to the gill implants. The sensors measured the rate of oxygen and carbon dioxide diffusion across the gills. Matsuda had to work around the blood-filled lines that emanated like tendrils from Styles's chest to the heart-lung machine.

Steinhardt nervously hovered over Matsuda, suggesting minute, almost imperceptible corrections to the placing of the sensors, afterward pressing them with a finger as one might assure himself that a postage stamp was firmly secure on a letter. Then Steinhardt straightened and muttered, "It's ready."

Bernstein and Harrison helped the two other men lift the patient. Styles was so emaciated that it required very little effort to lower him into the tank of saline solution. Steinhardt arranged Styles's limbs, a totally unnecessary fussing, since they floated freely. Then he stood back and stared.

Totally submerged, Styles's shrunken flesh was suspended and weightless, making it appear fuller, an effect that was further enhanced by the magnifying effect of the water and Plexiglas. He floated motionless as if set in an enormous transparent jewel, surrounded by shimmering bubbles that caught the light and reflected it back like a current of smaller jewels. The blood-gorged plastic tubes spouted from his abdomen like synthetic umbilicals to a creature, not quite of this world, who hung suspended in amniotic fluid as if awaiting birth.

It was a moment before Steinhardt could speak. Then he asked in a strained voice, "What amount of diffusion are we getting across the gills?"

Matsuda checked the read-out on a console of instruments set up across the room. "There's . . . there's no indication of any oxygen or carbon dioxide diffusion taking place."

Steinhardt was instantly at his side. "What? There

must be." He peered at the instruments. "Perhaps it's the sensors," he said. "They've shorted out in the saline solution."

"I don't think so," Matsuda said. "We're getting normal baseline readings. There's just no diffusion taking place across the membranes."

"Is there water circulation in the pharynx and past the gill combs?" Steinhardt asked anxiously.

"Yes, sir. A strong circulation. About one hundred cc per second."

"It *must* be the sensors," Steinhardt insisted, a note of desperation distorting his voice. "What else could it be?"

The panic in his voice and face galvanized the others. Without stopping to take off their jackets, Matsuda and Harrison plunged their arms into the tank and lifted Styles's head and chest out of the water while Steinhardt hurriedly replaced the sensors on the gills.

Then they all stared at the read-out on the instrument panel. There was no change.

"I don't understand," Steinhardt said. "On the animals we experimented on. The dogs. The monkeys. We always got a significant diffusion."

"Maybe he's too weak," Matsuda said. Then he added uneasily, "Perhaps man has evolved to some biological point of no return. He can't revert back to primitive organisms."

Steinhardt stared at his assistant, then looked over at the tank in which Styles lay, and his eyes filled with tears. It was a while before he turned back to the others, and when he finally spoke, his voice was little more than a whisper.

"Gentlemen, I would appreciate it very much if you

would please continue to take readings of the vital signs for the next few hours," he said in a flat voice. "Also the blood gases." He started to say something more, but his voice failed. He strode from the room.

The experiment's total failure devastated Steinhardt. He wandered the halls of the hospital, and it was as if each scene he encountered had been deliberately contrived to confront him with the waste of his life. A child with a congenital heart defect that would have normally killed him before he was ten was wheeled into surgery to correct it. A young man whose arm had been crushed and all but amputated in an industrial machine was prepared for an operation to rebuild his hand. A mother whose malignant abdominal tumor had been diagnosed and excised in time struggled to consciousness in the recovery rtoom and smiled wanly at the surgeon who hovered over her. In each case the healer might have been Steinhardt. *Might have been.* The words were a trembling accusation of guilt. Guilt for the children whose lives he had not saved. The suffering he had not relieved. But primarily guilt for the futility of his own life. Instead he had gone off in search of . . . what? *Secrets. Mysteries. Curiosities.*

Steinhardt found himself on a balcony above the black asphalt parking lot ten stories below. Off in the distance, beyond the squalid bungalows and the flaking stucco apartment houses and hotels that supplied the university hospital with the majority of its patients, Steinhardt could see the ocean. Once, Steinhardt had regarded the sea as the living blood of all life. Now it lay dark, implacable, and lifeless beneath the haze of brown smog.

Steinhardt felt dizzy. Far below him the concrete and asphalt seemed to swirl as if it too were a back-water of the distant ocean. Unlike the sea, the swirling mass ten stories below taught him no secrets of life, but staring at it all with distracted eyes Steinhardt had a vivid glimpse of death.

13

Matsuda conscientiously kept recording Styles's vital signs over the next few hours. Styles had been on the heart-lung machine too long—he was rapidly weakening as his blood cells were damaged and deteriorated.

When Steinhardt bolted from the room, Matsuda and the two surgeons had tacitly agreed that he needed time alone to absorb the shock of the experiment's total failure. But after several hours Styles had declined irrevocably toward death, and Steinhardt had still not reappeared. The three men became concerned.

They were about to launch a search for him when the old man shambled through the door. He looked as if he had aged ten years in the few hours he had been absent. His shoulders slumped. His skin had a lifeless gray hue, and his eyes were bloodshot with fatigue.

He gazed a moment at the tank, where Styles hung from the plastic tubes in his abdomen in a grotesque mechanical parody of life. Then he turned to Matsuda.

"There's been no change in the readings." Matsuda

answered the unspoken question.

"I had thought not," Steinhardt said. "What is the fundamental axiom of research?" he addressed the three men in the room. "There is no such thing as an unsuccessful experiment. Well, today we have proved nothing; we have discovered nothing; we have learned nothing. Except perhaps the folly of an old man's fantasies, his arrogance, and his conceit."

Bernstein put his hand on Steinhardt's shoulder. "Karl, it was a perfectly valid approach."

Steinhardt reached up and patted his friend's hand. "Thank you, Morris."

Steinhardt roused himself and leaned over Matsuda's shoulder to study the log of Styles's vital functions. Then he turned back to Bernstein. "Let us end this poor creature's suffering."

Bernstein walked over to the heart-lung machine, but then hesitated and stood staring at the switches and dials, his face drawn and morose, his eyes tear-filled.

"We've made a promise to the family," Steinhardt said in a soft voice.

The surgeon nodded but still stood motionless by the machine. Finally he reached forward and closed a throttle and clicked off a series of switches. The pump ceased rotating and the blood drained back into Styles's chest, leaving the returning transparent plastic tube blood-smeared and empty. The machine decelerated and then was silent as though the whirl were itself the sound of the life now rapidly dying.

"Dr. Harrison, would you please witness and verify the exact time we cease to get EEG and EKG patterns?" Steinhardt asked, and turned away. "It should take approximately three minutes before total anoxia and hypoxia take place."

"Of course."

Matsuda, still seated at his post at the diffusion monitor, lowered his head and wiped his eyes. The unflinching dials he had watched so intently for hours now blurred. The needles flickered. Matsuda dried his eyes with a handkerchief and blew his nose. The needle flickered again. Matsuda stared at it. Once again the needle moved, the fluctuation stronger than before.

He looked at the man in the tank. Styles's head and chest convulsed as if he had coughed. Again the needle registered strongly.

"Dr. Steinhardt!"

"It's just an involutionary spasm, Mark," Steinhardt answered, as if anticipating him, "as the medulla suffers oxygen deprivation."

"No, damn it, I'm getting a diffusion reading here."

"What!" Steinhardt was immediately over him. Both men looked back and forth from the dials to the man in the tank. The coughlike convulsions continued. They were irregular, with no pattern, but with each spasm, the needle jumped on the monitor registering the oxygen level of the blood.

Steinhardt sprang back to the tank and hovered over it, intently studying the man lying there. Then his eyes traced the path of the plastic tubes leading from the abdomen to the now quiet heart-lung machine. "Of course," he said softly to himself. "How could I be so stupid. So incredibly stupid. Davis and Potter."

"Who the hell are Davis and Potter?" Bernstein snapped.

Steinhardt didn't take his eyes off Styles. "Their work with human fetuses. It was published over a quarter of a century ago. I'd forgotten it. If the placental circulation is interrupted, or if the umbilical cord is tangled, the fetus makes exaggerated respiratory movements, aspirating large amounts of amniotic fluid. The same instinctive reaction occurred in the early as well as the more advanced fetus. Inadequate oxygen saturation of the fetal blood triggers the respiratory mechanism." Steinhardt pointed to the heart-lung machine. "Until we cut his umbilical circulation, he did not *have* to breathe the fluid in which he was immersed. Now he does."

"But for how long can he do it?" Bernstein asked.

Matsuda joined the three doctors alongside the tank. "The readings are still spasmodic," he reported.

They stared at the man in the tank. Styles's face was contorted, his eyes squeezed shut, and his mouth yawning wide like that of a child bawling.

14

Ruth Styles kept track of the almost imperceptible changes of season in Southern California by her roses. In April she began a program of deep watering, feeding, and spraying to prevent the infection of powdery mildew that plagued the flowers during the hot, dry summer.

In June she cut the flowers and pruned the sucker stems that had sprouted at the base of the bushes. She stopped watering in November to encourage the plants to go dormant in the winter, and in February she pruned the rosebushes to prepare them for the spring growth.

Ruth's pruning was brutal. She first systematically stripped away all the dead canes, twigs, crisscrossing branches, and the new suckers, cutting them off at the base of the plant. That done, she selected the three youngest, most promising canes and mercilessly snipped off all the others at the bud union.

Now behind her on the grassy border of the rose garden that ran across the front of the house there was a pile of amputated woody and green rose canes lying before each upright triad of young branches she had selected for the summer blossoming. For her work, Ruth wore a wide-brimmed straw hat that shaded her pale skin from the sun. The sun hat flattered her. It softened the dark shadows and etched lines of fatigue and tension that had in the past year marred her complexion. She gently fingered a bud, then snipped the cane a quarter of an inch above it, cutting the stalk back to that one promising bud.

The sound of a car pulling up made her turn toward the street. To her surprise the long figure of Steinhardt uncoiled from the passenger's seat and stood towering above the car, shyly looking at her as if he were reluctant to walk forward and greet her. A moment later Bernstein got out of the car and together they approached.

Ruth was embarrassed by their visit. She had been expecting simply a call from Bernstein. "Gardening is about all I can cope with right now," she said with a nervous gesture toward the roses. "That and getting the kids fed and off to school."

She looked at the pile of prunings at her feet, then looked back at Bernstein and asked, "Is Harry dead? Is that why you're here?"

Bernstein exchanged a look with Steinhardt. "No, he isn't. As a matter of fact, his condition seems to have stabilized."

Ruth shook her head. "I don't understand. You told me on the phone that Harry's other lung had been removed. And that you would turn off the artificial life supports as soon as the experiment was over." She looked from Bernstein to Steinhardt.

"Well, it's rather difficult to explain," Steinhardt said. "We don't entirely understand what is happening ourselves."

"Mrs. Styles, may we discuss this inside?"

"Yes, of course," Ruth said uneasily. She walked ahead of them into the house.

"Well, did you or did you not turn off the artificial life supports?" she asked as soon as they were seated.

"Yes, we did."

"Then what's keeping Harry alive?"

Steinhardt shrugged. "We're not exactly sure. For one thing the implanted artificial gill is functioning with much greater effectiveness than it had on any of the laboratory animals we'd used earlier. They usually succumbed to shock or pneumonia after being totally immersed. We fully expected that your husband would react in a similar way, but the heart-lung machine apparently modified . . ."

"What the hell is the heart-lung machine?" Ruth interrupted. She had prepared herself for Harry's death. The fact that he was still lingering in some grotesque limbo had her utterly bewildered.

"It's a machine that pumps and oxygenates the blood. It's used routinely in heart and lung bypass operations. The newer types with membrane oxygenators are, in essence, artificial gills, and that may have created a condition we simply did not anticipate."

"Dr. Steinhardt, I simply don't understand what you're saying. But I demand to know what's happening to Harry!"

Steinhardt held out his hands in supplication.

"Please, Mrs. Styles, I understand your confusion. Frankly, Dr. Bernstein, my colleagues, and I don't entirely understand what's happening ourselves. We only have a hypothesis at this point."

"Well, what's your hypothesis?" Again her voice snapped with anger.

"In our previous experiments with animals we didn't use the heart-lung machine. There was no need; we weren't removing the lungs. We were merely implanting the artificial gill."

"But the animals still died," Ruth insisted.

"Yes, but that was because of other complications, not the inadequacy of the gill."

"What about Harry?"

"He was totally oxygenated by the heart-lung machine. And since his lungs had been removed, he didn't experience the same complications. I suspect that being submerged weightless in a warm saline solution was, in fact, salubrious to his system rather than a shock. It is a form of therapy in several—"

"And when you turned off the machine?" Ruth interrupted impatiently.

"The technique of switching a patient's respiration on and off the machine has become sophisticated to the point at which it can be done with very old people or weak cardiac cases. The shock is minimal. As I mentioned, the machine incorporates a membrane blood oxygenator, and in essence your husband had already made the transition from his lungs to an artificial gill." Steinhardt looked at Ruth and shrugged helplessly. "When we turned the machine off, the function of the oxygenation of his blood merely

104

switched to the artificial gill. It was in fact physiologically more convenient and less damaging to the blood than the machine had been."

He looked at Bernstein for support, but Bernstein remained silent. "There undoubtedly will be complications. The gill itself may prove inadequate to support his system, in which case there will be a swift physical deterioration including irreversible brain damage. A blood clot or a postoperative infection may develop. We don't know yet what may happen." Once again Steinhardt shrugged helplessly. "But at the moment your husband's condition appears to have stabilized."

"What about the cancer?"

"We removed it," Bernstein said. It was the first thing he had said since they entered the room.

Ruth stared at him incredulously. "You mean Harry is just lying there in this . . . this . . . this fish tank . . . breathing water?"

Neither Bernstein nor Steinhardt said anything.

Ruth started to laugh hysterically, then began to sob. "Oh, my God. Oh, my God. Oh, my God." Tears streamed down her face. She trembled uncontrollably and sat hugging herself, rocking back and forth.

The trembling subsided as quickly as it had begun, and she sat shaking her head. "Oh, Harry. Harry, you compulsive son of a bitch. Now you've really gone and done it."

Bernstein silently offered her a cigarette and she readily accepted it, then wryly regarded the cigarette. "How quickly we forget," she commented.

There was a moment of silence while Bernstein lit it. "I watched my father die of cancer," Ruth said, wiping her still wet cheeks with the back of her hand. "What are the five classic stages that all terminal patients go through?" She held up her hands and tallied the five stages on her fingers. "First, they deny they're going to die. Then they get angry. Then they bargain for life. In the fourth stage they get depressed, almost suicidal. And finally, they accept that they are going to die."

She rose and walked to the built-in bookcase that covered the far wall. "It's all here in Dr. Elisabeth Kübler-Ross's book." She searched for a moment without success, then turned back to Steinhardt. "But you know all that," she said, and the edge of anger in her voice made it an accusation. "I'm sure you've seen it many times in your experience."

"Yes. With my own wife."

Steinhardt had spoken quietly, but the pain evident in his voice and in his eyes stopped Ruth short.

"I'm sorry. You mentioned that to me."

She paced nervously, quieter now, sensitive to another's pain. "You assumed Harry had accepted death. But you were wrong. You operated on a very willful, driving man who was at that moment enraged at the idea of dying. And he was *still* desperately bargaining for life. Bargaining with a medical experiment that was no more alien or impossible to his mind than the space flights on which he had worked."

The photograph on the mantel of herself and the children at Yosemite caught her eye. The other night the absence of Harry from the picture had seemed foreboding. Now she was struck not by his absence but by his enveloping, possessing presence, the loving eye that had staged, posed, and taken the photograph and painstakingly cropped and framed it.

She turned back to the two men. "Dr. Steinhardt, I don't give a damn what your hypothesis or prognosis is. But in that fishbowl of yours my husband is still fighting to stay alive. I don't know whether to laugh or cry."

Steinhardt stared at her, his face drained white, confronting for the first time the horror he had wrought.

15

That night Harry Styles regained consciousness. The cannulas from the heart-lung machine had been surgically removed, but the electrodes transmitting his vital functions were still in place. Bernstein was on watch. The surgeon sat brooding over the read-outs, then laboriously made notes in the medical log as if each inscription he made were painful, another burden of grief for his wearily stooped shoulders.

A nurse from the intensive care unit came in to check the catheter and intravenous feeding. Then she stood studying the motionless, naked figure suspended in the tank. "My God, what in hell are they going to do with him?" she asked.

Bernstein looked up at her and shook his head. "I don't know." The man in the tank was no longer just a surgical or medical problem. He had become an acute moral dilemma. The dilemma was reflected in the uncertainty in Bernstein's voice, the confusion in his eyes. He glanced at the nurse and his look was furtive, as if he were ashamed.

The nurse brought Bernstein a steaming cup of black coffee, and they both sat sipping their coffee, each for the moment more comfortable with silence than with discussing their extraordinary patient.

"Can I ask you a personal question?" the nurse finally asked.

Bernstein hesitated and then said, "Sure. Why not? I can always plead the Fifth." There was a forced levity in his voice.

"I've been a nurse, what, twenty years. I've seen the interns, the residents, the surgeons all come and go," she said. "They almost always fall into two categories. Those who want to save the world and those who want to make a million dollars. It's almost as if they've got it written on them. I can always tell which they are. All except you. I can't figure you. Which category are you in?"

Bernstein gave a short, quick laugh. It came out like a bark. "That's easy. I thought you were going to ask me something tough. You had me worried."

"Which are you?"

"Both. I'm both. I want to save the world and make a million in the bargain."

"You want too much."

"You sound like my wife Selma. That's what she's always . . ." Bernstein saw a movement in the tank. Styles shifted, if a man floating weightless can be said to have shifted his weight. The movement was tentative, the instinctive caution of a creature who has been terribly wounded and doesn't know what pain even the gentlest stirring might create. He was coming out of a deep, drugged sleep, still anesthetized with morphine.

Bernstein stood up but didn't move to the tank—he

109

was mesmerized by the fascination and horror of Styles's awakening. He tried to imagine what the man was experiencing. Styles's first sensation should be one of general comfort. The temperature of the saline solution was regulated so that he would experience neither heat nor cold. Styles floated just below the surface so that he felt no pressure, not even that of his body weight upon a mattress, the burden of gravity that in the days just before his operation had become increasingly painful as he was afflicted with bedsores. The only exception to the general feeling of comfort would be a dull aching pain in his chest and neck.

Hesitantly, still not fully conscious, Styles touched his chest, fingering the incision there. His hands drifted up to his neck and gingerly explored the stiff protrusions. His eyes opened—confused, unfocused, frightened.

Styles saw lights, colors, shapes, but everything was blurred and distorted, the surreal images of a nightmare. As he moved, he felt the water, the weight and resistance of it, its suffocation. Instinctively he groped for the surface to breathe. But no breath came.

He screamed, as if the alarm of his own voice would wake him from this nightmare, but no sound came forth. He thrashed in the water to get his head above water, his hands splashing about desperately for something to grab.

The nurse whirled about at the sound of the splashing. "My God, he's going wild!" she shouted at Bernstein, breaking him from a trance. "He'll rip out his I.V."

Bernstein leaped to the tank and grabbed Styles's shoulders. Gently he tried to push him back into the water. "It's all right, Harry. It's all right. Just lie back."

Styles was terrified. He pleaded with Bernstein. "Help me. Help me." His eyes and lips begged the doctor, but his entreaties had no voice. Styles suddenly realized that Bernstein was trying to force him under the water. To drown him. He fought back with panicked strength, inundating the room with great waves of water.

"Help me get him underwater, before he suffocates," Bernstein cried out to the nurse. He threw his weight on Styles, plunging halfway into the tank himself, while the nurse pressed on his shoulders.

Styles tried to struggle but he was too weak. He was forced underwater, into its warm suffocating envelopment, his nightmare totally realized.

"The sedative! Quick!" Bernstein commanded.

The nurse sprang for the table and in a moment was back at the surgeon's side with a syringe. Bernstein was half submerged in the tank holding Styles down with his body weight, one of the patient's hands clawing at his face, still trying to fight him off. Styles's other arm was thrust out of the water, the I.V. line whipping about, his hand futilely grasping at the air, trying to clutch anything. The nurse grabbed the arm and jabbed the needle into the nipple on the intravenous line.

After a moment, the hand ceased grasping at the air and slipped slowly under the water.

16

If Paul Buckley, director of the Institute of Oceanography, could have found a way quietly to murder Harry Styles and dispose of the body he might have seriously considered it that morning. Buckley had not known of the existence of Styles before the early morning phone call to his office. Now the institute was threatened by that existence, and his own career was not just threatened but possibly doomed.

He removed his glasses, rubbed the bridge of his nose, then replaced the glasses and continued to stare out his office window at the sea and pier. Buckley's office was on the second floor of the administration building of the institute, and the window framed a panoramic view of the ocean, the beach, and the quarter-mile-long research pier.

"The pier is an arrow pointing our way into the mysterious, still unknown depths of the sea," Buckley would say to visitors. He often said things like that to legislators, trustees, press, and potential endowers. His verbal flair was one of the reasons why, at forty-two, he was director of the Institute of Oceanography. He had done no significant research in over a decade, since he had organized a study of the petrology and plate tectonics of the East Pacific Rise. The expedition had been sponsored by three oil companies. Buckley's workdays were now spent in boardrooms and academic meetings; he dressed in tailored suits rather than coveralls for wrestling drill pipes aboard a research vessel or lab coats for analyzing sediment cores.

The door to his office opened and Steinhardt entered. The tall man's face was haggard and pale, but his eyes were bright with excitement.

The two stood silently facing each other.

"In God's name, Karl, what have you done?"

"It was just a continuation of my work on the artificial gill. I've been sending you regular reports."

"Yes, yes. I know." Buckley indicated several folders strewn over his desk in contrast to the meticulous neatness of the rest of the office.

"But apparently you only just now read them," Steinhardt added.

"With my schedule I haven't had a chance to keep up with everything," Buckley said, vaguely apologetic, then suddenly exclaimed, "My God, Karl, this time you experimented with a human being! You should have cleared it with me first. My door is always open to you."

"*Cleared* it! I am not in the practice of *clearing* my research at each step of the work with anyone," Steinhardt said rather stiffly. "I already had adequate funds, and the hospital human research committee had approved the procedure."

"Jesus Christ, we're not talking about some goddamn Rhesus monkey or a dog from the pound. We're talking about a human being. *A human being.* It's a hell of a time to start standing on academic prerogatives."

"It wasn't a matter of academic prerogatives," Steinhardt said, now more subdued. "You were at that ecological conference in Rome. There just wasn't time. The patient was terminal. He had gone into a final coma when we began the experiment. He wasn't expected to survive."

"How the hell am I going to explain that to a board of trustees of ex-bank presidents and oil tycoons? Not to mention a governor who is practically a Jesuit priest?"

"Since my work is of such acute embarrassment to you, you will have my resignation on your desk this afternoon absolving both you and the institute of any responsibility," Steinhardt said in clipped, imperious tones. He turned on his heel and strode to the door.

Buckley was shaken, but he jumped to intercept Steinhardt at the threshold. "Karl, for Chrissakes, you must realize that this has all come as a great surprise and shock to me. My first concern is for the institute. I apologize if I was overbearing with you." Buckley was stalling for time. The whole experiment had, truthfully, come as a great shock to him. He had not had time to evaluate it. Were the dangers worth the acclaim? The lines of responsibility between a scientist of Steinhardt's stature and the institute were, at best, delicate. Government research grants were made directly to specific scientists, not to universities or institutes. The scientists were, in essence, independent contractors. In Steinhardt's case he was supported primarily by the

Office of Naval Research and paid the institute a percentage of his grants for overhead. They provided him with research facilities and their prestige was a factor in his securing research grants. He, in turn, contributed the prestige of his name to the institute, helped support it, and provided work for the graduate students and faculty.

If Steinhardt resigned, Buckley as director of the institute would still share the infamy of the experiment, if indeed it became infamous, but he would be excluded from the laurels if the tide flowed the other way. In academic and scientific circles Buckley would be fingered as the villain who had driven Steinhardt from the institute. Steinhardt was a recluse, a maverick, an eccentric, an egotist, and a son of a bitch to deal with. But his discoveries about oxygen transport and fluid pressure in body tissues had been nominated for a Nobel prize. There was no question that the operation would create a great deal of excitement once it became known. Buckley had to stall and placate Steinhardt until he had more information. "You must realize that this is going to bring a great deal down on our heads," he rationalized.

"You're talking politics, not science," Steinhardt said with condescension.

Steinhardt's patronizing tone once again triggered Buckley's temper. "The facts of life are that this is a *political* institution," he snapped. "Of this year's budget of forty-one million dollars, less than a million came from our endowment fund. Another million dollars came from gifts and private grants. The rest—some ninety-five point five percent of our funds—

comes directly from a dozen federal government agencies and the state of California. Our lifeblood is controlled by politics, not science."

Buckley stared at Steinhardt, then jabbed angrily toward his desk. "When word of this Frankenstein experiment of yours gets out, that phone is going to be ringing from Sacramento to Washington. State assemblymen, senators, preachers, and rabbis are going to be screaming for your head. And mine. Despite your vaunted independence as a researcher, you're still officially affiliated with this institution. It'll come crashing down about our ears. And so will your career and mine."

"I think you're being melodramatic," Steinhardt said in an uncertain voice.

Buckley heard the uncertainty. He seized it. "Am I, Karl? Do you read the newspapers? Do you watch TV? Do you remember what happened when it came out that the Army and the CIA had performed experiments on humans with drugs? And those experiments had been over for twenty years! When the politicians and press get wind of this experiment, you're going to have TV cameras following you right into the men's room. Do you think the Navy or the National Science Foundation is going to touch your work? Let alone continue to fund you?"

Steinhardt was silent. He looked stricken.

Buckley turned his back on the scientist and stared out the window. He had succeeded in intimidating Steinhardt. For the moment at least the director was in control. Buckley clasped his hands behind his back and rocked back and forth on his toes and heels. "Now just what the hell do we do with . . . *Homo sapiens gillus?*"

116

He turned back to Steinhardt. "No, let's give credit where credit it due," Buckley said with a cutting edge to his voice. *"Homo sapiens Steinhardtus."*

"His name is Harry Styles," Steinhardt said lamely.

"Well, just what the hell do we do now with Harry Styles?"

17

Harry Styles lay immobile in the tank, his eyes open and only an occasional blink indicating that he was conscious. His stillness disturbed Bernstein. There had been cases in which a patient left too long on the heart-lung machine during surgery had suffered extensive brain damage. The thoracic surgery had been a success but the patient had lost his mind.

Bernstein now had Styles heavily tranquilized, with ten milligrams of Valium every four hours flowing directly into his bloodstream through the I.V. Technically, ethically, Styles was still his patient, although Steinhardt was now dictating the procedures and tests to be made. It was, after all, Steinhardt's experiment. Bernstein's work was to keep his patient alive as long as possible—prescribe the necessary antibiotics, the intravenous fluids, the blood chemistry tests—a task he viewed with increasing horror.

An underwater speaker had been placed in the tank, and Bernstein uncertainly lifted the microphone to his lips. "Harry. Can you hear me, Harry?"

Styles continued to stare straight ahead. Steinhardt had devised an operculum, a gill cover that fitted about Styles's neck and resembled the thick collars worn by victims of neck injuries. It protected the very delicate, capillary-thin membranes of the gill. It was open at the top and bottom and clefts at the side permitted the free flow of water. It made Styles look considerably less grotesque than he had with the exposed gill combs.

"Can you hear me, Harry? Please nod if you can."

For a long moment Styles remained still. Then hesitantly, like an arthritic who expects any movement to cause pain, he slowly nodded his head.

Bernstein turned and looked at Steinhardt, who stood beside him staring at Styles.

"Talk to him more," Steinhardt commanded in a low voice that was quick with excitement.

Once again Bernstein reluctantly raised the microphone. "I don't know what to say, Harry. We know this has been a tremendous shock to you. Quite frankly, the experiment has succeeded beyond Dr. Steinhardt's and my wildest expectations. We can only attribute it to your own unexpectedly strong constitution and adaptability. We're doing all we can to make you as comfortable as possible. Are you feeling any pain?"

Styles shook his head, but the movement was very slight, apparently restricted by the collar.

"Is there anything troubling you, Harry?" Bernstein asked. "Just point to it, if you can."

Styles pointed to his eyes, making a vague, confused gesture about them.

"Yes, Harry, your eyes. Everything is blurry, is that it?"

Styles nodded.

"We have some goggles that should clear that up. But we'll have to raise your head out of the water to put them on. Do you think you can handle that?"

Styles nodded.

Steinhardt and Matsuda quickly got on either side of the tank and, supporting Styles's neck and head, partially raised his head out of the water, while Bernstein slipped the goggles on. Then Styles slipped below the water again.

"Is that better, Harry?" Bernstein asked.

Styles turned his head slightly to look at Bernstein. Magnified by the interfaces of air, glass, and water, Styles's eyes were gargoyled—and infinitely sad.

"Can you see now?"

Styles raised his hand and made a circle with his thumb and forefinger indicating "okay."

"Ask him if he can see clearly enough to write," Steinhardt asked.

Styles overheard the question and nodded.

Steinhardt picked up a plastic-coated slate and a thick pencil, the type divers use to take notes underwater, reached into the tank, and placed them in Styles's hands.

"If you want to communicate anything with us, Harry," Bernstein said, "just print it out in large letters."

Styles held the slate and pencil right up to his face, examining them as if terribly nearsighted, then began laboriously to write.

"This is incredible." Paul Buckley stood behind Steinhardt, staring at the man in the tank, totally awed by the spectacle. "How long do you expect him to live?"

Steinhardt shrugged and pointed to the large electronic monitor displaying Styles's vital signs in a series of waves and digital read-outs. "He appears at the moment to be gaining strength. But it is, in all probability, a temporary recovery. It often happens in operations, especially any type of transplant. The expectation is that he will soon develop some sort of systemic complication or infection. Or he may still reject the gill transplant. In either case he would expire very quickly."

"It's a miracle he even survived the operation."

Styles finished writing and held the slate up out of the water.

Steinhardt took the slate. In large, sprawling, almost illegible letters was printed:

I AM the FIRSt one!

Steinhardt nodded and said softly, almost inaudibly, "Yes, indeed, you're the first." He took the mike from Bernstein and repeated into it, "Yes, Harry, you're definitely the first." Then for the first time since the operation itself Steinhardt turned and smiled at Bernstein, but it was a strange smile, one of triumph overlaid with deep tragedy.

Styles's hand reached out of the water, his fingers making little grabbing motions to indicate he wanted the writing slate again. Steinhardt handed it to him, and Styles immediately began scribbling.

Buckley studied the man in the tank, then turned to Steinhardt. "Karl, I don't know whether they're going to crucify you for this or give you the Nobel prize," he whispered.

The scientist looked with irritation at Buckley, then turned back to Styles. "It's the historical practice of the medical establishment to first crucify their pioneers," he remarked in a brittle voice, "and then canonize them a generation or two afterward."

Once again a hand rose out of the water, holding forth the slate. Steinhardt read it and silently handed the slate to Bernstein.

The crude letters, like those of a six-year-old learning to print, read:

I WANT my wife

Bernstein and Steinhardt exchanged a troubled look, then the surgeon spoke into the mike. "Your wife is on her way, Harry. I spoke to her as soon as we saw you were conscious."

Harry nodded, then leaned back and shut his eyes, all the effort having apparently debilitated him.

Bernstein himself felt exhausted. The events of the last several days had physically and emotionally drained him. Now he awaited the appearance of Ruth Styles with trepidation. Bernstein had strongly suggested that she not come to the hospital, but she had been adamant. If Harry was expected to die, what right did he as a doctor have to keep his wife from seeing him? Bernstein had had to yield to her.

"*Harry?*" Ruth Styles's outburst was a question, one registering both bewilderment and fear. Bernstein whirled around. Ruth Styles stood frozen by the door, staring at the tank. She took a hesitant step forward, frightened and confused.

"Harry?" Again the fearful question.

"Mrs. Styles." Bernstein stepped to intercept her, but the woman walked by him, moving slowly as if dazed.

"Harry?" She stopped at the tank and peered into it unbelievingly.

For the first time Styles recognized her, turned full face toward her, and smiled. He said something but no sound emerged. The face now turned to Ruth Styles was bloated and distorted by the water and glass like a reflection of a fun-house mirror.

"Oh, my God!" She sank to her knees in front of the tank, bringing her face level with his.

His mouth again formed desperate eager words that remained mute. She reached out a hand to touch him, but it was blocked by the glass. Styles pressed his hand on the glass opposite hers.

"Harry!" It was a cry of stabbing anguish. Ruth threw herself against the tank, pressing her face to the glass. Harry did too, struggling futilely to touch her through the hard unyielding wall between them.

Bernstein watched, helpless, and suddenly he began to cry silently, tears flowing down his cheeks.

The night attendant paused in his mopping and glared at Bernstein and Steinhardt as they tracked footprints on his freshly washed floor. They entered an office at the end of the hall. The office was a cramped, utilitarian room with two steel filing cabinets, a large sprawling desk, a couch wide and long enough for napping, and an end table. From its contemporary design the furniture looked as if it should have been relatively new, but heavy abuse by a succession of interns and resident doctors had prematurely aged it so that the pieces and the room had the feeling that they were decades older than the hospital itself.

Steinhardt sank onto the couch, leaning back and shutting his eyes as if the touch of the couch had dissolved the last fiber of muscle holding him upright. Bernstein withdrew a key from his pocket and unlocked the bottom drawer of the desk. "Schnapps?"

Steinhardt nodded, his eyes shut. His hands rested in his lap, atop several large X-ray photographs. Bernstein withdrew a bottle of Cutty Sark Scotch and glasses from the bottom drawer and poured two stiff drinks.

"Karl."

Steinhardt opened his eyes, sat up, and accepted the offered glass with a grateful nod. Both men drank in silence. Then Steinhardt sighed audibly, stirred from the couch, and reached for the telephone on the desk. He dialed a number, and while he waited for an answer he spread the X-rays on the desk, reexamining them for the tenth time, searching for some hidden symptom he might have missed before.

Steinhardt glanced sharply at Bernstein as the phone was answered. "Hello, Paul, this is Karl. I'm sorry to disturb you so late, but you wanted me to call you immediately if there was any significant change in Styles's condition."

He paused to listen to the other end of the line. He took a drink, as if fortifying himself, then responded. "Actually his condition is quite the contrary. It's entirely possible that Mr. Styles might very well live longer than I will."

He listened again. "No, I'm quite serious. In hindsight it's actually very simple. Styles was originally destined to die of lung cancer. In totally removing both his lungs we have effectively arrested the cancer. At least temporarily. Of course it may still have metastasized elsewhere. But no other organs were involved as far as we could detect at the time of the operation. There is a forty percent probability—almost an even chance—that the cancer will not recur elsewhere. That statistic is the opinion of my colleague Dr. Bernstein, who has had considerable experience with this type of malignancy."

Bernstein took a large gulp of his drink, as though to buffer an impending blow.

"Yes, well, the danger of infection seems to have passed," Steinhardt said. "In fact, this evening Dr. Bernstein and I discovered indications of natural cell growth beginning within the graft itself."

Steinhardt listened a moment. "Yes, in any case our original plan of my discreetly publishing an epoch-making paper after Styles's quick quiet burial is no longer operable."

"Jesus Christ, indeed," Steinhardt responded in a moment. "Whereas our Saviour had the miraculous ability to walk on water, he never, while in the flesh, had the ability to breathe it. Unfortunately, our hale and hearty Harry, through no fault of ours, no longer has the normal alternative of breathing air. And therein lies our considerable dilemma."

Bernstein took another compulsive drink. He listened vaguely to the rest of the conversation. After all, what more could Steinhardt say? He could merely repeat

125

himself, while Buckley, now stunned into silence, tried to absorb its significance.

Bernstein lit a cigarette and stared out the window. He was surprised to see it was raining. It was a heavy winter drizzle that smeared the red and white car lights, the street lights, the neon signs below, puddling the colors so that for a dislocated, nightmarish moment or two Bernstein felt he was a submariner looking out over a dark Atlantean city.

Steinhardt hung up the phone. Bernstein turned to face him. Neither said a word, then Bernstein broke the silence. "Well, 'nother drink." His own glass was empty.

Steinhardt shook his head. "No, thank you, Morris."

Bernstein poured himself another drink and raised it in toast. "Well, I'm a helluva doctor," he said. "I've saved my patient's life and I've kept him alive. What the hell."

Steinhardt didn't say anything.

"I've betrayed my patient," Bernstein said. "Betrayed his family. Betrayed myself." He stared at his hands. "I was a healer. A healer. This is not healing. It's some perversion of medicine. I've let myself be led down some goddamn primrose path of science."

Steinhardt nodded solemnly. "I understand how you feel, Morris."

Bernstein vehemently shook his head. "No, you don't." How could Steinhardt know how he felt? It was all so confused in Bernstein's mind. The guilt. Styles, unnaturally alive in that tank, evoked memories of grotesque Nazi medical experiments. He provoked half-forgotten ancient Talmudic prohibitions against the desecration, the mutilation of the human body.

126

Bernstein had committed a sacrilege.

He stared at Steinhardt. The narrow, fine-boned face had never looked so Teutonic as it did at that moment. "No, you don't understand," Bernstein accused him. "How would you. You're a goy."

"A what?"

"A goy."

"You mean a gentile?"

"A goy. A gentile. You're even an Aryan, for Chrissakes."

Steinhardt didn't speak for a while, and when he did it was in a quiet voice that cut with an edge of personal outrage. "I'm well aware that you Jews consider yourselves born in original virtue. I won't debate that point. But I resent very much being accused of leading you down some primrose path of science. You participated fully in this experiment for your own personal motives, which had nothing whatever to do with any four-thousand-year-old Hebraic tradition of healing. To advance scientific knowledge perhaps. To pioneer an entirely new field of medicine with all the attendant glory was undoubtedly not a minor consideration. Major experiments into unknown provinces can't be conducted without great risks. Risks to our reputations, our careers, even our lives sometimes. And perhaps, if we go too far, we risk our very souls. At this point we can't undo what has been done. If our damnation lies ahead, then let us get on with it."

Bernstein stared at Steinhardt. In the blaze of the man's eyes, and in his voice, there was no hesitation or regret. Bernstein was himself a proud, driven man. He too was willing to take great risks with his patients and himself. He had always regarded death as a very personal enemy. The death of a patient was not a natural thing, a consequence of his diseased state; it was a personal failure. He fought death with the burgeoning arsenal of medical technology—respirators, dialysis, pacemakers—often beyond any rational sense of life. Now he had saved Harry Styles from death. Styles lived, but he lived a grotesque, subhuman life. And that life brought into question Bernstein's own life, the pride and the motives that had sustained and driven him for thirty-five years of medicine. For the first time the life of a patient offended Bernstein. He looked down at his hands nervously twisting the glass of Scotch. His own hands offended him.

"We are damned." The eyes Bernstein raised to meet Steinhardt's were lost, bloodshot, despairing.

"Don't talk to me about medieval rubbish," Steinhardt snapped angrily. "You're a man of science. Of rationality."

"We're damned," Bernstein repeated hopelessly.

18

The boy was blond and tan, and trying to study. The girl was lovely, with cascading chestnut hair. Her mind was not on her book, and every few moments she would reach over and stroke the boy or whisper something with an insinuating smile, as if there were a flame she had to frequently stoke by an intimate touch or it would die out. They sat sprawled on the lawn outside the Institute of Oceanography library, under a broad ancient acacia tree that shaded them from the hot, dry afternoon sun.

Ruth watched them, gripped by the girl's almost compulsive touches and caresses. The scene opened channels of memories that brought tears to her eyes, the tears blurring the images and distorting the colors. Emotion dislocated her sense of time and place, and for a moment Ruth was the ghost of love past spying on herself and Harry as students at the University of Southern California. She no longer heard what Buckley was saying as he and Steinhardt, both very attentive, guided her around the grounds of the institute.

"You'll note we have facilities here, large tanks and medical equipment, that they simply do not have elsewhere," Buckley said. "Mr. Styles would have much more room to move around, as you can see."

Ruth saw nothing. She was still in a state of shock and only now gradually emerging from it. For days she had been numb. Her sensibilities and emotions had been traumatized. Her husband was still alive. She had seen him, touched him, and even talked with him. That is, she had talked to him, and Harry in response had scribbled brief notes to her on a slate. The grotesqueness of the conversation had upset her more than if she had not been able to communicate with him at all.

She had wanted to kiss him. His head had bubbled up from the water, his neck braced in that thick turtleneck collar, making him resemble a traffic accident victim recovering from whiplash, and she had kissed him on the lips and face. But his flesh, which had been so long immersed in the saline solution, had a smooth slick oily feel to it, and she had involuntarily recoiled. Harry had noticed, and he had been hurt.

"I'm sorry, darling, it's just that you feel so . . . wet, so . . . different, it surprised me." She had almost said "fishy."

Harry nodded and smiled wanly.

When she went home she had said nothing about Harry's condition to the children, or to friends, or to the neighbors. For some reason she felt vaguely ashamed. She had told no one about the experiment. Assuming Harry's death was imminent, everyone was afraid to ask about him.

But Harry hadn't died. The complications that Dr. Steinhardt and Dr. Bernstein had predicted had not developed. Suspended in the amniotic fluid of his tank like some giant fetus, Harry grew stronger. He put on flesh. His hair, beard, and mustache grew, the wispy blond hair covering his face and swirling in the water like filaments of algae.

Ruth was frightened. Not of Harry or his appearance but of her own future. Before, her future had been Harry's death. It was to have been her release. Now she could not even imagine the future, and when she tried she conjured up only nightmare images.

"Mr. Styles would be much more comfortable . . ." Buckley's voice faded in and out of her hearing like the sound of a radio with a dying battery. "And it would be, I should think, intellectually challenging for him." He nodded toward Steinhardt. "Dr. Steinhardt and he would be able to continue to work directly together."

Buckley paused solicitously, but Ruth didn't respond. "We'd like to transfer Mr. Styles to the institute." Again he paused. "We very much need your cooperation and agreement, Mrs. Styles."

Ruth was on a tree-lined walk, with Buckley and Steinhardt on either side of her. To her right was a narrow quiet street, lined bumper to bumper with cars, and beyond that a steep slope covered with slate-roofed ranch houses and red-tiled Spanish homes with luxuriant lawns and gardens of roses and camellias, lemon, orange, and avocado trees that defied the area's natural aridity with batteries of water sprinklers.

To her left was a three-storied brick building and beyond that the beach and the ocean. The afternoon offshore breeze was moist and smelled of sea and kelp, but Ruth was still in her memories—there was no ocean, only the trees and laboratory and classroom buildings around her.

"Harry and I met at Southern Cal," Ruth said vaguely. "We went together all through college. How strange it should all end on the same sort of bright, sunlit California campus."

"This isn't an end," Steinhardt said softly. "It's a beginning."

Ruth was suddenly enraged by Steinhardt's comment and turned on him. "Don't recite cheap song lyrics to me, Doctor. You're going to stick Harry in some oversized bottle like one of those laboratory specimens for the rest of the time he is alive."

Steinhardt looked directly at her, but said nothing.

After a moment Buckley repeated, "Mrs. Styles, we very much need your help and cooperation to transfer Mr. Styles here. Really, what alternatives do you have?"

She turned on Buckley now. "For one thing, I could sue you."

"For what? Keeping your husband alive after he normally would have died from lung cancer?" Buckley said quietly. "That's easily remedied, Mrs. Styles. We have only to remove him from the water. He would then suffocate and expire in a way similar to that when both his lungs had been destroyed."

"My God, he might be better off dead."

Steinhardt held up both hands, as if to plead with her. "Harry has the rest of eternity to be dead. As I will have. In whatever time he has, we could expand our knowledge of medicine and biology by quanta."

Buckley was still worrying the threat of a suit. "But you're right, Mrs. Styles. The legal profession and the courts being what they are, I have no doubt that you could mount an embarrassing suit for damages. And the institute would maintain we weren't responsible. Dr. Steinhardt is an independent contractor who exceeded the terms of his research grant. Together we could destroy the career of a great scientist. And the court battles and the legal expenses would go on for years. In which case what would you do with Mr. Styles?"

Ruth had no answer. She gazed about at the sprawl of stately old stucco buildings and the students hurrying to their next class. At the end of the tree-lined path, suddenly rising from the hillside sagebrush and manzanita shrubs, were the raw concrete, angular planes of the new research building, looking like some surreal space colony erected on an alien terrain.

Ruth looked back at the young couple under the acacia tree. They no longer evoked the nostalgia of past desire and regrets. She felt only a cold, hollow ache in her stomach, and she hugged herself, shivering violently from a deep chill despite the heat.

19

It had rained the night before in Arlington, and the slick of water covering the tarmac of the Pentagon's heliport gleamed and reflected back the flat dawn light that shone through the overcast, creating the mirage effect that Admiral Zachary Harris, the chief of Naval Operations, was walking on water. Indeed there was a righteous ferocity in Harris's stride and expression that gave the impression he might be able to walk right across the adjacent Potomac River into the city of Washington.

He pulled up abruptly in front of Rear Admiral Theodore Nelson and glared at the taller officer as if he were going to slug him. Harris, his burly body hunched in rage, stared silently at Nelson, while the latter grew increasingly nervous.

Twenty yards away Harris's two spit-and-polish aides, a Navy commander and a Marine lieutenant colonel, stood waiting, each holding tightly onto his cap. Their overcoats whipped about their legs in the whirlwind churned up by the giant rotor blades of a helicopter that also stood waiting. The chopper was a Boeing Sea Knight, whale-bellied and huge enough to swallow a platoon of Marines. Harris had to shout to be heard above the roar of its twin turbine engines.

"How the hell did a thing like this happen? The United States Navy does not perform medical experiments on human beings. The CIA does that sort of thing. The Army does that sort of thing. Even the Air Force may do it. But the United States Navy does not do that sort of thing. How in the name of Jesus Christ did a thing like this happen?"

Nelson blinked and cleared his throat. "Admiral, the Office of Naval Research has over two thousand separate research contracts with almost as many universities, foundations, and private companies. We can't sit on top of every crazy scientist at every moment." He shook his head in acknowledgment. "But I know the responsibility is mine. I take full blame for it." Nelson was chief of the Office of Naval Research. He was tall and thin, white-haired, a vivid contrast to the shorter, stocky man.

Harris was a tough, intimidating man, an impression due more to his aggressive posture and physical hardness than the thickness of his muscles. Every morning, rain or shine, he ran three miles around the grounds of the Naval Observatory, where his official residence, a large Southern mansion, was located. The self-discipline was manifest in his gaunt face, which bristled with thick steel-wool eyebrows, hard humorless eyes, and a narrow aquiline nose.

"Who the hell is this guy Steinhardt?"

Nelson nervously cleared his throat. "He's considered a top man. Harvard Medical School staff, Johns

Hopkins, Woods Hole Oceanographic Institute, Scripps. His specialty is respiration and comparative physiology. His work in tissue-fluid pressure and oxygen movement in body cells has twice been considered for a Nobel prize. He's done research and development work in the past for both us and NASA."

Harris grunted an acknowledgment. "We didn't know how close he was?"

"The basic mechanics of the artificial gill have been around since the early sixties. Apparently even Steinhardt didn't think it was going to work with the first implant. The patient was terminal. He had lung cancer."

Harris nodded, then his expression softened. *"It really works?"*

"Without even trying, I can think of a dozen operations in which the Navy can use it," Nelson offered eagerly.

Harris nodded again. "This gill-man, he doesn't have a family, does he?"

Nelson cleared his throat again. "A wife and three kids," he answered reluctantly.

"Oh, Jesus Christ. We can't touch this thing with a ten-foot pole. We have ecologists and the press all over us if we even experiment with dolphins. And those sons of bitches in Congress who attack us on anything just to get their faces on TV will have a field day with this one." He looked down at his feet. "Why the hell does it have to happen now? With the Armed Services Committee investigation, the carrier and Trident cutbacks, and the SALT mess. Jesus."

He looked back at Nelson. "Totally dissociate the Navy from that research project," he ordered.

"Yes, sir."

Harris pivoted on his heel and strode toward the helicopter. When he was abreast of his aides, Harris unexpectedly turned around and came back at Nelson. "Totally dissociate the Navy from that research project," he repeated. He paused for emphasis, then added, "But keep total control of it."

Then Harris strode back to the helicopter. The two aides jumped to catch up with him. The helicopter took off immediately, circling briefly to the west to gain altitude, then headed south toward the Atlantic Fleet Headquarters in Norfolk, Virginia. It avoided the low-hanging clouds over Washington as if they were deadly shoals.

20

Gunther Marx listened to Ruth's outpouring, his dark and sympathetic eyes never leaving her face. When she finished, he blurted out, "My God, Ruth, I can't start to imagine the emotional agony you must be going through."

Ruth was surprised. She had come to Gunther for legal advice, and his first concern had been for her feelings. Perhaps that was the reason she had come to him. He had been the same way when she had asked his legal help in settling her father's estate.

There was a teddy-bear quality about him that Ruth liked, a warm woolly comforting presence. He was stocky, and had thick brown eyebrows and curly hair, balding in spots, that he'd made no attempt to camouflage by blow-drying and combing, a vanity even Harry had practiced.

She and Harry had known Gunther, but not very well, when they had all been undergraduates at Southern Cal. When they saw him again, he was a partner in a prosperous Beverly Hills law firm. In addition to doing Ruth's father's estate, he had helped Harry with his own estate planning, drawing up the will to minimize taxes. he had done it all as a personal favor, since his firm handled mostly corporate accounts.

"It's an incredible situation," Gunther acknowledged. "A goddamn can of worms legally. Off the top of my head I'd say there are at least three legal quagmires here. One. Is this a case of medical malpractice? Or, and this is the second legal bog, was the operation an unlawful or justified human experiment? If that's the case, then who's responsible for the research? That's the third question. From what you've told me, this fellow Buckley's attorneys aren't too sure of their ground either."

"I haven't spoken to his attorneys," Ruth said.

"No, but you can bet your mortgage that Buckley has." Gunther got up from his chair and began pacing, an impatient bouncing movement. "To prove malpractice we have to show a dereliction of duty that caused damages," he mumbled, like a law student reviewing a lesson. "And to do this we'd have to bring in expert testimony on the issue of what would a competent practitioner have done in a similar circumstance. And if the practitioner had not met the community standards of competence, he would be liable. Of course, there's a whole other issue here. Does a human being who no longer has the ability to sustain life have a right to die a natural and uncomplicated death? Or may he be subjected to human experimentation by doctors who are employed to treat him?"

"You mentioned that this might be an unlawful human experiment," Ruth interjected.

Gunther turned back to her and nodded. "There are

federal government guidelines, even international guidelines to protect patients in experimental procedures. Every hospital that does major research has its own rules. Did Bernstein, Steinhardt, and the hospital follow them? But even if they did satisfy the guidelines, there is still a question of *informed consent*. Did they give you a complete explanation of the procedures involved, the risk, the likelihood of success? Did they really make clear to you how extraordinary the experiment was? What would happen if it did or did not succeed? And did any of the physicians improperly influence your husband to agree to a drastic experiment which caused him needless pain and suffering? These are the questions we'll have to answer just for opening arguments. We'll also have to find out the results of any animal experiments up to this point."

"Could we get one of the other doctors on the case to testify?" Ruth asked.

Gunther shook his head. "Most doctors are notoriously reluctant to testify against their colleagues. They feel, 'There but for the grace of God go I.' The reason there are so many external regulations over medicine today is that doctors have been notoriously bad at regulating one another's actions. They are a professionally delinquent community in terms of their ability to control one another's behavior."

Ruth felt panicky. Gunther was no longer holding her hand. In his quiet way he was forcing her to unemotionally and analytically examine the situation she was in. As he had pointed out, Buckley had undoubtedly been over the same ground with his lawyers and it had all boiled down to the same question.

140

"In his ruthless way, Buckley's being straight with me, isn't he?" she said. "We could sue them all. The doctors, the hospital, the institute. It would be a hell of a case. It would be in the courts for years and give them all a lot of headaches and bad publicity. But then what would I do with Harry?"

"The hospital ethically would have to maintain him as best they could in his present condition, but from what you've described, that's not the best of all possible environments for him."

"And the institute won't take him without a release against any liability."

"Have you discussed this with Harry?"

Ruth shook her head. "It's very difficult. Sometimes he scribbles me messages on that board, but more often than not he's too doped up. They have him heavily tranquilized."

"Is he coherent when he . . ." —Gunther groped for a word—"writes you?"

"He seems to be. But it's so hard to tell from just a sentence here and there."

"I'd like to see him as soon as possible."

"I'll arrange it with Bernstein. There shouldn't be any problem, although they seem to want to keep everything top secret."

Gunther grunted. He studied Ruth, silent a moment before he asked the next question. "What are you living on?"

"The company's disability insurance."

"Is it enough?"

Ruth shook her head. "Not quite. It's sixty percent of Harry's salary. We have some savings to cover the gap, but I don't know what'll be left after I pay the difference between the medical insurance and the hospital bills."

"Do I have your permission to negotiate on your and Harry's behalf?"

"Yes, of course. But what is there to negotiate?"

"I don't know yet. For one thing, we might release Harry to the institute but still not waive any liability they incurred in the operation. If Steinhardt and Buckley are sincere in that they want Harry at the institute in order to gain further scientific and medical knowledge, then they would go along with that. Steinhardt, incidentally, would have nothing to say about it. It would be strictly Buckley's decision as head of the institute. If I were their lawyer, I would oppose it."

"Why?"

"Because it undercuts the only defense they have. To wit, the Institute of Oceanography isn't responsible for Steinhardt's medical experiments. He's an independent research scientist working under a contract with the government, or whoever the hell is sponsoring his work. It'll be a moment of truth for Buckley. Is he really more interested in Harry and the research or in avoiding the liability for it?"

"What if he refuses to compromise, if you could call it that, and insists that we sign a total release before they'll take Harry?"

"Then I guess it becomes your moment of truth. Are you more interested in pursuing a suit that might make you and your children rich but let Harry languish at the hospital? Or will you release him to the institute to continue . . . what? . . . this . . . this great experiment into the great unknown?"

Ruth was about to blurt out her answer but checked herself. She took a deep breath to settle herself. On the wall behind Gunther's desk was a painting, the only piece of art in his law office. A clipper ship rode perilously on the heaving sea, its narrow racy hull half submerged in iron-blue waves, the forward mast shattered and its sail rent to tatters by the gale. Ruth slowly let out her breath.

"I don't give a damn about the money," she said. "Harry will go crazy if he has to stay the way he is now. We'll both go stark raving mad."

21

The storm fell on Los Angeles. The flood-control channels with their high perpendicular concrete embankments swelled with the runoff of the streets and became muddy torrents. Two young boys in Van Nuys sneaked under the fence to play in the water and were swept away and drowned. The North Hollywood and Burbank area were blacked out when lightning struck a power line. Street corners were flooded under a foot of water. The year's accumulation of oil floated to the surface of drenched freeways, creating a slick, greased surface, and the commuting traffic crept along like lines of great snails gliding on tractionless tires. Cars with wet brakes careened into cars stalled with wet distributors, colliding like rudderless barges in a river. Three people were killed in traffic accidents caused by the rain. Harry Styles, dressed in a black neoprene wet suit, sat upright in an aluminum-framed chair, watching the spectacle on the six o'clock news on television.

It was not a torrential storm with gale force winds. It was just an insistent rain whose ordained mission was to soak and replenish the parched land for spring. But Los Angeles, that very technically advanced city, used technology to bulldoze and defy the primal nature of the land. In Pacific Palisades a cliff, undermined by the cut of the Pacific Coast Highway, collapsed, burying a forty-five-year-old salesman in his Impala. Mud and rock slides closed the Laurel Canyon road, trapping several drivers in their cars. A new development of $100,000 homes in Bluebird Canyon slipped and lurched several feet, tottering on their cracked foundations. A high tide and heavy surf breached the sand at Malibu, inundating beach homes, the foamy seawater surging and ebbing through living rooms. The TV reporter, his trousers rolled up to his knees, signed off the story standing barefooted and calf deep in water in a ruined living room, grinning cutely at the camera as if the storm were a great joke he had personally contrived.

Like many convalescing patients, Harry spent a great deal of time watching TV. The television was set up against one of the viewing windows of his tank at the Institute of Oceanography. The tank, a construction of welded steel plates framing enormous, thick glass windows, was about the same length and width as Harry's study at home but half again as high. It had originally been built for a study of large pelagic fish.

The transfer from the hospital to the institute had been uneventful largely because Harry had been heavily tranquilized. In fact, he had been kept that way since the first night he had regained consciousness, and after that shock of awakening he had biologically adapted to his new form of respiration without experiencing any anxiety about it. Having fallen into a coma with the realization that he was dying, he was at first overwhelmed with the wonder of simply being alive. The pain that had stabbed him with every breath was absent. The extraordinary environment in which he found himself did not alarm him. His isolation in an oxygen tent, numbed by drugs, before the operation had in a way preconditioned him. In the weeks before, bound by pain and feebleness to a hospital bed, even the shrunken weight of his body had become intolerable, and he had developed bedsores. Now he floated free, free from pain and the drudgery of gravity, unfettered by anxieties, to drift effortlessly amid psycho-pharmocological mists and dreams. Once Harry was at ease in the large tank, Bernstein, still acting as the attending physician, began gradually to cut down on the dosage of the tranquilizers.

Although the dimensions of his tank were limited, they were a liberation from the imprisonment of his hospital bed and the first tank in which he had found himself. Harry felt his horizons were in fact expanding, and this feeling was strengthened by his improving health. Like all reprieved men, he experienced each new moment of life as an unexpected gift. And each day Steinhardt or Buckley arrived with a technical innovation and expanded Harry's mobility—a pair of water-corrected contact lenses, a zero-gravity toilet adapted from Skylab, and now the remote-control TV switch, encased in waterproof flexible plastic, which allowed him to operate the TV set himself.

"They've installed all the comforts of home, huh." Ruth was standing at once of the viewing windows holding the microphone in her hand, smiling at him. Harry had not seen her come in. The tank was located in a large, windowless concrete-walled basement room;

the only other occupant, a graduate student who sat at a desk by the door on the other side of the room.

Harry kicked out of his chair and swam over to the window, propelling himself with small sculling motions. He attempted to talk to Ruth by making exaggerated movements with his lips, although no sound issued from his throat.

Ruth studied his mouth very carefully, then shook her head. "I'm sorry, honey, but I can't read your lips."

Harry nodded. He picked up the slate board leaning against the window and began to write something out.

"Dr. Steinhardt tells me that they're already at work making you a special throat mike so that you can talk. He says they don't even have to invent anything special." There was a strained, false note of cheer in Ruth's voice, but the note was dampened out as her voice came over the speaker in the tank and was transmitted through the water.

Harry finished scribbling and held up the slate for Ruth to read:

Not quite All the comforts of home

"Can I bring you something from home?" Ruth asked anxiously. The strain of the meeting deepened the lines in her forehead and the webbing of fine lines about her eyes.

Harry nodded and immediately began writing again. His request only took a moment to write, and he held it up:

Your bikini

"My bikini. Oh, Harry." Ruth forced a smile. "I'm not getting in that water with you. You know what a chicken I am about the water. If I get my head underwater I panic." She studied Harry then, as if eager to change the subject, and quickly said, "You're looking much better. That wet suit is something new."

Harry nodded and bent to writing again. He had put on weight, but the distorting wide-angle effect of the water made him seem huskier than he really was. His blond hair, uncut since he first entered the hospital, was growing out long and full, billowing about his head, and his beard was taking shape. The saline solution had bleached all his hair to the color of tow to which Christopher's reverted in the summer, and the pale yellow hair and beard encircled his head, reflecting the watery light like a corona.

"The wet suit looks good on you. Very macho."

With the wet suit on, the gill cover looked no more extraordinary than a cowl collar. It no longer seemed the grotesque prosthetic device it had been in the hospital when Harry, naked and helpless, had first worn it.

They're conditioning me to colder water

"Why are they doing that?"

Harry pantomimed flexing his muscles and beating his chest.

"It will make you stronger?" Ruth interpreted. Harry nodded. "Build up your resistance." Harry again nodded.

"Dr. Steinhardt says you're eating better. You're getting the same food the astronauts ate when they were in space."

Harry made a grimace and wrote:

It's like eating toothpaste

He held up one of the metal food tubes for Ruth's inspection.

"But the doctor told me they've started you on bananas, cheese, even hamburger."

But No fish. I'd feel like a cannibal

Ruth laughed, a very uneasy laugh that verged on tears. She was having a great deal of difficulty talking to Harry. He sensed it in her posture, the phrasing and rhythm of her voice, the tautness in her expression. It was as if she were angry with him. In the past she would get that way when, with a contractual deadline pressing, he would have to work late, or round the clock, or over the weekend, or he would have to go out of town on business unexpectedly. There was no reasonable objection she could make, since it was his work, schedules interlocked with the deadlines of other space and defense subcontractors, irrevocably committed to the countdown of space shots. She never blamed Harry. Still he could always sense the suppressed anger, the attitude of abandonment, the resentment. It was there now.

"Is there anything I can do for you?" she asked.

Yes. I'm horny

"Oh, Harry, don't. Please." Ruth's voice broke and she covered her face with her hands.

Harry was confused. It was meant to be a joke, one of the bawdy intimacies he had often used in the past to break any tension between them. But the joke now had its tragic resonances. Ruth and Harry's sex life had ceased with his illness. He had been preoccupied with pain, the struggle for breath, and dying for over a year. His sensuality had not extended beyond the primal lust to breathe. What aching deprivation Ruth might be experiencing he did not know.

With his growing awareness, Harry felt an increasing need to touch Ruth, as if to reaffirm his life. He wanted his children.

I want to see the Kids

"I'll bring them next time, Harry. I promise." Ruth was uncomfortable. "It's just that I haven't . . . I haven't explained everything to them." There was guilt in her stammer, a confession. "Harry, it's so hard to explain."

What did you tell them?

"I explained that you were very sick. And that you had to have a special way of breathing. Harry, it's as if they're afraid to ask any questions."

Harry nodded. There were only a few inches of glass and water between him and his wife's face, lovely even in her anguish. For the first time it occurred to Harry that he might never be able to transcend that fragile barrier.

"I'll tell them, Harry. I promise. And I'll bring them next time. It's just that it's all so confusing. It all takes so much getting used to."

Harry nodded again, but he didn't try to say or write anything. He reached up and touched the glass, and Ruth pressed her hand on the glass opposite him. They stood there in silence, looking at each other, as if trying to make an extrasensory contact through the implacable surface of glass.

"I've got to go now, Harry," Ruth said after a while. "Mrs. Levine is sitting with Christopher."

At the door to the tank room, Ruth turned and gave Harry a cheerful smile and wave; then she was gone, and Harry stood staring forlornly at the closed door.

The attendant put down the papers he had been studying at his desk and came up to the tank, where he logged the readings on several gauges and drew a sample of water from a tap located at the bottom of the tank.

Neither Harry nor the attendant was aware that in the hallway outside Ruth had collapsed against the door, stifling her sobs so that they couldn't be heard in the tank room.

22

Dr. Steinhardt peered into the goldfish bowl set on an end table in the Styleses' living room. He intently studied the fish as though it were a rare biological specimen. Across the room Paul Buckley and Gunther Marx were conferring in low tense voices.

Ruth paused in the doorway to note the contrast in the two men. Buckley, impeccably groomed, was wearing a glen plaid business suit and a carefully blocked silk foulard tie. Gunther was dressed in a bulky turtleneck sweater and a rough tweed jacket. His hair was shaggy and his jaws shadowed. He looked more like a tough labor leader hammering out a work contract than a corporate lawyer.

It was Gunther who had worked out the arrangements with the institute in an extraordinary way that seemed, at least temporarily, to have satisfied everyone. Harry had been moved to the institute not as a patient or a guinea pig but as a paid consultant in underwater research. But Gunther had refused to give any releases from liability concerning the original operation. The institute's lawyers had reluctantly agreed to the arrangement. Harry's status at the institute was made an entirely separate situation from the operation and its immediate aftermath. In that way the institute's liability was somewhat mitigated. Lawyers, Ruth thought, live in a world of threatening suits as tangled as any form of life Harry might find underwater. But the arrangement gave her husband a certain dignity. For that she was tremendously grateful to Gunther.

He looked up and caught her eye. "Are the children all right?"

"Fast asleep. God, that I could sleep so easily and so peacefully."

Steinhardt turned toward her, surprised to see her standing next to him, his concentration on the goldfish had been so intent. "How did they take the news?" he inquired solicitously.

"They were confused. They don't really understand it. I don't think they will until they see Harry for themselves. I don't look forward to that."

"How about the older girl?" Steinhardt asked. "Is it Brenda?"

Ruth nodded. "She's out with a school friend. A boy. It's a sort of date." She smiled ruefully and shook her head. "They start dating so young nowadays. She wanted to stay at home with me. But I made her keep her date. Whatever else happens, my children are going to live normal lives."

Ruth sat down on the couch and looked from Steinhardt to Marx and Buckley. "You know, right after I saw Harry in that water tank for the first time, I thought of telling the children that their father was dead."

Buckley leaned forward. "Would that have been wise?"

"I don't know what is wise or unwise anymore. As far as science is concerned, Harry may have made another great leap for mankind. But as far as functioning as a father, or a husband, Harry might just as well be dead."

There was a heavy silence in the room. Then Steinhardt stirred and cleared his voice. "Ah, yes, well, as Dr. Bernstein and I have explained to you in the past, the odds are still very much against your husband surviving very long. There is still a better than even chance that the cancer has spread elsewhere and will redevelop in another organ. In any event, serious complications are inevitable in a pioneering medical procedure."

Ruth said nothing. She stared at Steinhardt and then at Buckley. The institute director's expression was sympathetic. Buth Ruth wondered just how sincere his concern was.

"Harry will be transferred to the institute only because Paul Buckley wants Harry there," Gunther had told Ruth after his initial meetings with the director. "If it were up to his lawyers they would let Harry rot in a tank at the hospital and let us sue. It would make an easier case for defending the institute. But Buckley's an ambitious man. He's not a scientist in spite of his Ph.D. He's a game player. A power seeker. He's carefully weighed the pluses and the minuses. If he abandoned Steinhardt and denied any responsibility for Harry's operation, he would gain nothing, but he still might be a party to a messy lawsuit. Believe me, he carefully examined that possibility long before you blurted it out. By bringing Harry to the institute he is sticking his neck out. But he also gains control of the

155

situation, and he can exploit it to his own advantage."

"What advantage?" Ruth had asked.

"Having his name linked with a major scientific and medical advance. The publicity, the scientific prestige, the research grants."

"But he had nothing to do with it."

"He will if Harry is brought to the institute."

That had been Gunther's canny evaluation of Buckley. Ruth studied him closely now. His features were as neatly composed as his foulard. He had wanted to talk to her, so he'd arranged this meeting. He leaned toward her now, as if the diminished distance between them automatically created an increased intimacy and trust.

"Mrs. Styles, we are going to have to make a formal announcement in the next few days. Some word about the operation and Mr. Styles seems to have leaked out to the media. We've already had several confused inquiries. We don't think we can put off an announcement of some sort much longer. We'd very much like your cooperation and participation. It will give the revelation and the operation itself more an appearance of, well, normalcy."

Ruth was suddenly frightened. "You mean reporters. Television."

"I'm afraid it can't be avoided," Buckley said.

Ruth shook her head vehemently. "It's out of the question."

"I think Harry would be much more at ease with you at his side."

"At his *side?* I'm afraid the normal vocabulary of nuptial loyalty doesn't apply here. I may or may not still have a husband, but I do have three children. And I

156

won't have them made part of some scientific sideshow. Step right up, folks. See Harry, the fish-man. One of the wonders of the modern world. He breathes water like a fish and crawls on his belly like a reptile."

"Mrs. Styles," Buckley protested, "we're hardly going to turn this into some kind of carnival situation."

Gunther cut him off. "We're simply going to have to respect Mrs. Styles's feelings in this matter. I'm wholly in sympathy with her wanting to keep her children out of this. For the time being we can give Mr. Styles another identity. It's done quite often in the reporting of special medical cases."

Buckley looked at Steinhardt as if for help, but the scientist only nodded, as if he were also in sympathy with Ruth. "We could simply call him John Doe," he suggested. "Or perhaps John Glaucus."

"Glaucus?"

Steinhardt gave a shy smile and shrugged. "It is what I've been calling it in my reports. The Glaucus Project. In Greek mythology, Glaucus was a mortal whom the Titans transformed into a sea god who could only live in the water."

Ruth stared at Steinhardt in amazement. She looked from Steinhardt to Buckley, then suddenly laughed. The laugh was bitter and mocking. *"Glaucus.* Lord, but you people love to name your hardware and your grandiose projects after ancient gods. Apollo. Saturn. Poseidon. Glaucus. It's as if you are deliberately trying to invest them with some primal, holy force. The high priests of modern science and technology invoking the protection of the old gods."

She stood up impulsively as if it were the first step to fleeing. She was angry, and frightened. She turned and the end table with the goldfish bowl was directly before her. The goldfish hovered, its fins as delicate as veils holding it motionless, its huge popeyes staring at her, the puckered mouth gulping water and the fragile gold gills undulating softly. The convex crystal side of the bowl magnified the fish face into a threatening gargoyle. Ruth was revolted, horrified. She violently shoved the bowl to get it out of her sight. It hurtled off the table, shattering on the floor in an explosion of glass, water, and sand. The goldfish lay at Ruth's feet gasping, the delicate gills quivering.

"Ooh!" She stooped to pick up the goldfish and in her panicky haste slashed her hand on a piece of glass. She stood and held out her hand, the goldfish convulsing in her bloody palm, Ruth's eyes pleading desperately with the three men in the room for help.

23

The human voice starts as an exhaled breath through the windpipe into the larynx, where it passes over two folds of mucous membranes called the vocal cords. The cords vibrate, producing a resonance in the air enclosed in the pharynx, mouth, nose, and sinuses. The *a, e,* and *o* sounds of speech are made by the reverberation of air between the vocal cords and the back of the tongue and in the mouth. *M, n,* and *ng* sounds resound in the nasal cavity. And the other consonants are articulated by the teeth, tongue, and lips as the breath passes out of the mouth. Without the breath of air there is no human speech. In Harry's case his speech organs were intact. The solution of the communications engineers was to substitute oscillating circuits for the vibrating air columns and amplifiers for the acoustical resonating chambers. No new technology had to be developed. The electric voice box developed for people who have had their larynx surgically removed because of throat cancer had only to be modified and adapted.

From the first day Buckley had seen Harry scribbling

on the slate board, he had assigned engineers to that task. The Hydro-Voice they developed was a marvel of miniaturized electronics. It was the size of a small transistor radio and merely had to be strapped across Harry's throat. But the electronic shrieks, howls, grunts, trills, and moans it produced had to be calibrated and registered to Harry's distorted speech patterns. If a diver breathes air compressed to four or five times its normal density, as he would in a pressure chamber, the vibratory range of the voice is altered and the person sounds like an animated duck. Harry was breathing water, and the vibrations he made produced no comprehensible sound.

Harry worked with the engineers, pushing himself to the limits of his returning energy. When the engineers had finished their experiments for the day, Harry sat in the tank talking to himself, practicing sounds, words, and sentences like a child left alone in his playpen. He did not try to talk to Ruth, however. He continued to write her notes. Like an adolescent whose vocal cords suddenly double in size and unexpectedly drop or soar an octave, Harry was still finding his voice. He was self-conscious about it. He asked Ruth to delay bringing the children to see him. Christopher could not read and communication with the four-year-old would be impossible. David and Brenda might be disturbed if he was mute. But there was more to it than he told Ruth, a changing perception of himself that he couldn't scribble out on his slate board. It was a view of himself that Buckley had revealed to him. Without his voice Harry was a victim, a medical guinea pig. With a voice he would become an explorer, communicating his discoveries about the strange new world he inhabited in body and mind.

The day the engineers announced that the Hydro-Voice articulated Harry's speech as well as it ever would, Harry told Ruth that he wanted to see the children. He did not speak to her, but scribbled out his request. The next afternoon Ruth, nervous and edgy, ushered the three excited children into the tank room.

Christopher immediately ran to the window in the tank and stared at Harry. The two other children stopped in the middle of the room and stared, rooted to the spot. Overhead spotlights illuminated the tank, and Harry hovered in their beams, suspended in the shining water like a transcending angel. His long swirling blond hair and beard were unfamiliar to them. They did not recognize their father, and he awed and frightened them. Ruth had to shove them forward.

"Chrissy . . . Brenda . . . David. I've missed you." The voice that emanated from the tank was deep, resonant, totally strange. It was not quite human, yet it was vibrant, and something about it suggested that the speaker had extraordinary, mysterious powers. Ruth and the three children were stunned by it. But then the voice took on a familiar cadence.

"Goddamn but I've missed you kids. Christopher, how's my big boy? David, you look as though you've grown three inches and put on twenty pounds of muscles. But it must be a visual trick of the water, because Brenda looks like Raquel Welch."

Brenda blushed and grinned, flashing her braces, then quickly closed her mouth in the self-conscious way of a teenaged girl.

"Still breaking ten hearts a day at junior high, honey?"

161

Both Brenda and David silently gawked at Harry. Christopher took a step back and turned to Ruth. "That Daddy in there?" The boy's eyes were wide with wonder.

Ruth nodded. "He has to stay in the tank to breathe a special medicine, as he did in the hospital."

"Like his oxygen?" Harry's oxygen mask had made a great impression on Christopher.

"Yes, like his oxygen."

Christopher turned back to look at Harry and then, as if suddenly reassured, he ran right up against the glass and began breathlessly jabbering away, exploding with news. "Stevey's got a new dog. It's a big black one, and it almost bit me. I tried to ride on its back. And it growled at me, *rrraaahhh!* Like that. Just like a lion."

Ruth put her arm around Christopher and gently moved him to the microphone. "Christopher, honey, you'll have to talk to Daddy through this or he can't hear you in the water."

Christopher held the mike with both hands. "It went *rrraaahhh!* Just like a lion. You gonna fight sharks, Daddy?"

Harry smiled at his son. "There aren't too many sharks in here, Chrissy. Or at least they're hiding pretty good."

"They can eat you all up. Just like Jaws."

"I'll be careful. I'll look both ways when crossing the tank."

Harry had no favorites among his children. They each delighted, touched, and troubled him in different ways. Christopher was an exuberant, talkative puppy dog. He had been born almost seven years after David,

162

and the other two children had treated him with amusement, deference, and protection. Of all the members of the family, Christopher was the most buoyant and resilient. He hadn't understood his father's illness and disappearance, but he was a child with resources. His father had always presented him with wonders—movies, the ocean, the new swimming pool, Disneyland. Here was simply another wonder.

Harry studied his other two children. Standing side by side David and Brenda looked like twins. Brenda, at some point in his illness of which Harry was barely conscious, had celebrated her fourteenth birthday. She was about to enter high school, and she was preoccupied with the paraphernalia of her adolescence—the boys, dates, grades, fads, fashions, pop music, and social stigmas. Harry had already evolved to the status of "parent," a pronouncer of restrictions and duties. With his illness he had now become a source of sadness in her abundant life, an awkward legacy.

Harry sensed that sadness in her, but it was David who filled Harry with pain. The boy was his first son. They had always had a close, special relationship, and Harry's illness had come when the boy seemed particularly vulnerable. He had withdrawn, silent and brooding, into himself. Of all the children he had been the least able to cope with Harry's illness. Christopher had often wandered into Harry's bedroom at home, and later, in the hospital, he would bring grave, excited news of the neighborhood or television programs he had just watched. Brenda fussed about him, gentle and motherly, playing nurse. But David had maintained a silent distance, watching him from the doorway or, on occasion, speaking to his father with an unnatural shyness. Of all the children, David had instinctively known he was going to lose his father; he could do nothing; and the loss was unbearable to him. He now stared at Harry with dark, hurt eyes.

"You getting along okay?" the man in the tank asked David in a strange, resounding voice.

"Yes sir." The boy's voice was subdued, hardly audible.

"You're the man of the house now, David. You've got to watch out for everything."

The boy said nothing. Harry looked at him a moment, then asked, "It's very weird, isn't it?"

The boy nodded timidly.

"I'm okay. Really I am," Harry insisted in that alien voice. "Just try to think of me as a kind of astronaut. Like the first man on Neptune. Only I've had a systems failure, and I'm having trouble getting back to earth."

"Daddy, can I go swimming with you?" Christopher broke in.

Harry laughed, and the sound came out like the chords of a bass guitar. "Gee, I don't know. I don't see why not."

"Harry, it's too deep," Ruth said anxiously.

"I can hold him up. The way I used to do in the deep end of the pool." Harry wanted to hold his younger son once more. He felt an aching need to hold or touch each of his children and his wife.

Ruth appealed to the attendant, the graduate student assigned to monitor the tank. But the attendant didn't see any reason why Christopher couldn't go into the tank with Harry. Dr. Steinhardt, Mark Matsuda, two of the communications engineers, and the attendant had all donned wet suits and jumped in the tank with Harry at one time or another to perform medical tests or adjust equipment.

Ruth looked worried. "You want to get in the tank with your father and Chrissy?" she asked David.

The boy looked at Harry and then back at his mother and shook his head. Christopher had already climbed halfway up the steel ladder leading to the top of the tank and was squealing with impatience. Ruth ordered him down and made him take off all his clothes.

Then the attendant, laughing at the chubby little white ass that bobbed energetically, climbed up the ladder with Christopher in front of him. At the upper level of the tank, Harry treaded water with only the top of his head and eyes above the surface of the water, holding his arms out toward the boy. Christopher squealed *"Daddy,"* yanked out of the attendant's grasp, and lunged for his father. He wrapped his arms about Harry's neck, and the sudden force and weight of the boy dropping on him drove them both underwater. Harry had miscalculated his own buoyancy. Without his lungs filled with air, he could not hold the boy up. They sank to the bottom of the tank.

The boy, frightened at being underwater, entwined his arms about his father's neck in a death clutch, shutting off Harry's gills. Harry struggled to loosen the boy's grip, but in his fear the child only held on more desperately to his father.

Ruth watched with horror at what was happening. She screamed to the attendant to get Christopher. The young man jumped into the tank just as Harry finally pried the boy's arms loose from about his neck and shoved the child toward the surface.

The attendant grabbed Christopher's arm and

hauled the boy, choking and panicked, to the side of the tank. Ruth had scampered up the ladder in the time the rescue had taken, and now she reached out and pulled Christopher out of the water. Still coughing up water and sobbing, the boy clung to his mother. Harry's thickly bearded face surfaced at the side of the tank and he reached up in a futile effort to try and assist Ruth. Christopher screamed and recoiled in terror from his father so violently he almost knocked Ruth off the ladder.

"I'm sorry, Chris. I didn't mean to hurt you." The child's scream and the deep electronic voice reverberated off the concrete walls of the tank room and echoed hauntingly. *"I didn't mean to hurt you."*

Harry, dismayed and sick at heart, watched Ruth carry the screaming, terrified child down from the tank.

24

There was witchery in the sunset. Steinhardt felt it with an ancient homesick longing. Above the Pacific the evening sun heated the caldron of air and moisture, and it boiled up into great puffs of cumulus clouds, towering thunderheads, and high ghostly veils of cirrus. The sun sank toward the sea, and at the horizon the light struck back through the clouds. Scarlet billows, magic magenta towers, and searing pink sheets covered the western sky. Once as a child in Norway, enchanted by a similar sunset, Steinhardt had mindlessly sailed his small skiff out of the leeward shelter of the fjord toward it. He sailed under an ancient compulsion. There at the line where the air became water and the light became the night, there was a place and time where all mysteries of man and earth were revealed. But the sun had fallen and night engulfed him on a black heaving sea. Only by luck had the boy made it back to a beach, wrecking his sailboat in the surf and almost drowning.

Steinhardt turned reluctantly from the window. "We

simply don't know what changes are now taking place in his body."

Buckley frowned. "I'm not sure I follow you."

"Harry has apparently learned to use his diaphragm, the constrictor muscles in his throat, and the sterno-mastoid and trapezius muscles in ways they've never been used before."

"What's it all about?"

"To create a flow of water over his gills. Higher fish have special muscles in their operculum to accomplish this. In Harry's case we created the flow by circulating the water in the tank with a pump. However, now his muscles are functioning in a way we don't understand yet. It's possibly a combination of automatic swallowing and the action of his diaphragm."

"Can't Styles tell you anything about what's happening?"

Steinhardt shook his head. "It's entirely an unconscious response. Probably a biofeedback mechanism of some sort. The muscles and nerves of the jaw and neck, the pharynx, even the striated muscles of the diaphragm, all originally develop from the gill arches of the embryo. Perhaps they've regressed back to a primordial function. We simply don't know at this point."

"You said something about his having developed new muscles."

"Again, it's speculation. For example, when a lung is removed, the diaphragm becomes thicker and stronger in order to pump more air in and out of the remaining lung to make up for the lost one. Or if a vein is transplanted to take the place of an artery, the vein will develop a thick sheath of muscle the same as an artery.

Just what changes are taking place in Styles's body we can only guess at until . . . until such time as we can perform an autopsy."

At that moment the phone on Buckley's desk buzzed.

"Yes?"

"A telegram was just delivered," the voice on the speaker phone said. "It's from the Navy Department."

"Please bring it right in." Buckley turned back to Steinhardt. "Have you discussed this with Dr. Bernstein?"

Steinhardt hesitated, then said, "Yes, of course."

Buckley's secretary walked into the office, handed him a telegram, and left without saying a word.

"I haven't seen much of him lately," Buckley said, opening the telegram and scanning it.

"He, of course, still has his normal surgical practice." Had Buckley been listening carefully he would have caught the total lack of conviction in Steinhardt's voice. Bernstein's behavior lately had puzzled and hurt Steinhardt. As Styles had grown healthier, Bernstein had become morose. He showed up at the institute rarely, and his phone calls to Steinhardt were brief and perfunctory. It was as if the sight of Styles had become increasingly painful to him. On his last trip to the institute, he had collapsed in tears in Steinhardt's office. "My God, Karl, what have we done?" he sobbed. "What have we done?" He had been drunk.

Neither depression nor alcoholism was uncommon among doctors, and Steinhardt had tactfully suggested that Bernstein should perhaps seek psychiatric help.

"What the hell can a shrink do about that?" the surgeon had yelled, waving his arm in the general direction

169

of the tank room.

"Those bastards!"

Buckley's exclamation broke Steinhardt out of his reverie. "Something the matter?" he inquired.

Buckley read aloud: "'It is the established policy of the Defense Department and the Navy not to conduct or sponsor experimentation on human beings. The radical medical procedure performed in the Glaucus Project was totally outside the parameters of the research authorized in the funding research grant.'"

"Is that from the Navy? Is that telegram addressed to me?" Steinhardt interrupted, outrage in his voice.

"It's addressed to both of us," Buckley answered evenly. "But listen, I've just come to the tricky part." He continued to read: "'However, in view of the humanitarian considerations the Office of Naval Research will make available whatever reasonable funds are necessary to maintain the subject and allow him to develop his full potential.'"

Buckley glanced at Steinhardt and then continued to read. "'It is expected that the scientific knowledge generated will be transmitted directly to the Office of Naval Research. The previously established security and classification procedures will remain in effect.'" Buckley put down the telegram and smiled.

"I don't understand. What does it all mean?" Steinhardt asked in confusion.

"Officially they disown us. As a practical matter, they own us. And they will liberally fund the research."

"Aach, politicians," Steinhardt said with disgust.

"Yes, indeed. They have abandoned us to suffer the slings and arrows of our outraged colleagues, congressmen, clergymen and—" he groped unsuccessfully for another alliteration and then added lamely, "editorial writers." Buckley was still smiling. He was in an expansive mood that greatly puzzled Steinhardt. The institute director turned, and for the first time he noticed the glorious sunset framed in the window.

"The tide is coming in," Buckley noted. "What's that line from Shakespeare? 'There is a tide in the affairs of men, Which, taken at the flood, leads on to fortune; Omitted, all the voyage of their life is bound in shallows and in miseries.'" He turned to Steinhardt, the conspiratorial smile having returned to his face. "On such a full sea, Karl, we are now afloat."

Buckley's pompous oration irritated Steinhardt. "No doubt quoting from *Julius Caesar* is quite impressive at trustee meetings," he said caustically. "Just what the hell does it mean here?"

Buckley merely smiled in response. There was something triumphant in his expression that disturbed Steinhardt. The deep red light from the dying sun inflamed his face, giving him a Satanic look.

25

The tranquilizer Valium loses its effectiveness when used continuously over an extended period of time. Before that happened Bernstein began to reduce Harry's dosage to allow his psyche to make its own natural adjustments to its unnatural condition.

Released from their psychopharmacological bounds, the nightmares now assaulted Harry. He awoke from all of them but one—the reality that he would spend the rest of his life in a tank. He became deeply depressed, barely responding to Steinhardt's queries. Then his mood suddenly changed and he became agitated, nervously churning about the tank.

Disturbed, Steinhardt conferred over the phone with Bernstein. "Perhaps we should put him back on Valium."

"He's having anxiety attacks," Bernstein said. His voice was unconcerned. "I'll tell you what a psychiatrist once told me. If you feel compelled as a doctor to prescribe something in these cases, fine, write the prescription, fill it, and then take it yourself. But the patient has to learn how to cope with his panic and overcome it."

"Frankly, Morris, I'm seriously concerned with the state of his mind."

"Acute depression is very common in cases like this," Bernstein said.

"What cases like this can you possibly be referring to?" Steinhardt snapped in an astonished voice.

"Well, parallel cases. Major surgery. Heart transplants. Pathological depression is what you have to watch out for. I've had patients who became psychotic after surgery and had to be sent to a mental institution. Christiaan Barnard had a heart transplant, a housewife the same age as Styles, who just walked out of the ward one night and jumped out of the window. Suicides are not uncommon." He said all of this in a flat voice.

Steinhardt spoke to Harry. He related his phone conversation with Bernstein, even mentioning the suicide.

"Why are you telling me all this?" Harry asked.

"Because I don't regard you as my patient," Steinhardt replied. "You are my colleague. Together we are embarked on an investigation which has no precedent in science. We must have absolute trust in each other."

Harry nodded and was silent. He looked at Steinhardt standing outside the tank. He remembered he had once been impressed with the man's height, the gaunt severity of his features, and the guileless, uncompromising look in his eyes. Now all that was muted by the barrier of glass and water between them. Harry's thoughts and emotions were in riot. He both feared Steinhardt and was enthralled by him. "Where's Dr. Bernstein? Why isn't he here?"

"I talk to him every day, Harry. There's really no need for him to be here. You have, after all, a full-time doctor and surgeon in attendance." Steinhardt allowed himself a small smile.

"It's not that," Harry said. "I got the distinct impression on his last few visits that Dr. Bernstein was very uncomfortable in my presence. Now he worries about my being suicidal."

Steinhardt did not say anything for a moment, then asked, "Do you feel suicidal?"

Harry shrugged. "I look around at the four walls of the tank and I keep saying to myself, 'Is this all there is?' I'm getting desperate. When I first regained consciousness, I was ecstatic that I was still alive. That I wasn't in pain. That I would see my wife and family again. It wasn't the tranquilizers you had me doped up with. If anything, they kept me down. My mood was joy. I felt I was reborn. But I wasn't really reborn. I can't forget what I was before this. It's a bitter irony, but the stronger and more alert I become, the more depressed I am. My visits with Ruth have become too painful for both of us. My children are shocked and confused. I try to visualize how I must appear to them, and in my mind's eye I have become my own nightmare. Perhaps what I feel now is not very different from what I felt when I was dying. But my feelings are more intense now, perhaps because I'm stronger.

"I said a moment ago I was getting desperate, and I am. I feel like a prisoner in solitary confinement with a life sentence. It's all so goddamn hopeless." Steinhardt started to speak, but Harry held up his hand. "No, please don't interrupt. I know what you're going to say. What you always say. We've got important work to do.

174

The work. That's the only thing that keeps me from losing my mind. You know what the high point of my day is? The blood samples. Yeah, the blood samples. The prick of the needle lets me know I'm still alive.

"Sometimes I float here, not feeling anything. I'm weightless. I have no body. I don't even feel heat or cold. I'm like a ghost. Ruth comes to visit me, and I can only look at her through these windows. I can't touch her or feel her hair or her skin. I'm not even in the same world she's in. I'm a being from another world lost between it and your world. And sometimes I feel as though I'm drifting away into the other world."

"And this other world, this other dimension you're caught between," Steinhardt said intently, "what's it like?"

Harry shook his head. "I don't know. I have no window to look into it. But it terrifies me. I'm so goddamn alone."

That night Harry hovered in his tank, trembling in the darkness. The attendant was out of his sight, dozing at his desk in the shadows across the tank room. Harry suddenly, irrevocably knew he was alone, cut off forever from the world. In the silence he heard only his ears ring. Then he heard the sound of his own heartbeat, the throb uncertain and skipping. He felt hot, flushed, and sweating. He had stomach cramps and a spasm in his bowels. He was light-headed and dizzy, not getting enough oxygen. He began to swim restlessly back and forth in the limited confines of the tank, his actions increasingly agitated, his need for movement panicky. He stopped and listened, hovering in the black silence. He heard only his heart pounding, roaring in his ears as if it were a bomb going to explode in the next instant, totally disintegrating him. Harry panicked. He began screaming.

He screamed but no sound came. He had taken off his Hydro-Voice. His scream was only a frenzied rush of water from his throat. Only he could hear his own scream. All his terrors broke out from their hiding places and now fueled that cry. He clenched his fists and screamed again, and again, until, exhausted, he sank to the bottom of the tank.

26

In 1970 a study of the plate tectonics of the East Pacific Rise, by Dr. Paul Buckley, had been leaked to the press. It had shown that certain offshore tidelands being considered by the Department of the Interior for leasing to the oil companies for exploratory drilling were geologically unstable. They were the locus of an earthquake fault. An oil company had leaked the report to a newspaper.

The oil company had had no interest in that particular area. They had, however, made bids on other tidelands which Buckley's group had found stable and suitable for drilling. The press in their follow-up stories had reported this.

The oil company had invited Buckley and his research associates on a pleasant outing to one of their established drilling platforms in the Santa Barbara channel. The site was known to be geologically stable. It had the added virtue of being very scenic. Several newspaper and television reporters and cameramen were also invited on the junket. They insisted on interviewing Buckley, and he told them what he and his colleagues had long known. But to the press and public now alarmed about earthquake faults, oil spills, and ecology, it was suddenly news. Buckley carefully analyzed how the oil company had dramatically manipulated the news to their own advantage. Had they held an official press conference or issued a formal statement, it probably would have been ignored or treated with great skepticism.

The evening he received the telegram from the Office of Naval Research disavowing experimentation on human beings, Buckley worked late at his office. Was he now drilling on stable or faulted strata? He studied the dangers, anticipated them, and formulated a plan of action.

The next morning Buckley telephoned a writer on the Los Angeles *Times* whom he had cultivated. Buckley told him just enough to pique his interest. The reporter agreed to meet with him at the institute the next morning. Then the director went to Steinhardt's office.

"I don't understand. Why is the reporter coming here now?"

"I can't put him off. He knows too much. He only agreed to hold the story because I promised him that he'd have an opportunity to interview us here and get the facts straight."

"But my paper's not quite finished yet," Steinhardt protested.

"Karl, one does not announce the first man on the moon with a paper in the *Journal of Experimental Surgery*. It's too sensational."

Steinhardt looked troubled.

"Perhaps it's better that it comes out this way, Karl. There simply wasn't time to publish first. The Navy might make an announcement to get themselves off the hook. We can't keep Harry Styles a secret indefinitely. If the story comes out without our control, it's going to be distorted, sensationalized, and made grotesque."

"And how are you going to stop that?"

"This Kenneth Livingstone is a respected science writer, as far as journalists go. You and I will talk to him. He won't see or talk to Styles. The emphasis will be on the scientific accomplishment. And it will look better if he *breaks the story*. If we held a press conference and made the announcement, it would look as though we were deliberately seeking publicity. It might create a backlash."

Steinhardt shook his head. "I don't understand these things. I never read newspapers."

"Never?" Buckley was astonished.

Steinhardt shrugged. "When I was a young man I read newspapers and journals passionately. For a quarter of a century, I closely followed the great crises of our civilization. But I gradually came to the conclusion that all my reading did no one any good. It changed nothing. It only upset me and distracted me from my work. So I stopped reading newspapers."

"What about television?"

Steinhardt shook his head.

"Well, it's not really necessary for you to understand these things," Buckley said. "You're a man of science."

"And you? What are you?"

"I'm a man of science also," Buckley said. Then he added with a hint of a smile, "At the moment my field is political science."

After conferring with Steinhardt, Buckley placed a call to Bernstein. His publicized participation would give the artificial gill transplant the appearance of a scientific team effort rather than the bizarre experiment of one scientist. But to Buckley's surprise the surgeon—when Buckley finally reached him on the phone after several tries—refused to be interviewed. In fact, he insisted that his name not be mentioned. The institute director was furious, but after a minute he regained his perspective. Bernstein's withdrawal created a vacuum for him to fill with his own presence.

Kenneth Livingstone, the L.A. *Times* writer, was a cadaverous-looking man with wispy gray hair and pockmarked cheeks. His lenses magnified his eyes and his smile was a beat too eager.

He listened thoughtfully, on occasion nodding his head in grave acknowledgment, as Buckley outlined the background of the artificial gill and the operation. "Fascinating, fascinating," muttered Livingstone, but it was a moment or two before he realized the full implication of what Buckley had just told him. "Wait a minute. You mean the operation has already been performed? This artificial gill's actually implanted in someone?"

Buckley nodded.

"Who? Where?"

"The man is currently being maintained here at the institute."

"My God, can I see him?"

Buckley shook his head. "I'm sorry. But you understand this man has been critically ill. He's especially susceptible to infections. The slightest germ might kill him. Maybe we can do something almost as good. Get you together with Karl Steinhardt, the scientist and surgeon who actually invented the gill and performed the operation. He's right here on campus."

"That would be terrific," Livingstone said eagerly.

"He's almost as hard to see as his patient. But maybe if I pull rank I can get him to talk to you. He's got diagrams of how the damn device works and even some photographs of it."

"That would be terrific," Livingstone said even more eagerly.

Buckley made the call, and then walked with Livingstone to Steinhardt's office. "By the way, what's the patient's name?" the reporter asked.

"Oh, Glaucus. John Glaucus."

"How do you spell it?"

Buckley spelled it. "It's a Greek name, I believe."

Steinhardt was impatient with several of Livingstone's questions, but that characteristic crankiness added to his ivory-tower-of-science aura and intimidated the reporter. At one point Steinhardt launched into a historical review of the research starting with the Scottish physiologist Haldane's experiments with drowning laboratory mice.

"Excuse me, Doctor, but I simply have to get this straight in my own mind," Livingstone interrupted apologetically. "This patient of yours, this Glaucus, he can only exist underwater, like a fish?"

"Yes, yes." Steinhardt nodded brusquely. "When we operated he had almost total pulmonary insufficiency. Both his lungs had been virtually destroyed by cancer."

"Without the operation and Karl's prosthetic gill,"

Buckley interjected, "this man would have been dead months ago."

Livingstone shook his head in wonderment. "This is fantastic." He scribbled notes, then looked up at Steinhardt. "One last question, Doctor. If you can make a successful artificial gill, why can't you make an artificial lung to allow this man to breathe air?"

Steinhardt smiled. "Technology recapitulates phylogeny."

"I beg your pardon."

"We must follow in the steps of our Creator. We must first solve the biological engineering problems of the gill before we can design a lung, which is a much more complex organ. It took two hundred million years of evolution from the first primitive fish of the Ordovician period until the first lungfish and amphibians crawled from the sea. Actually the first investigator to describe an artificial gill, Bodell, also implanted a primitive artificial lung in sheep and dogs the same year, but there were several technical problems. Other experimenters suggested that a water, membrane, and blood interface was probably the best transmitter for dispersing the carbon dioxide in the blood. Actually this intermediate water transfer of the blood gases still takes place in the lungs between the air cells and the capillaries."

Steinhardt had lost Livingstone. The reporter still smiled and nodded agreeably, but his eyes were glazed and uncomprehending. Buckley interrupted. "I think the important thing to remember in all this, Ken, is that one of the long-range goals of Dr. Steinhardt's research is humanitarian. It's a fundamental step in the eventual development of an artificial lung to benefit those people who have unfortunately lost a lung because of cancer, emphysema, tuberculosis." Here Buckley made a circling motion with his right hand as if to imply a never-ending affliction of deadly lung diseases. "But it has an *immediate* application to the marine sciences. Its effect on our ability to explore and develop the two-thirds of the world that is the sea may be more revolutionary than that of the submarine or the scuba."

Livingstone scribbled on his pad, then he hurriedly got up to go—he wanted to write up the story for the next morning's edition. He was very excited. As they left the research building, Buckley paused on the steps overlooking the Pacific. "A thought just occurred to me, Ken," the director said. "When Neil Armstrong took that first step on the moon, Dr. Wernher von Braun referred to it as the most significant event in human evolution since a creature first crawled from the sea." Buckley looked directly at the reporter, and then his eyes swept toward the distant horizon of the Pacific. "How would he classify this scientific development, I wonder?"

"It's really incredible," Livingstone agreed. He hurried to his car, head bent, still writing in his notebook.

When Buckley got back to his office he called the head of the university security and ordered the guard to be doubled in the research building and around the institute. He authorized the hiring of off-duty policemen. Then he called in the institute's public relations man. Buckley briefed him on the *Times* story and dictated the information the PR man could release. He wasn't to send out a story; he was only to answer inquiries. "Don't read off the information like a prepared statement," Buckley instructed him. "Be informal but authoritative. You are, as they say, the official spokesman for the institute. But don't embellish what I've given you. If anyone wants to know more, tell them a great deal of the experiment is still classified."

"Classified by whom?"

"That's one of the things that's still classified."

"Gotcha." The PR man headed for the door.

Then, almost as an afterthought, Buckley called Steinhardt. "Karl, if the story appears tomorrow, you may be getting a lot of calls from the media. If you'd like, I can have the switchboard transfer all your calls to the PR office or my own office. . . . Of course it's trouble, Karl. But it's part of my job."

Buckley contemplated making one more call. To Ruth Styles. He picked up the phone to tell his secretary to place the call, then immediately replaced it. Five minutes after talking to her, her lawyer Marx would be on his back dictating what Buckley could and could not do. To hell with that. Ruth Styles and Marx could get the news with the rest of the world. By the next morning it would be a fait accompli, and they would be on the defensive, asking Buckley's help.

27

The next morning Ruth dropped Christopher off at day school and returned home. She picked the Los Angeles *Times* out of the rosebush and glanced at the headline.

**MAN BREATHES WATER
WITH ARTIFICIAL GILL**
**Lung Cancer Victim First Transplant
Lives Underwater in Tank**

Ruth suddenly felt faint with fear. She skimmed the article hurriedly, her heart pounding.

By KENNETH A. LIVINGSTONE
Times Staff Writer

MAREJADA—The ancient myths of mermen and mermaids living beneath the sea like fishes have become a scientific reality. In a historic breakthrough, researchers at the Institute of Oceanography here have implanted the first artificial gill in a human being, the *Times* learned exclusively today.

The 36-year-old patient was a lung cancer victim with a pulmonary insufficiency that is invariably terminal. However, the successfully implanted artificial gills have allowed him to breathe oxygen from water in the same way fish do, according to Paul Buckley, director of the Institute.

The implanted artificial gill is the invention of Dr. Karl Steinhardt, a surgeon doing advanced research in respiration and comparative physiology at the institute. Steinhardt also performed the pioneering transplant operation. "We were totally taken by surprise by its success," Steinhardt told the *Times*. "We had hoped, at best, to get a significant transfer of oxygen and carbon dioxide across the gills between the patient's bloodstream and the saline solution. But we had not anticipated in our most optimistic speculations that it would sustain him as long as it has."

The patient, dubbed John Glaucus by the elated scientists, is being maintained in a tank of sterile, oxygen-rich saline solution, which is similar to seawater. The name "Glaucus," that of a mythological sea god, is an alias to protect the patient's anonymity, a common procedure in the reporting of pioneering medical procedures.

Paradoxically, the gill, which is expected to revolutionize marine research, is an almost incidental spinoff of the development of oxygenators now routinely used in operating rooms for open-heart and lung surgery.

Ruth dropped the paper. She felt threatened, as if the story were announcing some imminent holocaust. Her first thought was to leave immediately with the children, to drive north over the Santa Suzanna Mountains into the flat farmlands of Bakersfield. She knew such an action made no sense, but the compulsion to flee was strong. She took a deep breath to calm herself, then another. She sat very still, breathing with great deliberation.

The phone rang. It was Gunther Marx.

"Did you see the story in this morning's *Times* about Harry?"

"I just this moment . . ."

"There's no cause for alarm yet. They've kept Harry's identity a secret. I'll call Buckley immediately to make sure it stays that way, and that you and the kids are kept out of it."

When she hung up the phone, Ruth picked up the paper and scanned the rest of the *Times* story. It was a review of the research leading up to the development of the gill. She couldn't concentrate on it.

Gunther would soon be calling back. He would let her know if there was any danger to her and the children. Until then, there was nothing to do. There was no one else she could call. There was no one else in whom she had confided.

She wandered about the house, the little black dog Groucho following her, his claws clicking on the wood floors. She was suddenly aware of the silence. The house was so quiet since she had enrolled Christopher in day school. No longer did she hear the sound of his running footsteps, the banging doors, Groucho's growling and grumbling in the child's wake. Ruth had become so used to the racket of the four-year-old that she wasn't aware of it until he was gone.

Since the incident in the tank with Harry, Christopher had become unnaturally quiet. He had nightmares almost nightly from which he woke trembling and frightened, but he didn't remember them in the morning. Ruth decided to send him to the day school, hoping that the new environment crowded with other kids would occupy his mind. It had worked somewhat. Christopher had come home breathless with stories of new friends and games, but the nightmares had continued.

The night before Ruth had been wakened by a noise and gone into the boys' room. She found David cradling Christopher, tears streaming down the older boy's face as though he had shared the unspeakable horror with his brother. But the older boy shared nothing with Ruth. He kept his thoughts and fears to himself, a dark, beautiful, and silent child stalking through the house, brooding and heartbroken.

Ruth wept silently, the tears streaming down her face. She wept for her confused, frightened children and she wept for herself. She was as confused and frightened as they were. Ruth hadn't cried as much in her life as she had in the past few months. Not during her childhood nor her father's long illness nor when she thought Harry was going to die had she cried as frequently and uncontrollably as she did now.

She wiped her face and gasped, trying once again to

deliberately breathe deeply and compose herself. She suddenly felt a desperate need to talk to someone— someone impersonal, a doctor.

Once, when it was certain Harry was going to die, Dr. Bernstein had suggested both she and Harry get psychiatric counseling. "Look, we all need help at critical times in our lives," Bernstein had gently advised her. "Hell, fifty percent of the doctors I know need psychiatric help. They don't get it. Doctors always make the worst patients. The worst. We're uncooperative. We know it all. But most of us need help." Looking back, it seemed to Ruth that Bernstein too was suppressing tears—tears for her and Harry and all his psychically wounded colleagues.

Ruth could call Bernstein. He was someone in whom she could confide. He at least would be able to recommend a psychiatrist. She dialed his office. His receptionist said he wasn't in. She didn't know when he would be, but she would give him the message. Ruth hung up.

She started to dial Gunther's office, but then stopped. She would be bothering him unnecessarily. She wandered into Harry's study, went to the liquor cabinet, and took out a bottle of Scotch and a glass. She sat down at Harry's desk, started to pour a drink, then stopped, and stared at the bottle. Whatever might happen this day, she needed whatever wits she still had to cope with it. She put the bottle and the glass back in the cabinet.

Ruth turned on the radio to KNX, the all-news station. The "fish-man" was the big story of the day. The report essentially repeated the facts that were in the L.A. *Times* story, but once again Ruth felt panicky.

She thought of contacting Brenda at school. But what would that accomplish other than alarming the girl? Yet the number of people to whom Ruth could now speak had dwindled to her teenaged daughter.

There had been a time when Harry was sick and at home that Brenda had competed with Ruth, vying to nurse and serve Harry. The girl fussed about and redid little chores for her father that Ruth had already performed, like straightening the bed and plumping pillows, and she frequently criticized her mother. One day they had had a terrible fight over a Coke. Harry had asked for it.

"It's got awful gunk in it," Brenda had protested. "Chemicals and sugar. It'll make him sicker."

"Your father's a grown man. He knows what he wants," Ruth had tried to explain. He had a craving for something cold, something sweet. Maybe the taste evoked some now distant memory of youth when, hot and thirsty, he had trotted off a sun-baked sandlot to eagerly guzzle Coke with his playmates. "Oh, what the hell difference does it make anymore?" Ruth had finally cried out.

Shocked, Brenda had run in tears from the kitchen.

The telephone rang, snapping Ruth out of her reveries. It was Gunther. "It took me over an hour to get through to Buckley. Apparently every TV station in the area, the networks, the wire services, newspapers, *Time, Newsweek,* they've all been trying to get through. He promised me to keep Harry anonymous and keep you and the children out of it. I guess we'll just have to trust him. We haven't got much choice at this point." There was a note of tense excitement and frustration in Gunther's voice. He didn't say it, but his tone

190

implied Buckley was in charge and dictating events and the lawyer didn't much like it.

"How did the newspaper get the story in the first place?"

"Buckley doesn't know. They probably had some source at the university hospital. He said they called him up with just enough information to write a sensationalized story, so he gave them the straight facts in order to prevent it from being distorted."

"Why wasn't Bernstein mentioned in the story? I tried to call him but he wasn't in."

"I've been trying to get him for days. He probably thinks we want to sue him for malpractice."

"Maybe he feels like me. He just wants to crawl under a rock somewhere."

"Look, Ruth, this will all blow over in a few days. You know the media. Everything that's novel, they blow up for a couple of days and then they've gone on to something else. By the end of the week there'll be a new Mideast crisis or a murder and they'll forget about Harry. In the meantime, if you want to stay out of it, perhaps you'd better keep away from the institute."

"Why?"

"It's up to you, Ruth. There are reporters and TV cameras all around the area, according to Buckley. If you're coming and going, you're bound to attract someone's attention."

"What about Harry?"

"Buckley's got security guards covering the research building. He's told the press that Harry, or rather John Glaucus, is still in critical condition. He's especially susceptible to infections and contact with outside people is a grave risk."

"But Harry's been out of critical danger for over a month."

"I know, but for the time being the story is keeping the press at bay."

There was little more to say. When Ruth hung up, the compulsion to flee that she had felt earlier had returned. She placed another call to Bernstein's office, but the receptionist said she still hadn't heard from him.

At one o'clock Brenda came home from school unexpectedly. The girl was pale, distraught. "Daddy's in the newspaper," she said in a frightened voice.

Ruth nodded. "I know. But nobody knows it's *us.*"

"We have this teacher in school. This Mr. Otis. He's always getting on a soapbox about *some*thing. And this just set him off about experiments with human beings, the Nazis, the CIA, doctors in general. He went on and on. He made it sound like Daddy was one of the freaks in *The Island of Dr. Moreau* or something." Brenda was trying to hold back her tears.

"Oh, honey, it's not like that at all." Ruth took her daughter in her arms, burying her face in the girl's glossy black hair. "Did you say anything?"

"Are you kidding?" Brenda whispered in a cowed voice. "I just shrank down in my seat. As soon as the period was over I told the homeroom teacher I felt sick. I really did. But I told them I thought I was coming down with the flu. They're so terrified of a flu epidemic that they practically ran me out of school."

Ruth kissed her daughter's brow. The girl actually did feel feverish. "That's okay, honey. You stay home with me."

"Aren't you going to see Daddy today?"

"Not today."

Brenda went with her mother to pick up Christopher at the day school at three o'clock. He knew nothing of the newspaper story. Neither did David, who walked home after school. Ruth explained to both boys that there had been a story about their father in the newspaper, but his name had been kept secret so they wouldn't be bothered. Then she read the story to them. Christopher listened with enormous eyes fixed on her face. When she finished, he asked, "That's a story about Daddy?" There was glee in his voice. David said nothing. But at five he and Christopher came in to watch the TV evening news with their mother and sister.

"The First Man with Gills" was the lead story. There were interviews with both Steinhardt and Buckley. Steinhardt sat in his cluttered office holding up cut-away diagrams of the gill implant to explain how it worked, as he had once explained it to Ruth centuries before. It was obvious to Ruth that his statement was severely cut. Buckley by contrast was interviewed outside the handsome administration building, as if he had just exited and a stakeout of reporters had snared him on his way to a meeting. "Dr. Buckley, why was this incredible experiment kept secret for months?"

Buckley looked directly at the reporter, his expression one of mild surprise. "It was not kept a secret. The institute's first priority has been to keep the patient alive and healthy as possible. We've also been trying to maximize the scientific data generated by this extraordinary event."

Another reporter shouted, "Doctor, what about the morality of experimenting on a human being?"

There was a momentary hush as the other reporters crowded in to record the answer. "The morality of experimenting with a new procedure on a human being?" Buckley answered evenly. "As opposed to what? Just letting him die of lung cancer? I can't answer that. But I know someone who can. The patient himself. Hopefully, he'll give you his answer in the near future."

The film ended, and the anchorman turned to the reporter who had covered the story. "That certainly is an incredible development in the world of science, Bob. Did they give any reason why the press wasn't notified when they first made the successful gill transplant?"

"I asked Dr. Buckley just that, and he answered that he didn't think it was the job of research scientists to *notify* the press. In fact he kind of gave us all a slap on the wrist. He commented that if the media had a fraction of the interest in science and the work being done to extend human knowledge that we do in murder and scandals we would have had the story the first day."

"The good doctor probably has a point." The anchorman nodded agreeably and turned back to face the camera. "And a case in point is our next story. Los Angeles homicide detectives . . ."

Brenda switched channels. David got up, heading for his room.

"Aren't you going to watch the other stations?" Brenda asked.

David shrugged. "They'll all be the same stuff."

Ruth felt numb. They were talking about her husband on television, but they might have been discussing a complete stranger. She experienced no connection. Harry had been dehumanized into an event without personality, flesh, or blood. And David was right; the other local stations on the six o'clock news and the ABC network news at seven carried the same interviews, slightly different quotes. The ABC network correspondent ended his report leaning against the rail of the research pier with the surf behind him and a lone gull squalling overhead. "Dr. Wernher von Braun once referred to Neil Armstrong's first step on the moon as the most significant event in human evolution since a creature first crawled from the sea. Today's revelation is considerably more than one man's toe in the water. It may prove to be another great leap for mankind. Tom Stockard. ABC News. At the California Institute of Oceanography."

As the image of Stockard of ABC faded, Ruth sensed reporters, cameras, and microphones pressing in like the mob that had besieged Buckley. Their strident belligerent echoes and ghosts had invaded her home, now haunting the deepening shadows of the room and threatening her and the children.

Christopher suddenly materialized beside her. "When we gonna eat?" he asked plaintively.

Ruth had completely forgotten about dinner. "Right now!" she exclaimed. She gave the child a fierce hug, as if to still his hunger pangs with an embrace.

28

The next morning a television interviewer with the bland pleasant looks of a Sioux Falls Junior Chamber of Commerce president and a former Jesuit priest named Timothy Matthews, who now wrote best sellers on devil possession, sat in swiveled armchairs and speculated on Harry's soul for the benefit of seven and a half million housewives getting their kids off to school.

"It raises a definite theological question: Does this man still have a soul—that is, as we conceive of the soul as Christians?" the Jesuit asked. "In the Bible the existence of the soul is synonymous with the breath. The relationship is clearly spelled out in the first pages of Genesis: 'And the Lord God formed man of the dust of the ground, and breathed into his nostrils the breath of life; and man became a living soul.' In Biblical Hebrew the words *neshamah, ru'ah,* and *nephesh* have the dual meaning of both 'breath' and 'soul.' To the ancient Hebrews they were inseparable."

Harry Styles, his breast now aching with the

imagined surgical excision of his soul, watched the show from his tank. The night before, he had watched the first TV news reports with keen excitement, but contrary to his expectations, the news stories had deeply depressed him. They were not about him. Then, as now, he felt that the reporters and commentators on TV were talking about some alien being just discovered to be living on this planet.

"Again both in ancient Greek and in Latin we have the same root words meaning both breath and soul," Matthews continued. "The words *psyche* in Greek and *anima* in Latin."

The interviewer leaned forward. "But aren't you playing word games? Are you really changing the spiritual nature of a man simply by adapting him to breathe water instead of air?"

"I think so," Matthews said. "The Spirit of God, the Holy Ghost, is the *pneuma,* which again is another Greek word meaning 'breath.' This is not a word game. In the Gospel according to St. John, Jesus gave the gift of the Holy Spirit to the disciples by breathing on them." Matthews, his eyes bright with fervor under his bristling black brows, visibly straightened in his chair to quote the Gospel. "'And when he had said this, he *breathed* on them, and saith unto them, Receive ye the Holy Ghost.'"

Matthews paused for dramatic effect, then noticed that the interviewer wasn't paying attention to him but peering nervously off to his right, apparently getting an urgent signal from offstage. Matthews frowned and continued talking at a hurried pace. "This isn't just a Judeo-Christian concept. It's also fundamental to pagan and primitive religions. For example, the epics

197

of Homer represent the soul as the breath of life, as when Achilles encounters the spirit of Patroclos. The Romans even went so far as to regard it as a religious duty that the nearest relative of a dying man should catch his last breath at the moment it left the body to ensure the continued existence of his soul. Interestingly enough, the Seminole Indians of Florida had a similar custom, as do the Athapascan tribes in Alaska."

"This all leaves me quite breathless," interrupted the TV interviewer. "Thank you very much, Timothy Matthews, author of *The Unholy Ghosts*. We'll be back in a moment with Beverly Jeanot, the talented new toast of Broadway. Twelve and a half before the hour. Station break."

"It is positively medieval."

Harry whirled about. Steinhardt and Buckley stood at the window of the tank, their eyes fixed on the TV set. Harry wondered how long they had been standing there.

Steinhardt continued angrily. "In 1700 Swedenborg was searching for the soul in the spiritous fluid of the blood. This ex-Jesuit has it in the alveoli of the lungs. No doubt the Holy Office is about to reconvene the Council of Trent and issue a doctrinal decree on Harry's soul, and mine. Then they'll burn us both at the stake. After all, the church exiled Teilhard de Chardin and all he did was *write* about the evolution of man."

"Damn it, Karl, this isn't a laughing matter," Buckley snapped.

"No? Then you don't have a sense of the absurd."

"I have a pile of telegrams on my desk," Buckley said. "Including one from a group of rabbis in New York. They're outraged by what they feel is a grotesque medical experiment on a human being."

Steinhardt smiled faintly. "God gave Moses ten commandments. The Hassidim expanded it to six hundred and thirteen commandments. Now apparently they have six hundred and fourteen."

"For Chrissakes, Karl, this is sensitive as hell. It's no time to get arrogant."

"I'm not arrogant. I welcome their scientific inquiries. I even welcome their metaphysical inquiries. Perhaps we have surgically removed Harry's soul from his thorax, along with his cancerous lungs. I'd very much like to know if we have. Do the Courts of Inquisition have a new laboratory procedure for detecting the presence or absence of the Christian soul? Or will they use the old but proven test of trial by fire? I don't think trial by water would be appropriate in this particular case."

"I don't think we need overly concern ourselves with the metaphysical speculations," Buckley said evenly. "It might be enough if Harry just spoke to the press himself. That is, if he's up to it." He turned directly to Harry. "How are you feeling?"

"I'm mad as hell about all this, if that's what you mean. Do you want to hold a press conference?" The idea of confronting a battery of reporters and television cameras both frightened and excited Harry.

"I can set up a press pool situation," Buckley said. "We'll just let a few carefully selected reporters and cameramen in to see you. And they'll have to share it with the rest of the press. That way they'll all pretty much stick to the facts, and they won't be bending over backward to get their own angle or interject their personal opinions."

"Is all this huckstering really necessary?" Steinhardt asked.

"Yes, it is," Harry said sharply.

Both Buckley and Steinhardt looked at him in surprise.

"I'm not a goddamn freak," he suddenly shouted and then in a softer voice added, "We have to show people that."

"That's exactly what we have to do," Buckley agreed.

Harry's children would be watching TV. He wondered how each of them was reacting. Christopher would probably just be confused. He would have difficulty relating the TV news stories to his father. David, however, would understand, and the reports would make the already sensitive boy feel even more an outcast and alien. Harry felt sure of that. He wasn't sure how Brenda would react beyond embarrassment.

As for Ruth, Harry was already experiencing her reaction. Her absence. She was an intensely private person, and the television cameras and reporters she had seen on TV had frightened her away. Strained as their visits together had become, Harry acutely missed her. He ached for her presence. She was the contact with the base humanity of his life, and without her he felt himself inexorably slipping away.

Harry gazed about the tank, the bleak steel and glass walls and the tons of water pressing in on him defining his prison. "I am not a goddamn freak," Harry had shouted a few minutes before. "We have to show them that." That outburst had ignited an old feeling in him. He had to demonstrate that he was a pioneer. A hero. It wasn't only for his children. It was as much for himself. He had been given a reprieve, and with it he could make his life add up to something, something important.

Buckley elaborated at length on Harry's meeting with the press. Harry listened carefully, but his eyes drifted over the impenetrable walls that confined him. They were fixed on a vision that went far beyond those walls.

"I want an American flag on my wet suit," Harry said suddenly.

"What?" Buckley was confused.

"Have one of those American flag patches on my shoulder," Harry explained, slapping himself on the left shoulder. "The sort of patch that astronauts and test pilots wear on their coveralls."

Buckley thought about the idea and nodded vigorously. "That's exactly the image you should have. That of a special test pilot or astronaut," he agreed enthusiastically. "We won't just have a patch. I'll have a special new wet suit made up. A deep blue." Buckley silently studied Harry. "You'll look terrific," he decided. He turned to Steinhardt. "He looks strong enough to break down walls."

It was true. Mostly it was an optical illusion of the water, but Harry had put on healthy flesh and muscle. He had learned to ingest a great variety of foods underwater. As a thirsty child automatically masters taking quick short breaths between continuous swallows, Harry now ate and aspirated water almost simultaneously. His taste buds no longer registered the constant saltiness of his food due to the saline solution. His appetite had increased. Steinhardt had Harry on a program of carefully monitored exercises similar to those developed for the astronauts in the weightless environment of Skylab. Twice a day Harry performed a program of isokinetic exercises and endlessly pumped on the spring-loaded pedals of a stationary bicycle ergometer. But as Harry's strength and work capacity increased daily, so did his desperation.

When Buckley had left, Harry looked at Steinhardt, then smiled grimly. "Maybe they're right about my soul. I feel as though I'm in some sort of limbo on the border of hell. Sometimes, at night especially, I feel I'm falling over the edge, that I'm going to drop into hell itself."

Steinhardt frowned. "Are you in pain?"

"Not physical pain. I'm afraid. No, *afraid* is not the word. It's total terror. A terror so primal it's worse than any physical pain imaginable."

"What are you terrified of?"

"I don't know. Of becoming lost."

"What do you mean by that?"

Harry made a vague gesture with his hands. "It's something I just *feel* is happening to me."

Once more Harry surveyed his prison. You don't always get what you want, he thought. But you get what you need. No more, no less. He turned back to Steinhardt. "You and I have work to do," he said suddenly. "Let's get on with it."

Work, Harry demanded. Work to fill his loneliness and to preserve his sanity. Work to keep himself from plummeting into the terrifying abyss yawning at the edge of his mind and soul. For a man with a unique destiny, a prison cell has often served as an incubator. There, cut off from the normal world, his vision is stoked by the will, refining and defining itself. For Harry the metamorphosis had begun.

29

It was late the next day that Dr. Morris Bernstein first seized on the idea of the injection of potassium chloride. A myocardial infarction, a momentary stab of pain, and then it would be over—death seemingly due to natural causes. The thought held his tormented mind enthralled, but it also horrified him.

Steinhardt might ridicule the Jesuit speculations on Harry's soul and the outrage of the rabbis, but Bernstein took it all to heart. The stories had been picked up by the wire services and became black headlines that accused the surgeon at every newsstand. They recriminated him from the five-minute news briefs at the top of the hour on his favorite FM station. They condemned him from the evening TV news. Bernstein did not avoid the newsstands or broadcasts. He in fact sought them out. The media reports were the just indictment of his sins, and he accepted them with a bowed head. His name was never mentioned, but Bernstein knew his guilt. His father, an immigrant who had dropped dead at his sewing machine slaving to keep his son in college, he, too, knew his son's guilt. Bernstein had betrayed his father's labors and dreams, and his own. He had perverted the humane art of medicine. He had committed an unforgivable sacrilege. Where was atonement possible? Bernstein retreated to his study at home and searched for it in a bottle of Scotch.

When he had been in his study for several hours, Selma looked in. "A glass of Madeira, my dear," he greeted her.

Selma smiled at him anxiously. "That's Scotch."

"Yes, it is. I'm practicing to be in one of those classy Scotch ads. You know, profession—thoracic surgeon. Hobby—reviving the forbidden cabalist art of creating golems. Last book read . . . that's what stumped me. I can't remember the last book I read. I can't even remember when I last read a book. But hell, you read enough books for both of us. Maybe we can do the very first husband and wife classy Scotch ad. You'd look terrific."

Selma Bernstein was a woman whose slenderness had a martyred severity to it, since it had been achieved by rigorous dieting that went against her nature. Her handsome face was framed by graying shag-cut hair. "Have you seen Murray Einhorn lately?" she asked.

"What do I want to see Murray Einhorn for?"

"All this business, it seems to be tearing you apart, Morris."

"So what can Einhorn do about it? I saw him for four years. All we did was talk about my father. I knew as much about psychiatry as the psychiatrist. I could change practices. Besides, I read in one of the journals that traditional Freudian therapy doesn't work with doctors in a lot of cases."

"Why not?"

"If they knew that they could get it to work. Look, I'm all right. I'm a little tired. I'm having a drink, and I'll go to bed and I'll be all right."

Selma took a deep breath. "You've been taking more than a drink lately," she said.

"So?" He held up his glass and examined it as if it were a medical specimen. "Drinking is a growing problem with both doctors and assimilated Jews. I don't know what it does for doctors. But since Jews traditionally don't drink, I guess it makes them feel less Jewish."

"Is that the solution or the problem?"

"Ha!" Bernstein barked sharply. "That's the sixty-four-dollar question. Is it the solution or the problem?"

There was a long uneasy silence before Selma spoke. "So it starts again. I thought we were all through with it."

"What starts again?"

"The whole dreary pattern. I could see it coming already months ago. You work day and night and you don't sleep. You take amphetamines to stay on your feet and barbiturates to come down. Until you're ready to spin out and crash. Then you start with the drinking."

"It's not that at all." There was no conviction in Bernstein's voice.

"Morris, you've already been in three major auto accidents. It's a miracle no one's been hurt. But the next time the police stop you, they're going to take your license away."

"God bless the Los Angeles Police Department. They protect and serve. They'll make me walk to work.

I can use the exercise."

"For God's sake, Morris, talk to me."

"What do you want to talk about?"

"Why are you killing yourself like this? What's bothering you? Don't always keep it bottled up inside."

"Nothing's bothering me. I'm just having a drink." There was a sudden anger in his voice. "I'm not going on a goddamn Irish bender. I'm just having a drink to unwind. Is that all right with you?"

Selma stared at her husband, intimidated by his anger. "I'm going to bed," she said, and the statement was an admission of defeat.

He raised his glass in toast. *"L'chayim."* He drank.

His wife left the room and Bernstein remained seated. *"L'chayim,"* he repeated softly to himself. "To life." He finished off his drink. What must be done, must be done. He rose, the effort weary and labored, and went to the desk. From his black bag he withdrew a hypodermic syringe and began to prepare it.

30

The surf was phosphorescent, glimmering lines of silvery white. Beyond the surf the waves rolled in massive and black. Each explosion confirmed Steinhardt's premonition of disaster. He stalked the dark beach, plagued by his usual insomnia but also disturbed by a new, shapeless anxiety. The headlights of a car winding along Sea Cliff Drive momentarily illuminated a wave, the light making the water appear even blacker and more malevolent, an evil wall storming the beach.

As was his habit, Steinhardt had tried to read that night. He buried himself in Teilhard de Chardin's *Le Phénomène humain*. Teilhard's concept that the noosphere—the mantle of technology that man had consciously erected on the earth—was the next stage of natural evolution had once stirred Steinhardt. It had given him great comfort and hope. Teilhard, the paleontologist and Jesuit mystic, had poetically fused science and Christianity and envisioned man evolving technologically toward an ultimate spiritual unity. But this night the vision had abandoned Steinhardt. His mind refused to focus on the transcendent destiny of man. All the commotion in the press and on television about Harry Styles disturbed Steinhardt. He felt himself surrounded by unnamed mortal dangers.

At midnight he fled to the beach, trekking through the heavy wet sand to settle his mind. But even the sea was haunted. Each wave disintegrated into a column of ghosts, glowing white specters that surged toward him in an angry rumble and then dissolved into the darkness before they reached the shore.

Once again headlights glowed on the sand, conjuring up new ghosts. The car had turned off Sea Cliff Drive and was heading along on one of the institute's access roads toward the research building. Now alert to its route, Steinhardt watched the headlights. They turned into a parking lot, briefly silhouetting the building's angled buttresses, and then the headlights turned off.

It was very late for anyone to be visiting any of the laboratories or offices. Steinhardt had no reason to be concerned about Styles. There was now a round-the-clock security guard at the building entrance and an attendant in the tank room with him at all times. There was no logical reason for Steinhardt to be alarmed, yet he hurried through the sand, his every sense bristling with danger.

The old man was sweating and breathless when he slammed through the door of the tank room. Bernstein was on the tank, halfway up the ladder.

"Morris, what in hell are you doing here at this unholy hour?"

Bernstein turned toward Steinhardt, a look of panic

on his face. He clung to the ladder, balanced on one foot like a bird about to take flight. As he pivoted, the light on the tank caught and glittered off a shining object in his right hand. Steinhardt's eyes fixed on the hypodermic needle. "What in hell are you doing?" he asked again.

Bernstein didn't answer. He seemed befuddled. His eyes flicked from Steinhardt to Styles, now hovering at the window of the tank staring out at them. Neither Styles nor the attendant had apparently been disturbed by Bernstein's sudden appearance in the middle of the night to give his patient an injection. Attending surgeons are often known for their erratic hours. But now the alarm in Steinhardt's voice gripped them both.

"What is *that?*" he demanded and strode forward.

Steinhardt's sudden movement galvanized Bernstein. His foot groped frantically for the next step. He awkwardly clutched at the steel rung with one hand while holding the hypodermic away from his body and then clawed up another rung of the ladder. Steinhardt lunged at him and seized his leg. "Morris, stop this. What are you doing?"

"Let me go. I have to do this. Let me go!" Bernstein shouted wildly. He yanked his leg out of Steinhardt's grasp. But there was no eluding the towering old man's reach. Steinhardt again caught his leg.

Bernstein bucked and kicked, his foot viciously striking Steinhardt in the face. The old man staggered but still he hung on. Bernstein lost his grip on the slippery steel rung. He lurched forward and his head slammed against the tank. He fell backward on Steinhardt and both men collapsed sprawling on the concrete floor.

They lay stunned and breathing heavily, their panting amplified and distorted by the concrete walls and ceiling as in a cavern. Then the two men slowly rose up on their arms and elbows and stared at each other. Bernstein's dark eyes acknowledged defeat. He still gripped the hypodermic syringe. Steinhardt reached out and took it from his now unresisting hand as one might take a forbidden cookie from a child.

He examined the syringe, then squirted it on the back of his hand and tentatively tasted it with the tip of his tongue. There was a distinctive salty tang with the vague aftertaste of chlorine. He looked back at Bernstein.

"Morris, why?" Steinhardt's voice was soft, hurt.

Tears filled Bernstein's eyes and poured down his hollow cheeks. He heaved to his feet and lurched to the door. Steinhardt glanced over at Styles, who, wary and confused, was still staring through the tank's window. Bernstein hadn't had time to give the injection, Steinhardt decided. The surgeon was, at the moment, no longer a danger to Styles, but to himself.

Steinhardt got up and ran after Bernstein, but he was too late. The car roared from the parking lot in a squeal of smeared rubber. It careened onto Sea Cliff Drive, the beam of the headlights switching back and forth like the blade of a scythe as the car climbed the twisting road to the heights of the palisades that traced the sea north of the campus. Steinhardt watched until the car's lights cut to the right and disappeared around a hairpin turn in the road.

31

The television lights focused on the tank, brilliantly illuminating it, refracting in the eddies of water in strange ways so that John Glaucus hovered at the center of an explosion of light like some mythic god descending. His long flowing blond hair and full beard, bleached to a shimmering flax by its immersion in brine, swirled about his head iridescent with its own light. Stephanie O'Gara, the reporter for the pool of local Los Angeles TV stations was awed. She had come, as had the other reporters, to interview a patient, a sick and dying man who had been the guinea pig in an outlandish medical experiment. But the broad powerful body and the glory of golden hair and beard suspended in a burst of light seemed not to have materialized from a mortal hospital bed but from Mount Olympus.

O'Gara glanced about her at the cluster of reporters, cameramen, and sound and lighting technicians. They too were stunned by the sight of Glaucus hovering above them in his chamber of liquid light. Their questions were subdued, almost reverential.

"Mr. Glaucus, are you comfortable in that tank?" the reporter from Associated Press asked.

"Yes, I'm very comfortable. It's warm, buoyant, soothing. In many ways, it's like returning to the womb." The voice of Glaucus, resonant and electronically powerful, emanated from the speaker outside the tank. In the dramatic acoustics of the tank room his most mundane comment resounded like a pronouncement from the throne. O'Gara's soundman was having difficulty adjusting the sound level to record it.

All the local TV stations had been allowed only one news camera crew to cover the interview, and it would have to share the film with the others. As was the custom in pool situations, the competing reporters had drawn lots. O'Gara, a red-headed woman in her early thirties with sharp, handsome features, had won the draw. She alone would be reporting on camera for the local stations.

Buckley had carefully controlled the press admitted to this audience. There were only a reporter and a photographer from the two major wire services and the Los Angeles *Times* science writer Kenneth Livingstone. One electronic video camera was shooting for all three networks, but Buckley had allowed each of the networks to have its own correspondent present. His concession to the networks, O'Gara suspected, was a deliberate one to enhance the star quality of the press coverage.

But the appearance of Glaucus totally upstaged the network news stars. He wore a body-fitted, marine-blue wet suit of neoprene with a large American flag emblazoned on the left shoulder sleeve. A well-

212

proportioned man invariably looks more powerful in a wet suit; the thick taut layer of neoprene creates the illusion of a sheath of muscle investing the entire body. The wide-angle lens effect of the water and glass magnified the illusion. John Glaucus looked powerful enough to snap anchor chains with his bare hands.

The black cowl collar hiding the gill combs suggested the steel collar on a space suit, giving Glaucus the appearance of an astronaut.

"How do you feel about this radical medical experiment being performed on you?" one of the network correspondents asked. His tone was subdued, respectful.

"You're asking me if I'd rather be dead or alive at this moment. I very much prefer being alive."

Against three walls of the tank room mahogany-stained panels had been set up; the intended effect was that of a ship's cabin. On the panels were mounted large impressive photographs of leaping porpoises, dramatic seascapes of surf and rocks, and studies of crabs, shimmering schools of fish, marine research vessels cleaving the waves, divers at work on the sea bottom, white-coated scientists in a laboratory—a panorama of the work of the Institute of Oceanography.

But no display of art could transform the thick concrete walls, ceiling, and floor O'Gara sensed surrounding her, heavy and pressing as the walls of a cave. The illuminated tank threw out a watery light, transforming the room into a sea cavern—the grotto of Glaucus, god of the sea. O'Gara felt herself under a spell. The man before her must be an illusion, like some carnival attraction from her youth, one that she had never actually seen but was buried in the collective unconscious of forgotten myths and faded old movies. O'Gara shook herself. This was no carny hype. This was science. The man was real. "Where do you sleep?" she asked. The question was instinctive. She had not meant to ask it.

Glaucus made an expansive gesture with his hands that embraced the mammoth dimensions of the tank. "As you can see, I have the world's largest water bed."

There was something in that broad gesture that touched O'Gara; it was both humorous and a little sad. The humor, totally unexpected, galvanized the other reporters. They laughed appreciatively and clustered about O'Gara and the microphone all at once, as if the laugher had suddenly dissolved the inhibitions that had been binding them.

But O'Gara refused to give up the mike. "What about your family? Where do they live?"

There was a moment of hesitation before the answer. For O'Gara it was more significant than the answer itself. "I have no immediate family," the man in the tank answered.

"Don't you get lonely?" O'Gara persisted.

"Yes, terribly lonely."

Then O'Gara had to relinquish the microphone to another reporter. "You said a moment ago that the tank was very comfortable physically. But how is it mentally?" he asked. "It seems very claustrophobic to me."

"It is. But so are submarines and space ships. You have to keep busy."

"How do you keep busy?"

"I'm constantly involved in experiments. Right

now we're conducting a series to test and increase my work capacity underwater. In a few weeks we're planning to begin work with a hyperbaric chamber, one in which the pressure can be increased to simulate great depths. When I'm not working, like most Americans I just lie back and watch TV."

"What are your favorite programs?"

"The news mostly. I watch all the news I can every day. But 'Sixty Minutes' is my favorite show. I don't really like all the police programs. I don't think they're particularly healthy, with all their violence and sexual innuendos, especially for kids."

O'Gara was suddenly alert. Glaucus's response was not that of a man with "no immediate family." O'Gara herself was a divorcée supporting her two children by hustling as a TV newswoman. Now every maternal, feminine, and reportorial instinct was humming. She stared at John Glaucus, his hair and beard encircling his head like waves of sunlight, the seemingly Herculean physique. He had once been an all too frail and vulnerable human being whom science was now transforming into God knows what. But somewhere there was a wife. And there were children he wouldn't allow to watch "Hawaii Five-O" and "Charlie's Angels."

"Mr. Glaucus, I understand from both Dr. Steinhardt and Dr. Buckley that the gill had not really been expected to function as successfully as it has." Kenneth Livingstone was at the microphone, flustered by the cameras and lights. He stuttered out his question. "I . . . I understand that at first you weren't, well, how can I phrase this, you weren't expected to survive the operation."

Glaucus nodded. "No, I wasn't. But I'm rather glad

I did."

There was a burst of laughter from the press. O'Gara studied Livingstone. It seemed incredible to her that this apologetic, deferential man had ever ferreted out a major story like this by himself. "Well, how do you feel about your being alive as a s-s-sort of scientific accident?" Livingstone stammered.

Glaucus was silent a moment, and when he began speaking, his speech was measured and thoughtful. "I don't think I would use the word 'accident.' It was something that was unexpected. Dr. Steinhardt and I have discussed this at great length. We've developed a certain philosophy concerning it. Before my operation I worked in aerospace research and development, and I know from painful experience that experiments don't always go the way you anticipate. There is always the unexpected event. What you might call *an accident*. Columbus *accidentally* found a new world while exploring for a new route to China. In terms of his original expectations, his voyage was in fact a failure. In all explorations the difference between success and failure may simply be being imaginative and daring enough to exploit these *accidents*. The unexpected event. Dr. Steinhardt, Dr. Buckley, the staff here at the institute, and I intend to be that daring."

A network correspondent seized the microphone, shouldering Livingstone out of the way. "Mr. Glaucus, what do you think the future holds for you? Are you optimistic about it?"

"I am challenged by it."

"Would you elaborate on that, please."

"I will see and touch and experience things that no man has before me. I will go where no man has

216

gone before."

O'Gara hardly heard Glaucus's speech. In her mind only one phrase echoed and reverberated: *"Before my operation I worked in aerospace research and development . . ."* O'Gara pounced on it. It was the key that might open the door to Glaucus's past life. The male reporters were enraptured with Glaucus's vision of voyages into unknown worlds. Whatever domestic debris the man called Glaucus might have left behind in his wake was to them a sidebar story, but it was the story that tantalized O'Gara with its unanswered questions.

While the TV crews were packing their equipment, O'Gara sought out Livingstone. "Mr. Livingstone, I'm Stephanie O'Gara from Channel Three. I've been wanting so much to meet you. You really got the scoop of the century. It's really fantastic," she exclaimed, implying with her excitement that it was Livingstone who was somehow personally responsible for the whole event.

He nodded self-consciously. "Thank you, thank you."

"You did a landmark job of reporting. How'd you get your break?"

"My sources," Livingstone said mysteriously. "My sources. And a lot of old-fashioned digging around."

Somebody had leaked the story to him, O'Gara was convinced. She talked to the reporter for a few minutes, alternately flattering him and pumping him, but she was unable to get anything out of him she didn't already know.

As she was leaving, O'Gara noticed Buckley approach Livingstone and walk away with him. She watched them closely. The director was apparently briefing Livingstone, who nodded eagerly. Livingstone's obsequious manner confirmed O'Gara's suspicions. Buckley had fed the original story to him. His exclusive presence today had been a reward for the way Livingstone had broken the story. O'Gara frowned. Where there was news being carefully manipulated, there was also information being concealed.

32

There was a fertility figure from Nigeria on the bookcase—a tattooed woman with swollen breasts and udder-like nipples and a clinging child. It was one of several objects of African primitive art calculatingly placed about Helena Axelrod's office. A pair of wooden ancestral figures—a crone with spear-pointed, conical breasts from Mali and a bearded old man from the Congo with a potbelly and a penis that dangled to his knees—served as bookends. A water spirit of the Baga tribe on the Guinea coast, half man and half crocodile, crawled across an end table toward the afternoon sunlight streaming through the window. Like Dr. Axelrod's questions, or her silences, the figures were meant to provoke Ruth into revealing herself. What did she fear? What did she want?

"I'm so goddamn confused. I don't understand what's happening. Who to blame. Or if I should never have let it all happen in the first place," Ruth said.

"I think you're taking too much on yourself," Dr. Axelrod replied softly. "Some things can't be foreseen or blamed on anyone. They can't even be understood. They can only be endured." Helena Axelrod was about ten years older than Ruth, with long black hair that was relentlessly turning gray. Today she wore it in long braids. With her dark eyes and coloring, a tawny skin like a faded tan, she looked very much like an Indian. But she was dressed in tailored slacks and an orange pullover sweater with a wide soft cowl collar that reminded Ruth of the one Harry wore over his gills.

"If he was sick or crippled or had some chronic affliction, I could endure it. I would have to make great adjustments in my life. But I could do it. This way . . . sometimes I get so angry."

"Angry about what?"

"I don't know. It's almost as if he wanted this all to happen. He willed it. He sees himself as some sort of explorer. You saw him on TV. He acts like Neil Armstrong and Jacques Cousteau rolled into one."

Ruth fell silent.

"I almost envy him," she said after a moment.

"Why envy him?"

"You have to know Harry. He's totally fulfilled now. Before, he was frustrated in his work, an anonymous cog in the machinery. He said he developed systems within systems within systems. Yet he worked so hard at it. He would work without sleep, living for days on coffee and cigarettes to meet a development deadline. That's how he got cancer. I know it. He felt he had to drive himself harder because he didn't have his Ph.D. But now he *is* the system. What he calls a fundamental breakthrough. He's the invention, the research leader, *and* the astronaut. My God, it's his fantasy."

"You should share all that with him."

"I can't share anything with him. He's not there to share anything with. We are inexorably separated. All I would do is turn my life and my children's lives into some kind of sideshow. Since that press conference on television, I've been terrified that someone might discover who we are. I feel embarrassed all the time. Almost ashamed."

"Ashamed? What are you ashamed of?"

"I don't really know. But it all seems so freakish. Harry's in a bottle being exhibited. Like the bottles of deformed fetuses, the monsters, that they have in medical schools."

"I didn't get that impression from television at all," Helena Axelrod said softly. "Of course, knowing you somewhat mitigated my reaction, but my feelings were those of awe rather than any revulsion. But we're not here to discuss my reactions."

"No, please, I want to hear them."

"Well, basically I was very impressed. It was somewhat like when I first saw the three men who were going to the moon on TV. I had the feeling of an extraordinary man, a very courageous man."

Ruth shook her head. "He really is living out his fantasy. He sees himself—how did he put it?—as a marooned astronaut. As far as I'm concerned, he's been lost for almost two years. Only now it's nothing as mundane as cancer. He's a hero." Ruth's voice grew sharp-edged and bitter. "It's positively romantic. He's absolved of all responsibility for his wife and children." She began weeping.

"Oh, damn it. I'm becoming a total bitch. I was never like this before. But it's all so goddamn frustrating. I still love him, but I can't do anything for him. He's surrounded by professionals. They're the only ones who can help him or work with him now. There's just no point of contact between us anymore."

"What about the children? How are they?"

"I'm not sure. They've been very subdued. It worries me terribly. But since Harry was on TV, they're talking a little more. Not much, but even a question now and then is better than nothing. Brenda said it's as if the father they knew had died, and he had somehow been transformed into this strange man from another world."

"What about the oldest boy?"

"I don't know. Sometimes he looks so lost and hurt I want to cry. But since the TV appearance he's talked about going to visit Harry again. He's still very shy about it. I think he sees Harry now as some sort of superhero. He's awed and intimidated by him. That's the effect of TV. But he doesn't know how to relate to Glaucus. He can't relate to him as he used to to his father. He's very confused about it. Aren't we all?"

"And the littlest one? His nightmares?"

Ruth shook her head. "He still has them. He was terrorized in that tank. That strange bearded man from another world tried to drown him. His father would never have done that."

"Have you discussed any of this with Harry?"

"It's very difficult to talk to him, but I think he knows it. He senses it." She shook her head and broke into angry tears again. "I don't know what he knows or understands anymore. I'm not even sure it's Harry anymore."

Helena Axelrod didn't say anything. She nodded sympathetically. Ruth suddenly had a strange feeling she was taking part in a timeless ritual—a young woman seeking counsel from the old wise squaw. Was Ruth's dilemma really unique in history? The primitive figures about her varied from tribe to tribe in their tattoos, elongated ears, filed teeth, artfully mutilated cheeks, circumcisions, and beaded breasts, yet each was still a recognizable archetype of human experience.

Ruth wiped her eyes and blew her nose. "I've become the ultimate travesty of the wife whose husband abandons her to go off on some adventure and leaves her home with the kids." Ruth emitted a short humorless laugh of recognition. "My mother would be furious."

"Your mother?"

"She always used to warn me, 'Never marry a traveling man.'"

"Why? What did your father do?"

"He was a geologist. He was always off looking at mines somewhere. He was never home."

"How did you feel about that?"

Ruth shrugged. "I guess I felt as my mother did. If he really loved us, he'd be home more."

"Does Harry remind you of your father?"

"In some ways, perhaps. The humor. The preoccupation with work. They were both very good-looking men."

"No, I mean that he's left you and doesn't love you?"

"No, of course not. Harry couldn't help what happened."

"A moment ago you said you felt that Harry had almost willed what had happened."

"I was upset."

"It's something to be very upset about. But sometimes we're not just upset about what is happening to us now. It gets confused with things that go all the way back to our childhood."

"I understand all that," Ruth interrupted sharply. She found it uncomfortable to discuss the intricacies of her feelings, even her anger.

Dr. Axelrod remained silent. On the desk next to her was a crude wooden figure of a man almost a foot and a half tall with thick elephantine legs and feet. His hands were raised in supplication and his head thrown back, straining upward. Despite the figure's grotesque proportions, the yearning was so intense and physical, Ruth could feel it across the room.

"What's that?" she asked, pointing.

Helena Axelrod looked and turned back to Ruth with a slight smile. "It's a fetish from the Montrol tribe in northern Nigeria. It's very powerful, isn't it?"

Ruth nodded.

"The Montrol witch doctors use it to cure sickness."

"It reminds me of Dr. Steinhardt," Ruth said.

"Who?"

"One of the doctors who operated on Harry. The one who invented the artificial gill. It doesn't look like him. He's very towering and slender. But sometimes I sense the same feeling of yearning in him, that same intensity. It frightens me."

"Why? Don't you trust him?"

Trust. It was such a meaningless word to use to categorize Steinhardt. "I don't know. Gunther said that the man is incapable of being dishonest. If he told a lie, it would destroy him. It's all wrapped up with his being a scientist. His search for truth with a capital *T.*" It was Steinhardt's passion that frightened Ruth, and how

224

could she explain that to Dr. Axelrod? The scientist held her husband captive, enthralled in body and soul. And God only knew where Steinhardt's passion would lead them both.

"Who is Gunther?"

"Our lawyer, Gunther Marx."

"Oh, yes, you've mentioned him before. Have you been seeing much of him?"

Ruth was flustered by the question. Her face grew hot and flushed. *"Gunther?* He's our lawyer. I don't know what I would have done without him. He's the one who made all the arrangements for Harry at the institute and negotiated the finances."

"You're blushing. Why?"

"I don't know why. I feel embarrassed and I don't know why. I mean there's nothing between Gunther and me. We've been to dinner once or twice, but only so we could discuss things away from the kids or his office."

"Why away from his office?"

"There are always interruptions. Phone calls. Senior partners popping in. I feel like you're giving me the third degree. Why?"

"I'm just trying to explore your feelings about this Gunther. You've mentioned him several times."

"He's just a very old and dear friend."

Dr. Axelrod nodded and fell silent.

"Does it work?" Ruth asked.

"Does what work?"

Ruth indicated the intense, yearning figure on the desk.

"Yes, it works," Dr. Axelrod said. "For the Montrols. But I only use it for the most desperate cases."

She looked at Ruth. "You know, you're going to have to start consciously considering your options."

"My options?"

"The things you can do to make a new life for yourself, without your husband."

"A new life without Harry?" Ruth repeated it very softly, not really as a question but as a speculation. It was a thought that had hovered at the edge of her consciousness since he had gotten sick. But she had never brought her mind to focus on it. Never uttered the phrase out loud. But now Dr. Axelrod had given voice to it. It was as if it were a forbidden phrase, like the ancient Hebrew name for God, and once said aloud it had powerful unpredictable consequences.

33

Two sheriff's deputies had to rappel down the cliff to recover the body. They had to wait until low tide. The surf pounded the rocks directly below the cliff, and when it ebbed they were exposed, wet, black, and shining in the bright morning sun.

Steinhardt hung back from the cliff. He forced his mind not to speculate on the grisly scene below. He would have to confront it soon enough. He thought it strange that in Southern California special squads of police were trained in mountaineering and scuba diving just to recover bodies and rescue sightseers. Before he had come here, he had had the impression that it was a benign tropical land. He was surprised to discover it was an arid confrontation of mountains, deserts, and sea, and only great irrigation works and technology had made its sprawling population possible. In its primitive state the land was harsh and unforgiving. Automobiles often plunged off tortuous mountain roads or sea cliff drives and were not discovered for days.

There were several police cars gathered just off the road thirty yards from the cliff's edge. Seagulls soared overhead squawking at the intrusion of their sanctuary. One gull, a mussel clenched in its beak, rose above the others, then deliberately dropped the shellfish on the rocks below. Then the bird swooped down to peck and tear at the shattered shell and devour the exposed meat. Steinhardt shuddered. The shattered body of the man on the rocks had been there for days before the wreck had been spotted.

There was a shout from below. A winch on the front of the rescue truck was engaged and began hauling up a heavy load at the end of its steel cable. The wire body basket, filled with a dark form, appeared at the edge of the overhang, and then scraped up the steep incline. Several deputies gathered around the body and one of them motioned to Steinhardt. He moved forward to the basket, his limbs heavy and reluctant, his stomach queasy.

The corpse was bloated and soaking wet. The flesh of the hands and face was gray and bloodless, but relatively well preserved from immersion in cold water. The fish, crabs, and gulls had not yet gotten to the body. There was a great tear of cloth and flesh from the groin to the hip, exposing viscera, as if a great force had almost ripped off the leg. As the sun warmed the body, the blood that had congealed at death in the cold water now all at once began to flow from the tear and a dozen other wounds, soaking immediately into the parched brown sand.

A sheriff's deputy materialized at Steinhardt's side. He pointed behind them. "He must have been going fast and was out of control, 'cause he missed the turn and smashed into the guard rail there and ricocheted off, then rolled down this here incline. We can't find any skid marks but the dirt is too loose to show them up."

Steinhardt remembered the car headlights spiraling up Sea Cliff Drive. He had a vision of the car soaring right off the palisade, the lights blazing like twin meteorites arcing into the sea. He forced himself to stare down at the gray, grotesquely swollen face. "Are his glasses in the car, I wonder," he muttered.

"Then you can positively identify him?" one of the deputies asked.

"Yes, that's Dr. Bernstein," he said, knowing already that he would be haunted by that face for the rest of his life.

Late that night Steinhardt ransacked his desk, distracted, searching. He was trying to find an old photograph. On the wall behind him, the only one not completely covered by shelves of books, was a tableau of Steinhardt's professional life. The mounted photographs had been carefully arranged by Johanna. In the first, Steinhardt, thirty-five years younger, stood posing with a World War II B-29 bomber crew, each of whom held up a new oxygen mask. In a second photograph Steinhardt, bundled in furs, huddled with a family of Baffin Island Eskimos outside their igloo, and in a third picture he stood in an almost identical pose with a family of naked Australian aborigines in the Arnheim Land reservation. His studies of the two extremes of metabolic adaptation to freezing temperatures had been his first important publications.

In the desk drawer there were more photos. Steinhardt in tropical shorts and a pith helmet squatted up to his haunches in swamp water holding up the head of an alligator whose jaws had been wired shut. In an ill-fitting suit he stood squinting awkwardly into the sun amid a large group of scientists and engineers with three astronauts at Cape Canaveral. In a scuba mask and wet suit he explored a coral reef in the Bismarck Archipelago. He had been hunting for *Hyrophis,* the venomous sea snakes whose ability to obtain dissolved oxygen from swallowed seawater had been another Chinese box he had elaborately dissected only to discover another Chinese box within. On that expedition his assistant, Wilkie, a bright young Ph.D. candidate in marine biology, had momentarily mishandled one of the serpents and been bitten. There had been no antidote.

Steinhardt slammed the desk drawer shut. The picture of Bernstein and himself at Massachusetts General Hospital was lost. He wept. He wept not for the lost picture but for Bernstein and that part of himself that had also been crushed on those sea rocks and perished. After all his exotic expeditions and research he had come full circle. Bernstein, unknowingly, unwittingly, had always been his alter ego. No doctor, however skilled, is both a superb clinician and a superb research scientist. For Bernstein surgery was the art of healing, and if he could have healed with the laying on of his hands, he would have gladly forsaken his scalpel. Most surgeons cut the flesh with passion. Bernstein had operated with compassion. As a resident, Steinhardt had witnessed the young surgeon instinctively do things that were not correct procedure but had immediately worked. It was as if his hands were in communion with each organ and felt its suffering.

It was Bernstein, by his example, who had demonstrated to Steinhardt that his own passion was not for the practice of medicine but elsewhere. Once Steinhardt had learned and practiced a vagotomy or pneumonectomy he was bored with the surgical procedure. For him it was the end of his research in that area, his adventure of discovery. But for Bernstein it was then the beginning of the practice of his art.

Steinhardt could never have performed the gill operation on a human being if Bernstein had not assisted him. But it was more than the surgeon's skill and hands that Steinhardt had required. He had needed Bernstein's approval. His fiat. And there in the operating room, Bernstein had given it. With his hands he had instinctively sewn in the silicone structures and Dacron tubing as if they were natural fascia, the intimate connective tissue investing, supporting, and binding together the organs. And the body had accepted and nourished them. In those exhausting hours, the two physicians had synergized over the body of a dying man, fusing a scientific vision and a healing art that neither individually possessed.

Later Bernstein had accused Steinhardt of having seduced him into helping create a perversion of man. Steinhardt had been deeply offended. Now, unreconciled, Bernstein was dead, and his death had the stench of self-destruction clinging to it. The fiat had been revoked. Steinhardt was now alone. The old man wept uncontrollably for both Bernstein and himself.

34

In the early sixties, researchers at the State University of New York at Buffalo investigating the phenomenon of "fluid breathing" drowned twenty-nine mongrel dogs inside a U.S. Navy decompression chamber. Unknown to them, one of the bitches was about two weeks pregnant.

The experiments were among dozens of similar ones being conducted at the time in the United States and Europe. "Fluid breathing" had first been observed by John Scott Haldane, the Scottish physiologist who laid the foundation for the modern study of respiration. About the turn of the century Haldane reported a delay in the drowning time of mice when they were submerged in water with high oxygen tension. Later scientists got the drowning time of mice and rats up to eighteen hours by pressurizing buffered salt solutions. The animals were seen rhythmically inhaling and exhaling the water.

Paradoxically the return to air breathing proved more dangerous than the initial drowning. Pneumonia developed or the lungs collapsed. The pregnant dog in Buffalo, however, survived twenty-seven minutes of fluid breathing and the return to air. Forty-five days after the experiment she delivered nine healthy pups.

"If by some special arrangement men could be made to breathe water instead of air," the physiologist Johannes Kylstra speculated in *Scientific American* in 1968, "serious obstacles to attempts to penetrate deeper into the ocean and to travel to outer space might be overcome."

The Navy now wanted to test Harry in a pressure chamber.

"It's very dangerous," Steinhardt told Harry. "I don't know how pressure will affect the gills. It might rupture them." Steinhardt's voice was listless, without confidence. His skin, once the healthy pink flush of a white-haired vigorous old man, was now sallow and yellowish. He stood bent and stoop-shouldered before the tank, communicating discouragement and foreboding disaster. He had been that way since Bernstein's death.

"What about the rest of me? My body? Won't it be crushed?" Harry asked.

Steinhardt shook his head. "Sperm whales dive a mile deep and stay down for an hour just to hunt squid."

"But a whale has had sixty-five million years of evolution in the sea."

Steinhardt shrugged noncommittally. "How many years of evolution in the sea has a mouse had? Örnhagen and Lundgren pressurized liquid-breathing mice up to eight thousand two hundred and fifty feet deep—two hundred and fifty times normal atmospheric pressure—and some of them recovered and functioned normally afterward, even though no special efforts had been made to save them. Apparently the mammalian body has the inherent capacity to absorb tremendous hydrostatic pressures without injury. The pressure of the water itself is not the problem in deep diving. Breathing compressed gases under pressure creates the problems."

"How deep can divers go?"

"For scuba divers breathing compressed air, the record is only four hundred thirty-seven feet. However, using an oxygen-helium mixture, two divers swam out of a diving bell at one thousand feet deep off Catalina Island right off the coast here. French divers have *simulated* a dive to two thousand and one feet in the Comex Chamber in Marseille. They also breathed an oxyhelium mixture."

Harry grunted, the electronic sound deep and bull-like. Ever since the press conference and his appearance on TV he had been in a state of great excitement. He felt as if the enormous electrical energy required to transmit his image and voice around the world was being routed directly through him. The energy had emanated from the TV cameras, the microphones, technicians, and reporters, but mainly from spotlights. They were blinding and hot, sizzling with a power that separated him from those outside their aura. It had not been an unpleasant experience, but rather a feeling of greatly enhanced magnetism, a palpable charisma.

When he had watched himself on TV, he had hardly recognized himself or the resonant electronic voice.

The image on TV was infinitely more confident and powerful than he had felt. His own electronic image fed back to him that confidence and power and it now radiated directly from him. The vision of himself he had blurted out, the fantasy, had become his destiny. "Theoretically, how deep can I go?" Harry pressed Steinhardt.

"*Theoretically,* we simply don't know. We don't have enough information. We don't know whether the gill structure itself will withstand the pressure."

"But if it does, there's no reason that I couldn't withstand the pressure down to at least a mile deep?"

"The experiments with dogs and mice would seem to indicate that," Steinhardt admitted reluctantly. He was hesitant, unwilling to volunteer information. His eyes were red and his gaunt frame more drawn than ever.

"That's over two and a half times as deep as the French record."

"This is not an Olympic competition," Steinhardt snapped irritably. "This is a scientific investigation."

"You're wrong, Doctor. It's *always* an Olympic competition. To go higher, faster, farther. To build the fastest fighter. The deepest submersible. To be first. First at the North Pole. First on the moon. The first heart transplant."

Steinhardt shook his head. "No, it's for knowledge," he insisted. His voice fell to a strained whisper. "For knowledge."

"Is that what you want? Knowledge?"

Steinhardt looked surprised. "Yes, of course."

"Then get me deeper than any man has ever been before. And, dead or alive, I'll bring you back new knowledge."

Steinhardt stared at Harry, then held up his hands in a gesture of despair. "But there's no such chamber available. We don't have the equipment."

"The Navy can build it for us. They have the hardware, the chambers, multistage compressors, pressurization systems. It's just a matter of adapting and modifying them for me."

"It would be enormously expensive."

"Yes, it will be," Harry agreed. "And they won't do it to test rats or dogs for pure scientific research, Doctor. But they will do it to get a *man* a mile deep. Deeper than any diver has ever been before."

Steinhardt said nothing. He stared at Harry, grave doubts etched in his sallow, despairing face.

"But before we approach them," Harry continued, "we'd better first run a series of hydrostatic tests on an assembled gill to see how it stands up under the pressure."

Steinhardt nodded distractedly.

"Believe me, I know what I'm doing," Harry insisted. "You're the genius in medicine and biology, but now we've crossed over into my bailiwick, material and systems testing. Help me get a mile deep, and I'll get you new knowledge about life processes." The deep urgency in Harry's voice echoed in the tank room like the rumbling of distant thunder. "Get me to the bottom of the abyss and I'll bring you back the secrets of life itself."

35

Stephanie O'Gara's divorce had left her with her illusions of security shattered, her trust in men gutted, and with two daughters to support. Her ex-husband's support payments were, at best, irregular.

Before her first child was born she had worked for a small suburban newspaper. In returning to work, she had looked unsuccessfully for a newspaper or radio or TV news-writing job for four months and then had taken a job as a typist in the sales department of a Los Angeles TV station. She calculatingly made the acquaintance of everyone in the newsroom and had been on the spot when a production assistant's job opened up six months later. In three months she had moved up to news writer. It had taken her another year and a half to wangle a job as a field reporter. During that period she had had a brief, guilt-laden affair with a married assistant news director.

If she had felt insecure before, she was totally vulnerable as an on-the-air reporter. She looked into the mirror and her once soft, pretty features reflected back sharp anxious lines. Younger women with billowing manes of hair were being hired to sell news on TV as they pitched shampoo. Her job was subject to vagaries of personality, charisma factors, overnight ratings tabulated at fifteen-minute intervals, and the winds of station politics. O'Gara desperately felt she had to make a big splash. She needed a scoop, an exclusive. It was not a matter of vanity but of survival.

"If the fish-man does have a wife and child, it'll make a helluva story," Greenberg agreed. He was the assistant news director.

"He does. I know it," O'Gara said.

"What makes you so sure?"

"Just call it my feminine intuition."

"Feminine intuition. You and Lucrezia Borgia." There was an edge to Greenberg's voice that O'Gara caught. He still felt that she'd used him. She hadn't. She had been lonely and unsure of herself and their affair had simply happened. She was still lonely and unsure of herself, but she knew now that playing *Back Street* once a week with a man with three kids of his own was no solace.

"How're you going to track him down?"

"I have a lead. But I'll need a day in the office just to run it down on the phone."

"That's what we have editorial assistants and assignment editors for. What's the lead?"

O'Gara shook her head. "I'll have to do it myself. It's a touchy situation."

Greenberg stared at her, then nodded. "Okay, I'll rework the schedule."

O'Gara spent the next day on the phone. She began by simply calling the heads of press relations of the major aerospace firms in the Los Angeles area. She told them that a source had tipped her that the so-called gill-man John Glaucus had once worked for their company. She drew a blank.

O'Gara had automatically assumed that Glaucus had been referring to a local Los Angeles aerospace company. With a shock it suddenly occurred to her that he might have worked anywhere in the country. There were clusters of the industry in Houston, Orlando, Cambridge, Seattle, and Palo Alto. There was no way for her to check them all out.

She had to follow up on her original hunch. She searched through the yellow pages of the half-dozen phone directories for the Los Angeles area. There were pages of companies listed under *Aircraft Mfgrs, Missile & Rocket Component Mfgrs, Missile & Rocket Instrument and Guidance Equipment, Space Components and Systems, Space Research and Development.* O'Gara's heart sank.

Doggedly, with ebbing hope, she began calling the numbers in the columns. She tried ruses, ploys, pretenses. She called the personnel offices at Rockwell, T.R.W., Hughes, and Lockheed and said she was from the business office of the county hospital. She needed to know the insurance coverage of John Glaucus. She claimed she wasn't supposed to give out his real name unless the person on the other end of the line was authorized. The response on the other end of the line was total confusion. By the end of the day she had made over a hundred phone calls and still didn't have a ghost of a lead.

When Greenberg came to say good night, she felt humiliated. She was on the verge of tears. Her head throbbed and she was nauseated. She smiled at Greenberg. "If it was easy, any bum could get the story."

Greenberg shrugged. "I'm sorry it didn't work out. I can't give you any more time on it. Tomorrow you're scheduled to go out with the crew."

O'Gara nodded. She didn't say anything. She would dig out the story on her own time if she had to. But, damn it, she was going to dig it out.

36

Steinhardt, already on edge after Bernstein's death, felt threatened by the two Navy men. In his mind they represented massive machinery that would overwhelm and oppress him, Harry too. He found even their looks deceptive.

In his gray worsted suit the tall slender man with white hair and rimless glasses would at first glance be taken for a university professor. He was in fact Rear Admiral Theodore Nelson, chief of the Office of Naval Research. "Glaucus appears to be preoccupied with setting a world record," Nelson commented.

"It's the influence of his aerospace industry background, I believe," Steinhardt murmured.

"Ah, yes."

To Nelson's right, and a step behind, ambled a square-faced, beefy man. With his fireplug physique and blunt scowling face, Roger Morrison would be typecast as the boss of an oil drilling gang. He was in actuality a Navy doctor with the rank of captain, a specialist in diving medicine. Like Nelson, Morrison wore a civilian suit.

"We're not opposed to making some sort of world mark, mind you," Nelson continued. "But our primary consideration, as it is for all tests of this type, is the safety of the personnel involved." Nelson's tone was admonishing, as if he were criticizing Steinhardt for some unspecified fall from grace.

Steinhardt nodded. "I understand that is your official position." Despite Nelson's scholarly appearance, Steinhardt was intimidated by the man. This admiral commanded not a fleet of warships but one of the most powerful scientific organizations in the world. After World War II the Office of Naval Research had plunged deeply into underwriting pioneering work at universities on nuclear accelerators, solid-state physics, quantum electronics, computers, marine biology, and medicine. The Navy's aggressive policy became the pattern for the Atomic Energy Commission, the National Science Foundation, NASA, the National Institutes of Health—the alphabet soup of bureaucracies that now dominated science in the United States. But the Navy's roots in research were deep and historic. Charles Darwin's epic discoveries on evolution, Steinhardt now recalled, had been made sailing as a naturalist aboard the *Beagle* on an official naval expedition. The admiral carried the mantle of that tradition.

Nelson nodded his head toward Buckley. "I was just telling Paul here, Dr. Steinhardt, I'm as excited by the basic research you've done that might lead to a workable prosthetic lung as I am by the gill's potential to allow us to exploit the sea floor. My background's in electronics so I don't understand all the aspects. But my medical people are tremendously impressed with the

242

way you've worked out the problems of sufficient surface area in the blood-water interface. Also the countercurrent heat exchangers in the bloodstream to minimize loss of body heat."

"They're not my inventions," Steinhardt said. "Nature worked them out millions of years ago for marine animals. The breakthrough was our technology developing to the point where we could manufacture a silicone capillary small enough in diameter yet strong enough. Then it was simply a matter of programming a computer to design a mathematical model to achieve the necessary heat transfer and oxygenation for a man."

"It's a remarkable achievement. However, I would be less than candid with you, Dr. Steinhardt, if I didn't admit we were extremely reluctant to continue sponsoring your work when we realized how far you had gone."

"I simply don't understand your attitude," Steinhardt replied with an edge of anger in his voice. "I've done nothing unethical, disreputable, or inhumane. I followed the federal guidelines for human experiments. The procedure was reviewed by the hospital committee on research involving human beings."

"No one is implying otherwise, Karl," Buckley smoothly interrupted. "I think the admiral is only restating the Navy's official position for the record."

"Research involving human beings is always acutely sensitive," the admiral said vaguely. "There's no question but that you've made some historic studies in the Glaucus Project. What I hope we can now do is organize the research to better evaluate your work's full potential. I see the hyperbaric chamber tests as merely a beginning."

Morrison nodded vigorously. "Up to now your research has been aimed at evaluating an unanticipated event, an accident." His Texas drawl somewhat mitigated his emphatic speech. In the course of the visit Morrison had referred several times to "the unanticipated event, the accident." He seemed fond of the phrase. Steinhardt didn't know if he was referring to the gill itself or to Styles's recovery. In either case he found the phrase offensive.

Morrison bounced on his toes as he talked, as if straining for height amid considerably taller men. "The information on cardiopulmonary functions, maximal oxygen uptake, and energy balance is first-rate. First-rate." He frowned. "But I would have liked a great deal more psychological evaluation. Cognitive performance, reaction time, and personality changes. We have next to nothing in that area."

"I'm sure it would have made fascinating reading," Steinhardt said sharply. "But it would have been scientifically pointless. We would have data on a man who had fully expected to die and had, in fact, almost expired on the operating table. He was revived and sustained only through extraordinary means, then woke up to find himself totally submerged in water. From that point on—until our admittedly sketchy psychological testing and psychiatric evaluation began—he was heavily tranquilized and under intensive care. He is still experiencing a great deal of personal conflict and confusion, understandably so. I doubt if a daily MAACL profile of his anxiety, hostility, and depression would have any validity."

Neither Nelson nor Morrison said anything.

"There still remains the question," Buckley interjected. "Does Glaucus go to the chamber or does the chamber come to Glaucus?"

Nelson cleared his throat and looked pensive. "The logistics of the situation would indicate that it is more convenient, and *safer,* to set up the chamber here than to transport Glaucus back and forth to Bethesda. We have no facilities to maintain him there."

"I agree," Buckley said immediately, seizing the opportunity. "If you get the necessary contracts to me, I'll work out the arrangements with the university."

Steinhardt looked questioningly at Buckley. The Office of Naval Research policy was always to make their contracts directly with the scientist rather than with the university. The contracts had no deadlines and were renewed if the progress warranted it. Steinhardt wondered if Buckley was now maneuvering to place himself legally in charge of the next phase of the research. And of Harry Styles.

After Nelson and Morrison had driven off, Buckley turned to Steinhardt with a cynical smile. "Logistics, hell. They could build a habitat for Styles as easily as they can transport and set up a hyperbaric chamber here. They're afraid of his dying on them. That's why they want the depth tests run on the institute grounds."

He and Steinhardt walked to the research building in silence. When they reached the door, Buckley turned once again to make a point. "That Morrison's going to give us problems. He's the hatchet man. They're going to try and take over Glaucus."

"Yes, I anticipate so," Steinhardt said dully.

*　　　*　　　*

245

The Navy built a hangar for the hyperbaric chamber and a small holding tank for Styles at the north end of the campus. The speed and efficiency with which the construction was completed and the chamber installed impressed Steinhardt.

Morrison shrugged. "It's nothing. In the Tekite Project we built a small city on St. John. And that was only to keep four men in a habitat forty-nine feet down in the Caribbean. Who the hell knows where this will end. Look, we built a forty-billion-dollar empire to put two men on the moon." Morrison, like Buckley, had visions of empire building. He squinted up at Steinhardt. "There's a right way and a wrong way to go about experiments," he said. "We're going to eliminate the unanticipated events, the accidents."

In his career Steinhardt had studiously avoided such large-scale projects. He had, because of the brilliance of his work, been offered directorships of research institutes, chairmanships of committees. He had refused them all. As a researcher, he was almost medieval, the alchemist who searches for his truths in solitude.

Now here he was in the very situation he had always shunned—research by teams. Teams of hematologists, cardiovascular specialists, physicians, physiologists, psychiatrists, and psychologists. Buckley had even enlisted political scientists and sociologists. NASA had commissioned a study of public reaction to Glaucus. The space agency wanted to know if the public would accept similar surgical operations to adapt men to work in hostile environments in space.

Each day was crowded with meetings. There were conferences to plan experiments, make out schedules, anticipate emergencies, and formulate procedures. The demands on Steinhardt's time were excessive, unending. Yet as busy as he was, Steinhardt could not shake the despair that had engulfed him since Bernstein's death. The surgeon had died violently, convinced of their damnation. It was as if his friend had pronounced a dying curse, and no amount of rationalization could dispel the growing horror and doubt Steinhardt felt.

He conferred increasingly with Harry, even on medical questions in which Harry had no knowledge. It was from Harry himself Steinhardt now sought the moral justification, the fiat to go on with the work that Bernstein had irrevocably withdrawn.

"What's this associative memory test?" Harry asked.

Steinhardt had shown him the schedule of pressure tests in the chamber. "It's a standard psychological test used in diving-related research."

"Cut it out. We don't need it. It'll take too much time." There was no reason for his objection. It was merely a capricious exercise of control, as though Harry were compelled to assert that he wasn't simply a guinea pig but the final decision maker.

Steinhardt gave in. As the pressure trials loomed near, Harry became increasingly temperamental in his demands. He insisted all tests and experiments be cleared with him. Yet he seemed basically happier; his energy was manic.

If Harry Styles had indeed surrendered his soul for continued life and scientific immortality, he seemed at the moment content with his Faustian pact. The anxiety attacks had ceased; his psychological tests indicated less depression.

Puzzled, Steinhardt conferred with the psychiatrist

Shapiro. "It's really quite simple," Shapiro said. "His former life was very goal-oriented. His work was always geared to developing a piece of hardware within a specific deadline. He's a product of the system that payloaded a man on the moon, blasted probes to Saturn. After his operation his life didn't have that sort of specificity. He was just existing, and that existence was without meaning to him. Now he once again has a concrete goal he understands, one that is tremendously ego-satisfying to him."

Steinhardt didn't entirely accept the psychiatrist's explanation. He couldn't dispel the mounting anxiety he felt about the pressure tests. The Glaucus Project had developed a steamrolling momentum of its own, and Steinhardt had lost control.

The hyperbaric chamber was a long cylindrical steel structure like a boiler drum with the area of a medium-sized room. It was dry and air-filled but rested on top of an oblong "wet pot," smaller in size and filled with an oxygenated saline solution.

The pot opened into the chamber like a pool into a steel-walled room. Harry lay submerged in the pot. With him was a Navy diving medical officer, Dr. Daniel Gillespie, who breathed through a "hookah," an air regulator supplied by a hose that snaked into the chamber above. Steinhardt's assistant Mark Matsuda was stationed in the dry chamber.

Morrison had insisted that two men be present in the chamber with Harry as safety tenders. Steinhardt had agreed but not for Morrison's reasons. If the gill ruptured, there was little the doctor or Matsuda could do.

For Steinhardt's experiment, the two men breathing compressed air, both in and out of the water, were "controls," normal men against whom he could measure the success or failure of the gill. Gillespie was a slightly built man, thirty-five years old, who played tennis once a week. Matsuda, twenty-six, was considerably huskier, a muscular man who ran several miles on the beach almost every morning.

There was a loud hiss as valves opened and compressed air was released into the chamber. Slowly, pound by pound, the pressure was increased. Harry and the two tenders were each fitted with medical sensors. Steinhardt and Morrison continuously monitored their vital functions on a console outside the chamber.

"Harry, this is Dr. Steinhardt. How do you feel?" He spoke into a microphone on the console.

"I'm fine. Are you increasing the pressure?" Harry's voice came over a speaker, strained and anxious.

"Yes, we are."

"I have no sensation of pressure," Harry said.

"Dr. Gillespie?"

"I had a slight ear and sinus block," the medical officer in the chamber reported, "but I've equalized it. I'm okay now."

"Mark?"

"No problems, Doctor."

The pressure was stabilized at the equivalent of thirty-feet of seawater, a depth at which the pressure is twice that at sea level. At that depth any pocket of air in the body is compressed to half its normal volume. Like a passenger in a jet airliner descending for a landing, Dr. Gillespie felt this as a painful squeezing on his eardrums and sinuses. The air that Gillespie and Matsuda were breathing was twice the weight and density as that outside the chamber.

But water, even under great pressure, does not compress as air does. The water that Harry breathed and that filled the sinuses and pockets of his body did not change in volume or density as the pressure was increased. Steinhardt had anticipated this, and he wasn't surprised that Harry didn't have the same sensation of pressure that the two air-breathing men in the chamber experienced.

At the simulated depth of thirty-three feet Harry and the two divers were run through a battery of exhausting physiological, psychological, and medical tests. Then the pressure in the chamber was carefully lowered to normal, and Harry was minutely examined for any injuries or trauma from the increased pressure. The doctors could find none.

Steinhardt and Morrison agreed to wait several days to see if any problems developed. None did, and a second chamber "dive" was made to sixty-six feet. Then ninety-nine feet. After each dive the medical staff pored over the EKG tracings from Harry's, Gillespie's, and Matsuda's hearts and the EEG tracings from their brains. Urine and blood samples were analyzed. Rectal temperatures. Gillespie's and Matsuda's lung volumes and ventilation were computed and compared with Harry's gill-flow rates. Heartbeats, stroke volume, cardiac output, carbon dioxide output, and oxygen uptakes were charted and graphed.

After the third chamber dive Harry still showed no adverse reaction to a fourfold increase in pressure, and Steinhardt proposed accelerating the dive schedule.

"What the hell's the big rush?" Morrison snapped. As the depths increased, the conflicts between Steinhardt and the Navy doctor had increased mathematically. The relentless build-up of pressure in the chamber seemed to radiate its force beyond the cylindrical steel walls, generating a mounting tension between the two men.

Steinhardt realized that Morrison thought he was a crazy scientist who had performed a bizarre human experiment without the proper authorization. Now Morrison was assigned to oversee a series of extremely dangerous tests. If the trials succeeded, the success would be Steinhardt's. If there was a disaster, the responsibility would be Morrison's, as far as the Navy was concerned. As a career officer, he had been placed in a terrible position where he had nothing to gain and everything to lose. He lived in constant fear of what Steinhardt or Harry might do. The anxiety oozed from him as sweat, staining the armpits and collar of his khaki shirt.

"We're going to take it slow and sure. By the book," he said.

As the pressure sank to the 165-foot depth, six times that of normal pressure, the divers with Harry could no longer breathe compressed air. Air is 80 percent nitrogen, and nitrogen under pressure becomes a powerful narcotic similar to the nitrous oxide "laughing gas" dentists use as anesthesia. At two hundred feet deep, divers stoned on compressed air have tried to give their air hoses to passing fish. Breathing pure oxygen is also dangerous, because pressurized oxygen by itself has a toxic effect that causes convulsions. For work at greater depths, Navy and commercial divers use carefully controlled high-pressure mixtures of oxygen and helium. Harry, directly absorbing the oxygen in the water through his gills as a fish does, wasn't affected by these problems.

As the depths increased, the two men with Harry created another problem—exhaustingly·long decompressions. It took twelve minutes to pressurize the chamber to three hundred feet. It took Harry and the two divers three hours to perform the physical and psychological tests for that depth. It took over twenty-four hours to safely decompress the divers back to sea level. The deeper a diver descends, the more the pressurized gases he is breathing dissolve in his blood. If he is brought back up too quickly, the gases bubble in his blood like a bottle of Coke that has been suddenly uncapped. In mild cases the tiny bubbles cause itching, a rash, fatigue, minor aches and pains, and dizziness. In severe cases there is excruciating pain, paralysis, blindness, convulsions, and death. The bends.

Steinhardt carefully compared Harry's blood at three hundred feet with that of the divers'. The divers' blood, like bottled Coke, was charged with the pressurized gases they had been breathing. Harry's blood was not.

"The Navy decompression tables we're adhering to are meaningless for Styles," Steinhardt told Morrison.

The Navy captain glowered. "Not for the divers."

"The tenders are no longer needed, and now they're unnecessarily delaying the experiment. Styles doesn't need these long decompression periods."

Sweat bubbled on Morrison's brow. The perspiration on his scalp made his close-cropped black hair and exposed white skin gleam as if they were coated with oil. "We're going by the book here," he said, his voice tight with anger. "As far as I'm concerned, your gill-man is a medical patient in my chamber. According to the book, he undergoes compression with qualified tenders in the chamber with him. And we decompress by the tables. I'm in charge of the operation of the chamber, and that's the way we're doing it."

Steinhardt looked from Morrison to Gillespie, who stood behind the senior medical officer. Gillespie remained silent. His lank brown hair framed a pale, morose face. Both he and Morrison were totally pre-occupied with imagining what could go wrong. Steinhardt could readily understand why the Navy had selected Morrison to supervise the pressure tests. He was excruciatingly thorough and conscientious. But Morrison's ability to avert disaster was based on experience, and there were no precedents for Harry Styles. With no precedents to guide him, a scientist needs audacity and intuition. These were qualities Morrison simply did not possess.

"We're creating an unnecessary hazard," Steinhardt insisted.

"Don't tell me how to run these tests," Morrison exploded. "I get that every day from your monster."

"My monster?" Steinhardt was outraged.

Morrison looked away. "He's not a natural man," Morrison muttered. "He's a laboratory freak. We don't know how he's going to react to any situation. We're flying blind." He turned on his heel and strode away. Gillespie glanced nervously at Steinhardt, then dogged after the senior officer.

Steinhardt stared at their retreating backs. There had been something strangely fearful and furtive in

253

Gillespie's drawn face. It occurred to Steinhardt that Morrison and Gillespie each hated Harry Styles. It was not the physical revulsion that Morrison's outburst had indicated. Harry Styles was an alien life forcing Morrison to venture beyond the safe pale of his knowledge. And he was forcing Gillespie, who was locked in the pressure chamber with him, beyond the limits of his courage.

The surge of high-pressure gas into the chamber made a deafening blast. The chamber itself roared and trembled, seething in the center of the hangar-sized building like an enormous cylindrical bomb that threatened to explode at any moment. In the hangar the air was at normal atmospheric pressure, 14.7 pounds per square inch. Inside the chamber the pressure was six hundred pounds per square inch. The depth reading was 1,320 feet. For Gillespie and Matsuda each breath was a heavy labor to pull in and push out gases sixty times heavier and denser than the air outside. The pressure and the helium altered the vibratory range of their vocal cords. When they tried to talk, incomprehensible ducklike squawks came out of their mouths. They communicated with each other through notes and hand signals and their messages to the outside were tapped out on an electric typewriter.

Once again the tedious hours of tests began. Aerobic work rates and anaerobic limits were tested by pedaling a stationary bicycle to exhaustion. How long did it take before Harry, faint with the exertion and thigh muscles cramping, faltered and could not keep up with the pace? Or Matsuda? Or Gillespie?

The tremors in each man's hand, a symptom of high-pressure nervous syndrome, were measured by a transducer attached to the middle finger. Gillespie showed considerably more tremors than either Harry or Matsuda. But wide deviations in the high-pressure nervous syndrome between individual divers was the rule rather than the exception.

A second test for the syndrome was given. They picked up ball bearings with a tweezer and placed them in a tube of the same diameter. Gillespie kept dropping the ball bearings. He became visibly irritated and frustrated, swearing in harsh angry duck noises.

Each of the tests was a standard used in diving research. There were volumes of data against which to compare the three men's performances. Morrison moved on to tests for touch, hearing, eyes, and reaction time. There were problems to solve in spatial orientation and arithmetic.

The tests took several hours to complete, but the dive was far from over. The men in the chamber were hostages to the immutable laws of physics that govern pressure and gases. The decompression from 1,320 feet would take fourteen days.

The chamber itself was oppressively bleak—bare steel walls with only jutting pipes and pressure fittings for relief. The toilet facilities, bunks, benches, and tables were also of steel. Matsuda had brought with him photos of his wife and child, a tottering stack of paperback novels and magazines, playing cards, and a chess board. Gillespie brought only a few books. He declined the other man's invitation to play cards or chess, preferring to spend the decompression time reading and sleeping. Harry and Matsuda managed several difficult games of amphibious chess, raising and lowering the magnetized board into the wet pot after each move.

On the second day of decompression Gillespie suddenly threw down a book he had been reading and made an unintelligible comment.

Matsuda looked up in surprise and laughed. The laugh came out, "Quack quack quack."

Gillespie glared at him with a murderous look. He didn't speak to either Matsuda or Harry for the rest of the day but sat brooding. When Steinhardt or Morrison asked him a question, he answered with a curt nod or shake of his head or ignored them completely.

Morrison ordered the psychologists to decode the MAACL profile Gillespie had taken at 1,320 feet. They reported back that his measures of anxiety, hostility, and depression had greatly escalated since the previous dives. But there was no way the decompression could be speeded up without risking seriously injuring the three men. Whatever happened, they were trapped inside an oversized pressure cooker for another twelve days.

On the fourth day it was evident that Gillespie was sleeping fitfully when he slept at all. Rather than being exhausted, he was nervously agitated. He paced the chamber like a caged beast. He took four strides, hit the blank steel wall, pivoted, and took four strides to the opposite wall.

"Dr. Gillespie, perhaps you'd be more comfortable if you took a tranquilizer," Steinhardt suggested tactfully. He peered into the chamber through a small viewing port.

Gillespie squawked back, his voice further distorted by anger. Steinhardt couldn't understand a word he was saying.

Matsuda came up and placed a placating hand on the medical officer's shoulder. He said something in duck gibberish and pointed to the typewriter, suggesting Gillespie use it to communicate.

Gillespie violently threw off Matsuda's hand, sending the young man reeling against the steel bulkhead with a painful crash. The two men screamed at each other in horrible squawks.

Harry broke water and thrust his head and shoulders into the chamber. "For Chrissakes, guys, ease off. We've got ten more days to go and you're already going stir crazy." The helium and pressure didn't affect his electronic larynx.

The sight of Harry seemed to further enrage Gillespie. He flung himself at Harry, grabbed him by the neck, and tried to drag him out of the wet pot. Harry instinctively yanked back and pulled the other man into the pot with him. They furiously thrashed in the water, inundating the chamber with heaving waves. Matsuda jumped to the lip of the pot and struggled to pull Gillespie off Harry. The chamber resonated with their garbled frantic cries, a bedlam of battling geese.

Steinhardt watched horror-struck. He and the men outside the chamber were as powerless to help Harry as if they were on separate planets. Morrison bellowed into the microphone for them to stop fighting, but his loud panicked orders only added to the pandemonium.

Matsuda managed to haul Gillespie, choking and sputtering, out of the water. For a moment they wrestled, but Gillespie sensed he was no match for the

257

husky, heavier young man, and all the fight and fury suddenly went out of him. He slumped to the floor of the chamber.

Matsuda lifted him to a chair, where he sat sodden and listless, staring vacantly into space, his lank brown hair hanging in his face dripping water.

For the next ten days the medical officer was tranquilized. He remained silent, hardly functioning, moving about the chamber like a sleepwalker. On several occasions he burst into tears for no apparent reason. Matsuda had to gently prod him into eating and washing. Both men abandoned shaving. Matsuda had discreetly gotten rid of the razors in the garbage disposal. At the end of the fourteen days Dr. Gillespie had to be carried out of the pressure chamber on a stretcher.

For the next two weeks Steinhardt and the Navy staff minutely examined Harry and restudied all the medical data. They were like stress engineers searching for telltale cracks after a test flight.

"I want to go alone on the next dive," Harry suddenly announced. "All the way. Down a mile."

Morrison shook his head. "It's too dangerous."

"If we don't do it, all this has been for nothing."

"That's not so," Morrison insisted. "The gill has checked out. The tests all indicate it's at least equally as effective as our most advanced underwater breathing apparatus."

Harry looked toward Steinhardt, but the scientist remained silent. He couldn't dispel the deep apprehension he had always felt about the pressure tests. Something about them was inherently wrong, Steinhardt's sixth sense was warning him, but he couldn't put his finger on the danger.

Harry was vehement. "I won't let you stop now. I'll take whatever risk is necessary. But we have to go deeper. Deeper than any man has ever been before or will go for a long time. We have to be the first!"

Morrison shook his head. There was a dumb bull-like stubbornness in the gesture. Steinhardt suddenly knew what was wrong with the Navy's whole testing procedure. The knowledge came to him, as scientific breakthroughs often do, in a flash of intuition. It was like adding one drop of catalyst to a supersaturated solution; instantly the solution crystallizes. All the vague uncrystallized doubts and fears Steinhardt had been experiencing for the past several weeks suddenly took a tangible shape. He knew with absolute certainty what was wrong with the tests and what had to be done. And with that knowledge the despair that had paralyzed him for weeks also disappeared. "We will go ahead with the tests," he said quietly. "And Harry will go alone."

Morrison whirled on him angrily. "Who the hell do you think you are?" he exploded. "I'm in charge of that chamber. I'm responsible for it."

"You've been responsible for forcing a scientific experiment to blindly adhere to dangerous procedures."

"I've followed the book," he said adamantly.

Steinhardt gestured toward Harry. "A third-year medical student could analyze his blood chemistry and tell you that the book, the Navy decompression tables you slavishly follow, are totally irrelevant. You have created decompression problems where none exist."

259

"What the hell are you talking about?"

"You've insisted on divers who have to breathe pressurized oxyhelium accompanying Harry on every dive. Their gases contaminate the fluid he breathes and in turn saturate his blood the same as the divers'."

"But that's to be expected."

"Only because you've created an artificial environment of high-pressure oxygen and helium for the divers. But in the ocean, even at great depths, no such high-pressure gas exists. The gases dissolved in the water are essentially the same as they are at sea level. Fish experience no decompression problems. But under your artificial conditions even a herring would have to decompress by the official Navy tables."

For the first time since Steinhardt had met him, Morrison looked bewildered. He glanced from Steinhardt to Harry, his eyes confused and anxious.

"We *will* make a dive to one mile deep," Steinhardt declared. "But we will seal off the water with rubber matting so we don't contaminate it with high-pressure helium and oxygen. The gas levels in the water will be kept the same as they occur naturally in the ocean. There *is* no more book to follow, Dr. Morrison. We must take a calculated risk."

"Jesus Christ," Morrison swore, his voice almost inaudible.

"And we must have the courage to fail."

"Jesus Christ," Morrison repeated. He looked terrified.

37

The once carefully tended garden around the swimming pool had become a jungle. After the heavy winter rains it exploded in wild tangled growth. The hibiscus crowded and shaded the roses. The camellias, once spherical masses of broad glossy leaves and carmine blossoms, shot up like randy trees and produced dried brown buds that never bloomed. The bougainvillea crawled over the wall and roof of the garage, as undisciplined as jungle vines.

Ruth surveyed the backyard one morning after she had taken Christopher to school. The garden had once been her joy, but since Harry's illness she had neglected it. Today she suddenly felt guilty. The plants and flowers were like abandoned children. They had lain dormant during the cold, wet winter, but now in the late spring they seethed with unruly life. They needed watering, feeding, pruning. Otherwise, the roses, hibiscus, and azaleas would soon wilt and die.

Moved by pity as much as anything, Ruth changed into her jeans and an old shirt and went to work. The morning had started cool and overcast, but by noon the overcast had burned off and the smog built up, a choking, contaminating presence in the air. She was exhausted and soaked with perspiration. About the garden were tidy piles of cuttings stacked and bound with twine. It would take several more mornings of work, but she had made a good start. It surprised her to feel the energy to garden again; for so long she had felt exhausted, dulled to the point of total inertia.

She wiped the sweat on her face and neck and looked at the pool. Unlike the garden it had not been neglected. It was swept clear of leaves and recently chlorinated. Harry had assigned it as David's responsibility, and her quiet, conscientious middle child had steadfastly maintained it as if it were a memorial to his father. The water was blue and clear. Ruth had a strong urge to jump in with her work clothes on. She was hot and sticky and could still feel the cobwebs of the camellias on her bare arms. The idea of going into the house and pulling a tight bathing suit over her hot dirty skin was repugnant. Ruth had never swum nude in the pool before, but suddenly the idea of it was delicious, tantalizing.

The children were not due from school for hours and the yard was sheltered by a high redwood stake fence. A row of camellia bushes and split-leaf philodendrons further screened the pool. Ruth slipped off her clothes at the edge of the pool and quickly slid into the deep end, pulling the enveloping water about her like a protective cloak. It felt cool and marvelous. She hesitantly breast-stroked to the shallow end and immediately swam back to the deep end. The pressure and flow of the cool water across her breasts and buttocks as she dove and swam was a new experience, sensual and amazingly pleasurable. She swam slowly back and forth, doing laps with an Australian crawl. But she quickly tired and became breathless, her stroke awkward. She rolled over on her back to catch her breath. Occasionally she did a languid back stroke, savoring the water, but mostly she just floated, her face to the sun.

Like a child, she didn't want to ever leave the water, but finally she crawled from the pool. She sprawled on the sun-baked tiles, the hot, hard polished glaze warming the sensitive flesh that had never before been exposed to those textures. She lay motionless, the water dripping from her limbs, evaporating in the slight breeze that stirred the bushes and cooled her. The sun was a benign warmth. She felt mindless, sensing only the coolness and warmth and the confusion of excitement and vulnerability that her nakedness aroused.

Ruth had never before taken such a self-centered pleasure in the pool. It had been completed shortly before Harry had become ill, and they had never swum together. At least one of the children was always around when she had swum before. But now she was alone and, in essence, a widow, abandoned. She felt a new selfishness that was oddly liberating. She felt it in the sun on her bare breasts and stomach. She belonged only to herself. It was a self-possession, she knew, that would evaporate as soon as she started to the car to go pick up Christopher at nursery school. But, for the moment at least, the feeling was there. And because of it things formerly forbidden were now possible.

That night Ruth visited Harry. With the constant

flow of doctors, physiologists, medical technicians, and psychologists in and out of the tank room, her regular visits created no undue curiosity. However, at Gunther's advice, she scheduled her visits after dinner, when the great bulk of personnel had gone for the day. She was, at first, startled by the change in Harry. The golden-bearded husky man was physically more of a stranger to her than ever. But Harry was working again, deeply involved in a technical problem, and the air of preoccupation with which he addressed her was very familiar to her. Harry explained in great detail the pressure tests they were conducting.

"I don't understand all this about decompression, nitrogen, and helium," Ruth said in confusion.

"It's freshman chemistry," Harry said impatiently. "Dalton's law of partial pressures. In a mixture of gases, each gas exerts a pressure proportional to its percentage of the volume of the total."

"I didn't take chemistry in college. I only had to take a year of biology. Talk to me about zygotes and reproduction." Harry's impatience in explaining the highly technical aspects of his work to her was also familiar, an unpleasant characteristic she had forgotten during his illness but now sharply remembered.

"How're the kids?" Harry asked. It was presumably a safe subject. Harry listened avidly while Ruth talked about the children. She mentally edited what she said. The Christopher about whom she told anecdotes was the bouncing extrovert of the day school, but not the child who awoke in terrified tears from nightmares in the middle of the night. The David she described was the brilliant straight-A student, but not the boy who came home immediately from school and wandered aimlessly about the house. The Brenda of her stories was the teenager plunging into the confusion of adolescence, who asked her mother for advice on clothes, hairdos, boys, and dating, but not the girl who blushed and looked acutely embarrassed when neighbors asked how her father was doing at the hospital.

Ruth's visit with Harry was subdued and unemotional. It was a polite passing of information. They had learned through the pain and anguish of their previous meetings how to avoid feelings—the necessity of throttling all hope, desire, and even love.

"Harry, these pressure tests. Are they dangerous?"

Harry shrugged. "It's an unknown area. We don't know if it's more hazardous for me than other men or less hazardous. That's what we have to find out."

"Why?"

"Why what?"

"Why do you have to find that out? What's worth getting killed or crippled or becoming a vegetable? Just to find out how deep the gill will go?"

Harry stared at Ruth, as if closely examining her, then shook his head. "You've never understood. You've always thought that life was just about you and me and the kids."

"No, I never thought it was just that," Ruth said quietly. She looked at her husband imprisoned in his cell of water. What did he really have to lose?

There was an awkward silence, then Ruth volunteered, "I'm reading a book on marine biology."

"Oh, have you learned anything?"

"A lot. I've become an expert on the mating habits of the Caribbean tulip-shell snail."

"The *what?*"

"The mating of the Caribbean tulip-shell snail. It's a very dangerous courtship. If a female tulip-shell snail approaches a male who is bigger than she is, he'll eat her. And vice versa. A successful mating occurs only when both the male and the female size each other up and decide neither can devour the other."

Harry laughed, the deep bass sound resounding in the tank room. "Honey, you've always been too tough for me to gobble up. I wouldn't have it any other way."

When Ruth returned home that evening, the children were still up. Christopher and David waited in bed to hear about their father. The man called Glaucus had become a bedtime story, a fairy tale Ruth told about a superman who lived underwater.

Tonight she described the deep pressure dives Harry was making. "The pressure chamber looks something like the picture of the *Trieste*—you know, the bathyscaphe that dove to the deepest spot in the Marianas trench." Ruth had picked up *The Wonder Book of Oceanography* at the supermarket, and she and the boys had read it together. "Only the pressure is all on the inside, not on the outside, as it is at the bottom of the sea. Dr. Steinhardt took me on a guided tour. All the dials and machinery confuse me—you know how I am about technical things. But I think you'd be interested in it, David. Dr. Steinhardt said he'd be happy to show you around."

Steinhardt had really said that. In fact, to Ruth's surprise, he had been very concerned with David's problems in relating to his father, as if they echoed some deep personal conflict of Steinhardt's own.

"Do you want to see what your father's doing?" Ruth prompted.

David shifted uneasily on the bed. He shrugged. "I don't know what to say to him."

"He's still your father. Talk to him like you've always talked to him." Wonderful advice to give an eleven-year-old, Ruth thought. She couldn't even follow it herself.

"Nothing's the same anymore," David said. He shrugged again. "I don't know," he said lamely.

Ruth looked at Christopher. The younger boy was frightened. Stories about Glaucus entranced him, but the actual prospect of again visiting the strange bearded man in the tank now terrified him. Ruth wondered if they would ever reconcile the memory of their father with the man they now knew as Glaucus.

She tucked them in and kissed both on the brow. Christopher blinked, yawned, and finally nodded off to sleep. When Ruth left the boys' room, David was still awake, lying with his hands behind his head, staring off into space.

Ruth checked Brenda's room. The girl was in bed but reading a homework assignment. Ruth retreated to the study, closed the door behind her, and broke out a bottle of Scotch.

"You could try to get involved in his work," Dr. Axelrod suggested. "Understand and share his enthusiasm for it."

On the wall behind Dr. Axelrod was displayed a new exhibit of African primitive art. Two wooden masks, one male and one female, from the Bajokwe tribe in the

Congo. The female face was hauntingly beautiful and serene, the nose narrow and delicately shaped, the eyes Oriental and the mouth composed. The male mask, on the other hand, was ferocious. The sharp curving lines of the brow and cheekbones created a gargoyle effect and the mouth was grotesquely wide and gaping with sharp, serrated teeth. The Bajokwes' beauty and the beast.

"I've never shared Harry's work," Ruth said. "We shared a bed, sex, children, a home, weekend outings, even ice cream cones, but I never shared his work."

"Perhaps you should make an effort to expand your interests," Dr. Axelrod said.

"Oh, really!" There was a copy of the Los Angeles *Times* on the end table. Ruth grabbed it and ripped it open to the classified ads. After a brief search she read aloud a three-line ad placed by an aerospace firm. "Employment Opportunities. Systems Analyst—To provide algorithm design and statistical analysis and modeling on GEODSS. Areas of application include electro-optic sensor modeling, sensor data processing hardware, software performance and analysis.'"

"My God, is that in English?" Helena Axelrod asked.

"That's the sort of work you expect me to have shared with him. I couldn't do it then. And I certainly can't now."

Ruth sensed disapproval in the other woman's expression. "But I've been reading up on oceanography and marine biology," she added. "Are you familiar with the sex life of the angler fish?"

Dr. Axelrod shook her head.

"Well, the male angler fish swims about very freely in

268

his youth," Ruth explained. "But as soon as he matures he begins a desperate search for a female. When he finds one, he sinks his teeth into her and just hangs on. After a while his mouth fuses with the female's flesh and their blood systems become connected. Eventually the male's eyes are gradually absorbed into the female's body and finally disappear. He becomes a total parasite. His body degenerates until he's nothing more than a sack of reproductive organs, permanently attached to the female to periodically service her."

The psychiatrist stared at Ruth curiously. "Do you relate that to you and Harry?"

"Oh, my God, no," Ruth exclaimed. "I just thought it was funny. Don't you?"

Helena Axelrod nodded. She didn't smile. "I think you just described my first marriage," she said.

Gunther Marx called to ask if Ruth was free for dinner. There were some complicated legal matters concerning Harry he wanted to discuss with her.

Ruth was happy about the invitation on two counts. First, she wanted Gunther's advice. She was thinking about going back to work. She and Dr. Axelrod had talked about it at length. In the fall Christopher would begin kindergarten. Her days would get progressively lonelier. But, more urgently, she just wanted to see Gunther again. She was confused about her feelings toward him. After he called she experienced a curious excitement like that she had once felt as a young girl going on a date.

But when Gunther picked her up she sensed something wrong. Throughout the ride to the restaurant and while they were being seated, he was brooding and withdrawn.

"Ruth, we're totally at their mercy." Gunther's eyes were anxious and troubled. "I'm sorry."

"Gunther, what the hell are you talking about?"

"We simply don't have a case. I've researched all the precedents and conferred with a half-dozen other lawyers who are specialists in malpractice law, and the conclusion is that we don't have a case. If we brought a suit it would probably be dismissed." Gunther's voice was heavy with defeat.

"I don't understand why," Ruth said.

"It's just not a case of medical malpractice according to the precise legal criteria for malpractice. The operation wasn't therapeutic. It wasn't supposed to cure or alleviate a condition. Harry was terminal. There are depositions by all the doctors involved in the operation that he was in extremis and they had to rush him to the operating room. His lung had hemorrhaged and he was literally seconds away from death. He was kept alive only by mechanical means."

Ruth felt slightly faint. She put her hand to her head and took a quick sip of water. "I didn't know that."

"It's not something surgeons generally discuss with the family after an operation."

"But this was the first time this sort of operation was ever performed on a human being."

Gunther shook his head. "That in itself doesn't constitute a malpractice case." He launched into an earnest brief of the law, as if trying to convince Ruth with a wealth of scholarly detail how hard he had been working. He cited laws, precedents, *Karp v. Cooley,* the Helsinki Declaration, the National Institutes of Health guidelines. Since the 1947 Nuremberg trials of Nazi physicians, an extensive body of international and federal laws regulating medical experiments with humans had been developed.

"Since Steinhardt's research was federally funded, he was obligated to follow guidelines set up by the National Institutes of Health. They're essentially a system of reviews by other doctors," Gunther explained. "But Steinhardt did that. And there's no question of your *informed consent*. It's heavily documented. Steinhardt and Bernstein went into great detail explaining both to you and to Harry exactly what they were doing. They held out no hope. The most that could have been hoped for was to prolong Harry's death. Not to prolong his life in any significant fashion. It's not uncommon in medical research to briefly prolong a patient's death by artificial devices in order to obtain important data."

"But Harry's still alive," Ruth protested. "In a goddamn giant goldfish bowl."

"The fact that Harry unexpectedly lived would, if anything, weaken our case unless we could prove extraordinary pain and suffering." Gunther shrugged helplessly. "I'm afraid Harry's grandstanding on TV has pretty well shot down that argument. At this point a judge would probably dismiss the case. And there'd be no point in appealing. The Supreme Court has never heard a case of medical malpractice or human experimentation."

Gunther looked so dejected that Ruth instinctively reached out to take his hand. "I really didn't care that much about a suit," she said. "I just wanted *something*

271

to fight with. To make sure Harry and the kids are taken care of."

"But *I* wanted it," Gunther said in a thick voice. "A big fat settlement. Something that would take care of you for the rest of your life. I wanted to bring it to you on a silver platter."

Ruth shook her head. "Something like that might have created more problems that it would solve. As long as we have enough to keep the house, and we can maintain our privacy, we can keep our lives on an even keel."

Gunther looked down at the table. "I can't even guarantee that."

"What do you mean?"

"The institute or the hospital or anyone else can make public Harry's real identity, and his family, any time they want."

Ruth was suddenly alarmed. "I thought you told me that a patient and his family had a right to privacy. That the doctors and the hospital were forbidden to disclose personal information unless we authorize it."

Gunther continued to look at the table. "Normally that's true. They have what's known as an obligation of confidentiality. But it's not absolute. The law recognizes an exception. The exception is that an important scientific discovery takes precedence over a patient's or his family's privilege of nondisclosure." Gunther held up his hands in a helpless gesture. "Ruth, you have no right to privacy."

"My God." Ruth suddenly felt frightened. She looked anxiously about the restaurant at the other diners. She seized Gunther's hand. "That's the one thing I just don't think I could handle. My life, the children, we're all in such a precarious balance. We have our whole lives to rework. If we were thrust into anything now . . ." She didn't finish the sentence but just shook her head. "The press, other people, they can all be so cruel and stupid."

"I know," Gunther said. "I'll do everything I can."

There was something in his voice, a breaking quality that had been there when he had said earlier, "I wanted to bring it to you on a silver platter." It was a devotion that Ruth didn't quite understand. But she was grateful it was there. "You're much more than just my lawyer," she said softly.

Gunther nodded and smiled shyly. There was a confession in his smile and in that nod.

38

Each evening, as the sun set and the sky darkened, in the sea offshore of the institute swarms of dragonfish, spirula squid, hatchetfish, bristlemouths, and lanternfish migrated from the dark mile-deep abyss of the Marejada trench to the warm surface waters. There the smaller creatures grazed in the teeming pastures of phytoplankton, and they in turn were eaten by the larger fish. Every hunter became the hunted. At the first rays of dawn the survivors plunged back into the lightless depths. It was a nightly ritual, eons old, of primitive creatures. Yet a man with the most sophisticated diving equipment could not follow them. The rapid compression and decompression would kill him.

Harry was alone in the hyperbaric chamber, immersed in the narrow confines of the wet pot staring out the viewing window at the crowd of technicians in the control room. There were no divers in the chamber above him, and a mat of black rubber now blanketed the surface of the water to seal out the gases above. It made the wet pot seem much smaller, claustrophobic. Up until this moment Harry hadn't realized how much he depended on having the two other men in the chamber with him. He was now alone. He felt light-headed and a little nauseated. The sound of the high-pressure gas blasting into the empty chamber had a louder, roaring, more ominous sound.

Harry lay quietly in the water. He willed himself to relax. He had to read his body—separate the false signals generated by his fear from the real signs of physical stress or damage.

The pressure built relentlessly—three hundred pounds per square inch, five hundred pounds.

The living tissue of flesh, blood, muscle, and sinew are largely liquid, and like water cannot be compressed. Harry's body conducted the pressure as a bar of copper conducts electricity. He and the pressure were one.

"How do you feel?" Morrison suddenly asked over the speaker.

"Fine. No aches or pains."

"Any nausea or vertigo?"

"No problems." Through the viewing window, Harry could see Morrison's strained, anxious face and the sweat gleaming oily on his scalp.

At 1,320 feet, the greatest depth to which Harry, Matsuda, and Gillespie had dove before, the compression was stopped.

"Come to the window, please," Steinhardt asked. He closely examined Harry's face for any telltale hemorrhages, then held up an optometer. "Your eyes, please." Harry held his eyelids open with his fingers as

275

Steinhardt probed them with a light. It was a prelude to the tedious battery of tests he had taken on the other dives. He now repeated them all to establish the baseline data for the plunge into the realms of pressure where no man had ever gone before.

Seven hundred pounds per square inch.

Eight hundred pounds.

Steinhardt's voice suddenly crackled on the speaker. "Are you experiencing any difficulty?" There was alarm in his voice.

"I'm terrific," Harry boomed.

"Your pulse, blood pressure, and cerebral oxygen levels are all rising. How do you feel?"

"Excited as hell. We're about to break the French record—two thousand feet."

There was silence, then Steinhardt said, "Please try to remain relaxed, Harry. You're distorting the medical readings."

One thousand pounds. Twelve hundred and fifty pounds. Harry felt the pressure pulsing through him, galvanizing his nerves. His fear and excitement flowed into that current; it hummed and buzzed through every fiber and tissue of his being.

Fifteen hundred pounds. Seventeen hundred and fifty pounds. The descent now went rapidly, as the increase of depth from two thousand feet to four thousand feet would only double the pressure Harry had previously withstood. Helium, stored in huge steel tanks under enormous pressure, blasted into the chamber. The noise was as shattering as that of a jet taking off. At the four-thousand-foot depth Harry was under 122 times the pressure the men outside the steel chamber felt.

Two thousand pounds per square inch of flesh. Two thousand two hundred and fifty pounds.

Steinhardt methodically asked Harry questions, checking his mental alertness, coaching him to anticipate any medical problems. But the tension in Steinhardt's voice betrayed the man's own fears.

Two thousand four hundred pounds per square inch; 160 times the pressure of air at sea level.

"He's a mile deep," Morrison whispered. His voice broke as though he were afraid of speaking, like a man standing alongside an enormous, unstable bomb which the mere sound of his voice might set off.

"I want to bring him back as quickly as possible," Morrison whispered urgently.

"We will run the scheduled tests," Steinhardt insisted. "This is a scientific investigation. Not a stunt."

In the chamber Harry sensed the conflict between the two men outside as if it were a dangerous rise in the pressure.

BAM! There was a sharp explosion.

"My God, what's that?" Morrison cried out.

His panic instantly transmitted itself to Harry. "What's happened?" he shouted. His instant fear was that the chamber had ruptured. An explosive decompression—the sudden release of pressure in the chamber—would kill him.

"Oh, Jesus Christ," Morrison swore.

"What the hell's happening?"

"Champagne. Some joker opened a bottle of champagne." Morrison appeared in the view window holding up a bottle. He pawed at the sweat pouring from his face and took a deep drink directly from the bottle. "To the new world record holder," he toasted in a hoarse voice.

Harry was exhausted. He felt almost faint, at once giddy and exhilarated. "Save some of that champagne. I want a drink when I get out of this pressure cooker."

"You can't drink," Morrison said.

"I'm going to drink like a goddamn fish," Harry exclaimed happily.

Once again Harry plunged into the gauntlet of tests. He dropped a ball bearing. "I don't know whether it's high-pressure nervous syndrome or just my nervousness," Harry reported. His voice came in gasps. He felt as though he were about to explode.

"Are you experiencing any physical discomfort? Any pain?"

"No. But I'm a little dizzy."

"You're breathing too rapidly, Harry. Stop what you're doing. Now consciously force yourself to slow down your gill-flow rate," Steinhardt ordered calmly. "That's very good, Harry. Just keep that same slow steady flow for a minute or two."

Harry concentrated on slowing his breaths of water. The dizziness and the feeling that he was about to burst gradually subsided.

"You're still exhibiting signs of nervous syndrome, Harry. It may be due to the pressure or it may be the stress of the situation. Continue with the tests as soon as you feel comfortable. Make a conscious effort to relax and do everything slowly and methodically."

The tests took considerably longer than they had before. Then the decompression began. Theoretically, a diver breathing compressed gases should take a month to decompress from a mile-deep dive. Steinhardt's schedule called for less than a day. The champagne Harry had joked about earlier now became a deadly metaphor. The bubbles that exploded and fizzed when the cork popped might be reproduced in Harry's blood. His reaction to a rapid decompression was still unknown.

He lay quietly in the tank systematically surveying his body for the telltale symptoms of the bends. At one point or another he imagined he detected every one of them, but when he willed himself to relax and concentrate on his breathing, the symptoms faded. As the pressure gradually decreased, so did his fear.

As his fear abated, there came a great feeling of satisfaction. He had that day redefined his aloneness. It was no longer that of a leper unable to live among normal men. He was now a man with a unique strength and ability. Others would follow him as far as they dared. He had paid a great price. But then anyone who achieved a unique pinnacle was altered in some way in either body or soul. An Olympic weight-lifting champion was more grotesque to the eye than he was. And, as Harry had painfully learned from his cancer, life often mutilates men to no purpose at all. Lying weightless in the tank, quietly waiting for the decompression to sea level to be completed, Harry felt at peace with both himself and the world.

At sea level the pressure between the chamber and the world outside was equalized, and the hatch opened, Morrison rushed in, clambered to the edge of the wet pot, and yanked off the rubber matting. "Congratulations!" he boomed and reached his hand out to Harry.

The bearded blond head broke water, but Harry ignored Morrison's outstretched hand and reached out to Steinhardt, who had followed Morrison. The old man seized Harry's hand and arm fiercely in both of his old, pale white hands. Steinhardt was trying to smile but the effort became a grimace as his eyes brimmed with tears. He couldn't speak. Gripping his hand, beaming rapidly up into the old man's face, Harry too found it difficult to speak.

A flash went off. A Navy photographer posed Morrison and Steinhardt kneeling at the lid of the pot with Harry. Buckley materialized. The intensity of that moment of union with Steinhardt was shattered. There was a great hubbub of nonsensical comments, exclamations, shouts, and laughter echoing and ringing in the chamber. Finally Steinhardt, Morrison, Buckley, and the others withdrew outside the packed chamber to allow the corpsmen to transfer Harry.

The procedure was to quickly lift and carry Harry in a canvas stretcher from the chamber to his tank. It had to be done speedily, as Harry was a fish out of water. Two corpsmen plunged into the wet pot and arranged the stretcher for Harry to squirm into. Then with a corpsman at each corner, it was lifted up out of the water.

As he was rushed from the chamber, Harry suddenly ordered: "Wait. I want to take a picture standing with Dr. Steinhardt outside the tank."

"Harry, you're too weak," Steinhardt protested.

"Hell, I'm the strongest man in the world. I can bear more pounds per square inch than any man alive."

Before Steinhardt could intercept him, Harry swung off the stretcher. He heaved to his feet, but his legs immediately collapsed under him. He sprawled heavily on the floor. It was as if he had never walked or crawled on the ground before. He struggled to get his legs and arms under him, but they were too weak to raise the weight of his body. He flopped about helplessly. His chest felt heavy as concrete, crushing him into the hard implacable surface of the floor.

"What's happening?" Harry cried in terror. "I can't move!"

39

The seaplane, a fat-bellied Grumman Mallard, taxied into loading position at the head of the pier thrusting into Los Angeles harbor and now stood with its twin engines idling. The prop wash stirred Ruth Styles's raven hair, causing it to swirl about her pale face and shoulders.

Watching her brush the fine hair away from her face, Karl Steinhardt wondered if it was the hunger for that beauty that had driven Harry during the dangerous drudgery of the pressure tests. When a man is married to a beautiful woman he must do extraordinary things. Was each new heralded accomplishment Harry's desperate way of trying to maintain a hold on his wife? Had it now motivated him to dare the hazards of this new expedition?

At the moment Harry lay at the foot of the pier in a tub made of plywood and lined with fiberglass. It was about nine feet by three feet by three feet. A bottle of compressed oxygen was strapped to the side and attached by tubes to a filter and aerator, identical to those in a home aquarium, which emitted a constant stream of bubbles about Harry's head and gills. The tub rested on the blades of the forklift that had hauled it from the ambulance still parked at the foot of the pier.

Ruth bent over the tub. "Harry, stick your head out and look at the seaplane you're flying to the island in," she urged her husband. Harry's face emerged from the boil of bubbles. He peered first at his wife and then toward the seaplane and nodded.

"You're really traveling in style."

Steinhardt and Buckley had moved down the pier to give the Styleses a measure of privacy. But Steinhardt could still make out their conversation and detect the strain and false cheer in Ruth Styles's voice.

"The island's not that far away, Harry. Dr. Buckley said he'll arrange for me to fly or take a boat over any time I want. I'll be out next Sunday for sure."

Steinhardt didn't hear Harry's response, if indeed he made one. Harry had been in a state of depression since his collapse after the record-breaking pressure test. Steinhardt still felt guilty about Harry's collapse. It had simply never occurred to him to warn Harry about attempting to walk. His legs were no longer strong enough to support him. In fact, his arms and legs weren't even strong enough to crawl. Sustained weightlessness had weakened Harry's muscles to the point where he was helpless on land. Astronauts had similar problems on returning to earth, but none had experienced the long period of weightlessness that Harry had. Exercise on the bicycle had not been enough to prevent the deterioration. That work was only in the magnitude of tens of pounds. Human muscles must lift hundreds of pounds of body weight daily in order to maintain their strength.

Harry, in addition, had undergone another great physical change. His lung cavity, which was once filled with air, was now filled with serous fluid. The great increase in weight of his torso and the shift of the body's center of gravity was not noticeable underwater, but out of the water his body had become as unwieldy as a whale's. Neither physical change affected his health, but the discovery he could no longer walk had been a great blow to Harry. It eroded the heroic self-image he had constructed of himself. Steinhardt wondered if Harry had told his wife about his collapse; he doubted it. The humiliation would have been too great, especially after the success of the depth tests. That was a triumph Harry had wanted to present to her undiminished, like the first scaling of Mount Everest. But after the flurry of publicity and TV interviews, Harry plunged into despair. It caught Steinhardt and the psychiatrist Shapiro by surprise. They were dealing with a much more fragile and unstable man than they'd realized. There were emotional quicksands hidden just below the surface that all their psychological testing had not shown up.

"I don't know why you insist on flying over," Buckley suddenly exclaimed. "The institute has plenty of boats available for this sort of trip." He mopped at his brow with a handkerchief and eyed the seaplane with undisguised dread. Steinhardt had never seen him so agitated before.

"The channel's too choppy," Steinhardt explained. He gestured toward Harry. "In that sardine box he'd probably get seasick. In his case vomiting, if it got into his gills, might be fatal." He turned his attention back to Ruth and Harry Styles.

"I envy you," she said with an encouraging smile. "They say it's very beautiful over there. It's the closest place where the ocean is unpolluted enough to risk the experiment." She leaned toward Harry, her hair again tumbling across her face.

From the tub Harry's hand reached out to tentatively touch and caress her hair. "It's that ocean that will be between us."

"That's a strange thing for John Glaucus, modern science's answer to the sea god, to say."

Harry's hand continued to stroke her hair. Then the resonant, electronic voice from the tank said, "Ruth. We haven't kissed in months. We haven't even touched."

Ruth stared down at him. Out of the froth of bubbles, the bearded dripping head rose and leaned toward her. Ruth kissed him quickly, and yards away Steinhardt could sense the recoil from the contact, the slight shudder that she immediately fought to suppress.

"I'm sorry, Harry. You just felt so strange." She smiled. "You're very wet, you know."

Harry looked at her, the hurt showing in his eyes, then slipped back into the tank, the water once again coming between them.

In his own desperate way Harry Styles still courted his wife. He wooed her with heroic feats. Harry himself might be unaware of it, but Steinhardt saw it clearly. Harry brooded and waited anxiously for his wife's visits. And if he was sometimes impatient or picked quarrels with her, it was only because she failed to always recognize and applaud the ingenuity and courage with which Harry fought to live and even prevail. But Ruth Styles was the fountain of life for her husband. If he could hold on to her, still possess her love, however remotely, his life had purpose.

Steinhardt supervised the loading of Harry's tank aboard the seaplane. it was strapped down and secured in place with a luggage net. The tank had been used previously to transport a large shark to an aquarium in San Francisco.

"Are you comfortable, Harry?"

Harry, deeply preoccupied in his own thoughts, did not respond immediately. Then he acknowledged Steinhardt with a nod.

Steinhardt turned to the pilot. "Please keep your altitude as low as possible. The lower air pressure above sea level causes the oxygen in the water to bubble out too rapidly."

"Yes, sir, I understand." The pilot headed toward the cabin. Steinhardt took his seat beside Buckley and strapped himself in for takeoff. As the seaplane taxied into the harbor, he caught a glimpse of Ruth Styles through the window. She stood on the end of the pier, waving, the wind whipping her hair and dress, a forlorn and deserted figure. She waved goodbye to a husband who could not see her. How many other basic gestures of their life together had now become totally meaningless, Steinhardt wondered.

Both engines roared to takeoff power, and the seaplane surged through the water. Gathering speed, the plane violently hammered its way through the wind-churned waves of the harbor, alternately ricocheting off the crests of small swells and slapping down again with a shuddering thwack.

"Oh, God," Buckley cried. His eyes were clenched shut and he clutched the arms of the chair in a white-knuckled grip. His face was bloodless.

The seaplane nosed up and was airborne, climbing swiftly as soon as it broke free of the drag of the water. Over the stone breakwater that artificially created Los Angeles harbor, the plane banked west toward the Channel Islands.

Buckley opened his eyes but kept his grip on the seat. "How soon before we're there?" he asked. The question was almost a whine.

"The flight should take less than a half-hour." Buckley's fear of flying had come as a surprise to Steinhardt. The man was about to jump out of his skin.

Steinhardt looked across Buckley out through the window. The freighters and tankers in the crowded harbor, the smoking oil refineries of San Pedro, and the luxuriant hills of Palos Verdes Estates dipped beneath the right wing. The city of Los Angeles sprawled across the flat basin to the north, a baking plain of concrete and asphalt. From the perspective of the open sea of the San Pedro Channel, the smog was a clearly defined brown cloud smothering the city.

"God, the only thing I hate more than boats is flying," Buckley said suddenly.

"What a strange thing for an oceanographer to say."

"I've never shared all the romantic nonsense and mysticism about the sea. To me, it's a cold, hostile, suffocating element." Buckley's fear, bordering on hysteria, was making him giddy and talkative.

"What on earth ever led you into marine science?"

"It was a quite logical decision I made in college. I assayed the fields of science. Aerospace—the great glamour industry of the sixties—was already over-crowded and overfunded by government. There were bound to be cutbacks. There was obviously not going to be any significant economic return from space in my lifetime. On the other hand, as we quickly ran out of fuel, mineral resources, and food, the sea was the natural place for research and development. It will be the wealth and power base of the future," Buckley rattled on nervously, "as the colonies once were for Europe. And as our western frontier was for the United States."

The idea of pursuing science as a basis of wealth and power was repugnant to Steinhardt. It was as if a bishop had said that he was in the church for the money and the power. Steinhardt ignored Buckley and studied the sea below.

To the south Santa Catalina Island loomed up out of the mist, its rock cliffs primal and brooding. It was the only one of the Channel Islands that was inhabited. The other islands, scattered to the west and south of Los Angeles as far as sixty miles offshore, were deserted except for a handful of National Park Service rangers and Navy station keepers.

The ocean-assaulted cliffs and harsh peaks jutting from the sea were extensions of the Santa Monica Mountains, separated from the mainland after the Ice Age. Evolution had taken its own distinctive course here. Giant coreopsis with thick muscular tree trunks erupting into huge sunflowers covered the misty hillsides but grew nowhere else. The island bats, deer mouse, and gray fox were separate species unknown elsewhere. It was appropriate, Steinhardt mused, that man himself should now take a bold new step in his own evolution in these waters.

He rose to check on Harry. "Are you comfortable?" Harry looked up and again merely nodded. "Please talk to me, Harry. I want to hear your speech. Any signs of aphasia would indicate that you weren't getting enough oxygen."

"I'm reasonably comfortable," Harry said. "I'm sorry to be uncommunicative. I'm just depressed by my meeting with Ruth. I was hoping she'd bring the kids to say goodbye." He emitted a short mirthless laugh and even the electronic resonance could not disguise the undertone of bitterness. "I'm a heroic figure to the kids now, but the real sight of me frightens them."

"Did she tell you that?"

"Only that I'm a hero to them, not that I frighten them. Ruth is much too sensitive to tell me anything like that. But what's not said and not done now say a great deal more than any of her apologies or gestures." Harry was silent a moment. "I suppose this all answers your medical questions, Doctor. If I were anoxic I'd have this pleasant, don't-give-a-damn feeling of well-being. And there would be no pain." Steinhardt nodded. There was nothing he could say to Harry, no comforting platitude that wouldn't ring falsely in Steinhardt's own ears. He busily checked the gauge on the oxygen bottle and returned to his seat. Buckley pointed out the window at a scene below.

A behemoth supertanker, like an island unto itself, was moored in the calmer sea leeward of one of the islands. There were several smaller vessels attending it. They were lightering, transferring crude oil from the supertanker to the smaller ships for delivery to West Coast ports. Even these remote rocky Pleistocene islands were now threatened by oil pollution.

"Swimming through even a small spill would be fatal for Harry," Steinhardt said. "If the oil got on his gills, it would suffocate him."

Buckley said nothing but continued to study the oil tankers below with great interest.

The upcoming experiments worried Steinhardt. There were more unknown factors than known. In the open sea he would have none of the laboratory controls he had had in the chamber tests, and for that reason alone they were more dangerous. He had no way of predicting how Harry would react.

The seaplane swept low, parelleling a line of blunt dark cliffs that plunged into the sea. The plane's passage disturbed nesting gulls, brown pelicans, and cormorants, which soared into the air in great flocks and flapped away. A rookery of panicked sea lions swarmed over a rocky ledge at the foot of a sheer cliff and splashed into the sea for protection. As the plane slapped down on the water, Buckley emitted a low whimper.

The engines were cut, and the plane settled heavily into the water. It taxied sluggishly toward a long narrow pier that stabbed out from the beach of a shallow cove. There were a dozen men waiting on the pier. All were dressed in military uniforms. For the first time it occurred to Steinhardt that on this remote island he and Harry were in effect prisoners.

40

Stephanie O'Gara woke up at dawn with the answer. For weeks she had been obsessed with the one idea that someone in the aerospace industry knew Glaucus's real identity, and if she dug hard enough she could track him down. On her own time after work, on weekends, and in snatched moments between her other reporting assignments she had doggedly pursued this one lead. She had made hundreds of phone calls, searched down a dozen blind alleys. And she had come up totally empty-handed. It was only now when she felt beaten and exhausted that an entirely different approach occurred to her as she lay in bed half asleep.

She glanced at her watch. It was almost six. She wearily crawled out of bed, went to the phone and once again began dialing. On the third call she made contact.

When Greenberg drove into the TV station parking lot at eight-thirty, O'Gara was waiting for him. He uncoiled from the front seat of his car, a tall dark slender man. First thing in the morning, before the tensions and frantic work of the newsroom engulfed him, he had a sleepy, sweetly melancholy look that O'Gara had always found attractive and touching. He now smiled at her, his dark hooded eyes questioning why she was there waiting for him.

"The operation on the gill-man was performed at the University Medical Center hospital," she informed him without a preamble.

"How'd you find that out?"

"It suddenly occurred to me that it had to be done at one of the hospitals heavily involved in research, probably connected to a medical school. So I just started calling their surgical services. I told them who I was and said I just wanted to clarify whether the Dr. Steinhardt who had performed the gill operation was a member of their staff or just had operating privileges there. It turns out neither is the case. A bored, talkative nurse on the surgery desk told me he was only an associate of a Dr. Bernstein who performed the operation with Steinhardt. But Bernstein was killed in an auto accident months ago."

"Did this bored, talkative nurse tell you Glaucus's real name?"

O'Gara shook her head. "She didn't know it. But she did give me the names of four other nurses who assisted in the operation and a couple in the intensive care unit who also worked on the case. Apparently it's still quite a topic of conversation about the hospital."

"There's no way they're going to let you just waltz in and look through their records."

"I'm not going to. I'm going to go down there to research a feature story on nurses. Their daily life-and-death responsibilities, their overworked and under-staffed working conditions, their low pay. And we gals will just drink coffee and gossip, and I'll bet one of them remembers the name on a chart in the most fascinating case they've ever worked on."

"I hate to mention it," Greenberg said. "But it occurs to me that there's a question of invasion of privacy here."

"*Privacy?* This involves major public issues. A landmark scientific breakthrough. Medical experimentation," O'Gara insisted with passion. "But it's not some dull, wordy station editorial about ethics. It's a real life that's been turned inside out. There's a wife and children out there somewhere. And their confusion, heartbreak, tears, pride, loneliness—whatever the hell's going on with them—that's an important part of the story. We're not doing our job if we sit back and just mouth Navy or institute handouts that say look at the marvelous thing we've done. Everything is hunky-dory."

Greenberg held up his hands. "Enough," he said. "Go get yourself an Emmy."

O'Gara reached up and gave Greenberg a brisk kiss on the cheek, then strode to her car without another word.

41

Harry was frightened. It was a very deep fear that verged on panic. That was the problem—where does a man with gills flee when what terrifies him is the sea itself?

Lying in the plywood and fiberglass tub, his "traveling box," Harry eyed the stark rock cliffs that dropped into the lapping green sea on either side of the beach. He was in a little cove, a coarse sand beach walled by gray volcanic rock. The water beneath the cliffs was matted with giant bladder kelp, the blades an iridescent green-gold in the sunlight. The primordial landscape heightened Harry's fear. He felt he was the first man to plunge into these waters since the great glaciers melted, flooded the coastal basin, and created the island.

Behind him rose the marine biology station, a squat concrete block building in which his new habitat was housed. He had become restless and depressed with his existence in a succession of tanks since his operation, yet now he longed for the warmth and security of the tank. The ocean a few feet away was cold and forbidding. From his perspective on the beach the water stretched without end to the horizon. Harry dreaded it with the instinctive terror of an ancient, land-born animal. To awaken in an intensive care ward breathing saline solution was one thing. But this sea held the terrors that haunted his nightmares.

"Nervous, Harry?" Steinhardt knelt down beside him. He was wearing a black neoprene wet suit and scuba gear.

Harry nodded. Behind Steinhardt three other divers stood waiting, Steinhardt's assistant Mark Matsuda and two brawny Navy frogmen. In the distance Harry heard the raucous barking of California sea lions, out of sight beyond the rocky point.

"Your nervousness is certainly understandable," Steinhardt said. "But there's nothing to be concerned about. The water temperature and salinity are the same as in the outdoor pool in which we've been exercising. The oxygen content is very high due to the kelp beds and the natural wave and wind action. However, if you feel any signs of anoxia, give me a signal immediately and I'll aerate the water around you." To demonstrate, Steinhardt pushed the purge valve of his air regulator and it emitted a loud blast of air.

"The water's relatively free of pollution, but if it tastes at all unusual to you, swim immediately back to where it last tasted normal."

Harry nodded again. Steinhardt had briefed him a half-dozen times before, but he went over the procedure once more. The three divers overheating under their thick neoprene wet suits, the sweat dripping from their faces, restlessly shifted the weight of their heavy

295

steel scuba tanks. Overhead a gull circled, the white wings dazzling in the sunlight, then settled on the water just inside the cove. The gull bobbed lightly on the swells, looking toward Harry as though it were waiting for him.

Harry had asked not to be carried into the water. he wanted to go in under his own power. He took a last breath of water, then heaved himself over the edge of the tub and slid onto the sand like a reptile.

"Don't try to get up, Harry. Remember what happened before."

Harry couldn't even crawl. He floundered on his belly for a moment, then squirmed forward, his arms and legs churning in an aquatic motion like a three-month-old baby.

"Keep going, Harry. Don't let the sand get in your gills. Keep going."

Harry squirmed rapidly into the water, and as it supported his body weight, he got his hands and knees under him and frantically crawled into the deeper water. The cold was a shock, making him gasp. He hovered a moment, adjusting to the seawater, breathing quickly. He could taste and smell the sand and mud in the water. He gave a great porpoiselike kick and plunged deeper.

The sea floor of sand and scattered rocks sloped steeply, falling away into deep blue shadows. To Harry's left was a jagged rock reef that served as the holdfast for a forest of giant bladder kelp. It grew straight up from the bottom in long, slender, treelike stalks sixty feet high, the sun filtering through the gold-green columns like the light in a cathedral. Steinhardt and Matsuda materialized next to Harry. The old man circled his thumb and forefinger, a hand signal questioning if Harry was all right. Harry repeated the signal and nodded. He pointed toward the kelp, indicating that he wanted to explore in that direction. The two Navy frogmen deployed themselves on both sides as bodyguards.

With each breath of seawater Harry's fear gradually dissolved. The water about him was sunlit and clear and the kelp forest teemed wild life. A swarm of small bass hovered a moment, shimmering flashes of green and yellow, then shied away as Harry swam toward them. The sand underneath him suddenly erupted and five feet of halibut, its wide flat silver body undulating like a shining magic carpet in flight, rose up out of the clouds of sand and took off. For a moment Harry was as startled and frightened as the fish. Then he swam on to continue his exploration.

To his astonishment, Harry suddenly felt as if he had been released from bondage. He was no longer in bleak solitary confinement looking out on the world he could no longer enter. Suddenly he had plunged into an entirely new world, and it was his. The water itself had a cleaner taste, a sharper tang to it than that in the tank.

From behind the kelp stalks, large sheephead fish with blunt red brows peered at the divers curiously and backed away as they approached. Small golden garibaldis boldly swam right up to Harry's face. A bat ray with a three-foot wing span and a face as malevolent as a gargoyle bolted from the kelp and flapped away.

Matsuda made a cautionary sign with his hand and pointed to a crevice in the rocks. Far back in the shadows Harry spotted a moray eel, its beady rattlesnake eyes watching him and its vicious jaws with rows of needle-pointed teeth working as if it were about to rip into him. He made a wide berth of the moray's hole. But Harry had been confined to the sterility of glass and steel tanks in concrete-walled basements for so long that even the dangers of the reef excited him. He felt an exhilarating rush of energy.

Matsuda proved to be an excellent guide, pointing out the tentacled anemones that grew on the rock like yellow and coral flowers and the black sea urchins with their prickly porcupine quills. Tiny nudibranchs, marine animals with horned bodies of startling polka-dotted blue, green, orange, yellow, and purple, slid across the sea floor looking like creatures from Wonderland.

One of the frogmen suddenly seized Harry's arm and gestured with alarm. Harry looked up in time to see a huge dark torpedo-shaped body hurtling at them with frightening speed. There was no time to retreat or escape its attack. When it was just a few feet from them, the creature dipped its fins and banked like a fighter plane veering off from a strafing run. Harry had a quick glimpse of black pop eyes, whiskers, and a mischievous face. A second sea lion immediately followed the first in mock attack and sped back up to the surface.

Matsuda signaled that they should swim back along the reef in the direction they had come. Harry gestured for him to surface so they could talk.

The bedlam of the sea lion rookery just around the point of rocks assailed Harry as he surfaced. "They looked as though they wanted to play," he shouted happily.

Matsuda shook his head. "If you get too near their harem or pups, they get nasty. They bite."

Steinhardt surfaced. "You all right?" he asked with concern.

"Never felt better. I'm in my element."

"Any signs of anoxia?"

"None."

"We must head back now. We're at our midpoint of air."

"Oh, hell. I'm just getting into it."

"Don't swim quite so vigorously," Steinhardt warned. He was breathless. "You may build up an anaerobic condition by working too hard."

Harry looked about. Above his head the cliff rose straight up from the sea. Seen close, the basaltlike rock was not gray but muted shades of orange, umber, and rust. Green lichen rooted in every crevice. Great dripping stains of dried guano randomly painted the top half of the sheer stone face like an in-progress whitewash job. At the cliff's edge a dozen brown pelicans conferred together, their long beaks tucked down against their stately necks. It was a totally different world from the one on the reef, separated by only a transparent film of water, and yet they might have evolved on planets galaxies apart.

Harry suddenly tasted something foul in the water. A yellow-brown blob floated in the swells just a few feet away. Harry cautiously sculled toward it. It was a dead sea lion pup, its tiny pale whiskered face with its closed eyes hanging down in the water.

Matsuda poked at it with a gloved hand. "A quarter of the pups around here are born premature and die."

The dead pup had tawny, almost golden fur, and a fragile, pathetic quality to its expression. "What kills them?" Harry said.

"Chemical pollutants. DDT, lead, mercury."

Harry was shocked. "This far out?"

"It's not just in the water. It has built up in the food chain." Already a school of small opaleyes were nibbling at the seal carcass.

On the swim back and for the rest of the day, the image of the dead pup kept coming back to Harry. It drained the exhilaration he had felt on the reef. The death of those golden-furred pups with their premature, protohuman faces disturbed him.

In the weeks that followed, the Navy had Harry on a backbreaking program. They tested his work performance against that of divers under the same open sea conditions. At frigid depths his strength was gauged by the amount of force he could exert with a torque wrench and his manipulative ability measured by the time it took him to assemble a puzzle of steel rods, nuts, bolts, and washers. He laid out navigational grids on the ocean floor and salvaged with plastic foam a deliberately sunk jet plane. He patched a sheet of steel rolled to simulate the hull of a submarine and constructed an underwater oil wellhead assembly. For Harry, it was tedious and exhausting work. For the Navy, it provided data to compare with that gathered in their SeaLab studies.

Between tests Mark Matsuda taught Harry how to spear fish and they hunted for abalone, scallops, and spiny lobsters along the reef. They came across other dead sea lion pups, but the carcasses they chanced on were only a fraction of the toll. Most of the dead and dying pups were immediately devoured by the blue sharks and great white sharks that stalked the deep channels off Southern California. Harry couldn't shake his foreboding that the pups were an ominous omen. Without knowing why, he felt what was killing them now somehow threatened him.

42

The Santa Ana winds roared in from the Mojave Desert. Out over the sun-scalded griddle of rocks and dry salt lakes great caldrons of air heated up and boiled over the San Gabriel Mountains. The wind rushed into the canyons and funnels and blasted out in terrifying gusts that ripped across the San Fernando Valley, uprooting trees, toppling chimneys, and jackknifing trailer trucks.

As Ruth stepped from the shower, a violent gust shook the house. Perhaps she should cancel her dinner date with Gunther.

No, using the winds would be a lame excuse. The Santa Anas blew this fiercely each fall and the house had yet to be damaged. The children were used to the howling gusts that shook the trees and windows. Brenda, the baby-sitter for the evening, could always get help from Mike and Silvia Levine next door if there were any problems. Ruth had already made sure the neighbors would be at home. The hot blasts of the Santa Anas were not the cause of her nervousness.

As she dried herself Ruth examined her reflection in the full-length bathroom mirror. For years she had avoided looking in this very mirror. She had been full figured as a young woman, but three children had made her breasts pendulous, waist and hips thickened, and her thighs fatty. The long siege of Harry's illness— the worry, depression, loss of appetite—had burned the flesh from her, but the weight loss had not been altogether flattering. There were gaunt hollows in her face, shoulders, and hips.

However, Ruth's new morning regime of gardening, followed by a nude swim—increasingly longer laps of the pool until her arms and legs ached and her precise strokes faltered with fatigue—had had a rejuvenating effect on her. Her sunbaths were deliberately short, a sensuous rest in the sun while her limbs and flesh relaxed under the benign heat. The quality of her skin was such that no amount of baking would tan it. It would merely redden and blister. But under the sun the pimples and rashes "caused by nerves" had cleared up, the wrinkles and shadows under her eyes had dissolved, and the pale color of her skin had changed to the vibrance of old ivory. The exercise had improved her appetite and filled in and contoured the gaunt hollows of her body.

But her increasing energy and physical well-being made Ruth nervous; they awakened desires and hungers she wasn't yet ready to satisfy. And each succeeding meeting with Gunther now made her more anxious. Standing before the mirror by her bath she saw herself naked and vulnerable and there were no lies or deceptions with which she could cloak that vulnerability. Once again the walls and windows shuddered under the hot dry desert-spawned blasts outside. Ruth felt the tremble that passed through the house as if it were a fear that had originated within her and she pulled the towel tightly about her shoulders.

Three times on the drive back from the restaurant Gunther had to detour around a large broken branch or a fallen tree blocking the road. He pulled into the Styleses' driveway and killed the engine, and in the closed sedan the constant drone of the wind in the trees outside sounded like swarms of locusts.

"It was lovely of you to take your client out for dinner again," Ruth said nervously. "Your firm probably won't let you write off our dinners anymore."

"What if I asked you out on a real date?"

"What's a real date?"

"A show or a movie."

Ruth thought a moment. "That would be terrific."

"Really." Gunther's voice had an adolescent excitement. "You mean after fifteen years of my asking you're finally going to go on a date with me."

Ruth laughed. "You've never asked me before."

"The hell I didn't. We were juniors at Southern Cal. I asked you out and you turned me down cold."

"I don't remember you ever asking me out in college."

"My God, she doesn't even remember. I was so dejected I considered suicide. I OD'd on beer but I didn't die. I just threw up. I went into analysis. It ruined my marriage."

"All that. And I don't even remember this traumatic rejection."

"Hell, it didn't even register that I was asking you out. You said you'd ask Harry about it. You thought I was talking about a double date. So then I had to scurry around to find a date. Whom I hardly knew. I was frantic. I asked three other girls and got turned down. So, I told you I was coming down with mononucleosis. It was going around then. Remember? It was sort of a romantic disease in college because you supposedly got it from playing and working too hard."

"You're making all this up."

"I swear it's the gospel. And you don't even remember. I went out and got drunk and married Joan on the rebound."

"You told me you got married after law school."

"And divorced. It was a long rebound. It only proves how long I carried a torch."

Ruth stared out at the dark humming street. There was a bright full moon that cast strong shadows. The trees shaking violently in the hot winds animated the shadows, giving Ruth the feeling that a riot was going on all around her. "Tonight, when I was getting dressed, Brenda asked me if I liked you."

"What did you tell her?"

"I told her, of course I do. You're a very old and very dear friend."

"I don't think that's what she was really asking you."

"No, it wasn't. But I did answer the question she asked. I told her that you and I weren't having a romance, but that in addition to your being a very good friend, a man whose company I enjoyed, I thought you were an attractive sexy man."

"Well! I didn't think I was making that big a hit."

"You have. My sexual fantasies, such as they are,

305

don't run to Erica Jong's zipless fucks or Gothic rapes by tall dark handsome strangers. I like men who are warm, kind of cuddly, and definitely protective."

"Cuddly?"

Ruth laughed. "Oh, yes, you're definitely cuddly."

Gunther thought that over a moment. "Well, then, shall we go to your place or mine?" His tone was playful but there was a serious question beneath it.

"What I'm trying to say in my roundabout way—and I'm doing a really bad job of it—is that we're not going to either my place or yours. Not tonight. Probably not any time in the near future. And it doesn't have anything to do with you, or my attraction or affection for you. It has to do with me. And my own confusion."

"You mean about Harry."

"That's part of it. But it's not just Harry. It concerns me and it's entirely selfish. One of the reasons I was terrified of Harry's dying was that I had grown totally dependent on him. Emotionally and financially."

"But that's perfectly normal."

"Maybe so. But I felt it wasn't only the husband I loved and the father of my children who was dying. I felt I was dying also. That my whole identity was perishing with him, and that terrified me as much as anything. I don't ever want to go through that again."

"You have to make a life for yourself now."

"You're right," Ruth agreed emphatically. "You're absolutely right. And that doesn't mean transferring all my dependence over onto you. And I realize I've almost been guilty of doing just that."

"I haven't been exactly avoiding you."

"Oh, Gunther," Ruth said, "you're sweet and tremendously generous. But I think you're still a little bit smitten with a nineteen-year old girl at USC. If we were to get involved, in a few months I'd just be a clinging middle-aged woman with three children and a tendency to get fat and you'd start backing off. After all I've been through I don't think I could handle that."

"For Chrissakes, Ruth, you're a beautiful, intelligent woman."

"Thanks. Maybe I was fishing for that. But the fact is that I'm still very confused. I still feel a strong loyalty to Harry. I'm not Penelope weaving her endless shroud to stall suitors, waiting twenty years for Ulysses to come home from his adventures. Eventually I'm going to have to come to some sort of realistic compromise with that loyalty to Harry. But not just yet. Not until I've got a good running start on who I am and what I do." She shook her head. "It's such a strange paradox. Here's Harry encased in glass, and he's created this incredible new identity, a whole mythology about himself. Maybe that's why I'm terrified of people finding out who he is. It's not just the effect it might have on the kids and having our lives disrupted and exploited, though God knows that would be unbearable in itself. I'm afraid of being engulfed and drowned in Harry's myth before I know who *I* am."

"Are you going back to teaching?"

"No. I did that before Brenda came, and it was okay at the time. But I have three kids of my own now, and that's all I want to cope with."

"What are you going to do?"

Ruth studied Gunther a moment, smiling. "I'm thinking about going to law school."

"What? Are you serious?"

"Why not? Don't you think I can handle it?"

307

"It's not that. It just comes as a complete surprise." Gunther looked unhappy.

"You really shouldn't be surprised. You've been my inspiration. The problems with my father's estate and then all the business with Harry—the insurance, the house, the negotiations with the institute, and the malpractice suit. Above and beyond my personal involvement, I was fascinated by the law and how it works. Or often how it doesn't work. And understanding it made me feel less helpless."

"But, Ruth, law school's tough. Especially for an— well, let's be realistic—older woman with three kids."

Ruth shrugged. "Why's it so tough? I'm sure I can handle it academically. I got very good grades in college and my brain hasn't deteriorated that much. As for the kids, they'll all be at school." She laughed lightly. "We'll be a house of students. And the kids will just have to help out. Actually, I'll be home more than if I took a full-time teaching job." Ruth hadn't really thought it all out. It was a trial balloon, but the more she argued her case, the more she became convinced.

"There really aren't that many opportunities for older women who want to go back to work again. But people always take lawyers seriouly. Even lady lawyers. Even if I decide not to practice law, it's a great background for just about any business the way things are today."

She paused, and there was silence in the car, filled only by the wind outside, a deep, uneasy, turbulent sound. "Well, damn it, say something."

"I don't know what to say. It all comes as a surprise."

"You sound unhappy."

Gunther shrugged. "Why should I be happy? In two

308

minutes, I've had my fantasy of a romance with the girl of my dreams shattered, and I've been told I'm not only going to lose an old client but gain a tough, beautiful competitor. I already have too few dreams and too much legal competition."

Ruth leaned forward and kissed Gunther full on the mouth. "You and I, whatever happens, I hope we'll always be the best of friends."

She opened the car door and got out. Gunther walked her to the front door, and at the threshold he kissed her good night, a light, affectionate, undemanding kiss.

The temper of the Santa Anas quieted somewhat during the night. In the morning, before she took Christopher to kindergarten, Ruth made a quick survey of the house with the gusts still tugging at her hair and blouse. A few shingles had ripped off the roof. Small branches were strewn about the yard and leaves blanketed the lawn and glutted the pool, but there was no damage to the house. Driving to and from the school Ruth had to detour around power company work crews repairing fallen lines.

Broken tree limbs littered lawns and driveways and several large storefront windows were shattered, the long sharp shards of glass glittering in the morning sunlight. There was still a feeling of riot in the streets and the sound of angry siege in the air itself, pummeling trees and windows.

Once at home Ruth went directly to the study. There was the application to law school to be completed. She had yet to tell Harry. She had no idea how he would react to the idea, and she was apprehensive, but she was determined to go through with it. She had to start a life with its own direction and momentum. The front door chimes interrupted her thoughts.

At the door stood a handsome red-headed woman about her age. She looked very familiar but Ruth couldn't immediately place her.

"Mrs. Styles? Mrs. Harry Styles?" the woman inquired.

Because she was intent on the woman, it was a moment before Ruth noticed two men standing behind her and with a start realized they were a television news crew. The camera was pointed at Ruth, its cannon-sized lens zooming in.

43

Brenda Styles stared down at her textbook and then at Mr. Allen writing on the blackboard, but her mind wasn't on algebra equations. She heard the whispers around her. She looked straight ahead, but out of the corner of her eyes she sensed the other kids in the class staring at her. Mr. Allen, in the throes of transposing his equations, stared at her, distracted for a moment from his X's and Y's by her presence. Brenda blushed and lowered her head in embarrassment. The blood inflamed her cheeks like a scorching wind, and she buried her face in the textbook.

The bell ending the first period clamored, and the classroom erupted with the noise of scraping feet and kids heaving restlessly in their chairs until Mr. Allen dismissed them. In the seat beside Brenda a book slammed shut with a bang. Steven Ike grinned at her. Brenda disliked Steven Ike. He was loud and rough. She tried to avoid him but he always seemed to be bothering her.

Brenda had always been a popular and pretty child,

inheriting her mother's vivid black hair and pale, translucent skin. But she was self-conscious about the braces she wore to correct an overbite. She might have passed through this awkward period quietly except for another inheritance from Ruth—a voluptuousness that was now beginning to emerge. The effect on the boys in the class was galvanizing. They were silly, noisily attentive, sometimes vulgar, or they simply stared at her as if she were a new arrival from some strange land. But they never ignored her. She moved in a constant riot of small embarrassments. Her sensitivity had been heightened by her father's illness and his transformation to Glaucus. Now everyone knew about it.

Steven Ike said something to another boy and they both laughed. Brenda looked away and started leaving the classroom just as Suzi Pryor came up. Suzi was her best friend.

"I tried to call you all night, but the line was always busy," Suzi said excitedly, continuing the conversation she had begun before the class as if there had been no lapse for algebra.

"The phone kept ringing. My mom's lawyer was there and he and my mom were on the phone all night."

"Who was calling?"

"Everybody. TV stations, newspapers, some of my mom and dad's old friends. And just a lot of nuts."

"What did they say, the nuts, I mean?"

"I don't know. I didn't answer the phone. Just weird things. After a while Gunther, my mom's lawyer, just took the phone off the hook and left it off. Today my mom's trying to get an unlisted number."

"Janie Passen saw your mom on TV and called me." There was a note of reproach in Suzi's voice. "Why didn't you tell me Glaucus was your dad? I'm supposed to be your best friend."

"I couldn't. It was supposed to be, you know, a secret."

Suzi didn't quite accept that. Secrets were what best friends were for. "What's it like? I mean if your father has to live underwater all the time."

Brenda looked at her friend. "Hey, I don't want to talk about it all that much."

Suzi was hurt. "Well, pardon me." She turned and walked away.

Brenda went to her locker to get her books for the next class. Suddenly Steven Ike and two other boys surrounded her.

"Hey, it's Minnie the Mermaid," Ike said loudly for the whole hallway to hear. The boys laughed, and Brenda again felt the surge of blood to her face.

"She's growing gills too," one of the other boys said.

"Those are her titties, stupid."

The hot rush of blood flared to anger and Brenda swung the book in her hand at Steven Ike with all her strength. It caught the boy across the cheek and sent him reeling back.

Brenda whirled and fled down the hall through a crowd of astonished faces. She bolted down two flights of steps to the exit and out the door and didn't stop running until she was off the school grounds. For the first time she looked back. Nobody had followed her.

She tried to call home from a gas station pay phone, but the line was busy. She began walking home, struggling not to cry, staring at the ground. She was still a block away when she saw the crowd. There were groups of people standing on the lawn and sidewalk in front of her house. As she approached she saw several TV news camera crews standing around, apparently waiting for something. She was frightened but she kept walking toward them. There was no place else to go. All her friends were in school.

Brenda recognized Mrs. Levine, the next-door neighbor, talking to a red-headed woman. Mrs. Levine spotted her and pointed. "There's the Styles girl now." She waved. "Brenda, honey."

A man with a camera blocked her way. The red-headed woman was suddenly at her side. "Brenda, how does it feel to have Glaucus as a father?" She pointed a microphone at the girl.

"I'm very proud of my father," Brenda said slowly, primly, repeating what her mother had said. "I think he's very brave." She tried to walk on, but a second and third camera converged on her.

"When was the last time you saw your father?"

"I don't remember. I think it was a couple of months ago. Excuse me, please."

"Do you swim in the tank with him?"

"No. Excuse me, please. My mother's expecting me."

But the crowd about her grew thicker and more suffocating. There were people she had never seen before running across the lawn toward her, shoving and staring at her and gawking into the TV cameras.

"Who's that?" someone asked.

"I think it's one of the fish freak's kids."

"I have to see my mother. Excuse me, please," Brenda pleaded. She was close to tears. She kept moving toward the front door. She made the steps. The door was locked. She fumbled for her key and dropped it. It disappeared in the crowd of feet that pursued her.

Brenda grouped for the bell. "Ma, it's me, Brenda. Let me in." Microphones mounted on poles like spearheads jabbed at her. Brenda cried out again for her mother. She pounded on the door in desperation. "Let me in, please!" Brenda screamed and began to sob.

The door suddenly flew open and Brenda stumbled inside into her mother's outstretched arms. Ruth slammed the door shut and bolted it, then held her daughter tight as the girl cried uncontrollably.

44

Harry Styles hovered motionless in his tank and only the slow clenching and unclenching of his fists betrayed his emotions. His habitat on the island was considerably roomier and more elaborately equipped than his tank at the Institute of Oceanography had been. The new accommodations had been built specifically to house him and not pelagic fish. There was an organized exercise area with a stationary bicycle, barbells, and spring-loaded pulleys. On the wall a target was mounted and beneath it hung a spear gun with which he practiced his marksmanship. And there was a small library of books with waterproofed pages. But it was the six o'clock news report on TV that now mesmerized him.

The reporter, a red-headed woman, stood in the driveway of Harry's home, and behind her a mob of newsmen, cameras, and spectators was crowded on *his* front lawn. "For the second day in a row a stakeout of reporters and just plain curious sightseers laid siege to the Styleses' home here in Encino," the woman reported in an excited contralto voice.

"The crowds here have grown considerably since Channel Three exclusively reported that the fish-man whom scientists have dubbed John Glaucus is actually Harry Styles, a former aerospace engineer with a wife and three children." There was pride in the woman's expression and voice as though she had taken personal possession of Harry and his family.

The TV picture cut away to close-ups of the milling crowd. Harry was seized by their expressions. Most were utterly blank as if waiting for someone to entertain them. But others peered about, petulant and vaguely angry. A great many, mostly teenagers, simply joked about and poked one another. A small cluster of men, neatly dressed in white shirts and ties, picketed on the sidewalk with sharply lettered signs that read: "'God created man in His own image.' Genesis 1:27" and "Thou shall not experiment with Human Beings."

The camera focused on the house. The windows were all curtained. The voice of the woman reporter narrated the film: "Mrs. Styles has barricaded herself in her home and refused to talk to reporters since her brief appearance yesterday. The three Styles children today stayed home from school."

Harry felt enraged and humiliated. The sanctuary of his home was being violated before his eyes and he was helpless—and he was the cause of it all. He wanted to rush out and beat away the sensation seekers, vandals, and reporters mobbing his front lawn. But he could do nothing.

The camera had now invaded his backyard. The swimming pool was covered with leaves and twigs, empty except for an inflated plastic fish, one of

Christopher's toys that bobbed listlessly among the debris.

The camera abruptly cut to the front door, where Gunther Marx emerged, followed immediately by Brenda, David, Christopher, and Ruth. They were all carrying luggage, except for David, who cradled Groucho in his arms. Gunther carried a large suitcase in front of him like a battering ram to force his way through the crowd to a car parked in the driveway. Ruth had a vague smile frozen on her face. She ignored the questions shouted at her by the reporters and hauled Christopher along by the hand. The child looked up at the crush of people with a wide-eyed, frightened expression. The woman reporter knelt with her microphone to ask Christopher a question, but she was shoved by the crowd and knocked down, sprawling out of sight in the jam. The news film suddenly became shaky, the photographer himself now being knocked about in the melee. Two policemen wrestled with the crowd to clear a path. Ruth disappeared and then Harry caught a glimpse of her pushing the children into the sedan in the driveway.

"Late in the afternoon the whole Styles family made their first appearance, and possibly their last for a while," the report continued, but Harry no longer heard it. How often before had he dispassionately watched the same spectacle on TV involving people who were either strangers or celebrities. But this was *his family,* and now each scene was a torment.

The sedan inched out of the driveway, forcing its way through the cameramen and the pickets. As the car pulled away, Christopher pressed his face and hands against the rear window and the camera focused on him. The awed and frightened face of Harry's son peered out at his father, growing more and more distant until the boy faded from sight.

"Harry, we have some very special guests here to see you."

For a moment Harry was confused. He had been so stirred up that he had not noticed Buckley and two other men enter the habitat room. The three now stood side by side at the view window smiling cordially at him. One was an Oriental.

"Harry, this is John Chambers of Standard Oil and Mr. Hiroshi Tokugawa of the Japan National Oil Corporation. They're very impressed with your work." Buckley smiled at the two men as if sharing a private joke. "Especially with your construction of that oil wellhead assembly at depth."

Harry swam to the window and began talking excitedly but no sound came forth. "You'll have to put on your Hydro-Voice, Harry," Buckley said. "We can't read your lips."

Harry was in the habit of taking off the electronic larynx when alone because the strap chafed his neck. It was lying by the TV set. He dove for it and clasped the box to his throat. "Where the hell are my wife and kids? I want Ruth here!"

His charged angry voice exploded in the habitat room. The three men looked at one another in bewilderment.

Harry gestured toward the TV set. "Did you see what those crowds and reporters are doing? My God, they're destroying my home!" Harry slumped into a chair. "It's my fault," he muttered. "All my fault. I'm to blame." He sat hunched over, staring at the floor with stricken eyes.

Ruth flew to the island. She stood on the other side of the glass, and with tears streaming down her face she told Harry she wanted a divorce.

Harry felt as if he had been kicked in the stomach. He stared in silence at his wife. How long had they been unable to touch or hold each other? Harry had lost track of time. Now he measured the time not in months or years but in the anguish and hopelessness in Ruth's face. Finally his voice returned, and he pleaded, "Give it a chance, Ruth."

"A chance for what, Harry? What chance do we have together? Just tell me one. Just one. I'll cling to it. I'll pray for it."

Harry was silent. There was no hope he could offer her.

"Dr. Steinhardt tells me you're now perfectly healthy," Ruth said. "And they have a heavy schedule of important research work lined up for you. I have my own life to lead, Harry. And so do the children. This has been a nightmare for us."

"All the reporters hounding you. The TV. All the publicity. That'll settle down in a little while."

"And then what, Harry? Then what will the children and I have to look forward to?"

Once again Harry was silent. He had no answers to his wife's questions. No hopes to soften her despair. "What is it you want to do?" he asked finally.

Ruth shook her head. "I don't know. I haven't had a chance to work it all out. Right now I just have to get away from it all for a while. I spoke to my mother yesterday. The kids can start school there without losing any time."

"Colorado?"

Ruth nodded. "It will be good for the kids, Harry. Chrissy's having nightmares. He wakes up screaming. And the nightmares are about you."

"Colorado," Harry repeated. He said it as if she were going to the moon.

"We'll all always love you, Harry," Ruth said softly. "You'll always be a great hero to us."

After she had left, Harry stood slumped against the wall of the tank as if all the strength had ebbed from his body and he had to support himself. Once he had accused Ruth of thinking *only* about their family life. At the time he had been feverish with the idea of setting a mark. Of breaking scientific ground where no man had been before. And he had done it.

Now his sharp words to Ruth came back to haunt him. Even at its most shining moment his triumph had always had a black nimbus about it. He could never be with his family again, but he had consumed his despair like fuel. It became his energy. It was the warp and woof of what was regarded as his courage.

Harry felt no anger toward Ruth. She was merely formalizing the truth of their life. She was ending nothing but the illusion of their marriage and family. But that illusion had sustained Harry. It was the last tie to his own humanity.

"We'll all always love you, Harry. You'll always be a great hero to us."

Ruth had never looked more beautiful or in more

pain. Harry remembered the last time he had seen his children. David's and Brenda's awed, frightened faces still pained him when he visualized them. He once again heard Chrissy's terrified screams echoing off the concrete walls of the tank room. Harry leaned his head against the glass and wept. His convulsing throat made no sound. His contorted features, further distorted by the water and glass, were those of a grieving clown.

In his grief he pounded on the glass wall. The pounding was at first slow and senseless, then quickly built to fury. The glass cage itself became the object of his rage. His blows, heavy and violent, resounded through the building.

Two alarmed Navy guards came running into the room. "Hey, what's the matter?"

Harry kept pounding. His blows visibly shook the glass walls.

"Knock that off. You're going to break it."

The glass cracked. On the next blow it exploded. Thousands of gallons of water crashed into the room, breaking like a great wave, lifting up and throwing Harry and the two guards before it. The three men were slammed into the wall, and then they were swept back in a surge and crashed into the heavy steel electronic console. The monitoring equipment and electric fuse boxes shorted out, exploded, and flared. The lights went out.

The dark water flooded the room several feet deep, then began receding. One of the guards struggled to his feet, stumbled back down into the water, and fought to his feet again. The other guard lay unconscious face down in the water. The first man grabbed him and tried to hold the other's head clear, all the while coughing and choking for breath himself.

The water pouring through the open door rapidly drained the room. It left Harry sprawled unconscious on the concrete floor, the puddle by his head quickly reddening with blood.

45

Steinhardt, working late in his second-floor office, heard the pounding, but couldn't identify the sound. He listened for a moment, puzzled, and then went to the door. The sound of the tank bursting was a dull explosion. Steinhardt's first thought was that one of the steel bottles of compressed oxygen in the tank room had exploded. He hurried down the steps and on the first floor was confronted by water surging through the narrow corridor like a flash flood in a creek bed. He plunged in and reached the tank room in great splashing strides.

Near the door a Navy guard knelt over the unconscious body of a second sailor, trying to rouse him. The tank room was dark, but by the light from the hallway Steinhardt spotted Harry lying face down and seemingly lifeless on the floor. He ran to him and groped for a pulse. It was rapid but strong. At a glance Harry's head injury appeared to be a scalp wound, bloody but not immediately dangerous. He was at the moment more likely to die of anoxia than blood loss or shock. Steinhardt searched about frantically. Harry's traveling tub, the box in which he was carried to the beach, stood on its gurney alongside the wall. It was always filled with salt water to prevent it from drying out. Steinhardt shoved it alongside Harry, but he couldn't lift the sodden deadweight of his body. "Help me get him into the water," he shouted at he Navy guard.

The man looked up, dazed.

"Doc, Johnson needs help. He's out like a light."

"This man's dying. I'll get to your friend in a moment." The authority in Steinhardt's voice immediately brought the sailor to his side, and together they wrestled Harry into the tub. Steinhardt forced open Harry's mouth and pulled his tongue out to open the passage to his gill clefts. There was a spasm and a gasping noise as Harry sucked in water and air.

Steinhardt shoved the gurney into the lighted corridor. He turned on the tank's aerator, then examined the scalp wound as swarms of bubbles wreathed about Harry's neck and shoulders. The blood was oozing rather than actively bleeding. He checked Harry's eyes. The pupils constricted quickly in the blaze of the bright overhead light. Harry's pulse was still strong but slower now. Steinhardt tried to estimate the time that had elapsed from when he'd heard the tank burst until they had gotten Harry into the traveling tub. It seemed an eternity; it couldn't have been more than a few minutes. Harry's respiration now appeared to be normal, but Steinhardt had no way of telling if there was any brain damage due to prolonged lack of oxygen.

He turned reluctantly from Harry to the unconscious sailor. There was a large swelling at his hairline. His breathing was shallow, his pulse slow. His pupils reacted more slowly to the light than Harry's. Steinhardt opened the unconscious man's shirt and jabbed his knuckles into his breastbone. The man moaned and then fell unconscious again.

Steinhardt looked at the other man. "Are you all right?"

"Yes, sir. I'm just wet and a little shook."

"Bring Dr. Morrison here immediately. Tell him to bring two I.V.'s. *Two I.V.'s*. Do you know where Dr. Morrison's room is?"

"Yes, sir. Captain Morrison."

The man ran down the corridor, and Steinhardt turned back to Harry. To his surprise, Harry's eyes were opened and focused on him.

"Harry, are you all right?"

For several moments there was no reaction. Harry just stared at Steinhardt. Then he nodded almost imperceptibly and said, "I'll live."

The next day a team of Seabees flew out to the island from Port Hueneme to repair the habitat. They replaced the glass panel, reinforcing it with a steel plate.

On the same plane the psychiatrist Shapiro arrived at Steinhardt's urgent summons, but Harry refused to talk to him.

"What the hell can he do for me?" Harry yelled at Steinhardt, the deep electronic voice resonating in the concrete grotto of the tank room. "Can he make me walk on the land and breathe air again like a man? Can he bring back my wife and children to me? If he can do that, I'll talk to him. But if he's only going to use his psychiatric and psychological bullshit to try to reconcile me to this existence, then he's wasting his breath. I don't want to talk about it anymore. It's all been said. We have work to do. Let's finish it up. Just keep me busy." The last was said without anger, almost as a plea.

Steinhardt nodded. As he started to leave the tank room, Harry said, "If you want to bring me someone, Karl, find me one of the priests or rabbis who's worrying about my soul. A bearded messianic man who can lay his hands on my chest and make me whole again. Tell him my soul is still here, Karl. I know because it goes back and forth between hell and limbo, and I'm in agony."

Steinhardt spoke to Shapiro. "He's absolutely right, you know," the psychiatrist said. "There's really nothing I can do for him. Work! Your research. That's the only thing that gives his life meaning and purpose. But you'll have to watch him closely. He's suicidal. It's not uncommon in transplant cases. The body ego has been violated."

Steinhardt remembered that Bernstein had told him the same thing. But it had been Bernstein who had destroyed himself in the end. "Even before his wife's last visit he was restless and depressed," Steinhardt said. "Now his moods are swinging wildly out of control. It's not just a case of postoperative manic-depression. It never has been. And it's only going to get worse."

Shapiro nodded. "We're going to have to watch him very carefully," he repeated.

*   *   *

327

Two weeks later, at the completion of the sea trials, Harry was flown from the island to Los Angeles. Buckley and the Navy had organized a demonstration to show Harry off to a specially invited group of industrial and political leaders. Harry was in a manic mood, showing an unusual interest in his surroundings, bobbing his head out of the tub to peer around.

"They look like great black birds gobbling up the land," Harry said.

The tub was lying at the end of a pier in Los Angeles harbor waiting for transportation. Just across the channel, right at the waterline, there was a battery of oil pumps. The bird's-head-shaped counterweights constantly bobbed up and down at the end of a seesawing beam as if they were pecking at the ground.

"Yes, don't they," Steinhardt replied. There was something ravenous in the stark black silhouettes. But it was Harry's imagery of great black birds of prey that struck him. It was perhaps symptomatic. The peaks and valleys of Harry's moods had become much greater in the past week.

"Jesus, look at all this shit," Harry exclaimed. His gesture and his contempt seemed to embrace all of Los Angeles harbor. Directly ahead of them, at the southwest corner of the harbor, the sunken wreckage of a tanker that had blown up at dockside was being salvaged. At an adjacent dock a towering conveyor belt transferred iron ore from a barge to the top of a dark mountain of ore the color of dried blood just beyond the pier. All around them the water was streaked with oil refracting the light into greasy rainbows.

"It's not exactly our pretty, pristine little kelp-strewn island, is it, Karl?"

"It's a heavily industrialized port," Steinhardt answered.

"It's more than that. It's the belching factory town, refinery, slag heap, pipeline terminal, butcher shop, and cannery for the sea."

"I hadn't thought of it in those terms, but yes, I suppose it is."

Out in the center of the harbor, floating cranes and pile drivers were constructing the foundation for the giant new supertanker terminal.

"It's just the beginning," Harry said. "Just ask Buckley."

"Yes, Buckley's quite eloquent on the subject of the exploration of the sea."

Harry was silent a moment, and then began to sing.

> *"Many's the night*
> *I spent with Minnie the Mermaid*
> *Down at the bottom of the sea.*
> *T'was down among the corals*
> *That I lost my morals.*
> *Gee, but she was good to me,*
> *Oh, baby.*

"That damn song keeps running through my mind," Harry said. "It's an old college fraternity drinking song. I haven't thought of it for years. Now it keeps running through my head. I think I'll sing it to all of Buckley's VIP's out there. What do you think of that idea?"

"I think it would be quite lively."

> *"Many's the night*

With the pale moon shining
Down on our seaweed bungalow
That I pitched and wooed her . . ."

Harry's voice faltered as if he had forgotten the rest of the words and he fell silent. Steinhardt exchanged a troubled look with Mark Matsuda.

Matsuda was dressed in a black diving suit, but he had the thick airless jacket unzipped for ventilation. His air tank, mask, and flippers were at the foot of the pier, where Buckley was briefing two Navy frogmen. They all simultaneously looked down at their wrist-watches, apparently synchronizing them. Then Buckley strode toward Steinhardt.

"Sorry for the delay, Karl. Just getting everyone coordinated so that Glaucus rises up from the depths of the sea at eleven o'clock on the button." He bent down toward Harry. "Got your speech all ready, Glaucus?" In the past several weeks Buckley had begun to address Harry as Glaucus, as though the institute director had forgotten the man and now spoke only to the myth he had created.

Harry nodded and smiled. Steinhardt thought there was something disturbing about that smile.

"Great!" Buckley exclaimed enthusiastically. "You look just great."

Harry had on a new diving suit of vivid cobalt blue. It had been specially developed by the Navy to retain body heat during prolonged work at frigid depths and was made of layers of rubber and a new synthetic polymeric fabric. Harry's dive that day wasn't to be particularly deep or cold, but Buckley had insisted he wear the new suit. Its contoured bulkiness gave the illusion that

330

Glaucus was twice as brawny as even the muscular Navy frogmen escorting him.

Buckley picked up the pole spear that lay alongside the tub. "Don't forget to hold this up high," he said. The sun glistened off the three-pronged brass spearhead. "It's a great prop for the photographers. Symbolic as hell." The spear was, in actuality, a deceptively simple but effective underwater weapon—a slender six-foot-long steel shaft with a sling of rubber tubing at the butt end. Buckley hooked the sling on his thumb and cocked the spear by stretching the rubber loop as far as it would go while gripping the shaft in the same hand. His hand, in essence, became both the trigger and the barrel of a short-range spear gun. Buckley sighted along the line of the pole and his outstretched arm at an imagined target out in the harbor, then eased his grip and put down the spear.

"It's going to be an important day. A very significant day." Buckley nodded his head emphatically at Harry. He turned to Steinhardt. "We're running a bit behind schedule. We'll have to leave for the boat right now."

Steinhardt looked down at Harry. To his astonishment, Harry reached up and seized his hand and forearm, gripping it and squeezing it in both of his, as he had done once before, at the end of the pressure tests. Then he released Steinhardt's arm and slipped below the water that obscured the intense emotion in his face like a veil.

"I should be in the water with him," Steinhardt said as Buckley hurried him from the pier. There was a gray Navy sedan waiting for them at the foot of the pier. A uniformed driver held the door open.

"You'll be infinitely more valuable on board with

331

me. The oil men, congressmen, and others have specifically asked to talk to you. You've been avoiding them, Karl. Mark and the Navy men can take care of Glaucus in the water."

"Are all these military bodyguards really necessary?"

"They're just a routine precaution. After the incident when he smashed the tank, we don't know what could happen. I'll trust to your discretion, Karl, not to mention that to anyone here today."

The car sped along the access road to the Navy piers. On their right a nuclear guided-missile cruiser was moored. Its block-shaped monolithic superstructure loomed oppressively over Steinhardt. It suggested nothing of the sea or the wind, as if it sprang from a technology totally indifferent to nature. "I'm very concerned about Harry's state of mind," Steinhardt said.

"He'll be all right. He's always happier when he's in the ocean."

You're a fool, Steinhardt almost blurted out. But he remained silent. He slumped back in the car seat brooding. Something was about to happen. Steinhardt knew that with a certainty that was as inevitable as the tide. But he didn't know what it was nor how to prevent it.

"Is this carnival really necessary?" Steinhardt asked.

"*A carnival?* Yes, I suppose it'll be a celebration of sorts."

"What are we celebrating?" Steinhardt asked with an edge to his voice. "That Harry has become a virtual prisoner of the Navy. That all our research may be classified rather than published."

"I don't think you need concern yourself anymore with the Navy's restrictions," Buckley said.

"Oh. Do we have a wealthy new sponsor?"

Buckley nodded.

Steinhardt was taken by surprise. "Who are they?"

"A consortium of oil companies. Since Harry's sea trials, several corporations are interested in financing our research. I'm thinking of setting up an association of several companies to jointly fund an independent foundation."

Steinhardt was puzzled. "I don't understand the oil companies' interest. They have remote engineering systems for their sort of work."

Buckley shook his head. "In a subsea oil well there's no adequate substitute for a man underwater to do the final work. To make inspections and repairs. It's the oil companies who've been behind all the accelerated development of diving technology in the last decade. At least since the Arab oil embargo. That was the critical episode. Before that, we had little experience in working at depths greater than four hundred feet. Soon the wellheads will be a mile deep." He looked pointedly at Steinhardt. "We're not talking about pure scientific research now, Karl. We're talking about the immediate flow of billions of dollars of fuel. And a potential for incalculable disaster that may be prevented."

Steinhardt thought of the great black birds of prey devouring the land and said nothing.

"Quite frankly, Karl, there'll be more research money available to us than we'll know what to do with."

"That should serve your ambitions well," Steinhardt said in a withering voice.

"My ambitions!" Buckley was outraged. He stared hard at Steinhardt, and he was so tense with anger that

the scientist was intimidated. *"Goddammit,* I'm sick and tired of being cast as the convenient villain by you and Ruth Styles. I didn't perform the goddamn gill operation. And if I had known about it, I would have done everything in my power to stop it. But if it wasn't for me, Harry Styles would probably be dead now. Or a vegetable on some life-support system in a hospital back ward. You'd be disgraced and your career at an end. And the Styles family would be destitute. But I managed to maneuver the university and the Navy to support you and Harry. And at great risk to my own career. Belive me, it wasn't easy. You're not the most popular man with your colleagues."

Buckley rubbed his face with his hands. "Christ," he said, but the word was more a sigh than a curse. "Maybe that's the price of working with genius. Even Einstein's colleagues at Princeton considered him a heretic and an old fool." Buckley studied Steinhardt a moment, then said, "I probably shouldn't admit this to you, but, what the hell, it's time you knew the facts of life outside the ivory tower. I deliberately leaked the original news story on Glaucus."

"Why?"

"To protect you. To protect the institute. It was all bound to come out. And the press would have made you look like the mad scientist from a 1930s horror movie. This way I was able to control the story."

Buckley turned away and stared out the window of the car. Warships and submarines were tied up at the piers they passed, and out beyond them, in the middle of the harbor, a giant container ship loaded with Japanese automobiles waited to unload. "I suppose you're right," Buckley said softly. "I do have ambitions. Both for myself and the institute. That's not abnormal, unethical, or un-American. But whatever personal ambitions I have, they pale to insignificance beside your ambitions or those of Harry Styles. And I'd never do anything that would so devastate and hurt him as what his wife has done."

Everything Buckley said was true, thought Steinhardt. The two men rode the rest of the way to the ship in silence.

The *Richard Kenneth* was a handsome modern oceanographic research vessel the size of a Navy destroyer but broader in the beam. On an expedition it normally carried twenty-five scientists, but this day its supercargo numbered twice that many people. They bunched on the wide afterdeck bundled against the crisp morning air in a motley array of sweaters, windbreakers, mackinaws, yachting gear, and military surplus canvas jackets like weekend fishermen.

Mr. Hiroshi Tokugawa of the Japan National Oil Corporation—identified by the name tag pinned to his breast—wore a yellow nylon ski parka that reflected the sunlight so blindingly that Steinhardt was forced to squint.

"This operation, in a normal man with lungs, it would be reversible, yes?" Mr. Tokugawa asked.

"We have reversed dogs and rats back to air breathing," Steinhardt acknowledged. "But there are paradoxically greater dangers in the return than in the original gill breathing. The animals often develop pneumonia or their lungs collapse. What further complications might develop due to prolonged inundation of the lungs we simply don't know. We'd have to do considerably more experiments with animals. For instance, we don't know whether we should fill the lungs with a Ringer's solution and then surgically seal them. Or whether we should let them ventilate naturally with seawater. These would be the next logical experiments."

The next logical experiments. The phrase came as a shock to Steinhardt. He had subconsciously already projected the next areas to be investigated. His scientific training had programmed his mind for forty years and now it automatically fed back the next logical sequence.

"The gills, they can be removed, yes?" Mr. Tokugawa asked.

"It would require major surgery and reconstruction. All of which has its own inherent risks. But, yes, they could be removed."

"All new diving technology has inherent risks," Bob Spann of Spann Engineering Associates said. "Hell, if an air hose broke in the old hard-hat diving, the pressure would mash the diver right up into his helmet. Couldn't scrape him out. We'd have to bury him in the helmet."

Mr. Tokugawa blinked at Bob Spann as if trying to figure out if he had interpreted him correctly. Then he looked back expectantly at Steinhardt.

Steinhardt had nothing more to say. He searched the water to the north where the headlands of Palos Verdes and San Pedro thrust up above the brown haze. The entrance to Los Angeles harbor was already veiled by smog. The launch that was supposed to bring Harry and the Navy divers into position was nowhere in sight.

"We need a coalition of the universities, industry, the federal government, and the military." Buckley's emphatic voice carried across the deck. "We now have a unique opportunity to effectively exploit the two-thirds of the earth that up to now has been denied to us. We can carry out manned underseas activity to its limits. Not just oil but mining and agriculture also."

Steinhardt had no doubts about whom Buckley had in mind to head that mighty coalition. But who was he to criticize Buckley? The institute director was right—it was Steinhardt's and Harry's ambitions that had been outrageous. He turned to see the person Buckley was addressing. Buckley hovered over a shorter, balding, middle-aged man whom Steinhardt recognized as head of the U.S. Senate subcommittee on science and technology. "A fascinating vision." The bald head nodded. "Fascinating vision."

"It's not just a vision, Senator," Buckley persisted. "It's something we must start implementing immediately."

"I'm anxious to see your man-in-the-sea Glaucus."

Buckley checked his watch, then peered aft. At the stern of the ship a diving platform of steel grating had been rigged at the water level. "He should be here any moment now," Buckley said, then impatiently rechecked his watch.

Matsuda surfaced first, his black hooded head breaking water a few yards behind the ship. He scrambled aboard the platform and moved immediately out of the way. There was a shout about the deck and everyone jammed to the after railing. In the prerehearsed military drill the two Navy frogmen surfaced alongside the platform and swung onto it. They knelt

337

one on each side of the platform, each flourishing a pole spear as if it were a battle standard.

Between them Harry now surfaced. His blond hair and beard were a full thick mane that sparkled in the sunlight like wet gold. His cobalt blue wet suit shimmered. In his right hand he held the three-pronged bronze spear. With his left he gripped the edge of the platform, holding himself full shouldered out of the water. The effect was like King Neptune himself rising. Harry stared intently at the crowd on the deck, and they fell silent.

"I'm a new form of man, one that scientists, philosophers, and the writers of myths have speculated on since the dawn of mankind." Harry's voice was powerful and resonant. "In this age of technology I was an inevitability. Whether I am a man of the future depends on mankind's need to explore, exploit, and plunder the sea as you increasingly exhaust the resources of the earth."

Steinhardt glanced at Buckley. The blood had drained from the man's face and he gaped at Harry. This was certainly not the speech he had written.

"Some think I'm a monster. Perhaps I am. A monster in the original meaning of the word. I'm a warning from the gods." Harry's eyes searched the crowd as if seeking particular faces. "There are those who believe I'm an unnatural man. I don't know what's natural or unnatural for man anymore. But I do know that I now live an unnatural life among you. My family, all that I love and once lived for, is lost to me. In these extraordinary events, I've been a willing collaborator. And there's no one to blame."

His gaze settled on Steinhardt. "Our work is done,

Karl," he said, addressing the old man directly in a softer voice. "We've each achieved what we set out to do." He glanced briefly at Buckley and then back at Steinhardt. "The rest was to be exploitation and empire building. I've no desire or will anymore to go on with the work."

"What the hell's going on?" Morrison barreled his way to the rail between Steinhardt and Buckley.

Steinhardt acknowledged what Harry had said with a silent nodding of his head.

Harry blinked and his eyes left Steinhardt and once again swept the faces at the rail. "I no longer have a life among you," he said. "I'm going to whatever fate awaits me in the sea."

He reached for his throat mike, unstrapped it but held it pressed to his throat. "I guess I have nothing more to say to you," he said. He threw the voice box at Buckley. The director, rather than trying to catch it, threw up his arms as if warding off a blow. The mechanical larynx crashed on the deck at his feet, shattering and spewing out its electronic innards.

With a powerful kick and thrust of his arms Harry arced up out of the water like a great leaping fish. His body slapped down with a tremendous splash and he dove deep, the blue of his wet suit dissolving into the blue depths.

Morrison was the first to act. "Get the hell after him!" he bellowed at the two Navy divers on the platform below him. "Bring him back!"

Matsuda grabbed one of the frogmen by the arm. "Let the poor son of a bitch alone. Let him finally be." The Navy man wrenched away from Matsuda, sending him sprawling on the platform. Then the two divers sprang into the water. They hovered on the surface a moment getting their bearings. Then one of them pointed down and they simultaneously plunged after Harry.

It was not difficult for Steinhardt to reconstruct what followed, the immutable biophysics of tragedy. A few miles out from the Los Angeles harbor, where the ship was stationed, the gently sloping coastal shelf steepened, dropping three thousand feet into the San Pedro basin. In the first exultant, angry, mad rush of his escape, Harry dove deep. He was unaware he was being pursued. The two frogmen, impelled by Morrison's frantic order, doggedly followed. They were already too deep for safety when Harry first heard the harsh rasping and sucking sounds of their air regulators resounding in the water. He whirled about and gestured to them to go back. The two frogmen swarmed down on him like predatory creatures. One grabbed his arms and the other gripped him about the legs. Harry wildly wrestled and kicked free. The two were instantly on him again. Desperate, Harry jabbed at one, then the other with the butt end of his pole spear. But underwater the blows were ineffectual. The frogmen warded them off with their arms and grappled with Harry. The three frantically struggling men continued to sink rapidly. They were now over three hundred feet deep, in the realm of nitrogen narcosis, and the gases in their blood drugged the divers like opium. Their grip on Harry weakened. Their clutching became uncoordinated. Harry yanked his arms and legs free and broke away. One of the frogmen took a clumsy swipe at him, missed, and laughed in a burst of bubbles. He took the air regulator out of his mouth, looked at it curiously, then held it out to Harry as if offering a breath. He was entirely in the grip of narcosis.

Harry frantically signaled to him to swim back to the surface, but the diver just stared at his air gauge as if he were having trouble reading it. The other man, befuddled, sank beneath them.

Harry kicked down to him. He released the catch on the man's weight belt and dropped the lead weights to make him more buoyant, then yanked the emergency cord on the life vest to inflate it. In the squeeze of the great pressure it only partially inflated. The diver watched Harry, unresisting. His eyes behind the plate of his face mask were unfocused. Harry checked the air gauge. The needle flickered just above the zero mark. The divers had exhausted most of their air on the long swim to the boat. They didn't have enough left to make the slow ascent to the surface. It was a choice between drowning and the bends. The first was certain death. The other an agonizing probability.

Harry yanked the man's head back to straighten his windpipe and reduce the chance of an embolism, then pushed him up toward the surface hundreds of feet above them.

The other diver watched Harry and apparently something in his numbed mind clicked. He fumbled with the catch of his weight belt, dropped it, and yanked the cord on his life vest. Then he ripped off his face mask. There was nothing Harry could now do for them, and he watched helplessly as both men rapidly rose, their arms limp at their sides, their faces upturned like two black angels ascending to a brighter heaven.

*   *   *

"Will the divers be able to capture him?" someone askd Steinhardt. They were acting as though Harry were an escaped prisoner or a wild animal, Steinhardt thought.

At that moment one of the Navy frogmen burst to the surface. He popped halfway out of the water, then settled, floating in his Mae West with his head slumped forward. There was a cry on the ship just as the second diver popped up.

Matsuda leaped into the water. "Give him a hand," Morrison ordered a group of Navy men clinging to the platform. "We've got to get those men to a decompression chamber immediately."

In the water Matsuda felt for a pulse in one diver's neck. From the deck Steinhardt could see the stream of blood from the man's ears and nose staining Matsuda's hand and washing away in the seawater.

46

Along the Southern California coast the subsurface waters move up the shoreline, a great languid submarine current flowing northwest from the Mexican border to Point Conception. Harry drifted in that current. With his yellow mane and wild beard streaming, he sailed the subsea like a loony Neptune, still clutching his shining brass-headed trident. His mind was as adrift as his body on the offshore current.

In the solitary confinement of his tank, the sea stretching endlessly beyond the walls of his prison cell had called to Harry. In the last few weeks he had suffered from manic depression. At the heights of his mania he had heard the sirens murmuring of sunlight beaming through the golden cathedral columns of kelp and bursting in rainbows from iridescent fish. The sea was a world to which he alone of men had access and he had felt supremely superhuman. He would be the Christ wandering in a dazzling wilderness.

But his mood had been followed by deep depression, when Harry felt tortured by self-blame, guilt, and fantasies of suicide. But he was not insane. A madman loses touch with reality. It was the reality of his life that Harry had to escape.

In the nightmare of his depression the dark sea had whispered to him. He imagined himself drawn down fathom after fathom into the abyss until the darkness, the numbing cold, the silence, and the heavy black water finally crushed him, and he became one with the sea, all his pain and loneliness quieted.

The divers had checked his plunge into the depths of the ocean. His struggle with them had exhausted him. The mania was spent, but now he no longer had any desire or will. Harry simply drifted. The current carried him beyond San Pedro and Palos Verdes and up along the arc of glaring white sands that sprawled from Redondo Beach to Malibu.

The two divers were either dead or crippled—Harry felt that tragedy ruptured whatever fragile ties he might have had to other men. He was now an outlaw. An outcast.

Harry drifted. He was suspended, weightless, in a great blue void that had neither top nor bottom nor sides but only shadings of light. Above him the blue was pale and below it deepened to midnight. Gradually he became aware of another shading of light. To his right the water was darker, almost a slate gray, than it was to his left. And he knew, more by instinct than by reasoning, that it would soon be night.

It was then that he saw the first physical features he had encountered since his escape. It was a submarine reef. Instinctively, he sought a refuge among its crevices, and under an overhang of rock Harry curled up into a fetal position and fainted into a deep exhausted sleep.

47

The smog in Denver was worse than it was in Los Angeles. By eleven in the morning it was already seeping into the huge frame house, causing Ruth's eyes to sting. The paneled front hallway and the living room of her mother's house were not as enormous as Ruth remembered them as a child, but they were high-ceilinged and spacious enough to make them prohibitive to air condition. The hot smoggy air in the downstairs hall had a suffocating quality. But the phone was there, and Ruth had to call Gunther.

When she was a child there had been several health resorts and sanitariums for people suffering from lung problems in that section of Denver. The clean, dry, bracing Rocky Mountain air had then been regarded as tonic as vitamins. In her panic-stricken flight from California, Ruth had had a vision of a clean placid city and towering snow-capped peaks where the crisp pure air would purge her angry confusion. The children were all unhappy about the move, and on the plane she had told them stories about her girlhood—of swim-

ming in mountain lakes, skiing and sledding on the
street in front of her house, and the old-fashioned
snow-dappled Christmases she'd had there. The mountains, the change of seasons, the cool clear air had
taken on the quality of original innocence for her. In
her mother's home Ruth's children would relive her
childhood. She herself would start life anew.

But as the jet cleared the Rockies and began its let-
down to Denver's airport, Ruth looked out the window
and saw the smog. It hovered over the city in a thick
brown haze. To the east the Great Plains spread out
from under the blanket of smog flat and boundless into
Kansas. To the west the Rockies suddenly leaped up in
a jagged great wall fourteen thousand feet high. The
first sight of them had always thrilled Ruth on her visits
home. From Stapleton Airport one could see the Front
Range from Pikes Peak in the south 150 miles to Longs
Peak in the north. But not this way. Through the
mustard haze she could barely make out Mount Evans,
the closest of the great peaks.

"That's where your grandmother lives. Just below
that great big mountain," Ruth pointed out to Christopher, trying to drum up the enthusiasm that had suddenly drained from her.

"The smog's worse than in L.A., Mom," Brenda
said, and the statement of fact was an accusation.
David didn't say anything.

The freeways from the airport were jammed bumper
to bumper with fuming cars and angry drivers. The
immediate sights were billboards, forests of TV anten-
nas, tacky little tract homes.

By the time she stepped on the wide, wood-railed
front porch of her mother's house, Ruth knew that she

had solved nothing by running home. She had, at the most, gained only a temporary reprieve. The reprieve had ended with Gunther's shattering call about Harry the previous afternoon.

It was now ten o'clock in Los Angeles. Ruth's call to Gunther was relayed through the law office switchboard to his secretary. Gunther came on the line.

"Ruth, I was just about to call you. I just finished talking with Steinhardt. He's still aboard the ship. I had to get patched through by the marine operator."

"Have they found Harry?"

"No, not yet. But Steinhardt says it's just a matter of time before he shows up." Ruth heard the forced optimism in Gunther's voice.

"What about the two divers?"

Gunther was silent for a moment. "They both died."

"Oh, my God."

"Maybe it's a blessing. There was brain damage."

Ruth moaned and started to weep.

"It wasn't Harry's fault, Ruth. They were both experienced divers. They shouldn't have followed him that deep. They knew better."

She collected herself. "Gunther, I'm flying back there."

"Ruth, why? There's really nothing you can do here."

"I can be there when Harry comes back. I'm going crazy here just thinking about it."

There was silence on the other end of the line.

"And I can defend myself. I saw that son of a bitch Buckley on TV last night. He was putting the blame all on me, telling them, 'Glaucus was upset because of problems with his marriage. He and his wife were estranged.' He's damn right we were estranged. Harry's been estranged from the whole human race since he was wheeled into that operating room. That's what Harry was telling everybody. But Buckley doesn't want anyone to hear it. If they do it'll screw up his plans to become chairman of the board of the seven seas."

"What're you going to do with the kids?"

"Mom can take care of them for a little while. Just until things quiet down. But they're missing school. And they'll have to go back and learn to cope with their father. I guess we'll all have to learn that. Even if we stayed here, it would only be a matter of time until the reporters found us again. Glaucus was the headline in the Denver *Post* this morning."

"When are you coming back?"

"This afternoon. If I can get a flight. Can you pick me up at the airport?"

"Yes, of course. And I'll try to keep the press at bay."

"I'm not afraid anymore. Maybe because I'm a little numb right now. I didn't sleep last night. I'm tired and numb. But what the hell else can possibly happen?"

48

The reef, which had loomed up as a black barren formation of rocks when Harry had first spotted it, was now shimmering with sunlight when he awoke. He was cramped and slightly chilled, but the thick wet suit had kept him reasonably protected through the night. He was suddenly very hungry. He hadn't eaten in a day. His flight to the sea had first formed in his mind as a fantasy and then had become a compulsion. He had never thought out the logistics or consequences of his act. The sea makes no allowances for madness, but Harry had no need for rational thought. Instinct was enough to survive.

Harry swam low over the reef. There was a movement beneath him and a series of sharp snaps. He peered at the rocks, but he only saw algae and barnacles and tiny pink anemones that generated their own phosphorescent color. A quick movement caught his eye and with it came the sharp sound. A rock itself had moved. He closely examined it. It was the shell of a large scallop. Covered with barnacles, anemones, and algae, it was almost indistinguishable from the rocks. Harry could now make out the shapes of other rock scallops, six to nine inches wide, all about him. Many of the shells were slightly agape and all around their edges tiny tentacle eyes, the ocellus, glimmered in the water. As his blue hulk loomed near them, the ocellus immediately retracted and the shell snapped shut. If it hadn't been for that sound and slight movement, Harry would have swum right over the camouflaged scallops.

From the scabbard attached to the leg of his diving suit, he pulled out his utility knife—the blade as stout as a crowbar and the handle as heavy as a hammer. He pried open a scallop, cut out the muscle of succulent white meat, and devoured it. From his hunting expeditions with Matsuda, he knew the meat would be sweet and tender even eaten raw.

He wrenched open and ate a second scallop. A swarm of fish materialized, tearing and gobbling at any stray bits of food. In their feeding frenzy the fish followed him from scallop to scallop, darting in as soon as he cracked the shell and trying to snatch the white muscle of meat from his fingers. He consumed a dozen of the shellfish before his hunger was satiated.

For days Harry wandered along a bight of submarine reefs that paralleled the coast. The reefs, often the anchorings for forests of lush kelp, provided food and nooks and crannies in which to sleep. He didn't plunge into the cold dark depths of the abyss or swim near shore, where the tides and surf churned up the sand and made the water murky. In the clear deep waters of the reef he gathered scallops, abalones, and oysters. He speared sheepheads, perch, and rockfish and slashed the soft fleshy fillets from their sides and wolfed them. He caught red crabs and spiny lobsters, fractured their shells with his knife handle, and dug out the sweet meat. He needed great quantities of the low-calorie seafood to sustain himself, and the entire daylight hours were spent hunting. Clouds of small damselfish and wrasses hovered around him, scavenging anything he didn't eat. He wandered along the coast in a daze, a demented sea god and his retinue.

Harry existed as if trapped in an unending dream, suspended in a boundaryless blue twilight that was unbroken except for the reefs or jungles of kelp. He stalked a five-foot halibut through the kelp, the white fleshy underbelly appearing and disappearing amid undulating yellow-green fronds. A school of opaleyes scattered and then re-formed, hovering behind the fernlike leaves, all peering at him. Sunlight rippled through the wavering stalks. Harry suddenly saw a woman looking at him through the kelp. She was hidden by green veils and only her haunting eyes and long blond hair billowing on the eddies were visible. He swam to her. The face disappeared, but he glimpsed the white flesh of her legs swimming through the wispy feather-boa kelp ahead of him. Excited and stirred, he plunged after her. There was another flash of a lovely face wreathed in blond hair. A pale arm beckoned to him through the sea palms and then disappeared again.

Harry ripped through the seaweed, feverishly searching for her. Suddenly she floated before him, naked and voluptuous, a goddess garlanded with green feathery boas.

He reached out for her. She dissolved into the swirling motes of sunlight, then materialized again amid diaphanous membranes of green a few yards away.

He lunged toward her, tearing up the kelp, gasping in his excitement. But he couldn't catch her. She always eluded his grasp but still tormented his vision—the sinuous blond hair, lush lips, full buoyant breasts, soft flaxen belly, and long white thighs. Harry collapsed, faint and sobbing, at the edge of the kelp forest.

There was nothing beyond the reef and the kelp. An empty flat desert of gray sand stretched out before him. It was barren, lifeless, and unending. Suddenly Harry heard an eerie mournful cry. Then another. He listened, gripped by the sounds—terrifying lowings, moans, and roars that echoed through the sea as if heralding the rising of great monsters from the abyss.

49

Steinhardt stood at the top of the ladder of the *Richard Kenneth* waiting for Ruth. He held on to the rail with one hand, as if for support; he looked ten years older than when Ruth had last seen him.

"You look as though you haven't been sleeping very well," he said with some concern as he took her hand.

"I was about to say the same to you, Doctor."

His reply was a faint smile. "Men at my age either sleep too little or too much."

He led the way to the ship's lounge. When she was seated, Steinhardt said, "I've made arrangements for you to stay aboard. You'll find the accommodations spartan but comfortable."

"Is Buckley aboard?" Ruth asked.

Steinhardt shook his head. "We're in touch by radio. But he had administrative matters to tend to ashore. Besides which, he has a tendency to seasickness."

"Do you expect Harry to return to the ship?"

The old man looked her straight in the eye. "If he comes back, this would be the logical place."

Ruth's heart stopped beating for an instant. "You don't expect Harry to come back," she said at last.

"I think the longer he stays away, the less likely it is."

"But he could stay out there indefinitely if he wanted, couldn't he? I mean, there's food out there for him, isn't there?"

Steinhardt hesitated a moment before answering. "Oh, yes, there's a great deal of food in the sea."

"Well, how could he die out there?" Ruth said in a voice little more than a whisper.

"He might succumb to the cold, the pressure, or the lack of oxygen at great depths," Steinhardt said reluctantly.

Ruth had a strong feeling he was withholding something. "I want to know," she insisted. "I have a right to know what could happen."

Steinhardt nodded. "Below two hundred meters, about six hundred feet, the dissolved oxygen in the water varies a great deal. At its lowest levels it wouldn't be enough to sustain consciousness or even life. Harry would start hallucinating, then pass out and begin to sink."

Ruth felt a little faint. She excused herself and went out on deck. The sun was setting. The great red disk shimmered on the horizon a few moments and then was swallowed by the sea, leaving the sky to the west inflamed.

"Why don't you try and get some rest?" Steinhardt was at her side.

Ruth nodded. The accumulated fatigue of days leadened her eyes and body. She went to her cabin, stretched out on the narrow bunk in her clothes, and immediately fell asleep.

She awoke with a start, confused and disoriented by the strange surroundings, the creaks and sighs of the ship at mooring. The cabin was pitch-black. Ruth tried to go back to sleep, but she couldn't. She felt a familiar fear. If she fell asleep, Harry would die. It was a terrible anxiety. She had felt it before, what seemed centuries ago, when Harry was dying of lung cancer and she had insisted on staying in the same room with him. Now it was back. She tried to fight off the terror that came to her in a darkened room. She tried to sleep, but finally she groped for the switch for the bedside light and clicked it on. She sat up and wearily sagged against the steel headboard of her bunk. She stared at the cramped bare cabin. She didn't even remember going to bed.

Ruth got up and made her way on deck. The air was clear and the stars very bright. The lights of San Pedro and Long Beach flared across the water, giving the illusion the ship was closer to shore than it had been earlier. Despite her nap, Ruth still felt completely exhausted. She should go back to sleep. But she knew that as soon as she put out the light, the terror would come back.

There was no one around, but Ruth heard a voice coming from down the deck. As she approached, she recognized Steinhardt's voice emanating from a porthole. "I strongly object to your perpetuating this myth of Glaucus out there living on the great bounty of the sea. I won't be party to a deception."

Ruth was arrested by the tension in Steinhardt's voice. There was an answering crackle of a radio speaker and a voice that Ruth couldn't make out. Steinhardt was apparently talking on the radio-telephone. She stepped near to eavesdrop.

"Harry is swimming around in two hundred metric tons of DDT from the Los Angeles sewage outfall alone. It has permanently poisoned the sediment. The fish all about me suffer from tumors and fin rot. If you feed sea birds exclusively on fish from this area, they die of DDT and PCB poisoning. The scallops here contain three times the normal amount of mercury, and the shellfish in the vicinity of the oil spills are cancerous. Of course I realize the industrial interests you court don't want these matters brought to public attention."

"Karl, I appreciate the fact that you're greatly upset by all that's happened. We all are." The voice on the radio was low, placating. It was Buckley's voice. "But I think we've a great many more immediate problems. This isn't the most propitious time to go off on a tangent on an ecological crusade."

"Perhaps I am being overly concerned with Harry's diet," Steinhardt responded, his pitch still taut and angry. "The immediate danger is not what Harry eats, but what might eat him."

"Now I know you're being unnecessarily alarmist, Karl," Buckley said in the same unruffled, soothing tone. "The chances of a swimmer being attacked by a shark are as remote as his getting struck by lightning."

"For a swimmer frolicking in the surf at Santa Monica that may be true. But the majority of shark attacks in these waters are by great whites against skin divers wearing wet suits and fins. That much we have statistics on. Apparently the sharks mistake them for injured fish or sea lions. But the larger sharks don't venture into the shallow reef areas here in California. There aren't enough large fish to feed them."

"What the hell does all this have to do with Glaucus?" Buckley snapped, the self-control in his voice suddenly giving way to alarm.

"Our trawl studies show that below six hundred feet the fish average five times as large as they do in shallow water. That's the area the great white sharks inhabit. And the autopsies on the two unfortunate divers indicated that's the depth Harry may have plunged to. If that's so, then a shark attack is no longer an event as remote as being struck by lightning. His being devoured becomes an eventuality."

Ruth gripped the rail of the ship, trying to quell the shivering that seized her body. She felt cold, sweaty. The shuddering became violent. The shoreline lights blurred. She reeled and doubled over the rail, vomiting.

50

The strange melancholy songs of migrating great whales echoed through the sea around Harry, plaintive, moaning sounds of varying pitch and volume. Harry had never listened to the noises in the sea. Before, he had always been with scuba divers, and the loud sucking and rasping of their air regulators had drowned out everything else. Now, as he hunted, he became keenly aware of the multitude of sounds.

The water all around him vibrated with noise. Chirps, squeals, screams, roars, croaks, whinnies, gurgles, and growls. Some sounds, like the sharp, nerve-shattering shots of pistol shrimp, exploded right beneath him as he swam. Others, like the wails and cries of the great whales, reverberated through the sea from hundreds of miles away. Unseen dolphins clicked and whistled to one another. White croaker fish contracted their resonant air bladders and silver grunt fish ground their pharyngeal teeth. Harry listened carefully as he stalked through a kelp bed.

A large Dover sole suddenly flicked up out of the

sand where it had been feeding, partially buried and hidden on the bottom. Harry's spear impaled it right behind the gills. He laid the fish out on a rock and started to strip the fillet from its side, then stopped. Near the tail the fish's scales were all gone and there was a pink spongy tumor the size of a thumb. The tail fin itself was short and misshapen as if eaten away by disease. He violently hurled the fish away from him.

As he speared more fish, he minutely examined each one. He discovered sole and Pacific sand dabs with twisted ray fins and their tails completely missing, a chub mackerel whose flesh was covered with red sores, and a striped mullet with dark tumors dangling off its body like grapes. On a striptail rockfish the normally precise geometric mosaic of the scales was drunken and disoriented, as if the primal pattern from which the fish was created had gone crazy.

Harry's examination of each fish became obsessive. Even if the fish looked normal on the exterior, he cut it open, dissected it, and peered at its entrails. If any organ looked vaguely abnormal or diseased, and they often did, he flung the fish away. He poked through the viscera of scallops, abalone, lobsters, and crabs with his knife point and often found fleshy cancers perched on organs, devouring the fish from within. He fled from his discoveries, leaving behind him a slaughter of disemboweled creatures. They were quickly consumed by the scavengers and predators that followed increasingly in his wake. But Harry himself now went hungry. Even if a fish or shellfish passed his painstaking inspection, he ate with reluctance.

He trekked down the sea floor and reefs to greater depths, instinctively seeking escape from the poisons spilling out from the land. The water became colder and darker. A blue-green twilight enveloped him. The dark brooding rocks were covered with delicate lacy black fans that trembled in the current. The fans were a seaweed, plocamium, actually bright red in color, but at that depth all the red light of the spectrum had been filtered out by the water; only the faint blue-green rays penetrated. The plants' red pigment was an adaptation that allowed them to absorb every bit of blue-green light available. Since they reflected back no light at all, they appeared black to the eye and survived in the twilight world where green plants would perish.

The fish that swam around Harry were noticeably larger. The shellfish had disappeared and the rocks were covered with spiny sea urchins. The orange roe inside the black porcupine shells was nourishing but Harry disliked the taste. Instead he cracked open several urchins and just lay still in the water with his spear cocked, waiting for the fish to swarm and feed.

He singled out a large white seaperch and hit it just above the pelvic fin. It flopped convulsively on the spear several times and then was still. Harry looked at it closely. The scales and fins were regular and well formed. He cut it open and spread the guts on a rock for examination. Like a swarm of giant flies the other fish darted in to feed. He tried to swat them away but they boldly ignored his waving hand.

Suddenly all the fish scattered. Their disappearance was so swift that it startled Harry. He looked about and gasped. His mind went totally blank.

The great white shark that cruised slowly above him was so large its shadow darkened the reef. Its open mouth was as wide as a manhole. It drifted within a few feet of Harry, steadily staring at him with eyes as cold as glass beads. With a thrust of its tail the shark made a tight aggressive circle and, pectoral fins splayed out, came head on at Harry.

He was galvanized. He dove into the rocks, clawing and kicking frantically to crawl down into a crevice. But he was seized by the foot and ripped from the rocks. As if his body were the tip of a monstrous whip, Harry was violently snapped up and down. Then he was released and sank to the bottom. He scurried into a crevice, twisting and squeezing into it so that he crammed between the rocks. He felt no pain in his leg but he couldn't turn around to examine it. He sensed the shadow of the shark prowling above him but he couldn't see it. From where he lay between the rocks he could see only a narrow band directly ahead. And in that brief field of vision he saw the handle of his spear lying on the sand just out of reach.

Harry lost all sense of time. He stayed squeezed between the rocks, unmoving, peering out at his spear but unable to see the shark. Slowly he began creeping toward the spear. He squirmed an inch, peered out and waited. Then he repeated the move, inching out and waiting, slithering out of his hole like a spooked eel.

When the spear was almost within reach, he lunged out and grabbed it. Then he saw the shark. It was almost on him. He was caught in the open, half out of his hole. He tried to get back but couldn't move fast enough. Instinctively he pointed the spear at the shark. The shark took it in its mouth as if it were a toothpick, ripping it out of Harry's hand. The handle jammed into the rocks by Harry's head and for an instant deflected the shark's charge to one side. In that moment Harry scampered back into his crevice. The shark crashed into the rocks as if to bulldoze them out of the way. The sea floor shuddered under the power of the charge. The shark slammed again and again into the rocks, thrashing them with its body as if it were trying to pulverize them. Then it hovered right over the crevice, its body too thick to squeeze in. It stared at Harry with its giant mouth opened, as though to suck him right into it. Harry looked into the maw of the giant white shark and saw the rows of triangular teeth, each a serrated blade of ivory. The shark didn't move. It hung on the edge of the rocks, its implacable eyes fixed on Harry, the butt end of the pole spear still protruding from its giant mouth.

A midshipman fish darted into the crevice, spotted Harry, and darted back toward the shark. It fled inside the shark's mouth and then reemerged. For the first time Harry noticed the other fish hovering about the shark's head. They swooped in and nipped at the predator's flesh and then quickly backed off. Still the shark didn't move.

A shark *had* to move. It had to keep water moving over its gills or it suffocated. Sharks didn't have the muscles of the more highly evolved fish to pump water over their gills. It was the first rational sequence of thoughts Harry had had in days.

Harry shifted his position slightly. There was no reaction from the shark. He timidly raised his head, inch by inch. There was still no movement. Was the shark just waiting, catlike, to pounce on him? Several small fish bit at its head as if feeding. There was no flutter about the shark's gills. The shark was not even breathing. Harry raised his head out of the crevice another inch, then another.

At the upper side of the shark's head, just above its left eye, the three brass points of the spear stuck out. The fury of the shark's charge into the rocks had driven the steel shaft right through its head, apparently through its brain. The shark was dead.

Harry slowly eased out of his hole, still not believing it. His body was wedged into the rocks, and in order to get out, he had to slide forward to a point where his head was within inches of the shark's teeth. Only the presence of the fish now swimming freely about the shark, nibbling at it, gave Harry the courage to move.

He recovered his knife from where he had dropped it and then remembered that the shark had grabbed his leg. He studied it with wonder. The right flipper was severed a half-inch away from his toes. Only the shoe of the swim fin remained; the wide, thick rubber flipper had been buzz-sawed off.

Harry looked closely at the monster. It was at least twenty feet long and as wide as a rowboat. Even dead, with the spear harpooned in its brain, it terrified him. Gingerly he grabbed the spear handle and tried to yank it out. Suddenly the shark came alive. The great jaws snapped and the giant body convulsed, flinging Harry through the water like jetsam.

He fell on a flat rock table with no breaks or crevices in which to hide. But the shark didn't attack Harry. The daggerish teeth gnashed compulsively as if trying to chew up the spear, and the monster thrashed and writhed in a wild convulsion. Harry fled.

He kicked, crawled, and clawed through the rocks. From each safe shelter he warily peered about and behind him before scurrying on. His "crippled" fin caused him to wallow side to side when he swam. Harry limped through the sea, a frightened, wounded, hunted animal.

At the first sign of darkness he crawled into the rocks to sleep. He desperately wanted to sleep, yet he couldn't. He was too frightened. If he fell asleep he would die. Gobbled up and consumed by some black blood-thirsting monster. He shoved back into the crevice, pressing desperately against the rocks surrounding and shielding his body. He cowered in the dark and could hear his heart beating faster and faster. The sounds all about him were magnified. He didn't know where the noises came from, and like the darkening sea itself they were now terrifying.

The water became as black as ink, and from deep in the abyss rose wails and moans. Strange phosphorescent lights darted around Harry in the dark. He stared at them, his eyes wide and strained with fear. With the setting of the sun began the nightly migration of glowing nightmare creatures up from the deep toward the surface to hunt. Dragonfish, hatchetfish, viper-fish, spirula squids, and medusas. Carnivores and predators swarmed up from the depths beyond the light.

Schools of luminous skeletons darted through the blackness, teeth slashing and tearing at other creatures in a frenzy. They swirled around Harry, devouring one another. He cringed in the rocks, his terror so great it was a physical agony.

The night lasted an eternity. Harry didn't remember

its beginning nor did he recognize the first return of light. But gradually, almost imperceptibly, the creatures and the darkness faded away, as if Harry were rising from hell itself. The water above him became lighter and Harry broke from the rocks and swam furiously toward the light.

51

The *Amaroc Enterprise,* a tanker carrying sixty-six million gallons of crude oil from Valdez, Alaska, to Los Angeles, developed a breakdown in its hydraulic steering off Point Sur. The rudder stuck left. The captain stopped the ship's engines to prevent it from steaming into the rocky Big Sur coast and then radiotelephoned the ship's owner in New York for instructions.

At this point the ocean tug *Mary Emma,* hauling a lumber barge from Vancouver, British Columbia, to Los Angeles, offered assistance. The oil company in New York negotiated with the tug owners in Vancouver over the salvage price, usually a fixed percentage of the value of the ship and cargo. In this instance the haggling was complicated by the fact that the tug would have to set loose and probably lose its lumber barge in order to tow the tanker.

Waves and strong winds from the northwest, common to the Big Sur coast, had by now driven the tanker out of the shipping lanes dangerously close to shore. The captain dropped anchor, but even the drag of the anchor didn't slow the *Amaroc Enterprise*'s drift toward the rocks. The captain delayed sending out a distress signal, since that would put the oil company in a bad negotiating position. The Coast Guard in San Francisco radioed the ship as to its situation and received an "all is well." The Coast Guard couldn't dispatch a cutter to tow the tanker out of danger; by law they were forbidden to compete with a commercial company, and a tug was already on the scene. By the time the oil company and the tug owners reached a contract, it was too late. The tanker ran aground on an offshore reef and began to break up.

A dozen boats arrived to lay booms and skimmers to contain the oil, but the rough seas made them useless. The oil company dispatched a second tanker to transfer the oil but the ship couldn't safely maneuver close enough to the *Amaroc Enterprise*. Sixty-six million gallons of Alaskan crude streamed from the ruptured underbelly. As the ship broke in two under the pounding of the heavy northwest winds and waves, the oil gushed from the venting stacks like blood from severed arteries.

At the first taste of oil in the water, clusters of periwinkles, the lovely sea snails with turban-shaped shells, crawled to the top of the rocks. They retracted into their shells and waited for the poisonous black tide to pass. It didn't, and one by one the delicate periwinkles died and fell from the rocks.

* * *

"There's one! It's alive! Oh, please," Mary Ghio screamed.

From the pitch of her voice Resnick knew the girl was again on the verge of hysteria. She had gotten hysterical several times that day at the sight of clumps of oil-soaked birds and sea otters, most of them dead. The oil had overrun the sea otter refuge south of Big Sur. Weathering and photo-oxidation was now turning the oil into a thick glu that smothered rocks, plants, and animals indiscriminately.

Jay Resnick, a biologist on the faculty of the University of California at Santa Cruz, was himself angry, exhausted, and close to tears. But he kept a tight rein on his emotions. There was nothing that could be done except to survey, count, estimate. What does a beach ankle-deep in dead otters, birds, fish, sea urchins, crabs, and shellfish survey out to? Approximately sixteen million destroyed organisms per linear mile.

"Oh, a little closer, please," Mary pleaded.

Philip Wong, the other graduate student assisting in the survey, sat stoically at the helm, steering the outboard through the dark sludge. He maneuvered the boat alongside the floundering brown shape. The bird rode low in the water, hardly moving. From the long triangular shape of its head, Resnick identified it as a western grebe, although its brilliant black and white plumage was coated with oil. The girl basketed the bird in her hands, cooing to it. The bird didn't struggle. It was already in shock and half-dead. If ingesting the toxic oil didn't kill the birds, they died of exposure or drowned. The oil destroyed the insulating quality of their feathers.

The girl immediately started washing the grebe with

detergent. It was more important to keep the bird warm and feed it than to clean it, Resnick had explained to her. But the girl wouldn't listen. A blackened oil-soaked bird was a symbol of guilt that must be cleaned even if the ordeal killed the already weakened creature. The psychological needs of bird rescuers, Resnick had learned, often took precedence over the real needs of the birds.

The water alongside the boat suddenly exploded A man violently surfaced, covered with the thick brown sludge, choking and gasping into the air like a fish in a fouled pond.

"What the hell are you doing diving out here in this crap?" Resnick shouted at him. He reached out to give the man a hand, but the diver seemed to be in a state of shock. He just hung on the surface, gasping and coated with oil like some ghastly apparition. It seemed as if he would slide back into the ooze at any moment and be lost forever. Resnick screamed for the other two to help him.

He and Wong each managed to get a grip under the man's arms and they hauled him halfway into the boat. The swimmer was deadweight. He seemed hardly conscious at all.

Mary now seized one of his legs and together the three tugged and dragged the all but lifeless victim into the boat, where the man lay stretched out gulping the air like a landed fish.

"It's a hell of a place to go skin diving," Resnick said to no one in particular. The oil victim had on a wet suit and swim fins. Or rather a swim fin. The other fin was broken off.

Mary stared in awe at the prostrate man, then fell to

her knees beside him and tried to pull his oil-soaked beard and long hair away from his neck. "Oh, God," she whimpered.

"Goddammit, Mary, give him room to breathe," Resnick snapped. "This is no time for your angel of mercy hysteria."

The girl turned a stricken face to Resnick. "It's Glaucus!" she cried.

"What?"

"Glaucus. The gill-man who was lost."

Resnick dropped to his knees beside the girl to stare at the oil-drenched head and the thick collar about the man's neck. As a biologist he had been fascinated by the Glaucus experiment and had read every news clipping and scientific paper about it that had circulated through the biology department. "Jesus, he's suffocating in oil! His gills are covered. We've got to clean them."

Mary's bottles of detergent and rags materialized. "Be very gentle. The membrane is very delicate," Resnick cautioned. He looked at the girl and realized his warning had been unnecessary. Her touch would be soft as a feather, as it had been on countless birds. He had better heed his admonition himself.

Glaucus was unconscious, his mouth open, sucking in the air from which he could no longer extract oxygen. Even if they got his gills clean, what then?

"We've got to get him into clear water," Resnick ordered Wong. He gestured to the north, to the ocean beyond the broken wreck of the *Amaroc Enterprise*.

The young man leaped to the stern. The sudden surge of the boat at full throttle brought both Resnick and Mary down hard on their hands and knees. They ignored the bruising and immediately bent back to work over Glaucus.

"Won't the detergent clog his gills as bad as the oil?" the girl suddenly asked.

"I don't know," Resnick said with desperation in his voice. "I just don't know. The detergent will wash off in the water. The oil won't. It's the best idea I have."

"I can't get inside the gills to clean them."

Resnick stopped scrubbing and studied Glaucus. The girl was right. They were only cleaning the outside edges of the gill. The broad surface areas inside the operculum were still contaminated. "Hold his head back to keep his windpipe open," Resnick ordered.

He held the bottle to Glaucus's sucking mouth as if he were giving him a drink and poured the detergent down his throat. Soapsuds, oil, and blood streamed out through the gill clefts. Resnick washed the detergent down until it ran clear.

"We're in good water!" Wong shouted. The boat throttled back and settled in the swells.

"Help me get him over the side."

They tugged and hauled the heavy sodden body over the gunwale. Resnick jumped in the water, trying to hold on to Glaucus with one hand and the boat with the other.

"Splash water into his gills and mouth," he sputtered. "Help me hold on to him." Resnick was struggling to keep his own head above water and hold on to Glaucus at the same time. The heavy parka and jeans he wore were soaked and pulling him under. "I can't hold him!" he cried out.

Wong jumped into the water beside him and got a grip on Glaucus. The girl shoved Glaucus's head up and down in the water, creating a bobbing motion.

"That's it. Get the water going in and out," Resnick choked out. His hand slipped on the wet gunwale and he lunged to get a better grip, almost capsizing the boat. Both he and Wong lost their handholds and went under, dragged down by Glaucus and the sodden weight of their clothes. Instinctively they both let go of Glaucus and clutched for the surface.

"He's sinking. Grab him," Wong gasped.

"I can't reach him." In desperation Resnick dove down head first. He grasped Glaucus's arm and kicked frantically, but he couldn't raise the heavy, sinking body. Slowly Resnick was dragged down. The air burst from his lungs. He let go and clawed for the surface, coming up hard against the bottom of the boat. Wong caught him and pulled him, choking and gagging, to the side of the boat.

Resnick clung to it, gasping for air, and then began to sob. "I couldn't hold him. Oh, Jesus. I couldn't hold him. I lost him."

Below them Glaucus sank from view.

52

Karl Steinhardt wandered about his study, distracted, reluctantly taking leave of the warm familiar bookish clutter of the room. He didn't know when he would be back. He surveyed the dark musty hoard of volumes of philosophy, searching for one or two he might take with him. But none sparked his interest. What did any of them have to reveal to him now that he hadn't already learned with great pain? Could any of them tell him what he had wrought?

In a corner of the study on a simple oak lectern rested a large Norwegian Bible. It was Steinhardt's family Bible, willed to him by his father. The cover of the "Bibelen" was made of heavy wood decorated with an intricate hand-carved Gothic cross, covered with red leather and embossed with gold. Steinhardt opened the book, as if seeking his father's reassurance that there was an infinite wisdom that had created man and still controlled his destiny. Steinhardt's father, a cold, forbidding man but a devout Lutheran, had read to the family from this Bible every evening.

The frontispiece was an engraving that illustrated the Creation of Adam and the Garden of Eden.

Og der opgik en Damp af Jorden og vandede al Jordens Overdel.

Steinhardt could hear his father's voice, resonant and thrilling with the mystery and awe of Creation.

Og Gud Herren havde dannet Mennesket (af) Støv af Jorden og blæst Livets Aande i hans Næse; og Mennesket blev til en levende Sjæl.

The old Norwegian words had, for Steinhardt, a primal power that even the beautiful Elizabethan English could never convey.

But there went up a mist from the earth, and watered the whole face of the ground. And the LORD God formed man of the dust of the ground, and breathed into his nostrils the breath of life; and man became a living soul.

In the Old Norwegian the word for the soul, *Sjoel,* was derived from the word for the sea, *Sjo.* The connection was the same in all the old Scandivanian and German tongues. In Gothic, soul was *saiwala* and sea was *saiws;* in German, the words were *see* and *seele.* The Norsemen believed that the sea was the habitation of the soul and that both were part of the same divine force. For young Steinhardt, listening to his father in that dark, somber house while the spruce logs in the fireplace crackled and steamed, the mists of Genesis and the mists that shrouded the fjords outside were one. They were the breath of God leading from the sea to man's soul. They were the veils that hid the mysteries of life. The truths he sought were like those mists. He saw them before him, swirling and elusive. He could strive into their midst but he could never quite grasp them in his hand. Was that what his lifetime of medical studies and research into respiration had been? Just an awed Norwegian boy on his knees, hands clasped on his bed, praying fervently to understand the mystery of Creation.

Steinhardt almost laughed at the irony of it all. As a young medical student he had been openly agnostic. Such was the intellectual spirit of the times. "It is an illusion to suppose we can get anywhere else what science cannot give," Freud had convinced them. Steinhardt had been marvelously educated in all the tools he had needed to conceive, plan, and conduct important and exciting experiments. He had searched for knowledge according to the classical meaning of the word "science," but what he had sought to know transcended science.

There had been moments, lost in his meditations, that Steinhardt had experienced an ecstatic oneness with the nature he was studying. But the moments had passed, as if fleeing from the very "science" of his methods. Now, as an old man, he had all at once become aware that he had searched, irrationally, in tissue dissections, chemical analyses, and computer read-outs for the breath of God. As a scientist and physician he had succeeded brilliantly. As a metaphysician he was no further along than he had been as a boy.

Steinhardt broke out of his reverie. He must finish

packing and be on that road north. Buckley was furious about his leaving, which had all the more hastened Steinhardt's departure. He was admittedly getting to be a cantankerous old man.

But there was one person to whom he had to talk before he left.

French windows opened onto a small patio in the rear of the house. Beyond it Steinhardt could make out the swimming pool and the flaxen-haired boy who sat at the edge of the pool stroking a black, shaggy dog of indeterminate breeding. The pale gold head solemnly bobbed and nodded as the boy intently talked to the dog. The dog sat with his front paws nervously dancing as if he were about to leap away at any moment, and every now and then seemed to answer the boy with a sharp excited bark.

"It breaks my heart to watch him," Ruth Styles said.

"Oh, why is that?" Steinhardt asked.

"Ever since that time in the tank when Harry pulled him under the water, Chris has been having nightmares. I've explained to him that it was an accident. That his father hadn't meant to hurt or frighten him. I told him it was like the time when Groucho was a little puppy and David, our oldest, tried to teach the dog to swim by just throwing him in the pool. The puppy was traumatized, and to this day he's been frightened of the water and always shies away from David when he's near the pool. Ever since I made that connection for him, he's been trying to coax Groucho into the water. It's as though he feels if he could quiet the dog's terror, he could exorcise his own."

As he had often been in the past, Steinhardt was

struck by Ruth Styles's beauty. Her pain, her pleasures, her anxiety and anger were all quick and instantly measured in her eyes. Steinhardt, by nature a shy man, was somewhat in awe of her. "Your other children, are they well?" he asked.

A slight melancholy smile and a shrug. "Like me, they're learning to cope with anything and everything. They're back in school. I kept Chris home today because any news of Harry on TV gets him too excited. He won't shut up, and it tends to disturb the other kids. Or rather the teacher." There was a long moment of awkward silence, then she asked, "Do you think you'll find Harry?"

Steinhardt shook his head. "I don't know. I'm rather amazed that he's traveled so far up the coast. But the strength of the submarine currents and his hunt for food might have carried him that far north."

"But we've been getting reports of people having seen Harry from Acapulco to Seattle. He's becoming something like the Loch Ness monster. He's passing into the realm of legend and fantasy."

Steinhardt nodded. "Yes but this biologist Resnick and the others with him, they would have no reason to concoct such a story."

"If he's telling the truth, then Harry might have been killed by the oil."

"I don't know. I don't have enough information. We may never know."

Ruth looked sharply at Steinhardt. "Is that why you asked to see me? To tell me that?" There was a bitter edge to her voice.

"No."

"What was it then?"

Why *was* he there? Would what he wanted to tell this

377

woman make any difference now?

"I will not perform the operation again," Steinhardt said.

"And what will that accomplish?" Ruth asked. Her voice was flat and emotionless. "You've published your work. There are papers by you and Dr. Bernstein. And papers by you and Harry. It's hardly a secret formula that you've destroyed. And if men are desperate enough or curious enough or adventurous enough, it *will* be done again." She stared at Steinhardt. "Is that what you came here to tell me? That you'd never perform the operation again? Why? Are you looking to me for some sort of absolution?"

Was that what he was looking for? Bernstein had died cursing their work. Harry had totally abandoned him. Had Steinhardt now sought out the only other person who might remit his sin?

Ruth Styles shook her head. "I can't give you your absolution, Dr. Steinhardt. I'm still in pain. So are my children. And my husband is still out there somewhere, lost and confused, suffering his own agonies."

"I didn't come here for your absolution, Mrs. Styles," Steinhardt said. Whatever doubts he may have had, he was at least sure of that. "What your husband and I accomplished is its own absolution. We have proven that if men have the will and the courage we can transcend this body of a naked ape stalking the land. The whole world is ours. The universe is ours. We are created in God's image not in the flesh but in our spirit."

But Ruth Styles's anger recognized no piety. "I don't think Harry shared your spiritual pretensions," she said in a cutting voice.

"Not in those terms perhaps," Steinhardt said

378

quietly. "But he wanted to accomplish something with his life. What I think he would call 'a mark.' And he did. The part of his soul that strove for that is at peace. Would you feel less pain, or would he, if he had died miserably of common cancer, still unfulfilled and frustrated?"

Ruth's anger ebbed as quickly as it had flared. She shook her head and her "No" was hardly audible.

"I said I wouldn't perform the operation again not because I believe it's evil or unnatural. I don't view my work in those terms. Something is either beneficial or injurious to life. The gill was an investigation into the life processes that produced, almost as a byproduct, a device that allows us to investigate the depths where life begins. That was my purpose. Or perhaps my conceit. But the direction of our technology at the moment is toward a frantic exploitation of this planet that has become cancerous. Our rapacious technology itself has become a malignancy, consuming the earth and spawning other malignancies. And it's to those purposes I'm afraid my work will be directed. For that realization I have your husband to thank."

"Harry's dead, isn't he?" Ruth suddenly asked.

"I don't know. But I don't think we'll ever see him again. The operation was merely a temporary reprieve. His reprieve, I've reason to believe, has been canceled."

The implication of what Steinhardt just said hit Ruth like a blow to the stomach and she let out a gasp. "The cancer spread."

"I'm not certain. There were indications that showed up in the last examination. I'd have to perform a biopsy to be certain."

"Did Harry know?"

"I never told him. I've told no one else. But I think he

379

must have known. A man like Harry, who's been through it once before, doesn't need a doctor and laboratory tests to tell him he's dying. Even if he doesn't recognize the signs consciously, the knowledge is there in his body. He must be aware of it subconsciously. Perhaps that's why he went off by himself. To spare you the agony of watching him die again. To spare himself that indignity."

Ruth's cheeks flushed red and hot with shame. "That's why you came here. To tell me that."

Steinhardt nodded. "And to say goodbye. I'm leaving for a while and I don't know when I'll be back. At my age I've discovered it's best not to leave goodbyes unsaid."

"Where're you going?"

"After I speak to this fellow at Santa Cruz, I'm going to drive up the coast. North of San Francisco, it reminds me a great deal of my home in Norway. When Johanna was alive, we'd often go there on holidays. We own an old house, but I've been renting it out. I haven't been back there since Johanna's death. It's time now. There's some work I want to do there. I need the quiet and the isolation."

"Not more experiments with gills."

"Oh, no. It's somewhat in the realm of philosophy. It's an avocation of mine."

"Will it take very long?"

"Yes, I expect it will," Steinhardt said. The rest of my life, he thought.

In parting Ruth very gently kissed the old man on the cheek. She stood watching from the open door as the scientist walked to his car, got in, and drove away.

53

A thin morning mist hung over the sea so that the line between the air and water was obscure; it was as though they were hues of the same element. Harry floated near the surface. The once cobalt blue dive suit was oil-stained and torn in several spots. The cold water seeped in, chilled Harry, and washed out, draining away his body heat and strength.

He sculled just below the calm, dappled surface of Monterey Bay, warming in the sun. He was very weak. He had swallowed oil and had vomited steadily for a day. He had eaten very little since. But the weakness that now permeated his arms and legs had begun before the oil. A gull squawked overhead and Harry raised his head, searching for it. The gull flew low on the water, skimming the waves, then soared high into the sunlight, its whiteness so intense it was painful to Harry's eyes. Then Harry heard other sounds. They hovered over the water, vague and distant, almost as though they were memories rather than real sound. There was the music of a carousel. The laughter and shouts of people.

Harry listened and slowly swam in the direction of the sounds. They grew louder and more definite. Other sounds now came to him over the water. The ratchety mechanical clatter of a roller coaster climbing and then its plunging roar. A wave booming. He raised his head, straining, and off in the distance he saw the heaving framework of a roller coaster and the line of a board-walk suspended on the mist like a mirage. A Ferris wheel leisurely rotated, sparkling like the bits of colored glass in a kaleidoscope.

He drifted closer, kicking and swimming with a weak stroke, now carried in by the tidal surge. To his right, below a line of cliffs, he could make out a cluster of teenage boys straddling surfboards of brilliant Day-Glo colors. Harry thrust his head up again and saw the beach.

He swam more vigorously toward the shore, his head bobbing in and out of the water. With each movement his eyes focused on an image. Two young boys at the surf line squealed at each other and belly-flopped in front of the waves. In the shallow water a man held a young boy by the hands, trying to teach him to flutter-kick. A teenage boy and girl clung to each other in the foaming backwash of a wave and kissed. Each sight blazed into Harry's consciousness with a stab of pain and joy.

On the beach a mother wrapped a towel about a skinny shivering boy and rubbed him down. Two mus-cular young men tossed a football back and forth. Harry felt as though he were awakening from a night-mare into a rapturous dream. At the shoreline a small boy sculpted towers of dripping sand on a large castle.

The child was blond and about four years old. Harry focused all his attention on the boy.

He sensed the wave before he felt it roll beneath him. There was a change of light, an enormous shadow looming up behind him. The wave swept him up in its tremendous momentum and then crested. Harry thrashed about but was helpless in its violent churning power. It swept him to shore like a piece of flotsam and dumped him on the sand.

Stunned, Harry lay still, getting his bearings. He started to crawl back into the water but then stopped.

The little blond boy knelt in the sand before him, his eyes brimming with barely suppressed tears. At the child's knees was the ruin of the sandcastle he had so painstakingly built. Its towers crumbled away into the ebbing water. The child stared at Harry a moment and then back down at the ruin.

"Wave broke my castle."

Harry struggled up onto an elbow and knee and reached a hand out to the boy. He ached to touch the child, and by that touch finally end the long nightmare.

"Will you help me make it again?" the child asked hopefully.

Harry's fingers felt the warm downy cheek and the hot silky blond hair.

"Will ya?"

Harry nodded.

"Yay!" The boy gave Harry a quick impulsive hug. The child's embrace was like a burst of sunlight enveloping and warming him. Then the boy broke away and took Harry's hand as if to lead him farther up the slope of the beach, away from the incoming waves.

"We'll make the biggest castle in the whole world,"

the boy said very solemnly. He tugged at Harry's hand.

Harry nodded and smiled. Then he made a move forward and pitched headlong into the pile of sand.

"Mister?" the boy said in a frightened voice. He tugged again at the man's hand.

Harry's fingers closed on the little hand, held it a moment in a tight squeeze, then slipped off into the sand.

The little boy stared at the strange man lying so still on top of his broken castle and then ran off to find his mother. It was a while before a lifeguard noticed Harry lying sprawled on the beach just beyond the waterline, his blue suit ripped and stained with oil, his hair and beard matted, like a long-lost, shipwrecked sailor who had finally made it back to shore.